THE QUEEN OF LOVE

THE QUEEN OF LOVE

Sabine Baring-Gould

NONSUCH

First published 1894
Copyright © in this edition Nonsuch Publishing, 2007

Nonsuch Publishing
Cirencester Road, Chalford, Stroud, Gloucestershire, GL6 8PE

Nonsuch Publishing (Ireland)
73 Lower Leeson Street, Dublin 2, Ireland

www.nonsuch-publishing.com

Nonsuch Publishing is an imprint of NPI Media Group

For comments or suggestions, please email the editor of this series at:
classics@tempus-publishing.com

British Library Cataloguing in Publication Data.
A catalogue record for this book is available from the British Library.

ISBN 978 1 84588 358 4

Typesetting and origination by Nonsuch Publishing Limited
Printed in Great Britain by Oaklands Book Services Limited

CONTENTS

INTRODUCTION TO THE MODERN EDITION

SABINE BARING-GOULD WAS ONE OF the most prolific and versatile writers of the Victorian period. There is no definitive bibliography of his works, but it is clear that the number is extensive, stretching well into the hundreds. He was a man renowned for his somewhat unconventional lifestyle, behaviour and opinions, as well as the diversity of his interests and specialisms, and has, until more recent times, failed to receive the recognition that his vast contribution to literature undoubtedly merits.

He was born in Exeter in 1834, the eldest son of a land-owning family who possessed estates in Lewtrenchard, west Devon. He had a rather unsettled childhood, much of it spent travelling throughout Europe to relieve the boredom of a father whose career with the East India Company had been brought to an abrupt end following a carriage accident. Despite little formal schooling, he managed to complete his education at Cambridge University, where he became well known for his eccentric behaviour, as well as his anti-establishment views. After taking holy orders in 1864, Baring-Gould became a curate in Horbury, Yorkshire. There he met a young mill-girl named Grace Taylor, who, in another act of unconventionality, he decided to marry, after first sending her away to be educated. Their forty-eight-year marriage ended upon

Grace's death in 1916, and during this time the couple had fifteen children, fourteen of whom survived into adult life. Baring-Gould returned to his family home in Devon with his wife in 1881, where he was content to take up the role of squire and parson of the small parish of Lewtrenchard. Here he was to spend the greater part of his life, caring for the welfare of his parishioners, raising his large family, and continuing to travel as he had done as a child.

Baring-Gould's principal pursuit, however, alongside his other responsibilities, was the writing of a prodigious amount of literature. He was ranked as one of the most popular novelists of his day, though his work extended to a wide variety of non-fiction books, pamphlets and magazines, written on subjects ranging from archaeology, theology and history to folklore, travel guides and biographies. He was regarded as an authority on many of these subjects, his *Lives of the Saints* in particular becoming a standard theological work of reference. He is often recognised for his composition of the famous hymn 'Onward Christian Soldiers', the popularity of which surprised him as he apparently jotted it down in only a few minutes. It was certainly not regarded by him as amongst his greatest of achievements; indeed, his self-proclaimed most important work was the collecting together of the folk songs of Devon and Cornwall, published in 1889 as *Songs of the West*.

This endeavour occupied him for a total of twelve years. During this time he toured the length of the two counties, visiting the old people who knew the songs best in their homes and in the fields. The originality of the work can be attributed to the personal approach Baring-Gould took to it: approaching the people as his friends and his equals, and giving it the subtitle 'A collection made from the mouths of the people'. He was not always able to include every original word, as some were considered unsuitable for publication at the time, but he endeavoured to modify them while remaining true to his sources where possible. The book, which ran to four volumes, was the most ambitious of its kind, and has come to be regarded as invaluable for the legacy it has provided for folk revival singers in this part of the country. Appreciation of his role can be witnessed in the present-day societies dedicated to the study of his achievements, as well as the folk festivals which are held in his name.

Sabine Baring-Gould wrote thirty novels in his lifetime. These were usually inspired from his travel to a particular area, and as a result his stories were often placed firmly in the context of their settings, with a great deal of local colouring. His novels tell dramatic, exciting tales: of smuggling communities along the South Devon coast; of passion and obsession in the wilds of the Essex marshes; of a love triangle steeped in the romance and customs of ancient Dartmoor. All are filled with highly original and memorable characters who find themselves in extreme, yet realistic, situations.

The Queen of Love is one of Baring-Gould's lesser-known novels, but as typical of his style as any other. Set in the small salt-mining town of Saltwich, Cheshire, it tells the story of a rather drab, severe, industrial community, whose livelihood hinges upon the prosperity of the salt works. The staid, respectable leaders of this community are scandalised by the arrival of the circus of Signor Giuseppi Santi, whose insidious frivolity threatens the morality, and thus the very stability, of their town. Baring-Gould weaves a dramatic love story around this premise, skilfully conveying the nature of life in a small English locality dominated by one industry, and the constricted moral attitudes which prevailed there at the time. This is a novel by a remarkable and accomplished author, whose merit is gradually beginning to receive the reappraisal, and the level of recognition, that it rightly deserves.

I

THE DEPUTATION

A SINGLE CAB OR FLY—THAT was the sole equipage let out on hire in the town of Saltwich.

It had an arrangement whereby it could appear with a pair on very solemn occasions. Usually it wore shafts, between which shuffled one horse.

The fly was painted black, and when engaged for a funeral it had a cushion and valance of black for the box. The interior was lined with a very deep green, so deep that when the black trimmings were on the box it might be thought that the whole vehicle was plunged in the inkiest depths of woe.

But when the fly was required for a wedding, then the cushions and valance on the box were of a cheerful green, and the interior drapery brightened up into a corresponding smile.

But the fly was also engaged, occasionally, by such persons as did not keep carriages, to convey them to country houses to make calls. On such occasions the driver assumed a hat with a broad gold band, and a greatcoat with armorial brass buttons; moreover, the proprietor applied to the side a red lion passant, surmounted by a coronet. On being called out for a funeral, the driver wore a hat muffled in crape. When he conducted a wedding-party, he wore a favour of white ribbons. At elections he wore sometimes an orange and blue, sometimes a red rosette, according as he was engaged, along with his cab, by the Liberal or the Conservative parties.

The driver was out at the precise moment and day and year on which this story opens, lightly touching up his one horse between the shafts, and he wore no distinguishing badge of mirth or woe. The cab contained three men in their best suits—the suits in which they attended chapel on Sundays, and appeared on platforms at temperance or missionary meetings.

The driver, whose face was flexible as gutta-percha, had accommodated his features to his fare. He looked as serious as though engaged in the undertaking business. His nose was pointed along the axis of the spine of his horse; nevertheless, his eyes turned into the corners to observe an immense illustrated poster representing the achievements of horses, dogs and men belonging to a travelling circus.

"Stop! Stop!"

A head emerged from the right side of the cab. The head was that of a man of nearly sixty. He had very dark hair growing thickly over his head and neck, and below his chin. He was closely-shaved on the jaws and about the mouth. His eyes were dark, his face square, his features heavy.

"Stop! Stop!"

A head emerged from the left side of the cab. The head was covered with sandy hair, the eyes were of a watery blue, the cheek florid. The man was stout, and had a short neck.

The obedient driver drew up.

Both heads were drawn in.

Then the dark-haired man addressed a man with the face of a sheep, who sat with his back to the horses.

"Mr Poles! will you get out, and with your umbrella scrape down that abominable placard? It is indecent!"

"Do, please, Mr Poles. It will serve as a protest," said the sandy-haired man.

"Must I?" asked the gentleman with the sheep's head.

"Indeed, indeed you must. We will wait for you. Thomas shall not drive on. Consider the privilege, Poles, of putting away evil. Act up to your name. Be a Phineas; use your umbrella."

Thus adjured, the sheep-faced man stumbled out over the knees of the dark occupant of the back seat, and proceeded to efface the placard with the ferrule of his umbrella.

"It's rather large," said he, "and the paste is adhesive."

"Rip it down," advised the fair-haired man.

"Jump and lay hold of the shreds, and you will peel off large pieces," urged the dark man.

Some boys began to collect and utter protests. A handful of mud thrown by one urchin, who had secreted himself behind the carriage, struck Mr Poles in the small of the back.

"Poles!" called one of the inmates of the cab, "you had better return to us. The Moabites are upon us. We will drive on."

Accordingly, the sheep-faced witness to decorum re-entered the cab.

"Go on, Thomas," said the dark head at one window.

"You may drive on," said the sandy head at the other window.

Meanwhile, a labouring man, standing near the front wheel of the vehicle, asked the driver who he was conveying.

"It's a deputation," answered the coachman, without turning his head.

"And what monkey-tricks be this bloomin' deputation after?" further inquired the workman.

"It's goin' to protest agin' the circus, and stop it, if it can, from comin' into Saltwich."

"Thomas! I said 'drive on!'" called the dark-haired, interior passenger from the left window.

"Do you hear? Drive on!" said the fair-haired passenger from the right window.

The labouring man, looking steadily at the face on the left, said,—

"Oh! that's Jabez Grice." Then he caught sight of the sandy-haired man on the right, and said, "So! Nottershaw is one of this deputation. And Poles," he added, as his eye caught the side-face of the sheep-like man with his back to the horses.

The driver had described his fare concisely and accurately. He was, in fact, conveying a deputation commissioned by the Seriously-Minded of the town of Saltwich, and that deputation consisted of the quintessence of that body—the cream, the core of all that was respectable and sedate. Out of rude, common life, the ore was laboriously extracted by the efforts of the various ministers of the several denominations in Saltwich. The fine gold of perfect humanity thus obtained was run into the moulds of the different denominational chapels. But just as an alchemist who sublimates gold draws from it one essential, nay, super-essential drop, so did each congregation of the Seriously-Minded, on distillation, yield up a quintessence; and such drops of superlative excellence were the three gentlemen who formed the deputation—Mr Jabez Grice, foreman of Messrs Brundrith's Salt Works; Mr John Nottershaw, architect, builder, contractor and surveyor; and Mr Phineas Poles the paperhanger.

Saltwich was a Cheshire Jerusalem, whither the tribes of the Seriously-Minded went up to deepen their gravity, build up their self-assurance, and sharpen the severity with which they judged their neighbours.

Unhappily there were tares among the wheat, dross along with the gold—a certain number in the place who could not be purged of their grossness, however vigorously the bellows might be blown and the rakes applied. Resolutely and defiantly they maintained their levity.

If it had been possible to have accommodated all the Seriously-Minded along one side of the street, and relegated the frivolous to the other side, it would have been satisfactory. But practically this was not feasible. A veritable puss-in-the-corner, or prisoners' bass, was played in Saltwich. Some of the most worldly became for a while grave, and passed over to the side of the sedate; then some of the seriously-disposed relapsed, and were found in the congregation of the frivolous. It was not possible, geographically, to circumscribe or distribute the two classes. And yet, to a limited extent, such a separation had been effected, and one portion of Saltwich went vulgarly by the name of Jewry, another by that of Heathendom. The eminently serious had succeeded in securing most of the offices of authority and trust in the place, and they had established an outward semblance of gravity in the town. The only large hall in Saltwich was under their control, and no theatrical performances, no nigger-minstrelsy, no public dances were ever suffered to take place within its walls. Nothing was tolerated beneath its roof more sportive than a missionary meeting, more entertaining than dissolving views of Palestine.

A quiver of dismay ran through austere Saltwich when it was blazed abroad on every hoarding, and at every street-corner, that the circus of Signor Giuseppi Santi, with galloping ostriches, naked Indians, performing dogs, short-skirted dancers, clowns, trapezists, bounders through fiery hoops, was about to enter the town, erect its booths, and give a performance—and that, moreover, on the very evening upon which the renowned Rev. Dr Tallow of Jericho, U.S.A., was advertised to give an impressive undenominational and awakening exercise in the Town Hall, with the approval of all denominations in Saltwich.

It was such a privilege to have, for one night, Dr Tallow in their midst. It was so important to give him an united, an enthusiastic reception. It was so advisable to impress on the reverend doctor the intense seriousness of the inhabitants—and now, on that very day when the Rev. Dr Tallow entered the town at one side, slightly-draped damsels and men in fleshings, clowns in paint and powder, and piebald ponies would be entering it on the other side; and, what was worst of all, at the very time that the Rev. Dr Tallow was to coruscate in his most brilliant periods, pirouette at the apex of his loftiest elocution—at that very time, within a stone's cast of the hall, a circus with painted Jezebels and half-draped Bathshebas, and every description of allurement that the wicked world could offer, would be attracting to it the young and the thoughtless.

The sting of the consideration lay in the fact just alluded to, that the circus would be planted within a stone's throw of the Town Hall.

Owing to the frequent and protracted subsidences of the land as the salt rock beneath the town was extracted, the Old Town Hall had gone to pieces, and had sunk half-way up its first floor, and had to be pulled down. Then a New Town Hall had been erected on higher ground, on a space that was considered secure. As there was open ground hard by, the proprietor of the circus had obtained permission from the proprietor of the field to erect his booth thereon, and there display his attractions. It must be allowed that he had made his arrangements in complete ignorance of the fact that the Rev. Dr Tallow was to hold forth in the Town Hall that same evening.

The elect did not feel anxious for themselves. They feared for the wavering. They feared for the young. They feared for the nibblers. They feared for their own sons and daughters, for their domestics and shop-boys.

The Seriously-Minded put their heads together. What was to be done? To postpone the visit of the eminent American preacher would be an acknowledgment of defeat. To run Dr Tallow against Signora Muslina was risky. To the Seriously-Minded, of course, no hankering after the circus could occur. They would all be found on the benches or on the platform—but how about their young people? Would not they take advantage of the absence of their elders to rush to the circus?

Again, owing to the proximity of the circus, was it not likely that the strains of Signor Santi's brass band playing the "Rogues' March" might be heard within the hall, and overpower the sighs and groans of the listeners to the reverend doctor? that "Pop goes the Weasel" might disturb the effect produced by his most impressive applications? that the cheers and hand-clapping at some dexterous feat of a trapezist or hoop-jumper might distract the attention of the auditors and set them, in their minds, lusting after the vanities of the circus?

Accordingly, the various denominations squeezed themselves to produce their finest elixir, and this fine elixir was deputed to see Mr Button, the farmer owning his own land, to whom belonged the plot whereon the circus was to be erected, and to induce him to withdraw it from the equestrian troupe.

II

HOW THE DEPUTATION FARED

Mr Button was apparently a well-to-do man. He had set up brick gate-posts in alternating bands of white and red, and elaborate cast-iron gates at the entrance to his drive, and had planted his drive with shrubs, which, however, did not thrive vigorously, owing to the fumes from the chimneys of the Salt Works. He had rebuilt his house. It was as square in base as the pyramid of Ghizeh but not so secure, for the whole district of the Weaver Valley rested on beds of salt rock, and as that salt rock was corroded by water, and then sucked out in the form of brine by the steam pumps, the surface of the country sank correspondingly. Mr Button, prepared for this contingency, had built his house in the Cheshire fashion, with timber and brick. His foundations consisted of stout oak beams laid on the soil, extending somewhat beyond the lines of his walls. The advantages of this method of construction lay in the fact that, should a subsidence take place, his house would not split and fall about his head, but would lurch and settle either sideways or backwards or forwards, bodily, and then it would be possible to escape from it without danger.

The salt rock of the Cheshire beds is sixty-three feet thick; the height of Saltwich about forty feet above the sea; consequently the withdrawal of sixty-three feet of rock threatened, in time, to send that tract of country under sea level.

Consider yourself in bed and, snug on a mattress with a palliasse below, and that some practical joker were to draw the palliasse from under you; you would sink the full thickness of the withdrawn bed of straw. So, in the Cheshire district, the inhabitants rest above a matt of marl, lying over a palliasse of salt rock. The manufacturers draw out from under them this bed of rock, and down settle the inhabitants many feet deeper than they were before. Sometimes they descend slowly, sometimes they go down with a jerk.

The way in which this letting down of the surface of the land is performed is ingenious, and those whose properties are affected can obtain no redress. It is not brought about by mining—that is to say, no mining done by pick and shovel. What is done is to sink a shaft to where the brine overlies the rock, and pump it up. As this goes on night and day, so night and day the water is washing more of the rock till, the whole being dissolved, the whole has been removed in a solution and sent away in the form of salt. In time Mr Button must expect his entire estate to be submerged; but it would probably last his time. He must have a house to cover him, so he had rebuilt his dwelling-house in such manner as to let him down easily when it did sink. Meanwhile, Mr Button did what he could with his land, and did not do badly. He had a large dairy; he made butter, and would have made cheese, had not the consumption of milk and butter in Saltwich been so great that he could do more profitably by selling the raw and partially-manufactured produce of the cow, than by converting it into cheese. And though his land might be going down under his feet, as far as could be judged, his means were rising. He owned a parcel of land, as already said, close to the New Town Hall. Indeed, the site for this New Town Hall had been purchased of him.

The deputation drove in at Mr Button's entrance. The coachman had descended from the box and had rolled back the new iron gates; but somehow the catch did not answer, the fact being that the ground had given way since this catch had been set, so that the man was constrained to hold open the valve and call to his horse to proceed.

The horse dutifully walked forward.

"Way!" called the driver.

The horse did not hear the call, or mistook it, for it quickened its pace and began to trot along the drive.

"Halloo! you darned crocodile!" yelled the coachman, letting go the gate, and running after the cab. Then, considering this objurgation out of keeping with his appearance and the character of his fare, he called "Stay, my dearly-beloved brother!"

The horse, offended at the first epithet, and not mollified by the second address, trotted still faster. It did not halt at the door of the house, but trotted on past it, past the shrubs, out into a field, with the deputation behind it, flinging itself about through the windows, grappling at the door handles, shouting remonstrances to the horse in front, and cries to the driver running behind, and was suddenly arrested by a hand on the bit. The arrest was so sudden that Mr Poles was precipitated against the two other members of the deputation.

"Now, then," exclaimed Mr Button, coming to the door of the cab, "what are you gents after? Have you taken tickets for the bottomless pit, and are in a desperate haste to be at your destination?"

"Oh, sir, will you drag out Mr Poles? Take him piecemeal if you will. He is smothering us!"

Mr John Nottershaw butted at the paperhanger with his head, and managed by brute force to drive him back-foremost out at the door, and then he emerged himself in a somewhat rumpled condition.

"The horse ran away," he explained.

"The horse was curious, no doubt, to see what has happened. Justifiable under the circumstances."

"What has happened?" asked Mr Nottershaw.

"Come and see for yourselves. What! is that Jabez Grice? Halloo! What brings you here? Let me see—one, two, three of you all in your Sunday-go-to-meeting togs, and coming in the cab also! What's in the wind? Money? Subscriptions? I've none. I've lost one of my finest Jerseys. Come and see. I had her brought from the Channel Islands; she cost me a large sum, and now—I can't even get her hide for tanning, or horns and hoofs for gelatine. But, bless me! what have you driven in the cab for?"

Mr Button might well ask; the distance from Saltwich was inconsiderable. The fact was that the deputation had engaged the vehicle so as to give weight to their representations.

"We have not come for money," said Mr Grice with dignity. "We have come as representatives of a large portion of the inhabitants of Saltwich to lay before you our views."

"Let me lay mine before you first, man," said the farmer.

"We have a serious cause of complaint."

"So have I; I've lost my cow. Come along and look at my grievance. You are in the Salt Works, Jabez, and so are to blame, and should indemnify me. But I know better than to look for indemnification to you salt men. Brundrith says 'Prove that I did it, and I will pay.' But I can't prove that it was Brundrith, and not Hewlett or Elson. I go to Hewlett; he says 'Show that I did it, I'm a mile and a half from your place; try Elson.' Elson says 'Convince me it was I—not Brundrith. I am two miles and a half off. We all pump.' There is no redress to be got. I must bite my nails and bear it."

Several men were in the field standing about a conical gap in the surface, at the bottom of which water or mud was in a condition that looked like ebullition, though in reality it was cold.

"Don't go too near," said Button; "the surface is moving, cracking, and more will settle shortly."

"But where is the cow."

"There!" answered the farmer, pointing to the cauldron. "All at once the land gave way whilst my Jersey was cropping the grass, and in the wink of an eye she had disappeared. Where is my cow? You see a hole in the surface where my Jersey was, and she is going down, goodness knows where to, somewhere, below there in the bowels of the earth; somewhere, where salt rock was, there is now my Jersey worth forty pounds. That is what comes of your pumping, Grice."

"Well, sir! It's a great loss—but you must reckon that the salt works bring a market to your door. If you lose in one way, you win in another."

"I know that; I am sick of this concern," cried Button. "If anyone would pay me twelve thousand pounds, he should have the whole bag of tricks. I'll tell you what he ought to do—set up a salt work of his own. Why should Brundrith, Elson and Hewlett suck out all the rock from under our feet? Let us suck against them and make what we can out of our own salt, and that underlying our neighbours. 'Make hay while the sun shines' is the saying. Here we have it—'Get out the salt whilst you can, and the devil take posterity!'"

"You had best do that yourself, Mr Button."

"Not I; I have not the energy nor the experience. Come, Jabez, if you can find the money, you shall have the place, and run against Brundrith and Elson, and make your fortune."

"I have not the money."

"Well, mention my offer to those who have. If I were a younger man, I'd suck at one end and Brundrith at the other, and see which could suck the other down, and suck the wealth to himself."

"Now," said Jabez Grice, "will you listen to what we have to say?"

"By all means; but come from here—we can do no more than lament over my vanished, cow and the field which is going after the cow, and will soon be converted into a flash.¹ Come along, into the house, and I will listen to what you have to say."

He led the way to his square residence, the roof of which rose to a point with a block of central chimneys in the midst. The advantage of this arrangement was that the chimneys were propped up on every side. The cabman with his conveyance followed.

As soon as the party was in the nearly square sitting-room, the deputation opened the subject on which it was commissioned to wait on him.

"Oh! about this affair of the circus—I don't see how I'm to get out of it. I've promised the field."

Mr Nottershaw looked at Mr Grice, and the paperhanger looked at first one, and then the other.

"I suppose the agreement is hardly committed to writing?" said Jabez.

"No—but a man's word should be as good as his bond."

"Well—yes—in ordinary circumstances. But there are occasions when no man is bound. No man is bound to commit a sin."

"I don't know how, without disgrace, I can get out of a promise."

Mr Grice rubbed his polished chin.

"It depends on the wording," he said. "I suppose you promised the field by the Town Hall."

"Certainly."

"Did you specify which Town Hall?"

"There is but one. The other has been pulled down."

"That is true, but the situation still bears the name of Town Hall Field."

"The flash is there and the ground is full of cracks."

"I'll tell you what, Button," broke in Nottershaw, "you never did a worse job in your life than encouraging these mountebanks. There are two members of the Weaver Trust will be on the platform of the Rev. Dr Tallow, and they won't thank you; they won't propose you for a trustee at the next vacancy, you may be certain, and that won't be far off—old Whitley is on his last legs. I've heard from a bird who whispers in my ear that you have a fancy to be on the Trust—rather."

"And then," said Mr Grice, "many of the Serious-Minded get their milk and butter—"

"And eggs," threw in Mr Poles.

"Milk, butter and eggs from you; and it would be a pity—a great pity—to offend them. I don't say it would, but it might, affect your pecuniary interests—there is no knowing; it would be unreasonable, still there is no knowing; they might transfer their custom to Ruggles, get him to supply them with butter and milk."

"And eggs," added the paperhanger.

"Butter and milk and eggs," said Grice, again accepting the addition.

"You see, Button," said the builder, "I'm a man of business myself, and I know that it don't do to offend parties which hang together like bees. Honey-bearing they may be, yet sting they can. You'll excuse me, I'm a practical man."

"But what can I do?"

"The matter is clear as rock salt," said Jabez in a peremptory tone. "The Old Town Field is good enough for those ragamuffins. They shall have that or none. A parcel of tight-rope dancers have no right to pick and choose, to say 'We will have this site, to the disturbance and annoyance of the Seriously-Minded, and we will not have that, which will incommode nobody worth consideration.' Send them where they will be no nuisance."

"But," said the farmer with hesitation, "the old field is not safe. It is at the edge of the flash, and the ground is full of cracks, and is slipping in."

"So much the better—it may deter many from attendance."

"I don't know what to say," said Button, rubbing his head and looking with keen eyes at Jabez Grice. "You see—it was an understanding."

"A misunderstanding, you must let them comprehend. They shall have the Old Hall Field. Nonsense! Mr Button, you are not so foolish as to trifle away your interests for the sake of a set of mountebanks; they shall go beside the flash, and it will do for them; there will be water there for their horses."

"It is dangerous."

"No harm will come to them—they are there for one night only. Look here, Mr Button, you want to sell your scrap of land. I'll speak to Brundrith, he lays great stress on my opinion. I'll advise him to buy, so as to avoid the chance of competition."

"As you will, gentlemen," said Button. "Let me see, I'll go off to Chester. You must manage for me."

Still his twinkling eye was on Grice.

As the deputation prepared to leave, he crooked in his finger and winked at Jabez. He put his finger through his button-hole and held him back. When the other two were out of bearing, he said—

"I know there is something behind—do you think I'm a fool? I remember poor Joe Sant—I know him in spite of his Signor, his Giuseppe, his Santi, and all that sort of thing. I suppose, Grice, you don't like that he, your half-brother—"

"He is not even my quarter-brother."

"As you will—your reputed brother should appear in tights and spangles when you are haranguing. Well, it would be a scandal. I'll go away, and you shall block every entrance to my field. Settle with them that they are to rig up their show in Old Hall Field instead of New

Hall Field, beside the flash instead of near your meeting. And—mind–
—remember what you said about Brundrith. I'm sick of living on a
sinking soil."

1. A flash is the local term for a sheet of water where once was dry
    ground.

III

OLD HALL FIELD

THE LOSS OF THE FIELD near the New Town Hall did not greatly affect the spirits of the equestrian troupe, for it did not seem likely to materially affect their prospects. They were of a sanguine disposition, ready to make the best of very adverse circumstances, and the obligation to transfer the scene of their performances from one part of the town to another did not strike them as matter for concern. They were provided with an open space on which to pitch their tents, and this open space was nearer to the densest-populated part of Saltwich than was the site first agreed upon.

Where they now were was on the fringe of the ragged land near the old portion of the town—old, that is to say, comparatively, for the brine springs of Saltwich had not been discovered before the end of the eighteenth century, and the town had sprung up where had once been green fields. The most ancient buildings were comparatively modern and eminently ugly. They consisted of rows of brick cottages, and it was precisely these rows which went locally by the name of Heathendom.

These rows were regarded by the denominations of the grave, who held Saltwich in their grip, as all but hopeless as a hunting-ground. Its inhabitants were wholly given over to insolent, inconsiderate gaiety.

Their levity of conduct was a continual offence to the Seriously-Minded. The noise of Heathendom contrasted with the quietude of Jewry. The two moral hemispheres of Saltwich were in perpetual feud. Not a window in Heathendom contained a notice that the great American preacher was about to hold forth in the New Town Hall, and not a blank wall in Jewry displayed the attractions of the horsemanship.

In Heathendom congregated the poachers who ravaged Delamere Forest and provided the hares and rabbits and partridges for the local poulterers, to whom the Seriously-Minded gave their custom, without inquiring too closely whence all this game came.

Two streets had gone to rack and ruin, rifts had formed in the house-walls, and stacks of chimneys had fallen. The grave regarded this as a judgment on the gay who had inhabited them—whilst themselves pumping and steaming and sending away and converting into gold the salt rock that underlay these habitations. If the poor were turned out of their houses, or if they were forced to spend half their time in their bedrooms because their sinking kitchens were flooded—what did it represent to the imaginations of the serious of every denomination, who were themselves securely and dryly housed, but a call addressed by Nature herself to the frivolous to mend their ways.

In Heathendom were crushed and crowded together all such as had been driven out of the condemned and demolished houses; no room was given them in the new and spacious parts of the town, where the houses were of white brick and the windows of red brick, and every house had its little railed garden before its doors and its green Venetian blinds over its windows.

The portion of open land given up to the equestrians was precisely the site on which the demolished houses and the Old Town Hall had stood. It shelved down to a "flash"—a sheet of water occupying about a hundred acres—that had been formed by the subsidence of the soil. The surface of the field was singularly furrowed, as though at intervals a plough had been run through it. This open space grew but scanty, and that coarse, grass, and had the look as though blighted. It had been covered with buildings for half a century, and now that the buildings were demolished, it had not sufficiently recovered to resume its aspect of verdant meadow. Elsewhere, proximity to water would have produced luxuriant vegetation. It was not so here. What grass there was seemed to be dead, the bushes were stunted, and the trees were mere skeletons devoid of leafage. In all directions were strewn torn sardine cases, open empty tins of Ramornie beef, broken marmalade pots, scraps of newspaper, scale from brine pans, decaying rabbit skins, corroded saucepans and perforated kettles, mutton bones, old boots that seemed to have been exploded by dynamite, toothless hair-combs of imitation horn, and from the branch of a dead tree swung an abandoned crinoline, which, having gone out of fashion, had there committed suicide.

The erection of the circus was complete, and highly-coloured pictures representing the troupe performing their most remarkable achievements were displayed in front of it. There was to be a procession of the Queen of Love, drawn in a mother-o'-pearl shell by ostriches, with Cupid on the box. Wild Indians in moccasins, and with scalps flying at their girdles, were to hunt the buffalo. A horse rivalling that of Baron Munchausen would dance on a tea-table without disturbing the cups. The Pearl of the Indies, in the lightest of gauze drapery, would bound through a flaming hoop. Performing dogs would drink and smoke and play whist. The Modern Proteus would go through twenty transformations on horseback. The "Tailor of Brentwood" was declared on the posters to be a screaming farce, certain to convulse the spectators. Finally, the entertainment would conclude with a grand, and gorgeous, and hitherto unequalled display of the Queen of Love receiving the homage of gods, men and beasts.

Never, within the memory of the oldest inhabitant, were such attractions offered to the inhabitants of Saltwich. The outside of the great tent was contemplated by the assembled crowd with mixed feelings. Some of the eminently serious, who had descended—ay, condescended—to look at the erections in the Old Field, felt that Dr Tallow must be indeed a giant, in eloquence to contend with, and wrest from Signor Santi a congregation sufficient to fill the New Hall. They believed that they stood on the verge of a crisis, when a revolution threatened, if it were not imminent. Servant girls were asking leave to visit sick mothers. Boys were pretending to have influenza colds which would keep them from attendance at the New Hall. School children, instead of rushing home when class was dissolved, ran to the field to peer through the joints in the boarding round the arena, or to lose themselves in astonishment at the pictures displayed. The supremacy of the grave in Saltwich stood in jeopardy. The serious looked vastly serious. Their mouths went down at the corners, and their confidence sank to their boots. There would be no overflow at the New Hall. There would be backsliders—there was no possibility of captures; some who were infirm in their gravity would be seduced to see the show, and all who might be "brought in" would, to a man, be in the sixpenny seats at the circus. But that was not all. Father and mother could not go together to listen to Dr Tallow, and leave their children at home, for how could they be sure that their little ones would not forsake their beds and steal away to the Old Hall Field? What missionary boxes would be safe when the fingers of domestics were itching for the money that would entitle them to see dancing dogs, acrobats and ostriches in procession? How could a serious husband be sure, suppose he left his wife behind to keep guard, that she would not yield to the solicitations of the young people, lock the door and go off with them to the horsemanship? Or the sedate wife—how could she be certain, when her husband left her at home, under the pretext that he was going to hear the great Jericho preacher, how could she have any well-grounded confidence that he would not turn his back on the New Hall at the first corner, and be found applauding the damsel balancing herself on one toe, and roaring over the jokes of the clown? What seeds of revolt! What rifts in domestic confidence were like to ensue from this inauspicious arrival of Signor Santi with his troupe in Saltwich!

At a distance of a hundred and fifty yards from the circus and its satellite booths and tents stood a solitary van. It was large, it was long, and was gaily painted. It was carved with wonderful flourishes, all of which were gilt. It had glass windows, partly obscured by muslin blinds and by red curtains. A stove flue projected through the roof. From the door a set of four steps was let down to the level of the soil.

On the topmost of these steps, with her back to the door, sat a girl of seventeen; but she was small, childlike for her age, and looked younger by a couple of years. She was engaged in opening and eating walnuts. She was delicately formed and graceful, with flowing, golden hair that reached her waist, and very dark eyes and brows. The brows and lashes were, in fact, so dark that many a woman, certainly all of the serious persuasion, would be sure to assert that they were dyed. Had her eyes been blue or grey, then the brows and lashes might indeed have been justly taken to be artificially coloured, but they were not so in this case. Nature is always cunning in her harmonies; and the dark-brown eyes, with a golden sheen in the brown, admirably agreed with the still darker brown of the arched brows and the long lashes. The girl had a roguish look in her face, and dimples in both cheeks, but mainly in that on the left, for she had the trick of smiling more on one side than on the other. But though one side of her face might laugh more than the other, it was not so with the eyes, in both of which was an equally merry twinkle. The one of her smile gave a peculiar archness and special drollery to her sunny face.

Standing in front of her, below the steps, looking at her as she ate, with wonder in his great blue eyes, was a youth of one-and-twenty, with very fair hair, an open face, an expression gentle, and without force and strong individuality. Indeed, it may be said that there lay an evidence of constitutional or impressed timidity in the tremulous mouth and the quivering eyes.

He did not speak; he contented himself with staring. The girl did not resent observation. Every now and then she looked him full in the eyes. Then hers sparkled and the dimples formed in the slightly-flushed cheeks. Whenever she did this, the youth coloured to the roots of his fair hair, and lowered his eyelids abashed. After this silent homage had continued for some while, and the girl was tired of eating and being contemplated in mute admiration, though not tired of the homage, she said, glancing up slyly,—

"Are you fond of nuts?"

The young man started, alarmed at being addressed.

"Look," said she; "you shall share mine."

She took half a dozen, stepped down to him and thrust them into his pocket. He caught his breath and staggered back. She resumed her seat on the steps, and continued eating.

"What! No teeth to crack them?" she said. "I will help you again!"

Then she removed the upper shells of three, and placed them in a row on the step at her feet. They were fresh, yellow as butter.

"You are good," said the young man, shuffling from one foot to another; "but I will not deprive you of them."

He looked at the tempting nuts. He dared not put his hand so near her as to take one.

"Will you have one peeled?" asked the girl, flashing a glance at him, and puckering her funny little mouth.

Without awaiting a reply, she put a nut in her mouth, cracked the shell, then set to work deftly to remove the bitter skin. When the kernel was completely stripped, with a roguish look and her head a little on one side, and the golden hair flowing over one shoulder, she held out her palm, pink as a fan-shell, and with the kernel in it, white as an almond.

The boy recoiled in alarm.

"What! Do you think I am giving you poison? Oh, silly Adam! I am not Eve offering the forbidden fruit. This is quite harmless. There is no ban on walnuts. I thought you liked them—you looked at me in such a manner while I ate. Come! take and eat, you silly goose!"

Shyly the youth drew near, his face burning, his eyes on the ground, and his limbs trembling. He took the kernel so clumsily from the little, rosy palm that he touched the hand. A shock ran through him, and he gasped as though he had dipped his head under water.

"I thank you," he said.

"Why are you afraid of me? I am a teeny-weeny mite; you are a mighty fellow. Adam—"

"My name is not Adam, but Andrew."

"Andrew, if I were to put a walnut between my lips, and bid you come up close and bite it away, I believe you would die of terror."

He could not speak—the proposal made him giddy.

"No; but for all that I will not give you the chance. Take your three nuts, you toothless creature."

"I am ashamed; you have already put some in my pocket."

"You blush like a girl. We folks always give that we may take. I want something of you."

"What is that?"

"I want to know your thoughts. What were you thinking about me? What ideas were slouching about in that stupid head of yours covered with such a shock of tow, as you looked at me eating my walnuts?"

"I was thinking how pretty you were."

He reeled as he said this, astonished at himself for having paid a compliment.

The girl burst into a merry laugh and clapped her hands.

"We are getting on; this is famous. And your wishes—what are they? To come to the show and see me in all my glory—the Queen of Love? Well—it costs sixpence for the inferior seats; reserved seats, one shilling."

"I don't know—I am engaged."

"Engaged elsewhere? Where to?"

He hung his head.

"What a funny place this Saltwich is," said the girl.

"Saltwich funny! It is a very serious place. There are seven chapels in it of different denominations, besides—"

"Save me from the besides. I mean how funny it is that the place should live and thrive on salt."

"Yes—if there were no brine springs here, Saltwich would be nowhere; it has no other manufacture."

"How do you make salt?"

"We boil the brine."

"Where does the brine come from?"

"From the bowels of the earth."

"I should like to see salt made."

"Then," answered the young man eagerly, "come to the works to-morrow and I will show you everything."

"What are you?"

"A waller."

"What! a mason?"

"No; a waller with us means a boiler. I am on the day shift, and have to steam the brine, and rake the salt off as it forms."

"You are on the day shift?"

"Yes—I do not work at night."

"Then your objection falls through. You are *not* engaged. You will come to the show."

"It is not at the works that I am engaged," said the youth, colouring; "I have to go with my father to a meeting at the Town Hall."

"What! to the undenominational hop folks talk of as likely to spoil our attendance?"

"It is not a hop."

"What else can draw folks away? It must be a dance; that is the only other attraction I can think of that would take away the people from us. I suppose you Saltwichers love a hop. So would I if I had the chance—which I have not."

"You do not understand. If I could but persuade you to come to the meeting; it would do you so much good."

"I can't—I am engaged—in reality engaged. You can see that on the posters. Come and see me in my cockle-shell. Have you sixpence? No," said she, correcting herself, "from you I will have more—a shilling—and will reserve you the very best seat of all. Will you have the place? Give me the shilling."

"Here."

He extended a silver coin.

"And here in return is a ticket. Now, you must and shall come. It will be a grand show—it will be worth a bob to see me alone. I shall go about on two cream horses. I shall jump from the back of one to the back of the other, and all the while I shall look about for you. We have to keep very steady heads when we are performing, or dreadful things may happen."

"What things?"

"If I am not thinking of what I am about, but thinking of you, and why you have not come, then there is no saying, I may drop between the horses, and go under their cruel hoofs, and there would be the end of poor little Queenie!"

The thought that this girl would be concerned if he did not appear, that his absence might set her little heart in a flutter of disappointment, was too much for the lad. He put his hands to his head—it was spinning like a teetotum; then she spread out her arms, shaking the broken nuts over the side of the steps.

"What is your name?" she asked.

"Andrew Grice."

"And I am Queenie Sant," said she. Then putting her head on one side, and throwing a mischievous twinkle into her eyes, she said coaxingly—"You will come and see me? Promise, you good Andrew, and swear—"

"Hush, hush!"

"I vow and protest I will transform grave Andrew into a very merry Andrew; also, I will come to your salt works to-morrow. If I do not see you I will not come."

Then all at once a young man of rough exterior, with a shock of sandy hair on his head, strode to the side of the girl, and before she was aware, had bowed and lightly kissed her cheek. Turning to Andrew he said scornfully,—

"Stoop, fool, and pick up the nutshells offered; I, as a man, take what I can snatch, unasked—I—Rab Rainbow."

IV

RAB RAINBOW

THE GIRL SPRANG TO HER feet alarmed, incensed. The act of Rab Rainbow was so unexpected. Indeed, she had not even perceived the approach of the man. Nor had Andrew Grice observed him, so engrossed had he been in watching the circus girl, though Rab had been there for some little while, leaning his elbow against the van, with his fingers thrust through his light, bushy hair, looking down on the little Queen as she played with, and attracted the young waller.

The moment she had recovered herself, she sprang through the door into the caravan, and bolted it behind her.

Rab laughed, and cast himself carelessly on the steps, planting a foot on the ground on each side, beyond the steps, thrust his rough cloth cap to the back of his head, and picked up such nuts as were not broken, and such fragments of kernel as lay on the step where he sat, ready for consumption.

Andrew Grice thought it incumbent on him to remonstrate with Rab for what he had done. Rainbow broke a nutshell, looked up, and asked contemptuously,—

"What brings you among the tents of the ungodly?"

"I can go where I please," retorted the waller, "without asking your leave."

"What will the daddy say?"

"I am my own master."

"No, you ain't, or weren't. I am surprised to see you among the good-for-naughts, and larking wi' circus-girls. You, Andrew, oh fie!"

"I was not larking."

"Quite right. You haven't the spring and carol of a lark in you."

Rab Rainbow was a tall, strongly-built young man, with light hair, and features of no regularity of shape, and no special character, but he had a pair of good, clear, grey eyes. He was dressed in a sandy suit, short cut, untidy but not ragged, bulged and patched, and on his legs were breeches and gaiters. The coat was dragged out of shape at the pockets, which were obviously often burdened with heavy weights, or distended beyond their proper size.

There was a careless good-nature in the man's face, and this was all that was attractive about it; for he was far from handsome in feature, and his complexion was coarse and red. A gamekeeper would at once have set him down for a poacher, and, in fact, Rab's principal employment and amusement consisted in snaring rabbits and shooting pheasants in Delamere Forest. This royal forest at one time extended over 10,000 acres, but is now reduced to half that size. There are numerous noblemen's seats in the neighbourhood with extensive preserves. Five thousand acres of woodland, beside parks and preserves, afforded quite sufficient scope for Rab and those of his trade to pick up a livelihood. The poulterers' shops at Northwich, Saltwich and Winsford were kept supplied with game of all sorts by these free sportsmen.

"It would do you good, Andrew, to come to the circus to-night, and, as you've bought a ticket, come."

"I don't know. I am—"

"Yes; I know. The old "Hammer" will take you with him to the undenominational affair. I wouldn't go, if I was you. I'd come here. You've bought a ticket; it's a sin to waste a shillin'. I know, and you know, just exactly what the American doctor will say. There'll be so many anecdotes, so many illustrations, so much butterin' of the grave, and so much damning of the gay. I've gone through that sort of thing scores of times, and so have you. I hate it. You won't have the chance of horsemanship every week, and you can get serious flummery any day."

"You should not speak thus," said Andrew, indignantly. "if you are a backslider, you need not throw your taunts at those from whom you've slipped away, and who stand where you fell."

"Yes," said Rab, thrusting his cap further back on his head, "I am a backslider, sure enough. I dare say I'm a worse man for it; I ain't sure I'm a better. But one thing I do know—I'm a truer man now than I was when I was kickin' in your net."

"That is because you were never radically and sincerely serious."

"May be," said Rab, with a shrug of one shoulder.

"I don't think these travelling horsemanship people ought to be encouraged," said Andrew. "That is why I don't patronise the show."

"Why should they not be encouraged? ' asked Rainbow. "Don't you think life wants a little of the salt o' mirth strewn over it to make it taste less flat, and to keep it wholesome? May be they are just as useful in their way as are you wallers in your fashion."

"Anyhow, they are generally known to be a disreputable set."

"That's known to you, then, which is hid from me," said Rab, drawing his feet up on the step, and folding his arms on his knees. "Look here! You've been talkin' to the little lass in here, behind"—he pointed with his chin over his shoulder—"Do you know that she is the daughter of the manager? Do you think he ain't got fatherly love and care for her? Rats and mice have it for their little uns. Crows and jackdaws have it for theirs. You don't allow that mountebanks have what you know the beasts and birds possess. That never enters your serious noddle. You don't think that the Signor, as a father, would guard his child from every mischief, and eat his heart out with grief if ill came to the pretty mite? No; that never struck your dull imagination. And the young woman that goes through the fiery hoop, and dances on one toe on horseback—you mayn't suspect she's the wife of the clown, but I tell you she is so. If you'll come this evenin' and look at him instead of her, you'll see him wince every time she goes through the flames, and that he has his eye followin' her, and hands ready to catch her should she fall, all the while that he is crackin' his jokes and makin' grimaces, and cuttin' antics. If you'll come and see that, then you'll learn more of human nature than you will under the Rev. Tallow. And, somethin' more you may learn—or, at least, come to suspect—that the clown would not have his wife, for all her muslin skirts and bare arms, do anything but what is fittin' and decent in an honest wife and a good mother. You'll rub your eyes when you've learnt that; and that's what you won't get at the New Town Hall."

"I am very rejoiced to hear this," said Andrew.

"I'll tell you somethin' more," said Rab. "These poor creatures in the circus, they paint for an hour, and then wash it all off, and they are natural men and women, as God made them, for the other twenty-three hours. There's folks—I name no names—as wouldn't set their foot inside the horsemanship, who paint, and never get out of paint. They eat in paint, they sleep in paint, they talk and they walk in it. And the coorious sarcumstance is, that everyone else sees it is paint but themselves. There be some such in your show—I don't say all—and the thing that's remarkable about it is, that in your show everyone paints up to deceive his own self first, and he does it thoroughly. That paint, red-lead, gets into the veins and colours his blood; that paint, white-lead, gets into the head and is converted into brain. I'll tell you what is the great difference between these horsemanship folk and those I speak of—the real difference that goes to the bottom of all. Those who paint in your show deceive themselves first, and then, when that is thoroughly accomplished—with a deception never to be shaken off—then they take in others. The fellows in the circus paint, and they never—not for one moment—deceive either themselves or others."

"I don't understand you."

"Don't you? I don't suppose you do. I'll tell you what the symptoms are. The fellows in your show get to so believe in and worship their own painted-up and false selves, that they think and say that nobody can be right unless he be a reflection of themselves. If they likes beefsteak puddin', then cursed be he who has a fancy for mutton hash. If they walk on the shady side of the street, then may a sunstroke take him who prefers to go on the south side. They have such a likin' for the smell of a cauldron of biled cabbage, that anathema be to him who likes the scent of the flowering beanfield."

"I'm not one of that sort," said Andrew, sharply.

"Ain't you? You're on the highway to it—what did you say just now about these poor horse-riders being a disreputable lot? You have been galled when on horseback, yourself, I suppose, and so cannot allow anyone to be respectable who can ride."

Andrew turned to go away.

Rab called after him,—

"I've not done with you yet."

Andrew halted and reluctantly looked back.

"You don't often hear what is the opinion formed of you in Heathendom, so it is well to get it when you can. We're a wicked lot, we are, in them red brick cottages, and a wickeder lot was turned out o' them that tumbled down. We talk and we laugh and we have our opinions. Whether they be right or wrong, that's for such to say who holds the balances. I've been about in all coorses of life and conditions of men, and my notion is, there's a deal more good everywhere than you serious ones suppose, and there's good just where you don't expect to find it. Human natur' ain't all perfection in Jewry and all corruption in Heathendom. There are bad men, but the paint hides their badness, who'll be tonight gesticulatin' and haranguin' with the Rev. Tallow, and there'll be good and true men and women looking on at the horse-riders, ay, and ridin' the horses too! The human conscience is healthy and sturdy enough, and the fault I find with your Doctor Tallow and the likes of him is, they don't let it alone, but go pricking and poking at it, and whipping up a lather about it like them cuckoo-spittle insects on the young shoots in spring."

Andrew walked away.

Rab looked after him with a smile in his grey eyes.

"The chap ain't bad if let alone," said he.

As he sat, still smiling and looking after the retreating figure of the young waller, cautiously the window above his head was opened from within, without turning the door on its hinges; then a delicate arm was thrust out and took up Rab's cap from his head, so lightly, so gently, that he was hardly aware of the theft. He put up his hand and rubbed his head, looked about, saw no one, felt behind him, thinking the old bit of headgear had slipped down; then the cap was dropped on his rough locks again, and pinned into the side was a yellow rose.

V

"Hammer" Grice

Andrew walked home slowly and thoughtfully. He had been brought up in the straightest sect of serious-mindedness; his world had been one overcast by clouds, through which flashed no sun to throw the ripple of life into sparkle and laughter. He had been shown mankind as sharply cleft into two spheres, two camps—that of the good and that of the bad—ever at war, sometimes in active hostility, sometimes with that army to which he belonged drawn within Torres Vedras lines, prepared for attack, awaiting the opportunity of taking the field. Such a view of mankind as this is one which commends itself easily, readily, to such as are children in years, and to those whose hearts never expand with the experience of life. They have no idea of the blending of tints; the doctrine of equations is beyond the grasp of their intellects. It is a view which has been formulated into a dogma. Men grow to manhood, and pass through life and descend into their graves, possessed with the idea that their fellow-men are capable of broad and decided classification—into two hosts ranged against each other in internecine strife; into two states, in which the one is of light, the other of darkness. Humanity may be actually of one blood, but it is not, it never was, of one spirit. Not Adam and Eve, bound in mutual sympathies and loving each other to death, are the parents of the human race, but Cain and Abel, envying, hating, pursuing one another. Humanity is not, as a rule, penetrated by like emotions, moved by like ambitions, is not equally subject to caprices. It is not at one time prone to strive after high ideals, and then to sink to basenesses; not to be now generous and then mean; now brave and then cowardly; now true and then false. Far from it! All the loftiness, generosity, heroism, truth are to he found in the one army; and all the baseness, meanness, cowardice, falsehood in the other; and, should there appear in that other some tokens of what is accounted noble, and great, and liberal, then these are not to be accounted in them as intrinsic virtues, but to be esteemed as affectations and unsubstantial phantasms.

Teaching such as this is at home under the turban as well as under the triple tiara; it nestles into the heart under the Pharisee's phylactery and the preacher's gown; it is a teaching which accommodates itself to every creed and confession.

Jabez Grice was dominated by this teaching. It did not tincture merely, it constituted the very essence of his convictions; it petrified them to adamant, and rendered them as immutable as the rules of Nature. Jabez, or "Hammer" as he was commonly designated, had reared his son Andrew, a pliant youth, in this same aspect of life. Sometimes such teaching supplies to a naturally feeble character that iron which it lacks, but at other times it has a debilitating tendency and takes the lime out of the bones.

"Hammer" Grice occupied a house in a new row of cottages on a ridge of rising sandstone that ran no risk of settlement, and looked down with a frown on Heathendom. It was tenanted by exemplary individuals, all serious. No. 4 in Alma Terrace (Jewry, such was its slang designation) was the dwelling that was occupied by Jabez Grice.

From the height of Jewry the very serious sent forth skirmishing parties to hold street preachings in Heathendom, with the hope—a forlorn one—of effecting captures. But these parties rarely returned with spoils; they were usually followed by a groaning, cat-calling mob.

Heathendom retaliated by suborning men with barrel-organs, that ground off dance tunes, to perform along the length of Alma Terrace, and it sent forth its boys and girls to caper and waltz to these strains, under the horrified windows of Jewry.

Every available engine to annoy or discomfit Heathendom was set in operation by the very serious, who, being the respectable, the monied and well-conducted of Saltwich, had the command of the forces that could be employed against the disreputable, impecunious and noisy. They had them watched by the police; they harried them through the School Attendance Committee; they visited them through the Sanitary Officers; they had them dropped upon by the Excise; they worried them through the rate collectors. They made it impossible for a son or daughter of Heathendom to escape into respectability through any other door than that of the chapel. Should a young man from this quarter desire a situation in the police, or as a keeper, or in the army, or navy, no respectable man in the superior quarter would give him a character; and no girl had a chance, for the same reason, of obtaining a situation in a reputable house.

Saltwich was a town that had started up in the extensive parish of Scatterley, with a church at a distance of two miles. The Vicarage was occupied by a gentle, timid man, fond of collecting moths, an authority on lepidoptera, unable to cope with the difficulties of his position, and without the moral energy to attempt to do so. A good, kind man; but rather scientific than spiritual. He hunted beetles and moths, rather than souls. He was content, in face of the dominant nonconformity, to be left unmolested to minister to a couple of farmers, a sporting squire, and his own family. No man was of less account in Saltwich than the Vicar of Scatterley; and even had those whom Jewry had banned appealed to him for encouragement, he would not have dared to uphold them, lest, by so doing, he should offend the nonconformists, and the Serious-Minded of all denominations should conspire against him, and wrest from him one of the two farmers to whom he still ministered on sufferance. Over against the Reverend Edward Meek stood the layman, Jabez Grice, the most commanding power in Saltwich. He was not a man of means or of position. He was foreman at Brundrith's Salt Works on a salary of forty shillings a week, but he was a man of an intense and aggressive personality.

Giants are not necessarily great men, nor are mighty men always big in size. A man is not to be measured by the number of stones he weighs, and the number of feet and inches he stands. "Hammer" Grice was of moderate size, solid in structure, and with a firm head planted on a short neck and broad shoulders. He was not contained within the clothes that enveloped him. He filled every room he entered, he filled his own house, he filled all Jewry; it may almost he said that he filled all Saltwich. Certainly no man in that brine-pumping and steaming town had anything approaching his power. In the factory he was greater than Brundrith. In political influence he was a greater man than the Member of Parliament; in chapel, pastor and elders were his humble servants. No committee could be formed without Grice in it, and, when in it, the fellow-members did little else than register the opinions and resolutions of "Hammer." At an election he swept votes together with an irresistible force; on a platform he could sway his hearers and make them think and feel with himself. He was not an educated man, nor a logical reasoner. He carried his audience with him, not so much by argument as by assertion. No antagonist answered him with impunity. He crushed him under facts, or, at least, statements, or withered him with his scorn.

He was a man who never hesitated in the formation of an opinion, and who never wavered, when once his opinion was formed.

Andrew, brought up under this man, of an amiable, pliable disposition, was bent and moulded as his father desired. He saw, heard, felt through his father's organs. His father could not be wrong in his estimates, and could do no wrong. The strength of the superior nature, instead of infusing its vigour into the inferior, sucked from the latter what little force it possessed.

But Andrew had reached that age when the sap of youth is most vigorous, and he now, for the first time, began to be conscious of, and to feel impatience at, the restraints that had been put upon him, and which he had worn without a murmur as a child. He thrust from him Rab's sneers at the insincerity of "Hammer" and his colleagues. Andrew knew his father, and knew that he was genuine to the core. There was no question as to his earnestness. That Jabez Grice was one of those who imposed on himself before imposing on others, or who imposed

on others because he first thoroughly imposed on himself—this was an
innuendo of Rab's not worthy of consideration.

But there was something in what Rab had said relative to the
vagabond troupe that had stuck in the mind of Andrew, and the
poacher's words had fallen—come apt—on thoughts forming in the
brain of the young man during his conversation with the Queen of
Love.

He had been drawn against himself into this conversation. He had
stood looking at the girl, wondering at her beauty, and, in his own
mind, marvelling that the Creator should have sent such a creature into
the world to run to inevitable wreckage. Then, whilst these thoughts
were turning in his head, the girl had begun to notice him, and had
lured him on, with cleverness and coquetry, into buying a ticket for the
performance. She had some self-respect, some grace in her, for she had
resented the impudence of Rab Rainbow, had flushed with shame and
had fled from his advances. When the girl had disappeared, then the
poacher had spoken with him, and had said words which, if true, were
a revelation, such as is wrought by the rending of clouds, and the display
of a horizon illumined by sunshine and radiant with colour.

Was it possible that the daylight was not confined to Goshen, but
was diffused also throughout Egypt? Was it possible that the dew of
heaven fell on the herb of the field and forest as well as on cabbages
and Brussels-sprouts? Was it possible that there was sweetness of song,
and simplicity of life, and harmony of plumage in the wild bird of the
air, as well as in the caged canary and the fowls in the poultry-house?
As Andrew walked from the Old Hall Field, he saw an Italian playing
a hurdy-gurdy, with a monkey, dressed in trousers and a scarlet coat,
running up the blighted tree, swinging in the wires of the discarded
crinoline, then, at a word from his master, taking a tray and going round
soliciting coppers. Andrew cast in a trifle; but, as he did so, a spring of
gall welled up in his heart. Had he not been reared by his father much
as this monkey had been trained by the Savoyard? He had been taught
to foot it to his father's piping; he was held by him, chained from going
his own way; he was bidden by him do this and leave that, and he had
no option in any matter, and, even as this monkey, he was sent round

with missionary boxes and collecting cards. His brow coloured, and he turned quickly away. He became conscious of straitness, and, for the first time in his life, was inclined to strain his muscles and snap the bandages that were wrapped and knotted about him.

He had been a good boy—diligent in his work, regular in his hours, quiet in the house, docile before his father, and affectionate to his aunt who lived with his father, kindly, obliging to all. He had tasted nothing more stimulating than ginger-beer, had heard nothing more mirth-provoking than a humorous discourse at a chapel anniversary; the social gatherings which he had frequented had been all within the precincts of the Tabernacle or Temperance Hall. He had read nothing more exhilarating than a missionary magazine. Although living in a world in which the knowledge of good and evil (mainly the latter) is pretty generally diffused, and is acquired without the institution of Board Schools, yet Andrew was singularly guileless—as white in mind as blameless in conduct—so completely had he been kept, or had kept himself, within the circle of the serious. Now manhood was reached, and with manhood came a consciousness of innate power, a craving for independence. The imagination of Andrew began to plume its wings, his will to stiffen itself, and his mind to harbour the thought that it was not well for him always to live in abject subserviency, even to so admirable a father as was his.

On reaching No. 4 Alma Terrace, Andrew knew at once that his father was at home, by the fumes of tobacco that met him as he opened the door. He found "Hammer" seated by the fire reading his paper. Jabez recognised his son's footsteps, but did not trouble to look up, nor did he remove his pipe from his lips to throw him a greeting. Why should he? They worked in the same factory. Jabez was not one to trouble himself about the amenities of life; he contented himself with what was practical, substantial.

Andrew saw that the table was laid, and he put his hand upon it. In so doing he threw down a fork.

"Now then, clumsy!" called Jabez, without raising an eye from the line he was reading.

Andrew stooped to pick up the fork, and, in setting it on the table, rattled the cups.

The father growled.

"I should like a word, father, if disengaged."

"I am here."

"I have been to the Old Hall Field. They are there."

"Who are the *They* that are there?"

"The circus people. They have set up their tents."

"We sent them to the Old Hall Field," said Jabez.

"It is going to be an unusually good horsemanship."

"Possibly."

"I am fond of horses."

"Horses are one thing. Legs and muslin skirts are another."

"Father, I do not think I shall be able to accompany you to the New Hall to-night."

"Indeed."

Jabez did not raise his eyes from the paper, but Andrew saw his fingers clench the sheet more tightly, and heard him snort.

"I have so often attended this sort of thing," said Andrew.

"You have never heard the Rev. Tallow."

"No; but I have heard the female revivalist, and the negro evangelist, and the pugilistic apostle, and—'

"And what?"

"It's always very much the same. I don't feel any call to hear Tallow."

"Well—what more?"

The words fell from Jabez like lumps of iron.

"Well, father, and I thought—as a bit of variety, and as, somehow, I have got a ticket for a reserved seat—that—that I'd go to the circus to-night."

"So you are going to the circus?"

"You don't very much mind, father, do you?"

"And where will you go after the circus?"

"Well—I shall be home as soon as you."

"You will not come home at all."

A pause, during which the frizzle of frying onions in the kitchen could be heard. There was to be beef-steak for supper. The smell of the onions mingled with the smoke of tobacco.

"This is what I mean," said Jabez; "you ought before this to have taken lodgings where to stay. You do not stay here. This is not a house in which frequenters of circuses can sit down with chapel-goers. A house divided against itself, No. 4 Alma Terrace shall never be. I give you till half-past seven to remove your clothes. If every rag is not gone by half-past seven, I chuck what remains into the street. Bethulia! dish up!"

"Father, do you mean to turn me out?"

"He that heareth not the Church, let him be to thee as a heathen man and a publican."

"But, father, that's different. Do you mean to say you are the Church?"

"Yes, I am; what else is the Church?" Jabez put down the paper. "Dish up the steak and onions sharp, Bethulia. I'm hungry!"

VI

THE CIRCUS

Rab was in his place on a bench at the circus. He looked about him for Andrew, but could see him nowhere.

"I thought the fellow had hardly the dare in him," said Rab.

The benches filled rapidly. It was really questionable whether any would be left in Saltwich to sit under Dr Tallow, so numerous was the attendance at Signor Santi's rival entertainment.

One thing was, however, noticeable—that the reserved red baize-covered seats did not fill. A good deal of red baize was still exposed. Those who did speckle its surface were not Saltwichers, but country folk, the families of neighbouring gentry. They had sent their children with tutor and governesses, some had even come themselves. A rector was there with wife and offspring. A schoolmaster from a distance was there with his pupils.

Cheshire is famous for its horses; its heart beats high at racing periods. It is in the full glow of life in the hunting months. There are studs around Delamere Forest. The very high roads are furnished with soft trotting ground at their sides specially adapted for horses taken out to practice. From the stables had come grooms and horseboys in great numbers. The exhibition was, above all others, calculated to interest and delight them.

Some of the small shopkeepers of Saltwich were present; such, that is, as were not devoted hand and soul to the serious faction, and Heathendom, as far as its finances would admit, was there to man and boy.

The tent was sustained by a pole in the midst, around which hung a circular chandelier supporting oil lamps. The arena had been strewn with sawdust which, being slightly damp, exhaled an odour that impregnated the atmosphere. The structure on which the public was to sit, raised stage on stage, was simple to rudeness. The deal boards employed had been as few as was consistent with safety. The whole fabric was temporary and flimsy, but was calculated to sustain any amount of direct pressure exerted vertically, when occupied by a crowd of spectators. The boards were not jointed, and there was no flooring under the benches, consequently men who incautiously thrust their hats under their seats, or women their baskets of provisions, had them precipitated to the turf below. A mother screamed because her child had dropped into space, but it was recovered uninjured, having been caught by its frock. There was an outcry from a woman who, in counting her change, had emptied the contents of her purse over the benches and sixpences were dancing down the stage, and threepenny bits slipping between the joints. Some merriment was provoked by a Scatterley farmer who, on taking his place, removed and looked into his hat. It was surmised that he thought he was in church, and that he was saying his prayers.

Vendors went round with oranges and buns; ginger-beer bottles popped and squirted their contents into faces and over frocks.

Personal observations were made on all sides, as was inevitable in a place where everyone knew everyone else.

"My word! There's Susan Naylor in a new bonnet. Who ever is that with her? She's surely not picked up a fresh young man."

"Well, I declare, if that isn't Tommy Tinker! And he is in arrears at the shop. He might have paid for his 'backy, and stayed away."

"There are all the Suggars. Their business must be flourishing. Three whole tickets and eight children at half-price. That makes five-and-six. I'm astonished they ain't ashamed to show what profits they make out of us labouring people."

"Well, I never! There's the Townsends in the reserved seats. What swells they are become! What makes them strut such peacocks is, that they have come in for their uncle's money. But they'll soon run through that if they go reserved-seating it every day!"

"Why, surely the Linterns ain't gone to the sixpenny places, and they gave champagne at their daughter's wedding! I call that shabby—worse than shabby; it's positively dirty. I'd stay away, or go reserved if I gave champagne at a wedding."

The arena was not perfectly smooth. It had been brushed over more than once, but now a sort of ripple was observable on the surface of the sawdust. The manager noticed this and summoned a couple of work men in white jackets to sweep the arena once more.

When they had withdrawn, in leaped the clown with his familiar "Here we are again, and how are you, ladies and gentlemen, and all the little ones at home?"

He was greeted with applause and laughter.

The usual dialogue ensued between him and the manager, who cracked his whip, and made the clown jump and rub his shins. It was really astonishing to the spectators how little the jokes of the clown affected the manager. He spoke without a muscle moving; there seemed to be in him neither a sense of humour nor a spark of compassion. He laughed at no sally, and spared no stroke of the lash.

Then entered the little Queen of Beauty, as advertised, in her mother-o'-pearl shell drawn by ostriches. The birds and carriage were not by any means equal to what the public had been led to anticipate from the flaming posters. The ostriches were ruffled and frowsy; they wore a distressed air, and walked in ungainly fashion. The car was conspicuously of pasteboard covered with silvered paper, and somewhat battered. But the little Queen herself surpassed all that had been promised. She was clothed in white muslin, had a wreath of stars about her bead, and held a star-tipped sceptre in her hand. Her golden hair flowed over her fair shoulders in waves of sunlight; her complexion, perhaps heightened artificially, was brilliant; brighter than stars shone her merry eyes, full of light though dark in colour.

Rab set his cap on his head, with the yellow rose in front. The Queen was greeted with thunders of applause, a portion of which was contributed by Rab, who stamped and roared, and clapped his hands, till his face was red with exertion.

As the Queen made the circuit of the arena, her eyes roamed over the benches, and a smile lighted her cheerful face. When her eye rested on the young poacher, he flattered himself that she made him a slight inclination of her sweet head, that a brighter or more roguish twinkle kindled her eye, and that the dimples of her cheek deepened with a truer smile than that which had been accorded to the general public.

After that the Queen had retired as she came, Rab saw little of what followed. He was consumed with impatience for the reappearance of the Queen of Love and Beauty. The buffalo hunt passed before him unheeded. He hardly saw the wild Indians. He cared not for the performing dogs of the clown, nor for that buffoon's jests and capers. His eyes were riveted on the door through which the little Queen had disappeared, and through which she was to return. When the curtains of the entrance were raised and a horse issued forth, he hoped it might be that she was to mount, but when some one else— an athlete in fleshings, throwing balls and waving flags—leaped upon the sawdust, and with a skip was on the saddle, then Rab uttered a dissatisfied growl.

Andrew was not there—Andrew who had been specially invited; Andrew, who had been privileged to hold converse with the little fairy, who had been offered peeled kernels in her delicate palm, on whom words of favour and beaming smiles had been lavished—Andrew Grice was not there. Where was his heart? Was he a man of stone? Had he in his composition neither pluck nor gallantry?

If the Queen had offered Rab her empty nutshells, he would have worshipped her hand. If she had invited him to come, he would have spent his last farthing to be present. And this fellow Andrew, had she not told him she desired his attendance, that she would look out for him with her bright eyes; that, were he to disappoint her, it might even cause her to fall from horseback?

Rab's cheeks glowed. He swore, if he saw Andrew, he would beat him for disappointing that little heart. And yet he was glad Andrew was not there.

Had young Grice been on the bench, then, perhaps, on him would have fallen the eyes of the little Queen; to him would have been accorded the nod and smile, and he himself, poor Rab, would have been disregarded. The rose that Queenie had given him, Rab had placed in water till the moment he went to the show, then he had donned it with pride; in the hopes, that were not blighted, that by it the pretty circus girl might recognise him.

Rab's thoughts were diverted from their current—something was wrong. What was it that engaged the attention of the manager? He was pointing to the central pole, and had summoned the white canvas-jacketed men. The pole was not as it had been set. It was inclined so that the circle of lights touched it on one side. The workmen drove wedges between the base and the soil, and so restored it to uprightness.

Meanwhile Signor Santi amused the spectators by an interlude—an exhibition of the sagacity of his famous Arab mare, Black Bess. He made her leap a five-barred gate, he bade her dance on her hind legs; he summoned her to him, and she came, docile as a lamb. He bade her kneel and throw herself on her side and simulate death, whilst he fired a pistol over her head. Bess knelt as required, but tossed her head, snuffed the soil, threw herself down indeed, but, instead of lying prostrate and tranquil, reared herself to her knees, then sprang up again.

"Bess! What is this? I never knew you disobedient before. Down, Bess!"

Santi cracked his whip. The Arab hesitated, trotted away, came back, pawed the soil, snuffed at it once more, went down on her knees, but again sprang to her four feet and stood before her master, trembling, sweating and snorting.

Nothing would induce her now to go through her performance; neither threat nor persuasion were of avail, and Santi was forced to dismiss her to the stable.

"Ladies and gentlemen, I never knew Bess like this before. Something has alarmed her. Perhaps the workmen driving the wedges. We will find other animals more tractable."

He cracked his whip, fired the pistol into the air, and in bounded a pair of cream-coloured horses fastened together by their heads, with white and silver trappings on their backs.

In another moment the little Queen appeared dancing in, dressed in white muslin strewn with spangles, so that her every movement made her twinkle like a frosted bush on a sunny winter morning.

She ran to the horses, the clown offered a hand, and in a moment she was in the saddle of one, poised on a single foot, amidst the applause of the public, especially of Rab.

The manager cracked his whip and trailed the lash along the sawdust in a circle.

Suddenly, as by an enchanter's wand, absolute stillness was produced in that great concourse of spectators. Santi's arm was as though paralysed as he drew his whip along. The cream-white horses had recoiled; the clown, with his hands to his head, was looking, mouth open, at the chandelier.

The only sound heard was the straining and creaking of the timber structure occupied by the public, and the strain and creak were like those of a ship labouring in a heavy sea. Then ensued the tinkle and crash of the lamps that smote each other and went to pieces.

The hush was momentary, and then there rose a great burst of confused noises, first as a gasp, then as a roar. What ensued was a matter of a few moments only, though it may take a page in which to describe it.

The central tent pole was seen, in spite of the wedges, to lean, and then to be sinking into the earth. That this was the case was, however, hardly realised at once; it appeared as though the pole were collapsing telescopically. As it gave way, the vast stretch of canvas extended over the circus began to sag, to flap about and fall together. Simultaneously the lamps broke; some poured forth volumes of smoke; in others the light reached the oil, ignited it, exploded the receivers and poured down in liquid fire. The spectators on one side of the ring witnessed a strange phenomenon—they saw the other side lifted up as though a wave were passing under it, whilst those opposite were aware that the further side of the circus, with its benches and the occupants of those benches, was being swallowed up in the earth. The strain on the concentric rings of the structure was more than they could bear, the supports fell, the boards flipped out of their places, and the whole fabric began rapidly to go to pieces. Those spectators who occupied the highest benches were precipitated eight feet to the soil.

The barrier dividing the arena from the spectators was covered with crimson drapery; it was parted as though rent asunder by giant hands, and the drapery was torn across. A wave ran along the surface of sawdust from side to side, leaving a ripple, then the ripple changed into a rent, the earth gaped and the sawdust began to powder down into the fissure.

A north-west wind was blowing; it caught, bustled about the relaxed canvas, and breaking in through some of the gaps, assisted in the confusion by blowing out, or blowing to explosion, lamps hanging at the sides and hitherto unaffected, and by tossing the loose canvas against the benches over which it was falling, and sweeping from them the frightened people.

In a moment or two the whole fabric would be a wreck, a weltering mass of flapping canvas, dislocated boards, shrieking human beings, plunging horses, flaming oil and fluttering shreds of crimson baize. The terror was general. Men and women fought to escape, regardless of sex and relationship. They fell through the scaffolding; they beat at and tore a way through the exterior boarding. Screams, entreaties, curses blended with the crashing of timber, the snorting of horses, the bellowing of the bison, the yelp of dogs, the pistol-like reports of the tossed canvas, the crash of glass: these together formed a hubbub of sound, pierced at intervals by the shriller shriek of some lost and frightened child, shrill as the whistle of a locomotive.

Whether it were the vibration caused by the tramp of the horses, or the weight of such a multitude of spectators, or both combined, certain it was that the crust of earth that overlay a vacuum, caused by the exhaustion of the salt rock, had given way, as had previously other portions of the surface hard by, and the circus and the ground about it were going down into an unfathomed abyss.

VII

RAB TO THE RESCUE

WHEN THE EARTH BEGAN TO move, to slide from under their hoofs, the two cream-coloured horses linked together had been thrown into a paroxysm of terror, had leaped, plunged and flung the little Queen, who fell before their heads, on the sawdust.

Rab saw her danger instantly, and without regarding anything else, without questioning what had caused the panic, beat his way with fists and elbows through the rings of spectators that intervened, and who were up and struggling to escape, and leaped the barrier to her rescue.

The confusion was general before he had reached the arena, and to the experienced eye of an inhabitant of the salt district, there could be no question as to what the phenomenon was that was wrecking the circus.

As Rab threw himself over the barrier, the manager, Santi, sprang at the heads of the horses. These beasts, in their terror, had managed to snap the thongs that arched their necks and restrained their motions, and now, with heads free, they were plunging, striving to tear themselves apart, and menaced the prostrate girl with their hoofs. Queenie was insensible. Rab caught her up in his arms, brushed back her golden hair to see that her face had not been trampled on, and then looked about to determine in which direction he was to escape with her. On all sides the spectators were flying; some were still on the benches, running this way and that, bewildered, unable to find the entrance; others had fainted, and hung insensible over the seats, but the greater number had got down to the level of the ground, and had found, or were forcing, their way out at the sides. The interior was now dark—dense with whirling volumes of petroleum smoke, shot through with red flames.

The performing dogs stood, one on a barrel, the other on the barrier of the arena, howling with fear. Rab could see that the cream-coloured horses had gained the mastery, and were dragging Santi, whose hand was entangled in the reins; that the central pole was coming rapidly down with all its broken lamps.

He could see the fissure in the arena widening, like a great mouth that was breaking into a laugh of mockery at the ruin and panic wrought.

Not a moment was to be lost. He could not tarry to disengage the manager, nor reassure the clown who, in abject terror, had crept into the barrel, where he was sobbing and beating his hands together. He looked about him, assured himself of the direction in which the earth was subsiding, and, bearing the unconscious girl in his arms, made for the further side of the arena. The rift in the soil was between him and the point he desired to reach, its ugly edges crumbling down into the depth, with now and then whole clots of earth and sawdust dropping in a mass. It was uncertain whether the foot could find a hold to allow of a leap, and the soil be firm enough beyond to receive the feet without yielding. But there was no time available for measuring risks and calculating alternatives. Rab leaped the crack successfully, and reached the red-draped barrier precisely where one of the white performing dogs was perched, quivering with fear, and howling. At that same moment, down fell the awning, striking Rab, and precipitating him to the ground, throwing the dog down with him, and enveloping him, his senseless burden, and the wretched hound, in its cumbrous folds. For a moment or two Rab could not move, he was so weighed down and entangled with the canvas.

But Rab was a fellow of strength and energy. He laid his burden under the barrier which remained upright, and which, after a fashion, sustained the fallen awning, and, using both hands, with a knife hacked

and ripped at the canvas. In places this had caught fire. It hung over
the wrecked scaffolding, like skin on a wasted body, loose about the
bones. It flapped in the wind. The air entered below at the torn sides
and blew it out in bellies, then it collapsed again. Guys that had been
ripped out of the earth, or torn, slapped the canvas, as though some
one were lashing it with whips. In the arena it covered everything.
The struggling horses were seen leaping under it, the lamps were
burning their way through it; it began to sag down into the rift that
was gradually widening, as though the earth, having opened her mouth,
were mumbling and drawing in the cloth thrown over her face.

Rab left the still unconscious girl under the barrier that served to
stay up the canvas, whilst he hacked with his pocket-knife, and tore
with his hands at the smothering, all-enveloping cover. He speedily
ripped a hole in it. At once the dog leaped on his shoulders and sprang
through. Then he felt himself gripped at the heel, and, looking down,
saw the painted face of the clown, who had crawled out of the barrel
and wormed his way after him, with a dim instinct that by this means
he could escape. The man was crying like a little child, and the tears had
run the paint off his cheeks; as he wiped his face, he smeared red and
black together, rubbed the artificial eyebrows into a tuft on his nose, and
covered his white sleeve with stains.

"Help me, man!" said Rab. "Lay hold of that end of the rag."

"I can't do nothing, I'm so shook. Oh, my! is it the end of the world
come? I'll be good. I'll promise to be good. I won't drink no more. I'll
take the pledge."

"You fool! Stand on your feet and assist me."

"Oh! I can't! Is it the end of all things? If it is, I'll wear the blue
ribbon. I will—I swear I will! I will! I will! Oh! I'll be so good! I'll read
nothing but tracks."

"Out of the way! Do you see the little Queen there?"

"Is she dead also? Oh, dear! I'm not fit to die! I've been accustomed
to shave on Sundays."

"Let go!" The clown had laid hold of Rab's shoulders, and was trying
to climb on them so as to escape. "It's the end of nothing save your
show, you selfish hound! Can't you help me with the little Queen?"

Rab tore the sailcloth apart. The fresh air blew in on him. Above was the vault of heaven strewn with ten thousand stars. He looked round a moment, scrambling up the canvas over part of the scaffolding that seemed secure. In places, flames were leaping, ghostlike, high in the air above the oil or canvas that was burning. The confused mixture of voices of those outside the heap of wreckage filled his ears—the cries, shouts, objurgations, entreaties, orders, all mingled into a general roar. Outside, mothers who had escaped were seeking their children, strayed children were screaming for their parents, husbands called to their wives. Those spectators who had escaped were mingled with a crowd come down from the town to see the disaster and render help. They endeavoured to organise parties to search the wreck, and extricate such as were still buried, but no one was in authority, and none would obey self-constituted directors.

Some of the grooms and stable-boys had run to the subsidiary tent that served as green-room for the performers, and where also were those horses prepared to take part in the representation, and were assisting men in fleshings and velvet, the Signora Muslina in gauze skirts, and trapeze men half dressed, to lead away the animals. Wild Indians, talking cockney English, drove the ostriches before them; a mechanic had shouldered the mother-o'-pearl car, and was carrying it to a place of security. The buffalo was pawing the soil, bellowing, and would allow no one near him.

Rab now stooped and raised the red repp that covered the barrier. Queenie was still unconscious. He threw her over his left shoulder, and proceeded to thrust the coils of canvas under his feet and draw himself up to the surface. The clown persisted in dragging at him. He had lost all self-control, and was unnerved.

The course Rab had elected to take was by no means a safe one. He had to make his way over the fallen sailcloth that covered the scaffolding, some of which stood, some was down, and some was leaning and would yield with the least additional weight. Moreover, the wind under the canvas played with it, and made it most precarious where to tread.

"You go forward," said Rab to the clown, "straight as a line to where yon star shines afore your eyes, or as near a line as sarcumstances admit. Tread away, and I'll follow with my precious burden."

The white dog jumped about its fellow-performer and barked. The clown put down his hand and patted it.

"Glad you are saved, Tweedledum," said he. "P'r'aps it ain't so bad after all."

A shrill voice outside was heard calling,—

"Nelson! honey, dear! Nelson! where are you?"

"Coming! Coming!" screamed the clown. Then, turning his head over his shoulder, he said to Rab, "That's the Signora. That's Mrs Nelson. She is seeking me."

A little more confidence came to the poor fellow as he heard the voices of the crowd, and, above all, that of his wife. He could not see the people, for the canvas inclined upwards to the boarded side of the circus that was not broken down. As he looked back, he saw behind him the burning mass, and, beyond that, all was blackness—everything had disappeared.

He stepped along. Perhaps it was his costume, the absurd tufts of hair on his head, the high rolls for epaulettes, the out-stuffed thigh pads, but his every attitude was grotesque. He could not put forward a foot to feel if the canvas before him would sustain his weight, but he made an antic, and, as he stepped along, he continued shouting,—

"I'm coming, my poppet! I'm coming, my honey! Your Nelson is safe!"

Rab thought he was playing the buffoon.

"Have done with your merry-Andrew tricks," said Rab. "This is no time for fooling!"

"I'm not fooling. I can't help it. I'm doing my best," protested the clown, and he groped along, with the dog dancing at his side. "Coming, poppet! Coming, sweetheart!"

Every step he took, every inhalation of pure air, every strident call from his still invisible wife, served to restore elasticity to the spirits of the clown, and recover his mind of the fears that had oppressed it. He stepped firmer. He beat his breast, and said,—

"I won't! I won't! No; I won't!"

"You won't do what?" asked Rab, treading at his heels.

"I won't take the pledge. I won't read tracks, and I'll shave just when suits me—Sabbath included."

Then he reached the edge of the hoarding, looked over; a gas light illumined his face—some boys saw him and laughed.

"Here we are again!" shouted the man, and turned a somersault to descend to the crowd. "Poppet, here I am!"

Rab followed cautiously and descended slowly. He was greeted with questions, to none of which he replied, and with offers of assistance, none of which he accepted.

He worked his way with his right hand, thrusting men and women aside, till he got through the crowd. Then he made at once for the row of cottages entitled Heathendom, in one of which he lived along with his mother.

As he reached the door, the girl stirred on his shoulder, attempted to raise herself, and asked,—

"Father! where is father?"

"Lie quiet, little Queenie," said Rab. "My mother shall attend on you, and I will go back to look for your poor father."

"Who are you?"

"I am the chap to whom you gave the yaller rose. I'll do you no harm. Trust me."

VIII

NUTS

ANDREW WAS NOT PREPARED FOR open revolt against the authority of his father, nor was he ready to undergo major excommunication. In token that he gave way, he tore his ticket and threw the fragments into the fender, and his father accepted this act as one of tacit submission. But in heart Andrew was rebellious. "Hammer" believed that he had won a victory and riveted more firmly his domination over his son. He was mistaken; he had shaken his hold on the lad's conscience. The punishment threatened was out of all proportion to the offence. Andrew's conviction of the justice of his father had received a shock. He questioned his affection for him.

Andrew asked himself: Was a parent right in treating his son, when arrived at manhood, as the Savoyard treated his monkey? Was a monkey ordained by Nature to wear a red coat, to be controlled by a chain, to run up water-pipes, and hold out a begging-box? Would a monkey be justified *in foro conscientiæ* in breaking his chain, tearing off jacket and breeches, throwing aside his collecting box, and making for the green wood? The man and the monkey do not stand to each other in the same relation as father to son. That made a difference. What was lawful in the monkey was, perhaps, not sufferable in the son. In that the monkey was a happier, more privileged being than Andrew. It might assert its liberty without conscientious twinges.

In another point the monkey stood higher in the scale of happiness than Andrew. It was allowed to run and jump; it might stand on its head and stretch its little feet to heaven. It might dance and make grimaces; it might take without scruple anything—nuts—nuts!—(Andrew's breath came quick)—anything offered it. It was not obliged to go through the routine of missionary, temperance and undenominational as well as sectarian meetings.

Andrew had been eating his portion of beefsteak and fried onions. He laid down his fork, and lapsed into a brown study.

"What is up, Andrew?" asked his father.

"I was thinking," answered the youth submissively.

"Thinking of what?"

"Only that monkeys don't have—taking all into consideration—such a bad time of it."

His father stared, then turned to Beulah, his sister, and said,—

"I shall be on the platform. I suppose I shall be forced to say a few words."

"Oh, brother, of course, of course! What would the meeting be without an address from you?"

"I'll do what is right," said "Hammer," bringing his fist down on the table. "I'll do it, even though the Philistines be encamped against me with their host in battle array."

"The Philistines will not be there, brother."

"You are right, Beulah, they will not. They will be down at the Old Hall Field, with skipping ropes and butterflies and all the pomps! I'll speak tonight!"

"You always do, father," said Andrew.

"I do, yes!" answered Jabez. "Because I always do what I ought to do. Time is up. Get ready at once."

He rose from the table, without looking to see whether his sister and son had finished their meal; he ordered the table to be cleared. Then he remembered that he had not shaved, fetched hot water, and spent a quarter of an hour in polishing his upper lip and chin.

When he came downstairs, he found the other inmates of the house ready, and waiting for him. He thrust them forth and locked the door.

On the way to the New Hall they caught up and passed small parties of serious people, by twos and threes, walking silently and solemnly to the place of meeting.

From the lower part of the town pealed the brass band at the circus, and the flaring lights about the booth could be seen, even the black masses of people distinguished, who were crowding to the show.

"Look there, at the many," said Jabez Grice, sternly; "see here the few! I feel like Moses on the mount when he saw the people dancing and feasting. He broke all the commandments, he was in such anger. I could do the same."

Standing on the steps of the New Hall, and looking on the plain, the booths, the crowd, Jabez hastily, and with a jerk, opened his umbrella, shut it again, and opened it once more.

"I would," said he, "I would they was all swallowed up alive, like Korah and his company, them and their tents and their wives and their children. It'd be a lesson to some."

Then he turned and entered the hall and pushed his way to the platform, regardless of his son and sister, whom he left to settle where they pleased. The hall was very new, very white, and very glaring with the gas turned on full. It was but half filled, and the prospect of its filling was scanty. Already the hour for opening had struck, and those on the platform waited, hoping that more would arrive to replenish the body of the hall. Those who had come set up their greatcoats, mantles and umbrellas on the vacant seats at their sides to disguise, as far as might be, the emptiness.

On the platform were assembled the notables of the serious world at Saltwich. The chair was to be taken by Mr Nottershaw, architect, surveyor and builder. He stood well with the serious; it was his interest to do so. He spoke at their meetings, he subscribed to their charities, he appeared in their chapels, he sat on their committees, and he designed and erected for them their public buildings. He had indeed sent his children to the circus, with strict injunctions to sit in the cheap places with the crowd lest they should be recognised. The ministers of seven denominations were here sinking their differences and mutual jealousies. Dr Tallow, large, flat-faced, with bushy whiskers and very glossy black coat, and very starched white tie, was fanning himself with a printed copy of one of his own sermons.

As Jabez Grice ascended the platform, applause broke out from every portion of the room. Only the dummies of umbrella and greatcoat did not join in the ovation.

Andrew found it was impossible for him to collect his thoughts and make them wheel round Dr Tallow like the constellations about the sun. They wandered whilst the chairman was introducing the doctor and apologising for the smallness of the audience, with lamentations over the vanity of the minds that preferred circus-riding to the elocutionary gymnastics of the illustrious doctor from Jericho.

Andrew's mind was absent in the Old Hall Field, though his body was present in the New Hall. His father might command the one, he was powerless to control the other. He found himself listening to hear if he could catch, where he sat, any strains of the brass band wafted in through an open window. He found himself thinking over the programme, and picturing the scenes in the circus after the coloured posters. Was the little Queen now making her entrance in the mother-o'-pearl shell? How radiant, how beautiful she would be! and he was not there! She would look round for him—would miss him. She would be offended at his absence—she would not come on the morrow to see the salt works.

With an effort Andrew screwed his attention to Dr Tallow's discourse, and found that his mind was poisoned against him by the words of Rab—prejudiced against him by his own disappointment! That was true which Rab had said. He knew all the anecdotes—or others so like them that they were undistinguishable in their common silliness. He knew the illustrations—they were pointless. He could not endure the frothy eloquence. The topic of the discourse was commonplace, the delivery common place, the voice commonplace; he had heard it all a thousand times before, and he could find no interest in what he heard now for the thousand and first time.

He pulled out of his pocket a nut—it was one of those that had been offered him by Queenie. He looked at it. He fell into dreams over it. He turned it about. He held it up to the light. He saw in it the dints of her sharp little teeth—it was as though a squirrel had been biting at it. He looked closely at the depressions—No doubt about it at all. Those dints were the dints of teeth—of her teeth. Not considering where he was, what was going on, who was speaking, or whence the speaker came, nor what was the subject of his address, Andrew put the nut into his mouth and cracked it.

Those near him started. The lecturer paused. Those on benches and chairs in front turned, and, with indignant frowns, stared Andrew in the face. The sensation could hardly have been greater had Andrew discharged a bomb.

"When that young gentleman has finished his nuts, perhaps I may be allowed to proceed," said the doctor, with withering sarcasm.

The chairman interfered.

"There is a time for all things," said he. "If the frivolous choose to crack nuts at such a moment as this, under the outpour of such words as we have heard, let him go out from us—he is not of us."

"Turn him out!" was shouted from the further side of the hall, by those who had not seen that the culprit was the son of the respected Jabez Grice. Only the dummies of umbrella and greatcoat did not join in the remonstrance.

Abashed, Andrew took his cap, crept to the door, and slipped forth into the open air. He had as much as promised his father that he would not go to the circus, but he was free to prowl round it.

After the pause caused by the unseemly disturbance, the preacher caught up the thread of his discourse again and proceeded to draw it to an end.

Then rose Mr Poles, the paperhanger, to propose a vote of thanks to the American Demosthenes, the Jericho Chrysostom, who had come among them to deepen their seriousness. Mr Poles was a prolix speaker; his discourse consisted in a series of elocutionary festoons, and when done, no one could very well say what it had all been about. His place was at once occupied by Jabez Grice, who started to his feet and looked about him, not with diffidence, like Mr Poles, nor tremblingly holding to a chair back, but planted with his solid feet wide apart firm,

confident, like the Colossus of Rhodes, set to give light to the voyagers
the sea of life; he spoke, not with a thin, timid, quavering voice, like the
paperhanger, but with one rich, resonant and firm. There was nothing
apologetic in his manner, his tone, his attitude. He asked to be heard
because he insisted on being heard, and because he knew that he would
be heard, and heard with avidity.

"My serious friends," began Jabez, and he eased his arms in his sleeves
as he started speaking, and spread his breast; "it is a proud moment to me
to stand before you on this undenominational platform, and to second
the vote of thanks proposed to the illustrious stranger—who is yet not a
stranger, as his printed volumes are familiar to all the seriously-disposed.
It may be said that this undenominational gathering is unprecedented.
I ask—What is precedent? Why should we consider precedent? This is
the point to which I will address myself, and I pray you, lend me your
attention for two minutes. Precedents, my serious friends, are the rags
and tatters in which past ignorance enveloped itself, and which it hands
on to the imbecile and weaklings and unreasoning of the present day,
that they may cloak themselves in the same, when unable to give an
account in the face of the world for what they are asked to do, which
they know they ought to do, and yet which they dare not do. Respect
for precedent belongs to a condition of mind and to a state of society
out of which we have happily grown. We are not men of yesterday. We
are men of to-day!"

Here ensued a burst of applause.

"We are not concerned with the judgments of the past. Men may
have been fools then. If they did, and if they ruled foolish things then,
are we to do foolish things today?"

Cries of "No! no!"

"It is degradation—it is an absurdity for us men of the nineteenth
century to be ruled, not by reason, not by conscience, but by precedents.
Let each question that arises be judged on its own merits, and let
not the right or wrong of the question be obscured by the haze of
precedent. Drag it into the full blaze of light. Discuss it with unengaged
minds, and judge it as Heaven gives intelligence!"

Cries of "Hear! hear!"

"In the year 1847—let me tell you—the legislature of this country considered the introduction of a measure for the abolition of appeal to precedent. And let me tell you, there came up from all parts of Great Britain a petition, signed by seven millions of rational men and women, praying for the abolition of appeal to precedent. With what result?"

The audience held its breath. The speaker looked round.

"With what result? That the petition was ordered to lie on the table. There were found, my friends, in the legislature and outside of it, men—creatures, I should rather term them, with their tails turned to the present age of light, and their nozzles turned to the past age of obscurity—who raised objections, as such creatures always will, to every salutary alteration. And the measure was defeated on the grounds—on the grounds that there was *no precedent for rejecting the appeal to precedent.*"

The speaker looked round with defiance, his mouth shut, his brows knit, his hands clenched.

"The English people had said their say—and were silenced. This was in the beginning of the nineteenth century. They sat down and were content. They would not sit down and be content now. Why not? Because they live further on in the nineteenth century than did those memorialists. Now, if they say their say, and are not heard, they shout their shout; and if their shout be not listened to, then they roar their roar; and then heard they are. Heard they must be, for heard they will to be."

Immense applause, in which only the dummies of umbrella and greatcoat did not join.

Then some one, far back in the hall, stood up, and said,—

"May I be allowed to ask some particulars relative to this very remarkable bill brought before the House, of which I had never heard? May I ask where further particulars may be found?"

Jabez Grice was ready at once with an answer. "I know," said he, in his loud and resonant tones, "both whence this interruption proceeds, and what is its object. That gentleman who has put a question to me has deliberately distorted my words—I did not say, I purposely did *not* say, that this motion was debated in the House. I said that it was considered by the Ministry of the day. I have yet to learn that the deliberations of the Cabinet are recorded in the statutes at large, and the thoughts of the Ministry find their place in the 'Transactions of Parliament.' Let me advise that person who has interrupted with his frivolous question, in future to use his ears, and not allow his imagination to play; let me advise him to cultivate accuracy. I am not bound to meet captious questions. This is not the place in which to dissipate crass ignorance. But enough of this topic, and of this gentleman. I wipe him out of my memory. I return to the point from which I was drawn away."

"Father!" said Andrew. He was below the platform and had laid hold of his father's foot. "Pray, do come. You are greatly wanted. You are wanted immediately."

"What is it?" asked Grice impatiently.

"There has been a terrible accident. A subsidence at the circus."

"I said it—as I came in at the door I said it," shouted Grice with triumph in his face—in his tone. "I turned on the door-step of this hall and denounced the revellers, and said—'Let the earth open her mouth and let them go down quick into the abyss.'"

"Father, I beseech you, come! Your brother—Santi—"

"Well?"

"Is dying, and crying out for you."

IX

BROTHER OR NO BROTHER?

"You need not have shouted out that he was my brother," said Jabez, as he walked from the New Hall to Old Hall Field with his son at his side.

"Father, I did not shout. I thought that I whispered."

"Well, you whispered loud enough for all on the platform to hear, and interrupted me in the middle of my speech—and a very important speech it was."

"What was I to say? There has been a terrible affair. A subsidence where the circus was."

"That was right enough. I don't object to the subsidence, nor to your telling me of it."

"Signor Santi is frightfully injured, and is asking for you as his brother."

"Couldn't you have said he was asking for me, and have stayed there, instead of blurting out what followed, instead of proclaiming what is a lie and an insult."

"I knew nothing of that. I never supposed you would take the matter so, father. The dying man said he had no one in the world to ask for but you, his brother."

"He is not my brother—never was. My father married again after my mother's death, and took a young widow with her son by her first husband. That was Joe Sant. How can he be my brother when we don't share a drop of blood? All we ever did share were bed and bread and butter. He is no relation of mine. I have nothing to do with him. He took his road; I took mine—and his was the broad and evil way."

"But you are going to see him, father?"

"Of course, I am. I'll see him. I do what is right."

"Hammer" Grice said no more, but strode along.

At every step he took, he planted his foot on the earth as though he were taking possession of the soil for ever.

After he had gone forward some way in silence, he halted and said,—

"How has it come about? A subsidence?"

"Yes, father; I suppose the earth wouldn't bear the extra weight and the trampling. The Old Field has been held to be insecure for some time. But I suppose the poor fellows thought it would hold up as long as they needed it. Now the deepest point is not under the circus, it is between it and the flash, but the ground has given way, cracked, sunk; and the earth has begun to run, and as it ran, down came the structure, boards and canvas and all."

"Many killed?"

"I do not know, father. I was at the meeting as you know. When I went out, I ran down to the Old Field because I learned that something had happened there, and I could hear the screams and the general uproar from the steps of the Town Hall. I know very little more than what I was told when I asked—and then I heard that the manager had been extricated from under the tent, and that he was terribly cut about and crushed. I don't know whether the pole fell across him, or whether he was trodden on by the horses. He has been badly burned also, for there was fire that somehow broke out. Fellows were saying he had been taken to his van, and they had drawn that away out of danger of sinking, and they had sent for a doctor. They told me he was calling for you. He had no one in the world to look to but you, he said, and none to provide for but his daughter."

"He has a daughter?"

"Yes; the Queen of Love."

"The Queen of Love! He is surely not going to saddle me with her! The Queen of Love in my serious family! A hussy with short skirts in Alma Terrace!"

He remained stationary, brooding over the prospect.

"That would be a fine confusion! The Queen of Love—with her heathenish ways, her skipping ropes and butterfly habits, and all the pomps—in No. 4. Deliver us!"

He strode on.

Had he any idea of the sudden flutter of hope that stirred, the flash, the blaze, of an opening world of light and beauty and love, that broke on the imagination of the youth at his side as he said these words? None whatever—not an inkling. Jabez Grice had no thought of Andrew at all. He was considering the discomfort, the contrarieties to himself, the scandals that might ensue in his house, were this discordant element to be introduced into his serious family.

"Perhaps Joe Sant is not so bad after all," said he, drawing a long breath. "He'll move on, and take his precious set of belongings with him. The sooner the better."

On reaching Old Hall Field, it was found to present a scene of confusion from which it had not begun to recover. In the night light, the circus presented the appearance of a stranded and wrecked hull. Nor was it free from the attacks of wreckers. For it had occurred to a good many of the idle and unscrupulous that there were boards in the wreck which could be converted into poultry-houses with very little labour; that there was red repp and baize enough to make petticoats for whole families, and that there was rope that would come in handy as lines on which to hang clothes after washing day. One or two men were cutting slices out of the canvas, wherewith to make themselves jackets and trousers.

The police were there, but the number stationed at Saltwich was small, and they were directing search parties among the ruins to save lives, rather than spending their energies in the protection of property. The night was dark; they could not follow the proceedings of the depredators, though they might suspect that depredations were being carried on. Their first duties were towards such as were still entangled in the canvas, or were lying injured among the fallen wood work. Apparently very few persons had been seriously hurt. Some were bruised; here and there it was reported that bones had been broken. No one was missing—umbrellas, reticules, baskets of refreshments lay about under the boards, and these were the principal losses. Some children were astray, but their violent screams led to attention being directed to them, and, as they were able to give an account of themselves, to their speedy restoration to their homes.

The clown and Signora Muslina were the principal persons who seemed to be in grave distress. They could nowhere find the second performing dog, Tweedledee. They ran about, followed or preceded by Tweedledum. The dog was whining, the Signora remonstrating in shrill, harsh tones; the clown, her husband, screaming, because Tweedledee did not respond to their calls, and could not be seen or heard of on any side. The signora—her proper name was Mrs Nelson, Bell Nelson, in the troupe—had thrown a rug round her bare shoulders, but her spidery and somewhat exposed legs, encased in white stockings, under scanty muslin skirts, were everywhere distinguishable, running, jumping, climbing after Tweedledee; and the heart of the poor signora was sore under the spangles that overlay it, and she had screamed herself hoarse in her distress for the loss of the dear dog.

The workmen in white jackets belonging to the show, the trapezists, and one of the performers on horseback, the Modern Proteus, the man who balanced balls and waved flags, lent ready help; so did some of the grooms from the stables, cheerful and obliging. Boys and men went about with lanterns. It was as though a swarm of fireflies had settled down on the Old Hall Field. Some had brought together chips, broken pieces of deal and lumps of coal, and had made a fire, that threw light on the ruined circus and the crowd, wavering and interweaving in incessant change around it.

Andrew led his father in the direction of the gilded and painted van in which lay the injured man. About it were collected the horses, the bison, the ostriches that had been brought away from the endangered tract of land. The animals could not understand the condition of affairs. They made strange noises. The ostriches brayed like donkeys, the horses plunged and kicked out. The routine of their lives was broken in on, and they had lost their sense of obedience. The men who usually attended to them were those in white jackets, and they were engaged elsewhere. Their places had been taken by volunteers from various stables, but these did not understand circus beasts, or the beasts did not understand being handled by strangers.

Grice entered the van without a word to anyone. The van was divided interiorly into compartments. The first entered was the parlour; it had benches at the sides, stuffed and covered with leather. The windows were hung with pretty curtains. In the middle was a stove, and against one of the sides, under a casement, was fastened a desk, at which the director did all his accounts and correspondence.

Through a door opposite the entrance, access was obtained to the bedroom. There lay Santi, on his narrow pallet, as complete a wreck as his show. He had been trampled on by the cream-coloured horses, crushed by the falling pole, and burned by the overset lamps. A surgeon had been summoned, and he had stripped off the man's frock coat and waistcoat, and had examined him. One of the acrobats was kneeling at the sufferer's head and holding it on his arm. He was dressed as a wild Indian, painted brown, with red lips, and wore moccasins on his legs and a plumed head-dress.

The surgeon stood up and shook his head.

The Indian's brown face turned to him, watching intently.

"Done for, manager, done for," said the fellow in tones of deep and tender feeling. "You must try and bear it as a man, old fellow. We must all come to it some day. Shall I put your head a little more on one side? Are you easy? Or shall I stay you up in my arms, boss? You are as feeble and helpless as when you took me up."

"Thank you, Seth, it will do."

"Oh, boss, I wish it was I, crumpled up and done for, and not you. But, old boss, I'm afraid I wouldn't be as ready to go as are you. Boss, when you come to the place where we must all appear, you can hold up your poor achin' head and tell the story o' that there baby boy,

Seth—how you took and keared for the horphan, and fed and clothed him, free, gratis, when he could be nort but an expense; and how you taught him to know right from wrong. And if it please the pigs that I come to where you be going—Lord, it'll be all your doin'! For what would I ha' been but for you!"

Then the Red Indian began to sob, and the tears to stream down his painted cheeks.

"I've never had none but you, boss, and little Queenie to kear about in the world. Oh, dear! oh, dear! and what is to become of her?"

"Don't take on, Seth; you've been a good boy."

"I do take on, boss! I can't help it. And you're going to leave us and the hostriches and the 'osses, and that there darned idjot of a buffalo, as won't mind none of us, but your word only. But there, we won't think o' that. Put your hands together. You can't? That there old arm be broke, is it? Well, put that right hand up from off your heart, boss dear, and I'll put my left from under your neck against it, and we'll say the prayer together—as you taught me when I was a little creetur."

Then the Indian lifted the dying man against his breast, and put his palm against that of the other, and with sobs and broken voice repeated,—

"Meek and mild—look on me—a little child—pity my simplicity"— he wiped his face. "It don't suit altogether; 'tisn't that I meant. But it comes to my mind first, and yet old man, you're now weak as a babe, just as I was when you took me up, and keared for me, and taught me them words; and if it ain't quite what it ort to be, well, I daresay it will be overlooked."

"I think I can do better for the poor fellow than that," said Jabez Grice, stepping forward. "You don't seem to know what you're about. How can you? Grapes don't come of thorns and figs of thistles."

"My brother Jabez!" exclaimed the dying man—and held out the one hand he could command.

"I am sorry to see you like this, Joe," said Grice. He took his hand, then, turning to all who were present, said,—"He is not really my brother. We are in no ways related."

The dying manager looked steadily into the face of Jabez.

"You were always a serious boy," he said; "I suppose you're serious still."

"Certainly."

"Then I'm sure I can trust you. You were a good boy."

"What is right—that I do—of course. I couldn't do other," answered Grice.

"I want to speak alone with you."

The manager was in pain. It was with an effort that he gathered his thoughts; with an effort and manifest suffering that he spoke. His eyes were sunken. They seemed more sunken than they really were, owing to the shadow cast by the strong light of the lamp hanging from the ceiling of the cabin.

"Must I go, boss?" asked the Red Indian, from whose cheeks much of the paint had come away.

Santi nodded—then with his hand caught his arm, and said,—

"Her—my little Queenie. I haven't seen her! Tell me she is not hurt—tell me where she is. I want to say good-bye to Queenie—Seth, go and find her. Tell her—her father—Bring her to me!"

His head sank back on the pillow. He breathed with pain. His ribs were crushed on the lungs.

"I am sorry to say I can be of no more use," observed the surgeon, taking his hat; "if I could, I would cheerfully stay, but as—"

He left the room with the sentence unfinished

Grice waved a sign to his son to leave, and Andrew went outside.

When left alone with the manager, Jabez said,—

"I was afraid it would come to this. You never took my warnings when we were young together. I have gone my way—you have gone yours—and now you are struck down in your iniquities."

"Iniquities—what iniquities?" asked Santi, faintly.

"Skipping-ropes and butterflies, and muslin and fleshings, and all the pomps," said Grice, solemnly.

"I don't know," the dying man gasped. "I've tried to be true and just in all my dealings. If I haven't—I've been sorry. I mayn't have been all I ought to have been, and I don't deny it—I don't deny it. I feel it here." He lightly touched his heart—he was breathing painfully. "There was that picture of a boa-constrictor swallering of a man. I wouldn't have it up—outside the show. I hadn't a boa. Bell Nelson offered to lend me her fur one—and sew it up in canvas and paint it. But I wouldn't—'twasn't true." He remained silent awhile, breathing with labouring chest. "And I've tried to be just. If I haven't, by mistake it has been—not by intent. That's how I've made so much money."

"Money!" repeated Grice in astonishment.

"Yes—horses, and skipping-ropes and hoops, and muslin and all that—it has been my profession. The profession ain't amiss. I've made money. And I've always invested my savings every year—for Queenie. Stay—I can't speak." He seemed to lapse into unconsciousness, but rallied. "You were awfully strict and serious as a boy," said the manager, his great eyes turning searchingly on Grice. "Get a pen and paper from my desk. It's—in 'tother place. I can't trust Nelson—he drinks. Seth White is too young—I've no one else but you. I must trust you—for Queenie—little Queenie!" He turned his head. "I want to see her—to kiss her. Bring my Queenie here. I've worked, and slaved, and put by for her. Bring Queenie. There's a good deal of money."

Grice went into the outer compartment, and returned with paper and pen and ink.

"There is no time to be lost," he said. "Money, you said. A good deal of it. I shouldn't have thought it, brother Joe. My dear brother Joe."

X

AN ORPHAN

Q UEENIE SAT IN THE HIGH-BACKED chair by the fire in the cottage of the Rainbows. The walls of the chamber were painted sky-blue, and were of appalling brilliancy—the colour affected, possibly, as some contrast to the red-brick of the exterior. There stood a dresser against the wall, on which were ranged plates, jugs and bowls of Bristol lustre-ware that shone like burnished copper—or as the hair of the little maiden who leaned back in the chair.

She was in her white gauze dress, strewn with spangles. At every breath a flash, as of summer lightning, shot over her bosom, in the reflections of the great fire, and an incessant quiver of light was in her thistle-down skirts, produced by the slightest movement of her limbs.

She was recovered from her insensibility, but much shaken, and one ankle was sprained. Her arms were bare; one was raised, and the hand thrust behind her head. The little feet were crossed in their white satin shoes, and rested on a hassock.

Mrs Rainbow had put the kettle on the fire to boil, so as to make Queenie a cup of tea, after which she was to be put to bed. Sheets and blankets were tossed across chair-backs to air, and Rab's mother was on her knees with a pail, scrubbing the floor.

"Mother!" said Rab, in a tone of impatience, "why do you set to wash the floor now? Can't it wait till to-morrow?"

"No, it can't," answered the woman, standing up. She was a tall, handsome woman, very untidy in her person, and dressed incongruously, with an old hat on her head that had belonged to her deceased husband, and a tattered jacket of Rab's over her back. "No, it can't," said she. "If you choose to bring dirt in on your boots, I ain't going to let it remain ten minutes. Lor! the work you do bring on me. And never a thought for your old mother."

Mrs Rainbow was a person of immense energy; she worked, she verily slaved from morning till night; and yet was neither tidy herself, nor had her house neat. How, with all the work she did, so little result was visible—that was a marvel to her son. She did a little bartering with vegetables on a handcart she ran along herself; she had a little shop, that is to say, sold lollipops, peppermints, oranges and ginger-beer; she kept geese on the common, and fowls in the back-yard. She picked up pennies by this means, and professed that, but for herself, the house never could have been kept going.

"I'll clean up whenever dirt comes in," said Mrs Rainbow. "The kettle won't boil all at once, nor the blankets get aired of a jiffy."

Rab was on one knee before the fire, toasting bread, but his eyes were on Queenie. The girl's right hand was resting on her lap. Presently her cheek puckered with a smile, and, raising her finger, she pointed at Rab's cap.

He at once removed his headgear, put down the toast, and, unpinning the bruised and withered yellow rose said,—

"You gave me this."

He put his hand into his breast-pocket, and drew forth a much-used letter-case, in which were flies for fishing, and scraps of newspaper relative to races, and, folding the rose in a piece of clean paper, he threw out all the racing notes and flies, placed the rose within, and then put the case into his pocket again.

"There!" said he. "I shall not part with this flower till my dying day. Remember that, little Queen of Love. It is the first flower ever given me, and you gave it me when I had been very bold and rude, and by it showed you had forgiven me. When I'm dead, little Queen, then—if

I have not taken the yaller leaves underground with me—do me a kindness and strew 'em on my grave."

"I'll find you a better rose."

"I want none other. This will do for me. I am sorry I was rude, but Andrew angered me."

"Who is Andrew?"

"Oh, he is a good boy—an uncommon good boy; and I," Rab shrugged his shoulders, "I'm a shocking bad un."

"Ah, never was a truer word spoken!" exclaimed Mrs Rainbow, rising from her slops. "A precious life you have led your old mother, what with your idleness, and poachings, and drinkings and skylarkings."

"Do you drink?" asked Queenie.

"Sometimes—always on washing days, and when mother's tongue is loose at the joints."

"I'll tell you what it is," said Mrs Rainbow. "There will be no toast done at this rate—staring into a gal's face, instead of minding the bread before the fire."

Rab hastened to resume his operation of toasting.

"I am sorry you drink," said the girl.

"So am I," answered Rab. "But I can't help it."

"That's what our clown says. He'd be a first-rate clown and a good fellow, but he can't keep from the public-house. Father cautioned him over and over—he came fresh to the performances, and was not in the least funny then. He cried. So father has had to lock him up in an old monkey cage he bought of a menagerie man, who broke because his monkeys all got the influenza. Father locks him up directly we get into a town, and keeps him there till it is time to get ready for the performance. And Bell Nelson, she walks up and down with a switch and has the key. She does not let him out till he is summoned to paint and dress."

"A very good thing too," said Mrs Rainbow. "I'll treat you the same, Rab; I'll shut you up in the goose-pen—and serve you right."

"Does the clown submit?" asked the young man.

"He must—and he knows it's for his good. And Bell, she walks up and down and puts her nose between the bars, and gives him her mind.

He can't break out as before. It must be after a performance. Father can't keep him all day and all night in the monkey cage—"

"Now, then! Now, then!" shouted Mrs Rainbow. "I don't call that toast. You've got the bread against the bars. I'd like to make a zebra of you as you've been treating that slice."

"Where is my father?" asked Queenie. "I want to see him. Is he safe?"

"I brought you away," said Rab. "I really know nothin' more than that you are here."

"I remember the creamies turned restive, and they made a start."

"Yes—the earth cracked before them."

"Let me manage toasting the bread. Do, pray, go and ask after my dear father!" said the girl.

"Listen to the voice of nat'ral affection," said Mrs Rainbow, standing up with a scrubbing brush in one hand and a bar of soap in the other. "Hear her hollering for her father. It's a thousand years since I've heard my son call after his mammy like that, and I reckon it'll be a thousand years more before he comes round to know his duty to his mother." She rubbed her eyes with the soap, then, as that made them sting with the scrubbing brush. "As for Rab, if I but shows the end of my tongue, off he goes like a cricket before the light—to the public-house."

A tap at the door, and when the woman opened, she sprang back with an exclamation of terror. A Red Indian, hung with scalps, was in the doorway; he was dazzled by the light, and asked somewhat hesitatingly.—

"Is the little Queen here?"

"It's Seth! It's Seth!" exclaimed the girl, starting out of her chair, and then, finding her foot give way under, sinking back into it again.

"Queenie! Do I hear you?" said the Red Indian.

"I'm terribly grieved; you must come at once."

"Oh, Seth, Seth, what is the matter?"

"I am sorry to say—your father is bad!"

The girl uttered a piercing cry, and tried to limp to the door.

"You cannot walk," said Rab. "I carried you before; I will carry you agin. Mother, a shawl."

The young man carefully, tenderly, folded a great red wrap round the girl, so as to completely cover her, with the exception of her golden hair, which flowed out and over the shawl, and hung on Rab's shoulder like tresses of laburnum on a wall. He bore her lightly along, and the painted Indian stepped at his side.

"There's a lot of our chaps about the wan as wants to see the boss"— he looked significantly towards the bundle. "I mean, they've heard the signor ain't quite up to tune, you know, and they're all dying to shake his hand and say a word. But there's a fellow in the wan, as says he's the Signor's brother, won't let 'em in, not one of them. They take on dreadful about it."

"Are all your company safe?"

"Yes; I guess all but Tweedledee."

"Who's Tweedledee?"

"It's one of the performin' dawgs. There's a pair of them; they belong to the Nelsons, that is, to the clown and to her—the lady as goes through the fiery hoop, you know. The master pays so much a week for their services, and they're uncommon clever dawgs. But Tweedledee's amissin', so the Nelsons are in a pretty stew."

They had not far to go.

"Some chap said he'd seen the little Queen carried into one of them cottages," said the Red Indian; "and he told me 'twas that of the Rainbows. He—you know who I mean—he's been axing for her. I guess that brother who is there won't deny her admittance."

"I'll force open the door if he does," said Rab. They had reached the van. About the steps stood the members of the company. Some of those in fleshings had succeeded in getting coats to throw over them, as the night was raw. A curious mixture of persons was congregated before the van, in which a man was dying. Every face, as far as could be distinguished by a flaming light, showed signs of distress through the paint that obscured the natural features. A good deal of murmuring, and many a lamentation, broke from the kindly, affectionate hearts of these vagabonds.

"He was a master—a good un," said one of the acrobats. "He never swore at a chap on the trapeze till he lost his nerve, as I've knowed some do."

"Ay! he was a good chap!" said another. "Look what he done for that boy Seth."

"And he paid regular, down on the nail," said a third.

The clown was stealing away on tiptoe, in the shadow of the van; his wife was aware of the manoeuvre, and went after him, caught him by the roll on one of his shoulders, and dragged him back.

"For shame, Jim! for shame! you unnat'ral beast! when the dear master's dying! I know what you're after; you ha'n't got no money, but you think you can find chaps as will stand treat."

"I was going to have another look for Tweedledee," said the clown.

"No, you wasn't, you was after liquor. I won't have it! It's fortunate the monkey cage is safe. I've seed it! That's not swallered up, and I've got the key!"

"Oh, Bell, dearest Bell, darling, I'm never put in that after a performance."

"I'll put you in, and keep you in, if you demean yourself, and at such a time as this!"

Rab, with Seth at his side, pushed up the steps. Rab did not stay to knock—he opened the door. At once Jabez Grice started to intercept him, but Rab looked him straight in the face, and said,—

"Here is his daughter."

Grice drew aside, and allowed Rab, carrying the girl, to enter the inner room, followed by the Red Indian. Then, at once, the rest of the company pressed in. It was too late to repel them. One of the acrobats had planted himself against the door, so that Grice could not shut it. He hesitated, saw that it was not possible for him now to drive out the crowd, and they came thick on his heels, in all their motley, through the front compartment into the bed-chamber, and there spread out in silence, with folded arms and bowed heads. In the midst, by the bed, knelt Rab; he unfurled the red shawl, and let the girl, in her spangles and muslin, flash and twinkle in the eyes of her dying father.

"Bear up, child, bear up," he whispered.

The little Queen seemed turned to marble. She could not speak. She could hardly breathe. She could not move. It was all too terrible, too crushing for the childish heart. With great open, dark eyes, full of despair, she looked on her father's drawn face, altered by pain, haggard as she had never conceived his face could become. She put her hands over her eyes to shut out the sight, then withdrew them again. Then she caught his one hand extended to her from the bed, and squeezed it frantically to her glittering bosom.

The eyes of the dying man looked round the tiny, crowded compartment of the van, and sought Grice. Then he withdrew his hand from his daughter, pointed to Jabez, and said,—

"Listen all! I trust her to a good man, a good man. You will go to him, Queenie!"

He closed his eyes and laid his hand on his bosom.

"What is it?" asked Seth, stooping over the dying man.

"Meek and mild,
Look upon a little child!"

The words, broken, faint tremulous, were the last the manager, Signor Santi, uttered. To whom did they apply? To himself rendered helpless as a babe, or to his daughter left an orphan?

Then Grice drew between the bed, and the staring, frightened, stupefied Queenie, and said to Rab,—

"Take her away—it is over."

Suddenly a wave of gold poured over the poacher's face, dazzling, smothering him. The child had turned, thrown her arms round his neck with a bitter cry, and burst into convulsive sobs.

XI

ADA BUTTON

JABEZ GRICE WAS NOT THE man to yield in difficulties, least of all in such as were of a sentimental nature. When he made up his mind to a course, he neither swerved from it himself, nor endured that any impediments be put in his way by others.

Grice speedily made aware that the troupe had set their minds on making of the funeral of their manager a grand demonstration. They would attend in a body, and ride the circus horses. Some qualms came over them relative to the propriety of introducing the buffalo and the ostriches in the procession, none whatever as to the suitability of the creamies and a piebald pony. The late director's Arab was to walk, or rather limp, behind his coffin, with the boots reversed slung over the saddle.

Grice, with decision, put a stop to their scheme. He, and he alone, was responsible for the funeral arrangements. The interment was to take place with the utmost quiet and privacy. None were to attend save those related to the deceased. He would not even inform the troupe of the day when the funeral was to take place.

To prevent, as far as might be, any unauthorised accession to the ranks of mourners, Grice summoned the members of the company before him in the late manager's van, opened his books and paid every man and woman what arrears were claimed, and a month in advance, and requested them to make themselves as scarce as possible in Saltwich. The clown put in a demand for compensation for the loss of Tweedledee, but it was so extortionate that Grice refused to listen to it, and the clown was forced to depart, guarded by his wife, with their united salaries alone.

Jabez was a man of cool head, promptitude and practical knowledge. He resolved to make the best sale he could effect of the horses, vans and properties of the circus. He proposed advertising the whole in London and Manchester, and if no offer came within a fortnight, to dispose of the various lots, piecemeal, by auction, not at Saltwich, but at Crewe. If any of the old company were prepared with a bid they were welcome to remove the entire concern, only Grice would accept no promises to pay. Let it be clearly understood, he parted with the circus, and all belonging to it, cash down. Some of the troupe put their heads together and considered whether it were possible to put their pockets together as well. But proved that though they could furnish any amount of undertaking to pay, they were not able, singly or conjointly, to find the requisite sum for buying the stock. Money-lenders were shy of advancing money to a rambling band whose whereabouts was not always ascertainable.

The troupe again put their heads together. They felt it a duty to attend their old master to the grave. But there were difficulties in the way of their performing this duty beside those presented by the action of Grice. To attend a funeral necessitated mourning. Now, almost every colour was represented in the private wardrobes of the company but black. The principal acrobat affected blue trousers; the main performer on horseback, when in private, wore a very light, snuff-coloured suit and a Stuart plaid waistcoat. Bell Nelson's best gown was of copperas green. If they were all to go into mourning, a great hole would be made in the small available sum they had to maintain them till they could be re-engaged. Then, again, time was of almost as great importance as money. They must at once seek new situations, and, considering the competition in this, as in every trade, it was possible that those slow in offering themselves might be left out in the cold altogether. The only

men really unconcerned about their future were the two carpenters and
a fellow who had attended to the horses. These knew that they would
find ready employ anywhere; and, in fact, the latter was at once engaged
to one of the stud stables on the edge of Delamere Forest.

As yet, Queenie remained in the cottage of the Rainbows. Grice
had been unable to receive her into his house, owing to lack of
accommodation or of furniture, but he made provision for her removal
immediately after the funeral.

The troupe had pretty well dispersed before that took place. But Seth
White, who had personated a Red Indian, remained. No consideration
would induce him to leave till after the burial of the man who had
taken care of him when a helpless infant.

The day on which Joe Sant, or Signor Santi as he was professionally
called, was taken to his grave was not cheerful. The clouds hung low and
were unoutlined, forming one dense, dull canopy of grey, like dirty wadding.
Trees, fields, herbs had lost brilliancy of colour. The roads were deep in red
mud. There were no showers, nor continuous rain, but large warm drops
fell at intervals. Those who carried umbrellas never knew quite whether to
unfurl them or not. The hedges were dripping, the birds flew low; a crow
occasionally called, but no song-birds sang. The cattle stood moping in the
fields without spirit to gambol, without appetite to browse.

The air was warm, and dense with minute gnats, and wherever there
was garbage, swarms of long-legged flies wavered over the engaging
morsels. The gnats were everywhere. They got into the hair, into the
ears; they stung the temples and the wrists, they produced a sense of
general irritation.

The hearse that contained the body of Joe Sant, followed by one
mourning coach, was in the road to Scatterley Church, distant two
miles, and slowly progressed between hedges rank with docks, and
ditches choked with sting-nettles. The same vehicle and the same driver
that had conveyed the deputation to Mr Button, to remonstrate with
him on the concession, to the mountebanks, of the New Hall Field,
were now engaged to transport the mourners to Scatterley. For the
occasion, the driver had donned his weeper and drawn his mouth down
at the corners.

Jabez Grice, Beulah his sister, Queenie and Andrew, occupied the interior of the coach. Grice and his sister sat in the back part and held white pocket-handkerchiefs in their hands. Grice had a black suit always ready for such occasions, and Beulah had managed to contrive a bonnet and gown out of pre-existing materials; but Andrew had to be submitted to a tailor, and a dressmaker had been sent to the Rainbows' cottage with instructions to provide all that was necessary for the girl. Behind the carriage, unobserved by Grice and his sister, walked Rab Rainbow and Seth White. They had joined the funeral procession, uninvited and unnoticed, and were dressed up in such scraps of black as they had been able to scrape together. Queenie, weeping, half-blinded with tears, raised her heavy eyes, and looking at intervals through the window at her side, saw the figure of Rab lurching along in the rear, his trousers turned halfway up his calves, splashing through the mud; and bespattered by the carriage wheels in front. Horses are slower in their walk than men, and the two who were behind had some difficulty in accommodating their pace to the rate at which hearse and coach progressed. They could have walked the distance in half the time.

Rab's eyes were never off the carriage window, through which he could see the black figure of Queenie with her golden hair, which even the dullness of the day could not deaden; he could see how pale she was, how red were her eyes, and his whole frame quivered when he observed how she went into a convulsion of weeping behind the white kerchief that veiled her eyes.

He said nothing to his fellow-mourner all the way, and that way seemed interminable. They passed a red brick barn, with yellow lichen-spotted tiles on the roof, and a boulder of drift granite lying against the wall, with the water from the roof, that should have run in a shoot, as it settled or condensed, dripping over the stone.

As the carriage passed the barn, the bell of Scatterley Church was heard tolling.

About Saltwich there were no trees; the fumes from the brine-boiling works blighted, killed vegetation. But the vapours were comparatively innocuous at a distance of a couple of miles, and there were flourishing plantations of fir, some twelve to twenty feet high, about the parsonage.

Here the road made a rapid sweep, and in this sweep the hearse drew up at the churchyard gates. The driver descended from the coach and placed his hand on the door, to prevent those inside from opening, till the coffin had been removed from the hearse, the pall thrown over it, and the bearers were ranged in order.

Presently a nod from the undertaker gave the signal, and the driver raised his hat with one hand, and with the other opened the coach door and let down the steps.

Grice and Andrew descended first, then his sister and Queenie.

Now for the first time did Jabez observe the followers. He looked at them deliberately from head to foot, with an air of surprise, as though resenting their presence as an impertinent intrusion. Seth instinctively and apologetically touched his cap. Rab coloured, bent and turned down his trousers over his muddy boots.

The church bell had stopped. In the graveyard path could be seen the parson in surplice, book in hand, waiting to read the opening sentences. At that moment round the curve of the road in front dashed a pony carriage driven by a young lady in colours. The road was not broad. The coffin and the hearse perhaps occupied an undue portion of it, so as greatly to reduce that in which a carriage could pass.

In the steamy, heavy air, the sound of the bell had been lost. The girl was quite unprepared to encounter a funeral train. The suddenness of the meeting prevented her from using her judgment. Instead of at once backing as she ought to have done, though it would have been difficult, she whipped the cob so as to dash past. There was nothing intentional in this exhibition of disrespect. She was confused, and endeavoured to extricate herself from an awkward position in the way that seemed readiest.

But the horse would not proceed; he started back, and in so doing threw her on to the front seat. The sombreness of the vehicles, the black of the mourners, the flapping of the sable velvet pall, edged with white—perhaps the savour of death—had frightened the cob, and it was now almost beyond the girl's control. She gathered herself up on her knees on the front seat of the open trap, grasped the reins short and lashed savagely at the horse.

"Go on, you brute, go on! you shall!" she said.

The bearers drew aside, they were afraid the cob would strike them with his hoofs; moreover, by so doing only, could room be made for the light carriage to pass. The horse would not obey. Again the girl raised her arm and beat him, again, and yet again. Her face was white, her thin lips set. There was no token of fear in her countenance, but it was lined with marks of resolution. What she had made up her mind that the horse should do, that she would make the horse do.

The two men, Rab and Seth, behind the mourning coach, could ill see what was taking place ahead of them, owing to the bend in the road, and they had not ventured to follow close on the authorised mourners.

One of the bearers stepping forward said,—

"Miss! shall I lead him past?"

"No thanks, I'll make him obey." Again she thrashed the cob.

"Back him, miss," shouted the undertaker.

"He shall go on," said the girl; and then, finding that the beast would not proceed, in the blindness of one in anger, she struck at the coffin with her whip, and said,—

"Take that away. It frightens him!"

In a moment Queenie, limping, but forgetful that she was lame in her boiling indignation at the insult, ran to the little low carriage, snatched the whip out of the young lady's hands, broke it over her knee, and threw the pieces in her face, saying,—

"May you never have a coffin, never enjoy Christian burial—you hard heart!"

Rab and Seth had now thrust themselves forward and seized the bit. They led the foaming, trembling, panting beast past; and the girl who had been driving, with white, unmoved, or well-controlled face, resumed her place in the back seat, and said no word of apology or excuse.

"That is Ada Button," said Jabez, aside, to Beulah.

XII

RAB'S RIGHT

WHEN THE FUNERAL WAS OVER, Queenie returned to the cottage in Heathendom.

The quickly-kindled wrath had as quickly expired. The stroke of the horsewhip across her father's coffin had cut her quivering heart, and, in a spasm of anguish and rage, she had flown to resent it, had snatched the whip from this young lady, broken it and flung it in her face. On her way back in the coach to Saltwich, if her mind reverted at all from her great loss and sense of desolation to the incident at the church yard gates, it was with a pang of self-reproach. A generous, frank nature, such as hers, would not admit the idea that the act which had roused her anger could have been one of intentional insult, or would not admit it for more than the flash of an instant. There was no malice in the stroke; it was dealt accidentally in the struggle with the horse. In the moment of explosion of anger, her eyes suffused with tears and dazzled by passion, she had not taken note of the girl in the carriage. She would hardly recognise her again.

During the return journey, which was performed at a slow trot, Grice and Beulah made no allusion to the incident.

Queenie was driven on to Heathendom, where she was to pack up her few clothes, and such trifles as she could call her own. The coach was to wait for her and bring her uphill to Alma Terrace. Her sprained ankle was not sufficiently restored to allow of her making the journey on foot. Mrs Rainbow had been kind to Queenie after her fashion—talking incessantly, glorying in her grievances against her son, her neighbours, her customers. She was a restless woman, and, not content with being in a perpetual fidget herself she would allow no one in the house to be quiet.

Queenie was not sorry to leave. She felt that she could not have endured that woman many weeks. But she was not prepossessed in favour of Jabez Grice, who frightened her with his peremptory manner; nor of Beulah, in whom there was little to attract if nothing to repel.

The lonely girl hastily collected her goods and tied them up in a bundle, said farewell to Mrs Rainbow, promised to visit her again, and saw, with surprise, that this rough, restless woman was crying at her departure.

"My word! Whatever will Rab say at your going? Rab had made up his mind you would stay here. Rab will be angry with me for letting you go; and yet it is just as well. Rab is not a fellow to be trusted, and you are not a sort that would do for my boy to be with. I'll tell you the kind of woman he must find—one like that Mrs Nelson, who will lock him up if he misconducts himself. I am sorry you are going for my sake, glad for yours. You are going to tremendously respectable people, and we're not that—that's the fact. There's no denying it. Rab won't let us be. I tew from morning till night; but what can a woman do against a man? He upsets in one minute what it has taken me a day to order. I'm glad you are going. This ain't a fit place for a decent girl. You haven't seen Rab drunk yet. Wait till then, and you will pity me the life I lead. Yet—he is my own child, and I can't help myself. I suppose I must go on till he knocks my brains out with the poker. That's what it will come to some day."

The change to the house of the Grices was a change in every way. All things there were in order, everything scrupulously clean. There were some engravings in frames against the wall. Not one of them was an eighth of an inch on one side. There were knitted wool mats on the table; each was exactly at the same distance from the circumference.

When Queenie arrived, she found Grice at the table with a book open before him. On one side sat Beulah with her hands folded; on the other, Andrew in his glossy black suit, the stiffness and newness of which seemed to have entered into his soul, and glossed and stiffened that. A chair was placed over against Jabez.

"We will seek to improve the occasion," said he. "Will you take that chair?"

Chilled to the heart, with a sense as though an iron hoop were put round her temples and was being tightened, Queenie obeyed, and looked with piteous eyes at the great, solid face opposite.

"Before we begin," said Jabez, "let me call you, Andrew, and you, Beulah, to witness that, on the steps of the New Hall, I shook my umbrella against the Old Field and its skipping-ropes, and butterflies, and pomps."

"Indeed you did, brother. You always testify!" said Beulah with a sigh, opening her hands and then closing them again.

"And I lifted up my voice and prophesied," continued Grice. "I said—Let the earth open her mouth and swallow them up, they and their wives and their children—"

"And Tweedledee," said Andrew. "Indeed, father, it was only Tweedledee that went down."

"I have heard enough of Tweedledee," said Jabez Grice, sternly.

"Oh, brother! what a mercy it was no one but the dog went into the hole!"

"And that's not certain; some think he has been stolen and will turn up after all," added Andrew.

"I said, enough about Tweedledee," said Grice in a loud, commanding tone, and he looked with a dark face at his sister and son. "We will proceed to improve the occasion."

Grice had conceived that there was something more than coincidence in his denunciation of the circus and its immediate collapse. But the response from Andrew and Beulah did not encourage the view, and he said no more thereon.

The chair on which the child was seated was of hard wood—a kitchen chair, with a straight back. At the Rainbow cottage she had been accorded the arm-chair. She was weary, she had hardly closed her eyes the previous night. Her mind had been racked with painful thoughts, her heart full of despair, and now she could not collect her ideas to listen to what was being read or spoken. She strove to keep her dark eyes open and fixed on the massive face of Grice; when so doing she could see and observe nothing save the motion of the black ring of hair about his polished chin.

Then her mind rambled to Heathendom, and she slightly flushed as she recollected that she had left without saying good-bye to, without leaving a message for, Rab Rainbow.

Above the mantleshelf was a picture of Cain killing Abel—a chromo-lithograph, glazed. Queenie lifted her eyes to that, but the lids were heavy. She could not long maintain them elevated. Her chair had one leg a little shorter than the others, or else the floor was not quite level. Every now and then involuntarily, with a slight movement of the hard chair, in which she could not rest easily, the leg went down and made a slight noise on the oilcloth that covered the boards. Then she heard Grice's voice pause, and she dared not raise her eyes lest they should encounter his fixed on her in reproof.

Where was Rab? How was it that she had not been able to say a farewell to him?

Then she remembered that the carriage had returned to Saltwich at a very different pace from that at which it had gone to Scatterley. If Rab was walking he had been left some way behind, and he could not arrive at home till after she had left.

Would he be so very cross at her having gone away? She could not have endured to remain longer in that house. Rab was a warm-hearted fellow, but he was no companion for her. He was rough, violent, wild. His mother spoke ill of him and who would be more inclined to condone a lad's faults than his mother?

This house into which she had been brought—would that be more tolerable than the Rainbows' cottage? Queenie loved tidiness and cleanliness—she was accustomed to both. Her father's house on wheels had been the perfection of neatness. But how different it had been from this house in Alma Terrace. The little compartments of the van had been cosy. By no mental effort could she conceive of cosiness in the room where she now was. This improving discourse surely would not go on interminably! It might last for half an hour. Her head was spinning—possibly it might last an hour. Then she would be suffered to go to bed. She was sleepy, worn out. What sort of room were they going to give her? What sort of bed? Would Mr Grice come up with his great book and read her to sleep?

Her thoughts were becoming confused. She looked again at the picture of the first fratricide, and in her bewildered brain thought that the parts had become reversed, and that Abel was slaughtering Cain, and was knocking him about the head with a great volume. First he knocked his head to one side, then to the other, then he knocked it up with a blow under the chin, then he knocked it down with a blow on the crown.

Queenie's eyes sank to the floor, became dazed, and still saw Abel pounding at Cain with the big book.

She was losing consciousness. To recover herself she leaned forward, and in so doing altered the centre of gravity of the chair. As the short leg came down, there went a shock through her, and for a moment she was roused. Before her on the table was a wool mat, raised in little flounces of alternate violet and green and red, and at the tip of each little flounce was one steel bead. She timidly put forth a hand to this mat, and took one of the beads between her fingers. She felt its angles, she tried to count them, but could never tell at which she had begun. She was hanging on to consciousness by this one steel bead.

Meanwhile Andrew was watching the poor little girl, white, frail, battling with herself; now with her great eyes wide open, then with them closed, the long, dark lashes sweeping the cheek.

What a little nose she had! Just a bit turned up, just as though it were drawing itself away to allow the lips to be kissed. Andrew blushed as this thought entered his mind.

The golden head had sunk. The chin was buried in the black folds over her bosom. He saw the reflection of the lamp that had been kindled play in waves of fire over the bowed head. The hand had ceased to turn the steel bead. Then the arm fell, and the slender figure of the girl sank together in the chair.

"Andrew!" said his father peremptorily. "Where are your eyes?"

The young man recovered himself, and looked at the table.

"Andrew, you'll get no improvement looking at a girl, instead of listening to me. A backslider, a backslider you will be. Never was there an occasion such as this! What have I been speaking about?"

Andrew looked at the sleeping girl, then at his aunt, helplessly.

"I'm sure, father, I don't know."

"You don't know! On such an awful occasion as this! And you cracked nuts when the most famous orator from beyond the Atlantic was haranguing on the undenominational boards."

Then ensued a violent blow at the front door. It was opened from without, and a voice was heard.

"Where is Grice? Where is 'Hammer'? I demand my rights. He has taken her away. She is mine. I will have my rights."

Rab, flushed, partly with anger, partly with drink, stood before them.

"I have come to claim her. She is not yours; she is mine. Give me my rights."

XIII

No! No! No!

JABEZ GRICE ROSE SLOWLY FROM his chair and walked with decided step towards the excited and angry youth.

"You go outside at once!" said he.

Rab looked round the room uncertainly, and encountered the dreamy eyes of Queenie, who had been awakened from her sleep, but had not collected her faculties, and did not understand what was taking place.

"Go out quietly," said Jabez; "do not force me to throw you out."

"Throw me out!" repeated Rab, and looked at the massive man before him. It was by no means certain that, in a trial of strength, the young man would come best off. He had youth and agility on his side, the other weight and coolness.

Rab said sullenly,—

"I will leave the house if you will come into the garden. I do not wish to frighten her."

He pointed with his elbow towards the girl.

"Very well," said Jabez, and strode forward, the young man backing before him, till he was through the door, and in the little garden in front of the house.

"Now I am at your service," said "Hammer."

"You know who I am?" asked Rab.

"I have seen you before, Rainbow. What do you want with me?"

"Only a word, 'Hammer.' Stand where the light from the window falls on you, that I may see your face. That will do."

He put out his hand and moved Grice into a position where shone a streak of lamplight.

"You must give her up."

"Give whom up?"

"Oh yes! do not pretend not to understand me. You know whom I mean—the Queen of Love."

"I know no Queen of Love. If you mean Miss Sant, I will trouble you to speak of her in proper terms."

"As if I did not know her before you did! Did she ever give you a yaller rose? Have you ever carried her in your arms? Did you ever save her from death?"

"She is under my protection, and I will protect her from drunken and profligate ruffians."

"And who will protect her from you?" asked Rab. "I do not trust you."

"Not trust me?"

Jabez rose an inch and expanded two. That disreputable fellow did not trust him—him whom all Saltwich trusted, him whom it delighted to elect to committees, whom it made treasurer to clubs, secretary to societies, whom the member trusted at an election, whom the shareholders trusted to let the pews in the chapel, whom Brundrith trusted in the conduct of the Salt Works! It concerned Jabez little that this lout should not share the general confidence. What was the opinion of one man, and he a ne'er-do-well, against the current of estimation in which he stood?

"Do you know what I did?" asked Rab. "I saved little Queenie's life. She got her life fust from her parents. She got her life agin from me. Therefore I have now the right over her that once had father and mother. But for me she would ha' been trampled under foot, crushed by the tent pole, would ha' been burnt by the oil, smothered in the canvas, perhaps swallered up in the ground. I saved her. I saw her fall from the horses. When everyone else was dyin'—all thinkin' of themselves, how to escape the staggerin' tent and the gapin' earth, then I sprang to where Queenie lay. I took her up. I carried her away." He pulled out his clasp knife and opened it. "Look at this—with this I cut a way out in the great smash up. I carried her through and over it all, and never let go till I had brought her to my home. So she is mine!"

The fellow, in his excitement, gesticulated with the knife.

"Shut that and put it away!" said Jabez. "A tongue suffices wherewith to talk."

"I did all that," said the young man, obeying the command. "And so I say that she belongs to me who gave to her her sweet life. But for me she'd have been buried today alongside of her father. If she has eyes wherewith to see—she owes 'em to me. If she can still speak and hear—it is because of me. I gave her speech and hearin', after they had gone from her."

"You behaved, no doubt, in a courageous and unselfish manner," said Grice. "But, after all, you did only what was your duty, what any other man, worth the name of a man, would have done."

"Who did it but I? Every one else was thinkin' how to get out. No one had a care for the poor little Queen of Love, that lay as one dead on the sawdust. No one else jumped the barrier. The clown was concerned only for his dog. The Queen is mine, and I will have her back."

"This is absurd. The girl remains with me. I am her guardian."

"Who made you that?"

"Her father—my brother."

Rab was silent, for a moment perplexed.

"You gave her to me," he said after a while.

"I—I gave her to you?"

"Yes—when her father was dying you said, 'Take her away!'"

Grice laughed.

"You have been drinking, or you would not talk such nonsense. If you have any charge to make for what you have done, put it down on paper and bring me your account. If the bill be reasonable I will settle it, and so have done with you."

Rab did not hear or pay attention to these words. He proceeded:—

"She threw her arms round me when her father was dead. She knew she had no one else to go to—none who would so care for her and protect her so jealously as I—and she threw herself then round my heart, and none can tear her away from that hold."

"I am ready to praise and reward you for what you have done."

"I don't want your reward and I despise your praise," retorted Rab. "Give me up my Queenie—I must take her back."

"I do not acknowledge any right in you over her."

"You think I am a good-for-nothing chap. Well, I won't say but I have been a bit wild. I'm not to be trusted with the little Queenie—there, you don't know me. I'd never hurt a hair of her head, never look at her but as to my Queen; I'd watch about her that no harm should come to her. I'd think how I might make her happy. I'd work to find her all she wanted. She'd be safe enough with me. I'm not so sartain she'll be cared for and considered the same way by you. Yes, I've not been good for much, and mother always says I'm a trial to her. She's gone the wrong way to work to mend me. But Queenie can do with me what she wills. There is my sister married respectably to one o' the head-rangers in Delamere, and my brother-in-law—it's a lot of trouble and vexation I've given him, sure enough—he always says he'll get me an under-keeper's place if I like to take it. I've loved my freedom too much to accept that. But now, give me back little Queen of Love and I'll take the place he offers, and I'll live as decent as a chap can. I won't drink, I won't swear."

"It is of no use your talking, Rainbow. Promises are the most untrustworthy of coin. Performance is the sterling metal."

"Then try me?"

"I have nothing to do with you. The child is my ward and I shall act as her guardian. Neither you nor any one else shall take her away."

"Let me see her," said Rab.

"Here am I," said Queenie, standing in the doorway with her lame foot resting against the other, and her hand to one of the jambs for her support. "What do you want with me, Rab?"

"Come here! Come to me, little one!" said the young fellow passionately extending both his arms.

"I cannot, Rab, I am lame."

"Lean on me. I cannot speak before 'Hammer.' Let me take you ten steps—one to me, eight up and down, and one back—if go from me you must. Lean your hand on my shoulder. I will hold you up, and we will have it out, with no 'Hammer' Grice standing by."

She let go the door-post and stepped to him at Grice.

"You see!" shouted Rab, "Queenie ain't afraid of me. Queenie can trust me—the good-for-naught."

He put his arm round her waist and the girl rested her hand on his shoulder.

"Go in," said he to Jabez Grice. "We two don't want none to hearken—What is between her and me is for us alone, and we want none to look on."

He waited till Grice had retired into the house, but Jabez would not shut the door.

"Now throw your weight upon me, Queen of Love," said the young poacher. "Those people in there will make you serious; they'll take the laugh from your lips, and wipe the light out o' your eyes. They won't make you happy. Do not go back to them. One. When you've done the eight little trips, let me take you up in my arms and carry you away."

Pausing on one foot, leaning on his shoulder, the girl turned her head and answered,

"Indeed, Rab, that cannot be. My father gave me to them. It was his wish—I must obey him."

"Two!" said the young man. "It must out. Thunder and blazes! I can't be silent. I love you, Queenie, I cannot bear to hold it in no longer. I love you!"

"You have been good to me," replied the girl, slightly loosening her hold of his shoulder. "I must always thank you for what you have done for me."

"Thanks! I want no thanks! 'Hammer' says I did what any other man would do. 'Hammer' offered me money, gave me praise. I threw them away. I want love! Three."

"Oh! Rab, don't tease me. I am only a little girl. I give you my gratitude."

"I am not content with that. Four! See! I mean all fair and right. Lord! If anyone had said last week that Rab Rainbow would lose his wits because of a girl, I'd not have believed him. I would have said, 'Let the hares first run after the sportsman, and the sun rise in the west.' I can't help it, it is so!"

"Do not tease me, Rab dear; let me alone. You are asking what I cannot give. I am a child. Then think, Rab, you have no honest profession. You do nothing to earn a livelihood. You idle about, you drink, you swear, and poach!"

"Five. Do not let go your hold of me. I have a will. I will mend my idle, my evil ways. I will get work, honest work; I will work hard. I will never enter a public-house again."

"I would do much for you, Rab."

"Then be mine. Six. I will go to the parson to morrow and put in the banns, then you needn't stay in this house."

"No, Rab, no! Don't tease me. I can't help it; I must say it—No!"

"Seven. You cast me from you?"

"I do not that. I shall ever regard you as a dear friend, ever respect you, if with a good will you mend your ways. Will not that suffice? Do not tease me. I am a child. I cannot hold to you closer than I do now.'

"Then let us go through the world as we are."

She loosed her hold altogether and stumbled to the rails of the little garden and hung to them.

"Let me alone, Rab; you are too good to torment me. I give you what I can—my friendship."

He stood in front of her, and folded his arms and looked hard at her.

"There will mischief come of this. I cannot help it. I am a fellow who must have his way. There will come mischief of this somehow. How, I know not, but I feel it, like a thunderstorm comin' on. Oh, Queenie! do you put me from you? That will be bad for some—bad—worst of all, for me!"

XIV

BEGGAR-MY-NEIGHBOUR

QUEENIE WAS NOT UNCOMFORTABLE IN No. 4 Alma Terrace. On the contrary, she was well lodged, well clothed and well fed; and were human happiness assured by these three points of satisfaction, she would have been content. She had no longer to endure the irritation of the fussy interference of Mrs Rainbow, was no longer maddened by her incessant chatter; thus her overstrung nerves were given the repose they needed. And precisely so long as that was necessary was No. 4 Alma Terrace a place suitable for her. But no sooner had she recovered from her depression, than she found No. 4 Alma Terrace to be a place too strait for her, and its atmosphere not at all congenial.

As George Herbert well said, everlasting droppings young hearts can leastwise bear, and Queenie's mind was not one of the harebell order, but rather of that of the daisy, that holds up its face and drinks in the sun.

The twinkle came back into her eye, her droll little mouth began to curl on one side, all the flash and ripple returned to her glowing hair, and a tinge of colour painted her cheek. As there is spirit in wine, so was there fire in her blood; and in No. 4 Alma Terrace not only was alcohol forbidden in all drinks, but the life-blood was supposed to flow without passion, to produce no intoxicating effect when it rushed to heart or brain. Queenie had nearly the entire day to herself, for Jabez Grice and his son went to their work early, usually before six, and returned after four in the afternoon, when the pans had been cleared of their salt, or, if the boiling continued night and day, they returned when the day gang left and the night gang came on.

Only Beulah was in the house with Queenie for ten hours, and Beulah, though a good woman, was not an interesting one. She sighed over her work, not because she had a grief at heart, not because the work was too much for her, but because to sigh became her profession as an eminently-serious woman. She was a machine, performing her household duties regularly and well; she had but one absorbing idea, which was that her brother was the best and greatest of men. Queenie, unable to endure solitude, accompanied Beulah about the house, assisted her in her work, tried to make the good woman laugh, attempted a romp, and failed in all her attempts. Of entertainment to be got out of Beulah, there was none.

When Andrew and his father returned to the house, the girl tried her powers on the elder man. She drew a stool to his feet, and sat there whilst he read and smoked, pleaded for a whiff of his pipe, a peep at the pictures in his magazine. A little adroit flattery, a little coquettishness got him to unbend for a while, and make some clumsy attempts at humour, but he always became doubly grave and absorbed in his reading after such relaxation. Jabez was however, not much at home. He returned from the Salt Works to "fettle" a bit, put on his better suit, and then went forth to a committee meeting, or a political debating society, or else occupied himself with accounts at home, when no noise, no talking, hardly a whisper was tolerated in the room.

Andrew formed a more congenial companion for the girl. He was at home when his father was out, and then she had the field to herself. She liked Andrew; not only was he a very good-looking fellow, but his simplicity, his shyness, his ignorance of all the brighter side of life, amused and stimulated the little creature. She delighted in saying startling things, expressing novel opinions, telling droll anecdotes that made Andrew's eyes open and his mouth drop. She was to him a daily astonishment. She bewildered whilst fascinating him. He was in a flutter of doubt whether he was not wrong in liking her, wrong in listening to her, wrong in allowing her to lead him on to trifle and play and waste time, which is too precious to be spent otherwise than in getting up missionary statistics, or assimilating food for serious meditation.

She had extracted from him the story of the nuts at the undenominational meeting, and was incessantly poking fun at him thereupon, sometimes before his father, usually when they were alone together.

She had not been a fortnight in the house before she had upset the salt—put the fat in the fire. The occasion was this:—

"Where are you off to, Andrew?" she asked, one evening, when the youth came down, dressed to go out.

"There's a lecture on Behemoth, at the Young Men's Serious Association."

"Behemoth—who is he?"

"It is an animal."

"I never saw it in any menagerie."

"No; I don't think it has ever been caught. I question if it has ever been seen."

"Never mind about Behemoth. If there were one alive, and the lecturer would show him in a bath, like a talking seal, and if it would say papa and mamma, I'd go. But only to hear a lecture—bah!"

"I think my father would wish me to attend.'

"He has not ordered you to go and hear about Behemoth?"

"No; not exactly. He takes it for granted that I will go."

"Don't."

"I may never have another opportunity of hearing and learning about Behemoth."

"What does that matter? If he has never been caught, never seen nor heard nor smelt, I don't suppose the lecturer knows much that is reliable about the animal. You stay with me. Aunt Beulah will go to Behemoth, and we will have rare larks together. I'll teach you something better than about Behemoth."

"What's that?"

"You won't tell?"

"Honour bright."

Queenie crept to his side and whispered,—

"Beggar-my-neighbour."

"Beggar-my-neighbour! I never heard of it."

"Now, Andrew, choose—Behemoth or beggar-my-neighbour."

She put herself in a coaxing attitude, with her head on one side, her eyes half closed, full of malice, and the dimples deepening every moment in her delicate, rosy cheeks.

Andrew threw his cap into the corner of the room.

"Beulah is gone already," said he.

"So much the better; we'll make a night of it." After a little consideration—"Andrew, have you any money?"

"Yes; a few coppers."

"So have I. I have that very shilling you gave me for the ticket you never used. Go out and buy some chestnuts, toffee and ginger-pop. We'll toast the chestnuts, suck the toffee and be jolly. Blow Behemoth!"

"Queenie! for shame! Don't say such awful words."

"It's not swearing," protested the girl "Now run and get the chestnuts, toffee and pop. I'll get the other things ready."

"What things?"

"Cards, Andrew—cards."

The young fellow was aghast.

"Cards are sinful," he said, when he recovered from his dismay. "I can't stand this; I'll go to Behemoth."

"You shall not go, Andrew. Behemoth has already been trotted out. It would be bad manners and bad example to go late."

Then she used all her witchery to appease his alarm, to satisfy his conscience, and to excite his curiosity.

The lamp was lighted, the fire was burning, and on the hob the chestnuts were toasting. Now and then one popped and shot across the room. Then there ensued a scramble for it, and they knocked heads together under the table; or, as it burnt the hands of Queenie when she pounced on it, she tossed it to Andrew, who also let it go.

"We'll have a feast after the first round," said the girl, and she rapidly dealt out the cards.

"Mind, four for an ace."

"What's an ace?"

"A one, softie! Three for a king, two for a queen, one for a jack."

"A jack?"

"Yes, that little fellow with legs. The king has none and has a golden crown. Look—the queen has got a yellow rose, and I gave one"—she checked herself and coloured.

"To whom? Not to me."

"No—not to you—I'll give you one when I get it, but I have no rose-garden. Now begin."

For the first time in his life Andrew played a game of chance. Beggar-my-neighbour is not an engrossing game to experienced card-players, but to children, to a youth who had never touched card-board before, it is what a bull-fight is to a Spaniard, a gladiatorial show to a Roman, what roast pig was to the first Chinaman who tasted it. Andrew's cheeks flamed, he shouted, he grabbed at the cards when he made a set, he trembled when his pictures were swept away. He stood up in his excitement, watching Queenie's cards; he sat down with a bounce. He held his breath whilst Queenie counted out, "one—two—three, jack" to his ace. He groaned and flung himself back in his chair, when against her knave he was able to produce only a three.

Then there came a run of luck against him, and he was reduced to one picture card. But that one retrieved his fortunes. He cleared Queenie's hand out, and had started up with a cry of "Beggared!" when the door opened and in the doorway stood "Hammer" Grice.

Mr Grice had been at the lecture, and was appointed to speak a few words after it. But he found that he had left a little book behind him in which he kept notes, and there were some notes in it relative to Leviathan, who was held to be first cousin to Behemoth, and he returned hastily to No. 4 Alma Terrace for his little book. He stood looking at the card-players with astounded gaze. That this should take place in his house! That his son should be found with cards in his hands! But time was precious!

"Humph!" said "Hammer," and without another word he seized the pack from the unresisting hand of his son, and put it in his pocket. Then he went upstairs, found and pocketed his book of notes. Having done this he left the house.

"Now for the chestnuts and pop," said Queenie.

Andrew was too full of dismay to be able to speak. He dreaded the consequences too greatly to enjoy the toffee.

Had the matter ended there, it would have been bad enough, but there was a sequel that aggravated it.

Having returned to the meeting and heard the last words of the lecturer relative to Behemoth, Jabez Grice rose to thank the lecturer; and in the course of what he had to say, observed that there were a few facts relative to Leviathan which he had culled in his reading, facts which threw a flood of light upon the manners and habits of Behemoth.

Thereupon he put his hand into his pocket, and drew forth, before a hall full of attentive listeners and eager observers—a pack of cards. Still talking, and not noticing what he had done, Jabez proceeded to say that he would open his notes and read.

Then all at once he saw, staring him in the face, a knave of spades.

The shock was too great for even his iron nerves; his hand trembled, his fingers involuntarily relaxed, and away shot the cards, flying over the platform and snowing upon the audience in the front rows.

But Jabez Grice was not the man to be thrown off his balance for more than a moment by an accident so untoward.

Rapidly recovering his equanimity, in spite of the titters and commotion produced by the showered pack, he said solemnly,—

"The seed of Behemoth. Out of such as this proceeds that monster, *Play,* which consumes our people from the highest to the lowest."

When he came home, it was with his great mouth set hard, and his brows lowering.

Queenie saw that a storm was going to break.

"Oh, uncle," said she, "we have kept some roast chestnuts for you—and—and, as to the cards, we were only *playing* at beggar-my-neighbour."

XV

AGAIN:
BEGGAR-MY-NEIGHBOUR

"Auntie! There's a nice little carriage at the door."
Beulah went slowly to the window.

"It is Ada Button; she who whipped your father's coffin."

There was no necessity for this reference to the past. Queenie would not have recognised either the girl who was driving, or the cob she drove.

There is more mischief done in the world by stupidity than by malice. Beulah was wholly devoid of gall, but she was stupid to her finger-tips, and, because stupid, she said words that never ought to have been spoken, stirred a painful topic that should not have been retouched.

Had little Queenie been resentful and morose—one to harbour wrongs and to seek revenge—this revival of an ugly and distressing incident would have roused her passions. But the little horsemanship girl was of a gentle, forgiving nature, and already, on her way home from the funeral, had reproached herself for having resented an act which her sound sense told her must have been accidental.

Instead of flying into a fit of anger or turning sullen, Queenie said calmly,—

"That is she—is it? I am glad she is come. She has got no whip, only a stick—who is the saddler here in Saltwich?"

"She wants to come in," said Beulah. "There is no one to hold the horse."

"I will do that," said the girl. "I have not patted a horse, I have not spoken to one, since I came here, and I love horses."

Without another word Queenie hopped out at the door and went to the carriage.

"Shall I hold the cob, miss?" she asked.

"Thank you—for a minute."

Miss Button looked hard at the girl, and Queenie stared at her.

Ada Button was tall, with very dark hair and eyes, the latter hard as polished stone and as cold. She had a white face, regular, with thin lips. Altogether she would have been handsome, had not the lower portion of her face been too sharp and the mouth too large for beauty. The face was as stony as the eyes. She had no colour in her cheeks, her lips were too narrow to show strips of rose, and the only tinge of pink discernible in her face was about the nostrils. She had long, narrow hands, and Queenie saw that she had also singularly straight, narrow feet. She observed this as Ada stepped out of the carriage.

"You want to see Aunt Beulah?" she asked.

"Yes; I want to see Miss Grice. Will you drive the cob up and down? He is warm, and the wind is cold. You, I suppose, are the—the—I don't know the name—but you were—"

"The merry little wandering Queen of Love—now I am the moping, sitting-at-home Miss Muffet."

"I suppose you find a change. Dull, perhaps?"

"Awful!" Then thinking she had said an ungracious thing, she added, "They are very kind, but No. 4 Alma Terrace is not a circus. It is not even a menagerie, for they are all of one kind here, and no monkeys, no parrots, only solemn owls. They have been very good to me; it's no fault of theirs that they are not comic. It's their misfortune."

Ada Button put the reins into Queenie's hands, and entered the house. The circus girl went to the horse's head and talked to him, coaxed him, and whispered secrets into his ear. The horse flicked his ears, turned his head and rubbed his nose against her cheek.

"I knew we should be friends," said the girl; "all horses like me. And I'll speak a word for you to your mistress when she comes out, if she gives me the opportunity."

Then she hopped into the carriage.

A quarter of an hour later, when Ada Button issued from the house, she looked up and down the terrace, but could not see the carriage.

"Come inside again," said Beulah; "she's driving about to prevent the horse catching cold."

"She is doing more than drive about," said Ada in a hard tone.

At that moment Queenie was visible flourishing a whip; when she saw that the mistress of the little trap was waiting, she cracked the lash without touching the horse, and came on at a trot. When she drew up, it was with a smiling face and merry eyes.

"There!" said she, "I did wrong the other day. I have bought you a new whip. It cost three-and-six. Take it. I broke the other. But the cob does not want one, he goes very well with a word."

Ada Button drew back.

"You never intended it," said Queenie. "It was quite accidental that you struck father's coffin with your lash."

"Of course, I knew nothing about him, nothing about you. I did not know there was a funeral when I came round the corner. I did not hear the bell. My cob dashed up, and shied."

"There is your whip."

Looking into Ada Button's cold, inflexible face, Queenie noticed a dark mark on the cheek bone.

"I hope I did not hurt you when I threw the bits of stick in your face."

"You struck and bruised me."

"I am very sorry; I am, indeed. If you will let me, I will kiss your cheek where I bruised it."

Ada shrank away. She answered coldly,—

"You are good—the injury is nothing. I will not trouble you."

Miss Button entered the carriage and drove away. Queenie looked after her, shook her head and said,—

"There's not much fun in her, poor thing. But she can't help it. Aunt Beulah, now I'm beggared. I haven't any money left. The saddler wanted four shillings, but I had only three-and-six; as it was ready money, he took it. I must ask uncle for more."

"Ask for more! What can you require money for?"

"You see—I bought a whip."

When, somewhat later, Jabez Grice returned from the Salt Works, and seated himself by the fire, lit his pipe and took his newspaper, Queenie placed herself on a stool near him, and gradually sidled to his knee, laid both her hands on it, and her chin on her hands, and so looked up.

The newspaper was between her and the face of Grice, but Jabez was well aware that the twinkling eyes were fixed on him athwart the sheet—it was as though the fire from them shot through the paper.

For some while he pretended to ignore her, but the consciousness that she was looking and waiting took off his attention from a speech in the House that he was reading. Then her forefinger, Queenie began to scratch slightly at his knee, just sufficiently to tickle and tease.

"Well!" said Grice, raising his paper. "What's up?"

"It's all up with my pocket-money, uncle."

"Didn't know you had any."

"Yes, my dear father was so good. He always put up a nest-egg in my pocket. It was never quite empty."

"You want no money."

"Indeed, uncle, I do."

"Yes, indeed, to buy chestnuts and ginger-beer and playing cards. Chestnuts are harmless—ginger-pop is—well it makes for seriousness—but cards are wicked."

"Set the cards against the pop, uncle, and we are squared off."

"You are best without money. Don't bother me."

He lowered the paper.

Queenie was quiet for a few minutes, and then she began to scratch his knee again.

"Come, will you leave my knee-cap alone?"

"Uncle, I spent three-and-six on a whip."

"Where is it? I'll lay it across your shoulders."

"I gave it to Miss Button in place of that I broke."

"It is well; now you cannot get into mischief with money. No more cards."

"No, uncle, but I should like to have a little money. I'm fond of brandy-balls."

"Brandy—what?"

"I do not think there is brandy in them—only peppermint. Some people call them humbugs."

"You are better without them. They will upset you. And besides, I don't choose to have you running about the town into all the shops."

"Oh, uncle, I cannot run; you know I've sprained my ankle."

"Well, hopping about. If you have no money, you will be forced to stay at home; at all events, have no excuse for going out."

"Uncle," said Queenie, and now she laid her cheek on the hands that were crossed on his knee, and her golden hair flowed down over his leg. Her roguish eyes were peering up at him sideways.

"Uncle, you have sold the circus horses?"

"Yes"—answered reluctantly.

"Did you sell them well?"

"Middling."

"For how much? They cost father pots of money."

"I really do not carry details in my head."

"And the vans? Our beautiful van with the paintings and the gilded work? Is that sold, too?"

"It is on the way to be sold."

"Will it fetch a tidy price?"

"Middling only."

"And all the properties, have you sold them?"

"Yes, in a lump."

"Did they go off well?"

"Miserably—old rags."

"How much did you get for all together?"

"I really cannot say. The expenses were heavy. I had to pay off all the troupe, and there was the keep of the horses and other beasts till the sale, the advertising, and so on. You do not understand these matters. Take yourself off. Don't peer up at me from under my paper. Don't tickle my knee."

"But I do understand, uncle, and I'm awfully interested in the matter."

"Indeed! Why so?"

"Because it's my money."

"Your money!" Jabez Grice dropped the paper on his knees; in so doing he covered the little head. He noticed this and drew the paper aside. "Your money! Fiddlesticks!"

"I suppose it is mine. Didn't father leave it to me? I'm his child."

Grice was silent. His mouth closed and his brow contracted. Then he said slowly,—

"Understand this, once for all. I am your guardian. Your father put you unreservedly into my hands. Nothing is yours but what I choose to let you have—and mind this, I don't let you have anything which I am quite sure will not be spent profitably and in such a manner as my conscience will allow. I am responsible for your money—I am responsible for you. If you wanted to buy a box of matches wherewith to set fire to your clothes, do you suppose I would let you have it? There is something much more precious than your clothes. I must take care that the money I have in trust—mind me—in trust, is not so spent as to imperil your happiness in this world and the next."

"Five bob, uncle?" coaxingly.

"I do not mind a trifle, but not such a sum as that; and mind—no cards!"

"Pop, uncle, pop!"

Then he gave her a couple of shillings, and resumed his paper.

She turned her head on his knee and looked into the fire. Thus she did not irritate him. She had, moreover, ceased to scratch at his knee.

Presently he said, raising his paper,—

"You are laughing, or crying—which is it? You shake my knee, and that shakes the paper, and I cannot read."

"I am laughing, uncle."

"What at?"

"At you and me."

"Indeed; what is there in me to feed your mirth?"

"Oh, uncle, we are playing at beggar-my-neighbour, you and I—and I am rather afraid I'm going to be cleared out!"

XVI

THE TIGHT-ROPE

THE DAY WAS SUNDAY, THE time evening.
Jabez Grice was upstairs washing and burnishing himself for chapel.
For this process strong yellow soap and a rough towel were employed.
After the process a veritable gloss was over his forehead, cheeks, chin, as
though he had been gone over with beeswax and turpentine—even his
nose shone. Beulah was arranging herself in her best gown and bonnet,
both sober in colour, and getting her hands with difficulty into gloves.

Andrew was ready first. He came down into the sitting-room, in the
grate of which no fire burned on the Sunday, to economise labour.
Queenie was there standing on one toe.

"Andrew," said the girl, "put down your ear. I want to whisper
something—a secret. You won't tell?"

"No; I can keep a secret."

"Put your ear lower. My ankle is better—is all right."

"I am very glad to hear it. Next Sunday you can accompany us to
Little Bethel."

Again Queenie put up her mouth.

"Bend your ear again, Andrew. You don't know all."

"What more?"

"I am shamming."

"Oh! Queenie, what for?"

"I don't want to go to chapel."

Andrew pulled himself upright, and drew from her. He was shocked. She knew that what she had said would shock him. That was precisely why she said it.

Presently, down came Mr and Miss Grice in full plumage, with hymn books in their hands.

"You will find improving literature in that cabinet," said Jabez to his niece. "There are some volumes of sermons, a book on prophecy, and—some missionary reports. Occupy yourself seriously and profitably until we return. It is most unfortunate that your ankle is so bad."

Queenie looked out of the corner of her eyes at Andrew, and a dimple formed in her cheek. He became uneasy and shuffled with his feet.

"Now and then, Queenie," said Beulah, "look at the kitchen fire; see that it is all right, and that there is enough water with the potatoes that are boiling."

"She can take her books with her, and read in the kitchen," said Grice. "Mind, child, no wasting of time. Use the hours in which you might have been with us in something that will do you good."

Then the three left. As Jabez departed, he turned the key in the front door, and then carried it off in his pocket.

"I declare, he has locked me in! That is mean!" said the girl. "I don't care. I can get out by the back yard if I choose, or through the parlour window. And I will!"

As soon as she thought Grice was well on his way to Bethel she threw up the sash and jumped out into the garden in front. The height was but three feet. Then she went forward and sat on the dwarf wall supporting the railings that enclosed the garden, and watched the good people of Alma Terrace go by with their hymn books in hand. After a while the flow of the seriously-disposed ceased. Alma Terrace settled into silence as of death. There was hardly an inmate of the row left behind. Then up came the lamp-lighter. A gas lamp was in the road immediately in front of No. 4, and the lighter halted at it and turned the tap.

He observed the girl and nodded, paused and said,—

"Well, little miss, left alone?"

"Yes—but it's my own doing."

"Waiting for somebody?" asked the lamplighter in a sly tone, winking with an eye and with his lighter at Grice.

"I don't want somebody. I want everybody," answered she. "It's deadly dull here."

"I suppose it is."

"Awful!"

"Well, I'm sorry I can't stay to keep company with you."

"You're very kind. I'm Queen in name, but a queen without power. Do you know what I would do if I were a real queen?"

"Raise me to share your throne?"

"Not quite that, lamplighter. I'd turn this terrace into a grand parade, like that at Scarborough. And I'd have smart ladies and gentlemen to march up and down; and a shooting-gallery, and a photograph booth, and donkeys to ride, and goat carriages, and soldiers, and everything that is beautiful. Would it not be sweet?"

"That would not suit the Alma Terrace people; they would go off in a swarm and take you with them. Now, good-bye. We'll have another talk together next time I come round. I've got twenty-six more lamps to light before half-past seven."

No. 8 Alma Terrace was the most aristocratic in the whole row—it maintained a whole servant. In the other houses charwomen appeared occasionally to help in the washing, or at a spring cleaning, but No. 8 rejoiced, and puffed itself up with pride, at being in a position to maintain a salaried domestic. This domestic, Mary Jane, had, so she informed her mistress, received a letter to say that her grandmother was dying, and she had asked leave to go that evening and receive the last blessing of the expiring and venerable dame.

After the departure of the lamplighter, the milkboy from Button's came that way in very dapper get-up, with a check waistcoat and a spotted tie, and put his fingers into his mouth and whistled outside No. 8.

Thereupon Mary Jane sallied forth in all the gay colours she could muster, and went off accompanied by the milkboy, no doubt to see her dying grandmother.

Now Alma Terrace was completely lifeless, and Queenie was tired of sitting on the dwarf wall and peering between the rails, so she scrambled through the window again into the parlour.

How could she amuse herself? She had the house—she had the whole of Alma Terrace—she had all Jewry to herself.

She put chairs round the table, and proceeded to jump over them, and continued doing this till out of breath. Then she threw herself down in her uncle's chair and panted,—

"What am I to do?"

Should she pull out the serious books, make a circus of them on the table, catch black beetles in the kitchen, and make them run in the improvised circus? No, black beetles smell—are disgusting creatures. If she could be sure of crickets, she would do it. But crickets are not common, nor are they easily captured.

She jumped out of the chair, weary of inaction, ascended the stairs, went into Aunt Beulah's room, dressed herself up in the garments Miss Grice had just taken off, and began to pirouette, curtsey, dance, and make grimaces before the looking-glass. It was infinitely comical in Aunt Beulah's cap, in her stiff gown, and with a certain affectation of the old woman's manner, to go through this outrageous pantomime.

Queenie tired of this amusement. There was no one present to see how droll she was, and it palled on her. She resumed her own gown, went to her box and pulled out her spangled dress—that in which she had last ridden; that in which she had been rescued by Rab.

Then a wave of desolation swept over her heart, and the tears came into her eyes. Oh! the merry days of the circus! Oh! the genial, good-hearted company that had composed the troupe. That funny, tiresome clown, and the routine of locking him up in the monkey cage. The severe and censorious Mrs Nelson—severe and censorious only to her husband, gushing with tenderness to her. And Seth—that vulgar, good, stupid lad. And her father, so cheerful, so fond of her, so exact in all his dealings, so beloved by all who came in contact with him.

Tears fell among the spangles.

Then Queenie jumped up.

"I must not be out of heart," she said. "If I'm not jolly now when they're all out of the house, when can I be jolly? But Andrew is not a bad fellow; one can get fun out of him."

She seated herself on her bed and considered, with her finger to her cheek. How was she to kill time till the return of the Grices?

Queenie thrust both her hands into her hair and held her head as though afraid it were going to roll away from her, so full was it of lively, quicksilver thoughts; and that poor little body, in its black gown, must remain imprisoned in No. 4 Alma Terrace.

What nonsense it was of Uncle Grice to lock the door! Did he think that it would not be possible for her to get out through the window? Or did he lock it so as to prevent anyone coming in? Who but Rab was to come? She would hardly have let him in by the door, and she most assuredly would not admit him by the window.

"I do wonder," said Queenie, "when I am a little more grown up and am wiser, whether I shall be able to earn my own livelihood, and so not have to stay always in deadly dull Alma Terrace? I could go jumping about on the flat saddles upon horses in a circus. There's no great art in that. I wonder whether I could dance on a tight-rope? That would be an accomplishment."

It occurred to her that there was a very stout cord in an outhouse in the back yard.

There would be no harm in trying if she could steady herself—she had run round on the barrier about the circus often, and had not tumbled. Why would it be more difficult on a rope, and on one stretched in a direct line?

There would be no harm in trying. If she failed, she failed. If she could manage it, then she might practise again till perfect.

But where could the rope be strained?

There was the lamp-post, there were the railings. It could be fastened across the garden, and at no great elevation above the grass, so that she would incur no risk. But how make it firm at the other end? Alma Terrace was deserted, and would be a solitude till the chapels disgorged—and that would not be for an hour.

She descended from her room, went to the outhouse and dragged the rope indoors, into the parlour. She went to the window, drawing it after her. Yes, the lamp-post would serve famously as a strainer. It was not possible to fasten the other end to the water pipe that drained the rain from the roof. She could not have passed the cord between it and the brick wall. If there was anything in the room to which she might fasten the rope, then it would pass over the window-sill, and that would be like the bridge of a fiddle—help to hold the cord in position, and precisely at the right height above the soil. The chiffonier would not answer; it occupied the space between the window and the wall.

Of course—the bars of the grate. There was no fire burning! Nothing could serve her purpose better. There were three strong steel bars; she would make a noose and attach the rope to them. They would never give way; then the line would pass under the table and out at the window that was immediately opposite the fireplace, and so in direct course to the lamp-post. She went down on her knees and fastened the cord to the bars of the grate, crawled with it under the table, popped out with the end in her hand over the window-sill, and heard an exclamation of—"Queen of Love!"

"Oh, Rab! This is famous! Oh, I am so glad!"

She dropped her end of rope, and ran through the garden to the young poacher and shook hands with him athwart the railings.

"Queenie! I thought you might be at home, and I have brought you something."

"You good Rab. What is it?"

"Your silver wings! They were bent and bruised. You left them at mother's; I have been trying my hand at them." In a low and doubtful tone—"It was a labour of love, Queenie," then, in his ordinary voice he proceeded,—"I straightened the wires and, with the help of mother's needle and flat-iron, I have got them to look as well as they did when on your back."

"Oh! you dear Rab, you are a beauty!"

"I am neither one nor the other—not to you," said the young man in a tone of dissatisfaction. "I wish I were. But I thought I might give you a pleasure, and it kept my hands out of mischief. So I have put them to rights, and here they are!"

He held out the little wings, and fluttered them in the night air, and in the light from the gas flame.

Oh, Rab, you are a good old boy!" She took her wings and capered for joy. "Rab, I want you to help me. I can't do what I wish myself. I am going to try a little tight-rope dancing. I have fastened the cord inside—it is quite firm, a slip-knot to the steel bars of the grate—but I do not think I should be strong enough, alone, to make the other end firm to the lamp-post."

"I will do that for you, as well as I can. Pass me the poker and I'll use that as a twister. I'll get the cord taut."

"Rab, it wouldn't be proper for me to go on the tight-rope in my mourning black—would it?"

"I suppose not; put on the wings."

"I'll do more. Whilst you are tightening the cord, I'll go up and dress in my spangles and muslin. I have got a balancing-pole out of the back yard—one of the stretchers Aunt Beulah uses for the line on which she hangs the clothes after Monday's washing."

Queenie departed, and was absent for about a quarter of an hour, during which time Rab had done his utmost to strain the rope.

When she returned to the parlour, she was in her muslin, and had adjusted the wings to her back. A lamp burned in the little front sitting-room. The girl had to stoop under the sash to get through the window. Outside, there was a ledge on which she could stand upright.

"Is all ready, Rab?"

"As ready as I can make it."

"Rab, I shall never do it without music."

"I cannot get together a band."

"You can whistle, and hammer on a tea-tray."

"I haven't got a tray."

"You shall have one in a minute."

Queenie dived back into the parlour, and presently reappeared with Aunt Beulah's best japanned tray; she jumped into the garden, ran across the sod, and passed the tray out to the young man, who at once seated himself on the dwarf wall, and began to pipe between his lips, and strike his knuckles against the metal.

The girl ran back to the window, assumed her balancing-pole and mounted the ledge.

She took one step. Then a second.

The rope bowed under her. She righted herself; took a third, then quickly another, and down she went with the rope upon the sward.

The fall was inconsiderable. She was not in the least hurt.

"Oh, Rab," said she, "something has given way. I have not pulled over the lamp-post? No—nor broken the rails. It must be at the other end."

She went to the window, and, leaning her elbows on the sill, looked in. The rope lay loose on the turf of the garden, slack over the window sill, and limp on the floor of the parlour.

She turned her head over her shoulder, and signed to Rab to come to her.

He opened the garden gate, and joined her at the window, put his hand over his eyes and looked in.

"Rab," said Queenie solemnly, "here's a go!"

"Rather!" responded he, gravely.

"What is to be done?"

"Nothing."

"I shall catch it."

"He will not dare to strike you?"

"Oh no!—not that but he will look—awful! And he will speak—awful! I should prefer smacks."

What Rab and Queenie saw was this—the strain of the rope, with the additional weight of the girl, had not indeed broken the bars, but had pulled the entire grate out of its place, over the fender, and had precipitated it into the middle of the room, which was strewn with coal; whilst the hearth was cavernous, ruinous. A mass of broken bricks, mortar and soot was heaped on it and scattered over the hearthrug.

The two young people looked at the wreckage in dismay. What Rab had said was true—nothing whatever could be done by them, nothing could be done till the morrow, and then masons must be called in.

The two were both leaning on the sill, looking into the room—Rab in his rough and untidy fustian, his shabby cap at the back of his head, gaiters on his calves. Queenie was in her fairy costume, the wings fluttering at her back.

Thus they stood dismayed at what had been done, and both dreading the consequences; Rab regretting that he could not relieve his little companion of them, when they were startled by voices in their rear on the pathway before the terrace.

The congregations in the chapels had dissolved, all the serious were on their way home.

Those who came first were arrested—some by the cord stretching from the lamp-post to the rail, others by the astounding picture before them at the parlour window of No. 4!—save the mark, of No. 4!

So astonished were they that they could not speak. More arrived, a little knot was formed and increased.

Then came Jabez—he looked, dashed the garden gate open, strode through to the window, grasped Queenie by the shoulder, and said in quivering tones,—

"What is the meaning of this? Good Heavens! if I had taken a rhinoceros to my bosom it might have proved more inconvenient, it could not have occasioned one-thousandth part of the scandal caused by this dreadful girl!"

XVII

NOTICE TO QUIT

"YOU DID WHAT WAS WRONG, Queenie." Andrew said the words on the Monday afternoon, when he had returned to Alma Terrace after his work at the factory. "I have been thinking of you all day, and have hardly been able to attend to the brine-pans."

"I am glad you thought of me," answered the girl. They were in the front parlour. The grate had been replaced during the morning; a smell of wet mortar pervaded the room. No fire was kindled, as the mason had advised that the mortar should be allowed to set slowly.

"You did what was wrong, Queenie."

The girl seated herself at the table. Her mouth was screwed into a pout. She put her elbows on the board and began to pick to pieces a bit of flower that was between her fingers.

"Andrew, I have had the catalogue of my offences read over my head by uncle and aunt—mainly by him. I am all that is bad. First of all, and that is the worst of all, for it was repeated five times, I am a Sabbath-breaker," Queenie took one of the bits of flower stalk and placed it before her on the table. "Then I am a hypocrite because I shammed lameness. This little bit of stick stands for hypocrisy. Next, Andrew, I am heartless, because I put off my black dress and went into my fandangles for a quarter of an hour. You, little bit of stick, stand for heartlessness—ugh! that is a nasty crime. Fourthly, I am ungrateful, because I went against the feelings of Uncle Jabez"—again she marked her delinquency with a particle of flower-stalk. "Fifthly, I am disobedient, because I did not read the goody-goody books I was ordered to read. That twig stands for disobedience; do you see, Andrew? Then comes dishonesty; I took the rope with which I had no right to meddle. And in addition I am brazen-faced for talking with Rab. Let me consider how many crimes that is. I must count the bits—one—two—three—four—five—six—seven—eight. Eight wickednesses! Oh, horrors Andrew, that is not all. Aunt Beulah reported my ninth. I am unreliable because I did not attend to the kitchen fire, let it go out, and so the potatoes were not boiled for supper. Ah, me! then came a shower—untruthful, profane, rebellious, wilful, pert, disreputable! Oh, Andrew! do look at this little pile of sticks! Is it not a heap? Well, that represents me—a little bundle and mass of vices."

She poked the accumulation of particles in the direction of the youth, put her head down on the table, and looked slyly at him out of the corners of her eyes.

"Seriously, you have done what was very wrong!"

"I know it," said Queenie. "Don't you scold me, Andrew. I've had uncle and aunt jumping on me. I'm down. Don't you drive your heels into poor little Queenie as well."

"I do not want to scold you," said the young man.

"Then why did you say I was in the wrong?"

"I say what you admit, but you do not look at the matter seriously enough."

"Frivolous! frivolous! You have hit it. I knew there was another naughtiness I had not remembered, and now I have done with the stalk. Get me another bit of stick to set in the middle of my pile to represent frivolity."

"Do be serious, Queenie. This is either put on, or it shows a really ill-balanced mind."

"I know, Andrew, I did what was wrong," said Queenie with gravity. "But when uncle goes on at me, I feel that I don't care; I'll do worse!"

"Let us talk over what happened last night, and what the consequences will be. I will not scold."

"That pleases me. I should like to talk with you; I have no one else of whom I can make a companion and speak to concerning what is in my heart."

"Well, and the beginning of all is—you ought not to have done this."

Andrew drew a chair to the table.

"I know I ought not, but I did not suppose that anyone would have found me out."

"Whether you ran the chance of being found out or not, you should not have do it. It was not honourable, Queenie, to act behind my father's back, in his house, in such a manner as you knew he would disapprove of."

"Now I have you!" exclaimed the girl, raising her head and clapping her hands. "Why, then, did you play cards?"

"Then I did wrong. I have felt so ever since."

"I was Eve, and I enticed you."

"If your foot were well, you ought not to have pretended that you were lame. Then had you come with us to chapel, nothing of this kind of thing would have occurred."

"I don't like chapel."

"It is not a matter of like or dislike, but of duty. Queenie, you act on caprice and not as conscience dictates."

"Why should I go when I hate it?"

"Queenie, you might have been killed when your poor father was!"

"So I might if Rab had not saved me."

"Did you thank him?"

"Of course I did."

"Well—was it Rab, and Rab only, who delivered you from death? Rab and Rab only whom it was your duty to thank?"

The girl was silent, considering. She played with a lock of her golden hair, turning it about her fingers. A little hastily now and with manifest nervousness.

"And if you have enjoyed health and strength," proceeded Andrew. "And have had a home and shelter, and clothing, and all your faculties—is it such a hard matter, and a thing to hate, to return thanks for it all, once a week?"

"Give me your hand, Andrew," said the girl impetuously. "You are right, I'll go to chapel with you next Sunday."

"I fear you will not have the chance of going with me."

"Why not?

"Father is terribly discomposed at what has taken place—first the beggar-my-neighbour, then the tight-rope dancing. I never saw him in such a state of mind before. He says that this condition of affairs cannot continue, and that he cannot live in the same house with you."

"Is he going to bundle me into the street?"

"Not that—but he has been to the Buttons to see if he can place you there—at all events for a while."

Queenie was silent; she bit the ends of her hair. Presently she drew a long breath—it was hardly a sigh, for there was a touch of relief in the manner in which she breathed.

"I am a pickle," she said, "a pickle, even though I have never been steeped in your brine. I really cannot help fidgeting."

"It will be too terrible to lose you," said Andrew.

"It will be worse for me to be parted from you," answered Queenie, and suddenly she burst into tears. "I can talk to you, and hear you talk; and you do not ruffle up all my feathers as does uncle. When he begins to lecture me, I bristle all over. I cannot help it. Our clown used to get tipsy, and then, instead of being brimful of fun and nonsense, he became dolorous and tearful. With some folks all things go contrary. So is it with me. I ought to become humble and docile when your father has pounded at me. But I don't—I become just the contrary, exactly as our clown, when charged with ale and spirits, became what was least expected of him. When your father is talking to me, I am all over the shop with my thoughts. I can't keep my eyes still, nor my feet, nor my fingers, and the more he scolds me the worse I feel. If I stay here much longer, he will make a little devil of me."

Andrew was, and looked, distressed.

"All that is good in me," said he, "I owe to my father."

"We are made differently," said Queenie. "There was a fellow at a show once that I saw. He had three glasses before him, and what he poured out of the same bottle turned red as blood in one glass, green as grass in another, and in the third yellow as the sun. It is so with you and me. What changes to gold in you, makes verdigris in me."

Andrew sighed and looked sad.

"If that be so," he said, "then there is no help for it. It may be best that this little company should be dissolved, and that you should go to the Buttons. This I know, Queenie, home will no longer be the same to me after you are gone. I shall have nothing to look forward to when work is over."

"Do you look forward to seeing me, Andrew?" He fixed his great blue eyes on her, and his mouth quivered.

Queenie put her hand forth and took his, drew it across the surface of the table, and patted it.

"And I am happy when you are in the house. We are friends, are we not, Andrew?"

"Yes, and ever will be so."

"Ever, Andrew"—she pressed his hand.

Then he clasped hers tightly, and she could see that his eyes were filling. He turned his head away, and looked towards the window to hide his emotion, and said,—

"I cannot bear to think that you should go"—he paused. Then with a gulp he continued—"When I am on my way home after work, I ask myself—shall I see a little rosy face with gold hair at the window, looking for my return? And, sure enough, it is usually there. Then, before I have reached the garden gate, I see the door fly open, and out you come to meet me. I shall have but a blank window to look to, and no welcome at the gate after you are gone."

"You will come and see me if I am sent to the Buttons?"

"Yes, Queenie. But that will not be the same thing. I cannot go there every day. And how would Ada Button like it—to have me there continually asking to see you, and detaining you from your work? And if she were obliging and suffered it—well I should be in a strange house, and she would be in the room, or Mr Button, or a servant, and we could not talk in the same easy way that we do now."

"Oh! we are cousins."

"We are not really cousins. My father is not really your uncle."

"That will be awkward. Say you are my young man."

Andrew could not help laughing.

"That would be a funny way out of it," he observed.

"Yes—and, Andrew, you shall be my very own Andrew some day, and I, your little wife—that is—" she swept the heap of stalk fragments together and thrust them into his hand—"if you will be responsible for such a bundle of iniquities as I am. But really, with you I will be good. I won't go tight-roping any more, and cards—Andrew—if we play for love, there can be no poison in them. If you say there is—I'll give them up."

She spoke in such a droll fashion, with her face puckered up to laughter, that her words might be taken as a jest.

Andrew sighed.

"I wish it could be so," he said.

"Why not?"

"I have never even thought of such a thing."

"Why not? You earn enough—you told me what your wage was. And we will keep house together. Oh, famous!" she was up out of her chair and jumped over it—once, twice, thrice, and then reseated herself.

"I don't know what father would say," observed Andrew.

"Look here!" said Queenie. "I wouldn't care one snap of the fingers"—she suited the action to the word—"for what was said by that old iron man you have as a father.

> If you love me as I love you,
>   No knife shall cut our love in two."

"Humph!"

The young people looked round. There was "Hammer" Grice, filling the doorway. If the knife would not cut the young nascent love in two, fresh as the flowers of spring, "Hammer" would pound and break it to pieces. This he said with his eyes; he said it by the set muscles of his jaw.

When he spoke he made no reference to Queenie's last words, but said,—

"I know but too well that you do not care one snap of the fingers for my wishes, my words. Therefore I give you notice—this day week you leave, and take up your abode with Miss Ada Button. It is settled."

XVIII

"A Bag of Salt"

THE MANUFACTURE OF SALT IN Cheshire dates from the days of the Romans. It was carried on in rude fashion during the Middle Ages—nobles and country gentlemen had their "wyches" in which they steamed the brine to supply their own tables with salt.

Old Camden says that: "Near the brink of the river Dane there is a most beautiful and deep brine pit, with stairs made about it by which they that draw water out of it in leather buckets ascend half naked unto the troughs, and pour it thereinto, by which it is carried into the wych-houses, about which stand on every side stakes and poles of wood." The brine was then steamed over fires of log and of brush wood.

There are no strong brine springs in the district, as the salt rock lies below the sea level, consequently it can not waste naturally.

In 1670 the salt rock that was discovered was not drowned under a subterranean sea of brine. Thenceforth mining was begun, and the rock was excavated till the water broke in, flooded the mines and converted them into reservoirs of brine. But the quarrying of salt rock was a different branch of industry altogether from the salt making. In the town of Northwich, the principal centre of the industry, the town-pit was an artificially-constructed well, some 120 feet deep, sunk into the underground sea—or, as it is locally termed, brine-run. From this pit in former times the drawers toiled up the steps carrying leather buckets on their backs, and decanted the brine into a tank, whence it was conveyed by wooden gutters laid in the middle of the street, and supplied the several wych-houses. In these houses were little leaden pans, measuring three feet six inches by two feet six inches, and under these fires were kindled. But no "waller" or "boiler" was suffered to light his fire till the town bell on the top of the Court-House sounded the signal for firing.

As long as matters were carried on in this primitive fashion, no great harm was done. It was quite other when, in the first quarter of this century, steam pumps were introduced, and the little leaden boilers were exchanged for large pans, measuring some thirty-four feet by twenty-four feet, and when the demands made on the salt beds were increased a thousandfold. It was now no longer a matter of supplying salt to the gentry and the people of Cheshire; the salt was required for all England, Scotland, Ireland, the United States, Canada, and the East Indies. The pumps worked hard, the fires burned night and day, the steam of the brine rose in volumes, and formed a perpetual mist over the country.

Then a remarkable phenomenon ensued. As the brine was withdrawn, down went the face of the land in grand collapse, carrying with it fields and orchards, houses and churches. And this process begun with this century is continuing and will continue till the entire salt bed has been dissolved and drawn away in brine, and has been steamed and is exported, and then, where was a fertile land, and where were towns and villages, there will be an inland lake of unsounded depth.

When a salt factory is started, then the first thing done is to sink a shaft through the red marl and gypsum till a somewhat harder substance is reached, called "flag" or "beany metal." The moment this is pierced, up the shaft boils the brine of the underground reservoir. Then a pump is let down the shaft, and slung at the surface. It rests on no foundation below; it is simply let down, like the proboscis of a fly, into the sea of brine. This is now pumped up into large tanks, open to the sky, lined with brick. From this tank pipes communicate with the several iron pans, in which the brine has to be boiled till all the water it contains is driven off in steam, and it has yielded up all the salt it held in solution. How strong the brine is may be realised when we are told that in sea-water there is but three and a half per cent of salt, whereas in the brine pumped up, over one quarter, or twenty-six per cent is salt. Fires are maintained under the pans, at one end, night and day. As the brine boils and parts with some of its water in steam, a corresponding amount of salt crystallizes on the surface, and as it crystallizes is raked to the side and put into moulds. If the salt scum be not at once raked off the surface, it sinks to the bottom. The salt that forms round the sides of the pans is termed "cats." Once a week the fires are let out and the pans are scraped. It is found that a crust or "scale" had formed on the bottom, of gypsum, white as snow, but so hard that it has to be removed with hammer and chisel. The men who attend to these pans are termed "wallers," i.e. boilers—each waller is expected to keep his pan in clean condition, free from scale, and receives no extra wages for so doing.

On each side of the pans are the "stand insides," i.e., troughs about eighteen inches below the platform—or, as it is locally termed, "hurdle"—that intervenes between them and the walls of the building. A slightly elevated rib, two inches in height, rises at the extremity of the hurdle, dividing it from the "stand inside." This occasions accidents; when the steam is very dense, a man sees imperfectly, and, tripping on the rib, falls forward and goes into the pan.

But though the waller is subject to chance of accident, his trade is remarkably healthy. He laughs at cholera, smallpox and scarlet fever.

When the salt has been placed in moulds, it is left for a short while to drain, and then the blocks are removed to the stove, or hot chamber, there to become thoroughly dry.

The unmoulded salt, locally termed "butter salt," is sent to the East Indies. The "cats," or salt that has become encrusted round the edges of the pan, is despatched to the pottery works for glazing pipes and pitchers.

Andrew was engaged at his pan.

The air that day was chill and heavy, charged with vapour, and it refused to take up into it the dense steam emitted by the boiling brine. The white cloud filled the walling (boiling) houses rolled about in it, and now and then only, through an open door or vent-hole, did a cool draught enter, and set the steam in revolution. It was as though an invisible arm were stirring flocks of wool.

The fires are maintained at one end only of the pans, and, as the brine boils, it sends ripples down the length of the vessel, and these ripples become covered with a formation of salt as they reach the further end. A little glue or soft soap is put into the brine—this is called "poisoning" it—to collect the impurities which exist along with the salt, and this is skimmed off with wooden ladles.

Andrew's work was, to a large extent, mechanical—the raking of the fine crystals in a snowy foam to the side, and then casting the mass into "tubs" or moulds, which, when full, are set to drain on the "hurdles" or platform behind.

It was quite compatible with doing his work properly that his mind should be engaged elsewhere—with little Queenie.

Her childish solution of her difficulty—that he should marry her and set up house for himself—would not go out of his brain. It turned and rolled and clung therein, as the coils of steam turned and rolled and clung in the walling shed.

The idea of marriage frightened Andrew. He had not considered such an eventuality. Queenie was thoughtless, and in mind not a woman. She had neither weighed what her proposal meant, nor did she, probably, understand what it involved. To her it suggested itself as the pleasantest way out of a very unpleasant condition of affairs. She had no home. She was tossed from the Rainbows' cottage into the house of the Grices, and now thrown from that into the farm of the Buttons. Hitherto she had led a wandering life, but had carried her house about with her.

Queenie liked Andrew, and Andrew had admitted to her that he was very fond of her. What more natural, therefore, to her simple mind than that they should take each other for better, for worse, and so she would be provided with a settled home.

Andrew had never met any girl previously who had in the least touched his heart. Those whom he had encountered at anniversary teas, school treats and missionary bazaars, had been but re-editions of himself on a smaller scale, and in petticoats. But this little creature, this madcap, this witch, with her frolicsomeness, her vivacity, her eccentricity, her coquettish ways, was so opposed to himself in character, in habits of thought, in bringing up, that she had laid hold of his imagination with both hands, and had coiled herself about his heart before he knew where he was. He had no doubt whatever as to the condition of his affections, but Andrew was not the man to rush headlong where his passions urged. He had common-sense and principle, and it was precisely because he doubted whether these two qualities were lodged in Queenie's soul that he held back, and entertained grave doubts whether she could be formed into a suitable wife for himself.

She was volatile, obedient to impulse alone, in considerate, simple to childishness in some ways, precocious in others.

Of the sort of life she had led in her former career he knew nothing; what the moral atmosphere of the circus was he did not know. And to take a girl to his side, to be his companion for life, without any guarantee that she would be faithful and high principled, that she had balance to carry her steadily through all life's waves and storms—to do this, he was not prepared.

He could not, he would not, believe that there was evil in Queenie. He had seen enough of her to be satisfied that she was guileless and fresh. But guilelessness in a woman is not sufficient to satisfy a man. He desires not an empty watch-case, but a watch-case with a main-spring inside. Was there any law, any conscience of duty in the heart of this child, to fill and to hold it? An empty heart may become, by its mere voidness, a harbour of dragons.

Every day that Andrew spent with Queenie, she the more surprised him. He was ever making fresh discoveries in her, and these discoveries only served to further perplex him.

She was in contravention to all those ideas he had been taught to cherish as essential. He was not prepared to go the length of his father, and to condemn her for being in opposition. He thought his father's judgment was overstrained, but not that it was radically vicious.

What Andrew had been taught from infancy to respect, received no regard from Queenie; what he had been cautioned to avoid, she ran into with eyes open and without scruple.

What possible security could he have that a girl who broke the Sabbath would not violate other commandments with as light a heart and blunt a conscience? One who was so indifferent to her duty of homage to her Maker, might, as caprice took her, neglect her duty to her husband. She was moved to do what she did by inclination, not by a sense of responsibility, and to shirk a duty the moment it became irksome.

Whilst these thoughts were rolling in his brain, Andrew—happening to look up at a somewhat unusual sound—a laugh—saw the delicate face and golden hair of Queenie shining upon him through the volumes of steam.

"Andrew, I have come to see the works."

"Queenie! How did you get in? What will father say?"

"I walked in. I asked nobody's leave. I had found out the way for myself. I have been some while with the women in their packing shed, and have seen them sewing and tying up the bags of salt, and I have helped—and here is one of the bags I have done myself."

"You should not have come without permission."

"What a cloud of steam you have here, Andrew; it is a thousand times worse than Aunt Beulah's back kitchen on washing-day."

"You have done wrong in coming.'

Andrew was annoyed, and he spoke in a tone of vexation.

"Now, don't scold me," said Queenie, hopping to his side. "Don't, dear Andrew. You yourself invited me when first we had a little chat together."

"Yes, but then I intended to ask leave for you to see over the Salt Works. Now, if my father were to find you here, I would get into trouble, and he would be most seriously offended with you."

"How was I to know? There was no dog at the door to say 'Bow wow! no admittance, miss! bow wow!'"

"Common-sense might have told you—"

"That," said Queenie, "is just what I have not got. Look here, Andrew! Fancy yourself suddenly put into a circus among horses and acrobats and ostriches and pearls of the Indies. Would you know what to do, and what to leave undone? Would your common-sense, without experience, help you? Would not you be making all kinds of mistakes? Well, it is just so with me. I am brought into a place of which I don't know the ways and the rules, and what I may touch and what not, where I may go and where I may not, what I must do and what is under ban."

"That is true enough, my poor, dear little Queenie. But then—that which is to me a daily anxiety and distress, is that I cannot say whether you have any notion whatever of what is right in principle and what is wrong, not in this place or in that, under one condition or another, but in all places and always. That is why I think of your future with such sinking of heart. Out of mere ignorance and thoughtlessness you may commit some terrible fault, step off the right line of action and plunge, heaven knows, into what!"

"Oh, Andrew, you do not understand—I know what is right, I know what is wrong—at least, I know something about it. But you have such a lot of rights and wrongs in Alma Terrace that I get sheer bewildered—you make a sort of fog about my eyes, like this thick steam, in which one can hardly see anything clear."

"I hope it is so, as far as you are concerned," said the young man.

"Andrew, what is that trough you are in?"

"It is called the *stand inside*," he answered, and thought—that is Queenie all over, jumping from one thing to another and avoiding all serious thought.

"And is all that great boiling sea brine?"

"Yes—brine being converted into salt."

"Andrew—look!"

Suddenly, before he suspected her design, Queenie had sprung on the little ledge round the pan, balancing herself with one hand over the steaming surface, the other she held above the trough that surrounded it, that in which stand the "wallers."

Andrew looked at her, paralysed with horror. One false step, the slightest deviation from the perpendicular, and the little creature would be over in the boiling brine. The pan was but eighteen inches deep, but to anyone once fallen in there is no recovery.

His first impulse was to shout to the girl to descend from her perilous position. Then he checked himself. A shout might give precisely that shock to her which would unnerve her, and make her lose her equilibrium.

A dense volume of steam, thick as cotton wool, rolled between him and her. For a moment he could see nothing. Had it blinded, confused her? He had known such a thing happen—a sudden hot gush of steam take away the breath, disturb the understanding, and a man had reeled and fallen in.

Andrew's second impulse was to follow Queenie, to catch her up, lay hold of her by the arm, by the waist, by the hair—it mattered not by what—and to drag her from where she stood.

He stepped along the trough; he passed through the coil of vapour, and again he saw her. She was walking along the ledge, a ledge no wider than an inch, and rounded, with arms extended; she intended going the entire length of the pan, thirty-six feet. Thirty-six feet; and at each step she advanced eight inches. She was creeping along, one foot before the other, towards the end of the vessel, under which was a furnace, where the brine heaved and foamed, threw up bubbles and spouts of steam.

The waves ran past her, ran past Andrew, the scum of salt formed over the surface like cataract over an eye, and Andrew let it remain undisturbed and sink. He made no attempt to remove it. He could hear the hiss and ebullition of the brine. He could hear the stoker below heaping on more "slack."

He strode along the trough after her. She turned her head to look behind. She tottered. A cry of terror and pain broke from Andrew. He felt at that moment a scalding sensation over his whole body, as though he himself were immersed in the boiling fluid.

She righted herself and went on. Andrew followed circumspectly— he kept well behind. He hardly breathed, he feared to alarm her.

Again a roll of steam swept between him and the girl, and he halted, panting, trembling, his sweat as tears rolling over his face.

Then a cool waft from an opening drove the vapours apart, and again he saw Queenie. She had reached the end of the pan, and instead of stepping down from her ledge, had turned the corner, and was balancing herself as she worked her way along the breadth of the pan—twenty-two feet.

There was another workman in the wych-house. He raked the salt crystals on the further side of the boiler. He had not seen what Queenie was about. Now, if she were not content with walking the width of the pan, and chose to descend its length, reversing the direction in which she had started, she would come upon him. What might he do?

Was it not possible, was it not probable, that directly he perceived the peril in which the child was, he would run to her to remove her from the ledge? And she—might she not shrink from him and fall? Better leave her entirely to herself; let no movement on their part distract her.

Andrew retraced his steps hastily, and went round, at the further end, to the fellow "waller" and grasped his wrist.

"Whatever you see, do not stir."

He stood, holding the man, unable to trust him otherwise, and waited till Queenie appeared—if she ever should appear—emerging from the white vapour. Andrew's heart beat like a sledge-hammer welding the plates of a waller's pan.

The time seemed to him an eternity. He could hear nothing, save the ripple and lap of the wavelets flowing and depositing their salt. Round the pan formed a snow-like crust—"cats"—each wavelet adding to the foamy formation.

Then he and the man with him saw the girl coming on towards them, upright as a wand, flexible as an ozier. She saw Andrew, and smiled. She hastened her steps and leaped into the trough, then up to the platform or "hurdle," and laughed joyously.

"Andrew! there was no danger! There really was none at all. See; I had in my hand a seven-pound bag of salt, which the women let me take away. I held that on the side opposed to the pan, and so I was safe—quite safe. Andrew! why are you so dreadfully doubtful of me? Don't you think my father gave me more than a seven-pound bag of salt to keep me steady? I can walk where I see my way. I can walk steadily even through all the clouds and mists your father and you throw up to blind me. Why are you so convinced that I walk without anything to keep me steady?"

XIX

A Salt Scheme

"Andrew! Fettle up. Put on your new black cloth coat and your top-hat, and look sharp about it."

Obedient as was Isaac to Abraham, and without asking his father why he was to be thus dressed, Andrew hastened to array himself.

When he was dressed and had descended, his father was not quite ready. He found Queenie below. Her golden hair was wonderful. The salt had crystallised in it, and she wore a halo about her head of mingled silver and gold. Andrew took forth his kerchief and dusted the salt out of her hair.

"Andrew," said she, "do you know that Mr Poles often comes here? Did he do so in old times?"

"Sometimes—not frequently."

"He comes in very often now, on all sorts of excuses. Do you think he is after Aunt Beulah?"

"He is a widower. There is no saying. Does she receive him graciously?"

"I do not know. He is very civil to her. But so he is to me—more so to me when she is out of the room. He is very funny."

Further conversation was cut short by the entrance of Jabez Grice.

Father and son now walked in the direction of the Button's farm. In due time they reached Button's, and there they turned in at the gate.

"Very handsome gates these," said Jabez.

"Yes—if only the gate would fit the posts."

"That's the fault of the settlement."

"If I had the gates, I'd have something done to put them to rights."

"Very fine drive this," said Jabez. "There, laburnum, golden chains. There, syringa, that tastes like cucumber. There, yew, laurel and rhododendron. What do you think of the drive, Andrew?"

"Very fine, but the shrubs want cutting back."

"And the house," continued Jabez, standing in front of it. "That is my idea of what a house ought to be, square as a die—one window on one side of the door, one window on the other, and three windows upstairs, one over the door, one over each of the windows below. All the chimneys gathered into one flue—there's saving of bricks. No gables nowhere—there's saving of slates. No crinkum-crankums nowhere—there's saving of lead gutters. That is just what a house ought to be."

"It is rather ugly, is it not?"

"Ugly! you don't build a house to look at, but to live in," retorted Jabez. "Very nice people the Buttons are, to whom all this belongs. Old Tom—he has his wits about him. Ada is good-looking, sensible and will be his heir—Andrew, if you can make your self agreeable in that quarter, you may look to some day being able to set the front gate to rights, trim the bushes and alter the house."

"Have you come to see Mr Button?"

"I have; and I want you to entertain Miss Ada whilst I am engaged with her father. That is why I've had you put on your best suit and box hat."

"How long shall you be, father?"

"Half-an-hour—nothing under."

"Half-an-hour! Am I to talk to the girl all that while?"

"Yes, you are; and make yourself as agreeable as you can."

"It is rather a long time, father. I want to get home."

"I know what you are after—you are hankering to be home with that girl Queenie. Andrew, it is high time this were put a stop to. She is not suited to you. Ada Button is different. She has never kicked her feet about on horseback, and worn skirts that hardly reached below the knee. She's no painted Jezebel. She knows nothing of skipping-ropes and butterflies and the pomps."

They were now at the front door.

Mr Button was within. So was Ada.

"She'll show you her cows and her dairy," said Jabez to his son. "I'll go into the office with old Tom."

Mr Button looked as unlike a substantial yeoman as a man well could. He was cadaverous in complexion, and had small, cunning eyes. There was a slight stoop in his back, a little grey showing in his short-cropped hair. He wore mutton-chop whiskers. He might have been taken for a lawyer, a banker's clerk—not for a farmer.

Jabez Grice was a man who never beat about the bush. If he had something to say, he said it without preparing the ground for its reception. No sooner was he alone with Tom Button than he said,—

"I've come about that proposal of yours."

"What proposal?"

"The sale of your land."

"What—have you the money for the purchase?"

"I have money—perhaps not enough. But I can do better than buy it. If you and I can pull together, we shall make our fortunes."

"Glad to hear that. I've found myself for the last twenty years getting further and further away from that consummation."

"I don't propose exactly to buy the land."

"But, bless me! where did you find money?"

"I have been left trustee for my niece, and there is a good deal more money than I expected, locked up in unprofitable securities. We can do better with it than South American bonds."

"What! Santi's money! And the saint wants to spend it?"

Button's eye twinkled.

"Nothing of the kind," answered Grice. "You don't know me, or you would not say that."

"What will you do with it?"

"I will tell you what my idea is. If we two can work together, we will bore for brine, and run up a salt work here. Salt is under our feet."

"What will Brundrith say to that?"

"He will probably try to buy us out. One thing of two will happen, and either way we shall make fortune. When we have begun to pump, and have got into working order, then you shall enter into negotiations with Brundrith. If he will pay us what we have laid out, and something more, and take us both into partnership, then that is well. Our fortunes are made. If he refuses—but that he will not—we will undersell him. We will draw his custom to us. I have not been in Brundrith's Works so long without having my fingers on the keys and being able to play my own tune. I know all his customers, and can make it so unpleasant for Brundrith that he be driven to come to terms—and to our own terms—money down, and partnership for the future."

"You will use your ward's money to this end?"

"There is absolutely no risk. We know that there is salt under your land. We know it by the settlements and subsidence. Your cow has pioneered the way. Then, to bore and tap the brine-run will not cost much. A few hundred pounds will do it and start the pump working. The main cost is the buildings. But salt-work factories are not so expensive as others. There is no machinery to speak of. There are the pans—there is the tank; there is, worst of all, the chimney. You are on the Weaver Canal, and a couple of hundred yards of rail will put you on the line."

"Have you enough capital for all this?"

"No, I have not. But I propose to let Nottershaw into our scheme. As a builder, he can build cheaper than anyone else. He has made a good deal of money, and he will risk it when, at the end, the profits are so secure."

"What, have him in partnership also?"

"Not that. He will be paid off."

Button screwed up his little eyes, and began to drum on the table with his thin, white, bony fingers. Presently a smile played about his lips and he said,—

"I like it. So—you will build on my land, sink a pump and suck up gold. I like it."

"You like it, doubtless," said Jabez, quickly, "from the point of view from which you are looking. But I must have your land secured to me as guarantee for the girl's money. I'm not quite the fool to sink her capital on land that is not hers or mine."

"Then I don't like it," said Button.

"There must be some security given to satisfy each. Here is money lying idle. Without injury to my niece I can turn it over and over, so as to enrich both myself and you. At the end she shall have the same sum back that her father left—it shall be secured to her on the land and building."

"If you buy my land and pay me a sum down, I shall be content, without any partnership, and without any bother."

"I cannot do that. We want the land and the money. The land without the capital, and the capital without the land, are paralysed."

"Then I don't understand. If you buy the land of me and do not pay, but spend the money on the salt factory—I shall be no better off—I shall be done out of everything."

"No—the money of my niece shall be secured on the land and buildings—to be hers when she shall require it; in the meantime it is at our disposal. It is quite true that there must be some mutual guarantee. Let this be it. Marry my boy to your girl. Let Andrew and Adie make a match of it. Then our interests are one."

Mr Button considered a while.

"Humph!" said he, pulling at one of his whiskers, "I can't answer for Ada. You may say to your son 'Do this,' and he does it. 'Marry such an one,' and he goes head foremost to put in the banns. But it is not the same with me and Ada. She has to be consulted, and I have to do what she wishes, not she act as I desire. I suppose there is no hurry?"

"There is decided hurry. I must make use of my ward's money whilst I may. Why, if she were to marry—and there's no controlling her, she would be out of my hands, and the money also. I could secure the money at once if I chose. Andrew would take her if I gave the word, but she is not one I could endure as a daughter-in-law, and she would he the ruin of my son in this world and the next. Then, again, what is the money without the land? We must have a suitable site on which to sink the money. Ada is the wife for my boy—orderly, all that I could wish—and as I suppose I shall have to live with the young couple, or rather the young couple with me, I naturally look out for a daughter-in-law who will suit me down to the ground."

"Naturally—and you think Ada will do that?"

"I do."

"Oh, do you? How interesting."

Button looked between his half-closed eyelids at Jabez, and chuckled.

"You take your course—are firm," said Grice. "A child must accommodate itself. The young mind is a blank page. You write on it what you will."

"And you will be firm with Ada?"

"Certainly."

"Indeed—how interesting. I would give my ears to see you. Have you a back? Never broken, eh?"

XX

"I Love my Love with an A"

IF COMING EVENTS CAST THEIR shadows before them, so, naturally, do coming persons. What made Queenie speak to Andrew about the visits of Mr Poles, the paperhanger? Naturally, it was his shadow cast before, thrown athwart her brain or spirits.

The little Queen sat in the parlour. Aunt Beulah was out. She had gone to a Dorcas meeting. Uncle Jabez and Andrew had just departed, as we have seen, on a visit to the Button's.

The time was late in the afternoon. Queenie had the house to herself. What should she do to pass the time till Andrew's return? How should she occupy her hands? Were there any legitimate games at which she might play? She remembered what Andrew had said—that it was dishonourable, behind the back of her uncle, to do in his house what she would not do to his face. Her conscience consented to this proposition. What Andrew had said was right, and she would do nothing that might offend the Grices. Skipping-ropes were classified by her uncle with butterflies and the pomps of a wicked world. A girl can skip when alone, and entertain herself with a rope—there are not many games that can amuse for long a solitary child. Battledore and shuttlecock were impossible—she had no shuttlecock. She could have extemporised a battledore with one of Grice's half-bound missionary magazines, and a cork might have served as shuttlecock, but the rooms were low.

At the door appeared Mr Poles.

"Alone, my dear?"

"Yes, Mr Poles; uncle and aunt are out, so is Andrew. You will have to call again."

"I am warm with my walk up the hill. May I sit down and breathe?"

"Oh, certainly, any message for Aunt Beulah, she will be sorry to have missed you."

"Oh none, thank you." Mr Poles seated himself; placed his hat between his feet, closed his knees, and hung his hands over them. "I've brought my photograph. I thought you might like to see it."

"Thank you, Mr Poles; Aunt Beulah will be charmed. I will give it to her."

The paperhanger put his hand into his pocket, and produced an envelope, presented it to Queenie; again swung his limp hands over his knees, and protruded his sheep's face towards the girl.

"It is very nice," said she.

"You like it?"

"It is very good—of you."

"Pray keep it."

"I will put it on the mantelshelf."

Queenie got up, and did as she proposed, looked, in so doing, into the mirror over the chimney-piece, and laughed at herself in the glass, then made a little face at Mr Poles, whose back was towards her.

"I find you all alone," said the visitor. "Are you dull? Perhaps you will allow me to do what I can to entertain you?"

The paperhanger had arrived at that period in life when love blows with its second bloom. Most men are like roses in that. They have their spring flowering, and their autumn bloom.

"Thank you—it is quite true I was dull. I was thinking what I could do; I wanted to find something to make me laugh, and so, most aptly, in you came."

"You are fond of amusement?"

"Very. Andrew and I were playing cards one evening, but uncle caught us and carried the cards away. Do you know any game we could play together, Mr Poles, so as to pass the time till Aunt Beulah returns? Puss-in-the-corner requires more than two. So does kiss-in-the-ring."

"Oh, Miss Sant."

Mr Poles became pink in the face.

"Let us play at I-love-my-love-with-an-A."

"I think I know that; I used to play it with Duckie."

"Who is Duckie?"

"Duckie was—she belongs to remembrance only. She was my first wife."

"Have you a second?"

"I mean my deceased wife. I always called her Duckie."

"And did she call you Goosie?"

"She called me Sweet P. You know I am Phineas Poles, paperhanger. It was a pretty name, was it not? Sweet P. It is a curious coincidence that P and Q come so close together. Your name is Queenie, and I am Phineas."

"Yes; but so also do O and P go together, and O means nought. Shall we play a game, Mr Poles?"

"Certainly. Charmed."

"I will begin. You must follow. I love my love with an A because he is Amiable. I hate him because he is Absent at the present moment when I particularly want him. I took him to the sign of the Anchor, and treated him to Apricots. His name is—no, Mr Poles, I will not go on further than that; you begin."

"I love my love with an A," said the paperhanger, looking sentimental, with his head on one side, and his languishing eyes on Queenie, "because she is 'andsome. I do not 'ate her, because that is impossible. But if there be a fault to find with her, I should say she was too Arch. Her name is Adorable, and she lives in Alma Terrace."

Then in at the door came Rab, with his cap on the back of his head, and a pair of rabbits in his hand.

"There, Queen of Love," said he, "I have brought you something."

"Oh!" Up jumped the girl. "How good you are! I love my Rab with an R because he is a Rascal, and has brought me Rabbits, and Phineas Poles, paperhanger, brought me only Photographs. Sit down, Rab."

Mr Poles looked disconcerted. The poacher took no notice of him, and seated himself on the table, with one foot on the ground, swinging the other, and with his hands in his pockets.

"Well, Queenie," said he, "how are you getting on in Alma Terrace?"

"Not very happily, Rab. I get into trouble whatever I do. And now I am to be turned out."

"Turned out, Queen of Love! Then come to me." She shook her head.

"I am given a billet on the Button's."

"The Button's! You won't be happy there. I have come to tell you good news—news that will please you, little Queen."

The girl turned to Mr Poles.

"I am keeping you from your shop," said she. "I fear Aunt Beulah will not be home for an hour. She is Dorcasing."

The paperhanger looked at Rab, then at Queenie, then at the rabbits.

"Shall we go on with the game?" he asked. "We did not get very far in it."

"Oh, Mr Poles, not now. I daresay Rab will pursue it. And I saw Mr Nottershaw go by with a roll under his arm. I think he must have been on his way to you. Perhaps he wishes to consult you about re-papering his house. I am a naughty little girl to detain you from your business. I will not forget about the photograph. I will give it to Aunt Beulah with your love. You said with your love, did you not? and desired hers in return?"

"I did not say that," gasped the paperhanger. "And I do not think Mr Nottershaw was going to my place."

"He may have been. In business one must snatch at chances."

"I am bothered," said Mr Poles. "It would seem that you wanted to get rid of me. It is very kind of you, my dear, to take such an interest in my affairs. But, have you forgotten that we have begun and not finished a game?"

"A game! Oh yes, but you did not enter into it with spirit, I suppose, Mr Poles, you are too old to care for games."

The paperhanger, looking more sheepish than when he came in, rose, took up his hat, and somewhat sulkily departed.

"Now, then," said Queenie, "we are alone, Rab. Let me hear the good news."

"I have taken a place as under-ranger," he answered. "You need not fear for me any longer. I will not drink. I will not swear. I will not poach. I will not idle. I am going to be a steady, industrious man."

"I am very glad to hear it," exclaimed Queenie, jumping up. "Pull your paws out of your pockets and give them me—both." She clasped Rab's hands in hers, and shook them. "Oh, you are a good fellow! A real, true, good fellow—I always felt it."

"And yet I live in Heathendom!"

"That has nothing to do with it, Rab. Your heart is in the right place."

"My heart!" he sighed, and Queenie felt that he was drawing her towards him She snatched her hands away. "It is for your sake, Queenie. I can't bear to be thought ill of by you. I can't bear that folk should say—that is the drunken blackguard, the poacher, the good-for-nought—who saved the little Queen of Love, who carried her in his arms out of the fallen circus. Queenie! I've had a fire burnin' in me ever since that night. I feel it here on this arm that held you, on this shoulder where you rested, on this breast to which you clung. There the fire is consumin'—there it is! and will never out. Nothin' will quench it—not water, not snow—death alone!"

"Poor old Rab, I do like you!"

"Yes, I daresay! I can git no more of you than likin' and gratitude. I must be content with that."

"Rab! if that will satisfy you, I tell you that I like you better than anyone else in the world—except—"

"Except whom?"

He looked up from the floor, on which his eyes had rested.

"Never mind, Rab. I like you as much as I can like anyone, short of—"

"Short of what? Say it out, Queenie!"

"Don't bother me, Rab!" She put her head down on her shoulder, and peeped out at him through her eye corners—it was a trick of hers, as was that of laughing on one side of her face. "I like you very much indeed. I can say no more but this, that it will give me the greatest possible happiness to know that you are doing well. If I dare think I have been the means of making you live an honest and sober life, I shall hold up my silly head and think there is really something not altogether wicked in me. And, Rab, I have had such a list of my sins read out to me that I had begun to think I was an utterly bad, abandoned little mass of iniquity."

Rab swung his foot and remained silent, looking broodingly before him for a few moments. Then he said,—

"Queen of Love! I do not know how you will get on with the Buttons. She—Ada—folk ain't over-fond of her. I don't know what it is in her, or whether it is somethin' not in her, but they do not speak well of her. If you are not happy at Button's, then come to the forest."

"What forest?"

"Delamere. Miles of trees, and there are meres there. 'Tis a wild place, and you would be happy there with the birds and the hares and the trees and bushes. I don't say 'run to me'—that can't be. I know it. But there's my sister there; she is married to a head ranger; her name is Gerard. She is a clean, good woman, very different from me. I suppose she learned to be natty from mother, only did not take so much in hand that she can do no one thing well. Mother is always doing five or six things together, and one doin' gets to undo another. You will like Martha. Martha has been often at me to leave off my idle life and take to something. Now I have somethin' to make me listen to her. I wish to earn your respect. I do not choose to forfeit your liking."

"You are good, very good, Rab. Now, you really must go."

"Why should I go?"

"Because I wish it."

"May I not play the same game with you, you were playing with old Poles? If it serves to amuse, I will play!"

"No, you cannot play. I am uneasy. I do not wish to have you found here, and there—there, Rab! I see them coming—Uncle Grice and

Andrew. Do go out at the back door and I will put the rabbits in the kitchen. Oh, do go, Rab! my uncle would be so angry if he saw you here—after that affair of Sunday night!"

Rab reluctantly departed through the kitchen.

Then Queenie ran to the window, looked out at Andrew as he came, clapped her hands, laughed, danced from one foot to the other, shook her golden hair, and said,—"I love my love with an A because he is Amiable. I don't hate him at all now that he is no more Absent; his name is Andrew, and he lives—come in, Andrew! I am so glad you are home—he lives in Alma Terrace!"

XXI

ON A GATE

THE DAY HAD ARRIVED FOR the change of quarters. What Jabez Grice decided on, that was to be carried out, without the smallest alteration. "This day week," he had said, "you go to Button's."

He had said this on the Monday after the affair of the tight-rope; and on the Monday following, Queenie was to shift her place of habitation. Not a day's grace was accorded. Punctual to the day, she and her belongings were to be transferred to the farmhouse. Not till she was out of Alma Terrace could Jabez breathe free, certain that no fresh scandal would ensue to be a trouble and offence to him.

The little Queen had been very submissive during the week, but still waters run deep, thought Grice; a child when making no noise is hatching mischief. He had heard, as was inevitable, of her visit to the works. It greatly incensed him, but he did not consider it worth his while to rebuke her for it. She was unaccountable for her actions. She was a conscienceless, soulless, lost creature, under the bondage of evil, moved to mischief by demons, dead to all good influences.

In vain did Beulah entreat delay. Some articles of clothing ordered for Queenie were not ready. The dresses she had worn in the van were altogether unsuitable for one in a farmhouse; she must be re-clothed from head to foot. It was true she had her suit of mourning; but she had no ordinary working dresses at all proper for her position. Therefore Beulah asked her brother to allow the girl to continue at No. 4 for a few days longer; but Grice was inexorable. Moreover, he insisted on the destruction of the muslin dress covered with spangles, and the silver wings.

When Queenie heard that her circus dress was to be consigned to the flames, she was in great distress. She entreated that it might be spared. She wept, she coaxed, she sulked. It was all of no avail. Then she appealed to Andrew. He also endeavoured to move his father, but without much hopes of gaining the point. At last a compromise was effected. Andrew had been made to understand that his father required him to pay attentions to Ada Button. Andrew ingeniously took advantage of this, and promised, if his father would lock up the gown instead of destroying it, that he would visit the Button's at least twice a week, and that he would do his utmost to be agreeable to the young lady.

"I haven't been quite honest about it," said Andrew to Queenie, "for I should have gone to Button's whether the frock were burned or preserved, for I could not rest without seeing you and making sure you were happy. To save my conscience I must be extra polite to Ada."

Queenie inquired of Jabez in what capacity she was to be received at the farm. Her uncle told her that she was to make herself useful there. In Alma Terrace there was not much for her to do, and the devil always finds work for idle hands. She must learn to work. Heaven forbid that she should spend her time in play, and that her mind should be given up to frivolity! Ada would find her employment. For all that was necessary she should have money, but Jabez told her she must have what was allowed accounted for in a satisfactory manner to himself and Beulah. No spangled dresses, no packs of cards, nothing connected with pomps and vanities were to be allowed for in her expenditure.

Queenie delayed her departure till the return of Andrew from the salt pans on Monday afternoon. Her box had been sent on in a wheel-barrow, but she had a bundle, and that she made Andrew carry for her.

The day was bright, there had been frost in the air. The leaves of the trees were touched. Button's farm was at a sufficient distance to the west of the factories not to be badly poisoned by the smoke. In Cheshire, the prevailing winds are from the sea, and the fumes of the slack burned under the pans blight the vegetation to the east far more than in another direction.

The sun was setting. A haze was in the air, and the air was musical with green and gold-backed flies that congregated against every sunny wall, in parliaments, to discuss what was to be done with themselves during the approaching winter. Dock leaves in the hedges had turned blood colour, and bramble leaves were of rainbow tints. The maples were sulphur-yellow, the sycamores had shrivelled to a dirty ash-grey, and the leaves were speckled with black as though ink had been squirted over them. A plough man was breaking the glebe in a field by the road-side, and as he ploughed he sang,—

> "The farmer turns round with a smile and a joke,
> 'Tis four o'clock past, boys, 'tis time to unyoke!
> Unharness your horses, and rub 'em down well,
> I'll give you a mug of my humming brown ale.
> With rubbing and scrubbing, I swear and I vow,
> We're all jolly fellows that follow the plough!"

Andrew and Queenie walked along, listening to the man's song. Their hearts were full. She felt, more than she cared to show before her uncle and aunt, that she was unhappy at being turned out of the house at Alma Terrace. In her heart, she knew that it was best so. She and the elder Grices could never agree. Yet there was humiliation in being summarily dismissed from the only house that could, in any fashion, be regarded by her as a home, and it was a grief to her to be separated from Andrew, the only one whom she really regarded, now that her dear father was no more. It was, perhaps, with her as with Andrew, the complete contrast in their characters which made her hold to him; but that was not all. There was in the young man a something which she admired, and which exercised considerable power over her—his strong conscientiousness. She respected moreover, whilst she wondered at his submission to, his reverence for, his father.

Andrew's heart was a prey to mixed emotions. He really loved the little girl, but he knew that it would not be fitting for him to marry her. He was infinitely distressed at losing her, yet he was obliged to allow to himself that it was best for him that they should be separated.

Now that the moment for parting had come, he could hardly speak, so full was his heart, such a lump was in his throat.

They had reached the gate into Button's drive, and both leaned on it, looking in at the bushes, rank and overgrown, and smelling of decay under the withering touch of autumn.

"Don't let us look in there," said Queenie. It is all so dismal."

"Well—shall we part here?"

"No, Andrew, not yet!"

Without more ado, the girl climbed on the gate and seated herself on the topmost bar.

"See, Andrew! So we can look at the sun, and watch him go down. Is he not red—red as a dahlia."

He leaned on the gate, and looked up into her face. The evening sun was on her, suffusing it with rose, and glowing with incomparable glory in her hair—every strand of which seemed luminous with an inner fire. Her dark eyes were kindled; two suns were mirrored in the agate-brown orbs.

"Come up on the rail," she pleaded. "Then, here we will sit till the sun is quite set; and when the last spark goes out, then I will go away to my new lodging. Home I have none. My camp is always on the move."

"I do not think the gate will bear us both."

"Yes it will. Silly Andrew, do you not see it rests on the gravel, not solely on the hinges."

He could not refuse her. Their intimacy, which had been so frank and guileless, was to come to an end. They might meet again, but hardly in the same way. They could not be alone together as frequently as they had been.

So Andrew gave a leap, and he was perched on the top rail of the garden gate beside Queenie, with the setting sun in his eyes.

The western sky was gorgeous with colour—amber, copper, scarlet, carmine, primrose; and above the glory that was wrapped about the declining orb was a tract of the purest translucent green. Bluish-white mists hung over the earth.

Another minute and the sun would be behind a dark belt of cloud that lay on the horizon.

"Hark!" said Queenie. "Do you hear that little finch in the bushes? She says chink! chink! I can make that noise and hold conversation with her. Listen to me!"

She closed her palms, interweaving the fingers, and then brought her hands down on one knee sharply. The air between her palms, in escaping, made a sound like the call of the bird.

"I can do better than that," said Andrew. "Listen to me."

He began to rock on the gate.

"Don't do that, Andrew; you will bring the gate down."

"Not I—listen. Do you hear? As the gate swings, it squeaks out Quee—nie, Quee—nie!"

"Nothing of the sort. Let me rock the gate. It says quee—quee! Quee—nie!"

"To me it is Queenie!"

"If nothing speaks to you of Queenie when I am gone, other than creaky gates, I won't say much for the remembrance of me you bear away."

"On the contrary, everything will say Queenie, Queenie, to me."

Then he sighed, and she sighed in response.

"Hark!" said the girl. "The ploughman has ceased his song."

"Yes. I hear the clank of chains. He is unharnessing, and will go home; a summons, that, to me, to do the same."

"The sun is not yet set."

"I think so."

"No, it is behind that black cloud. Wait, and it will peep out again. Look! look! a spark of fire!"

The sun, which had been obscured by the cloud-bar, now suddenly flared up in a great conflagration; it sent flames over the whole landscape, it fired the trees, it blazed in the clouds, it rolled like a sea of glory over the young people seated on the gate, dazzling them, and forcing them to lower their heads. The ploughman went by, driving his team, and, as he went, he sang,—

> "Unharness your horses, and rub 'em down well,
> I'll give you a mug of my humming brown ale!
> With rubbing and scrubbing, I swear and I vow,
> We're all jolly fellows that follow the plough."

The sun was in his eyes, he did not notice those perched on the gate to Button's drive.

What shadows were cast by the man and horses! After they were round the corner, the shadows were still spun out, grotesque, monstrous.

"It is the last glow," said Queenie, sorrowfully. "Hold me, Andrew, whilst I turn on the gate."

He put his arm to her—it wound itself round her waist as Queenie lifted her feet and revolved on the top bar, so that her face was directed in the opposite direction to that of Andrew.

"Now I can see our two shadows," said she; "and the sun on the drive. When the light is extinguished, and the shadows all melt together, then I shall slip down on one side of the gate, you slip off on the other, and we part."

"Meantime, we are side by side."

"For one half second."

His hand was under her heart. He felt it beating.

Oh, little Queenie, little Queenie! thought Andrew. If only—if only—matters were other than they are. Now her golden hair, hanging down her back, caught the glory of the sun.

Andrew's eyes were on the setting orb. Already the conflagration was reduced. A great slice out of the red globe was taken. Slowly, reluctantly, the sun swelled to thrice its wonted size as he went down in the west. Now half was gone. The light on the road was less brilliant. The beech and maple were no longer trees of flame. Peering through the railings was a bush of white berries, commonly called the snowball tree. Every snowball had been converted into a ball of gold. Now each was reverting to its original whiteness.

A wild duck went by, high aloft, on her way to one of the great meres in the forest; the sun blazed on her white plumage. Neither Andrew nor Queenie saw her. His eyes were on the expiring sun; hers on the gravel walk, on the fast-fading shadows.

"Queenie!"

Andrew turned his head.

"Yes, Andrew?"

She turned hers.

"The sun has set."

His voice shook. He drew her closer to him, and their lips met. Then, without another word, he slipped down on his side of the gate, she on hers. Neither looked back, neither spoke again, but each, with bowed head, went on—Andrew towards Saltwich, Queenie towards Button's.

XXII

"A CHANCE CAUGHT"

As ANDREW WALKED SLOWLY HOMEWARDS, his conscience was uneasy. He had kissed Queenie, not with a light and laughing kiss that was half joke, but seriously, with overflowing heart; and he felt that he had done wrong. Weak he was, and his love for Queenie had overmastered his judgment. He had done her a wrong. He had encouraged that affection for him which had sprung up in her innocent heart, and he ought to have done what lay in his power to check a passion which was foredoomed to be blighted. He must go forward in this course, or at once retreat, and, as far as possible, stop the mischief done. Could he trample down his scruples, blind his eyes to the consequences, turn his back on his principles and defy his father? This was a step too bold for one such as Andrew to take. Reverence for his father had been ingrained in him. His principles were dear to him, constituted the best part of him; and his intelligence told him that the bringing up of a circus girl, or rather the sort of bringing up he supposed a circus girl must have had, was not such as could make of her one calculated to assure his happiness. If he were to marry Queenie, he must step out of the society of the Seriously-Minded and descend into that of the worldlings, the frivolous. He must break with old associations, do violence to old, deep-rooted convictions. He would place himself on an incline on which he could not maintain himself, but must slip further and further down, losing the respect of his old companions, and forfeiting what was worse—his own self-respect.

Queenie had shown herself so different, if not hostile, to the principles and decent order which he had come to regard as forming the essence of religion, that he could not hope to bring her round to a more sober and serious view,.He was too diffident in himself to believe that he had the power to turn her about to see as he saw, feel as he felt, think as. he thought. He was, perhaps, conscious that there was in her more strength of purpose, notwithstanding her childishness, than in himself. He knew her roguish ways, dreaded her fascination. It was far more likely that she would seduce him to take a lower course than that he should be able to persuade her to step to his higher platform. What was to be done? He regretted that he had promised his father to visit Button's twice a week. It would have been expedient for him and for Queenie that he should stay away. A visit to Button's entailed a sight of Queenie; and, if he saw her, he was sure his affection would reawake, after he had attempted to send it to sleep.

When Andrew reached Alma Terrace, he found that his father was out. He was glad of this. He did not desire a conversation with "Hammer" just then. His heart was too much in commotion, his brain too full of clouds. He took up a book and pretended to read. But his mind was too much occupied for him to pay attention to the words before him; and Beulah, who looked up from her work occasionally, saw that he turned over no pages, and that his eyes were fixed on vacancy.

On Tuesday evening Mr Grice was at home. No committee required his presence, no platform claimed his eloquence.

It was obvious to Andrew that his father had resolved to come to close quarters with him that evening. He knew it from the way in which his father eyed him, from the way in which he cut his meat, stuck it into his mouth, closed his jaws when satisfied, and folded his lips inward on his teeth.

Nothing, however, was said so long as Beulah was engaged in removing the plates and cloth. Jabez took up his newspaper as soon as he had done eating, and lit his pipe, but Andrew could not stir without his father's eye travelling beyond the sheet in his direction, and watching what he was about. He had risen from his place to remove little Queenie's chair, and put it away between the end of the chiffonier and the wall. It would be no longer needed, and its presence was a reminder that gave him pain.

Had Andrew attempted to leave the room, he was well assured that a peremptory word from his father would have arrested him. He therefore remained where he was, awaiting what was imminent.

Beulah was now in the back kitchen.

"Shut that door!" ordered "Hammer," waving his newspaper in the direction in which his sister had retreated. "Have you been to Button's to-day?"

Andrew answered,—

"No, father, this is but Tuesday."

And he crossed the room and did what he was ordered.

"Do you know how Brundrith became a millionaire?"

"Yes—I have heard he once had a flat" (barge).

"Right—and his sister Sally kept a little shop, oranges, lollipops; and sold salt-herrings by the pennyworth, and peppermints by the ounce."

"So I have been told."

"And now they do not know what to do with their money. Brundrith had a chance. He took it. To every man a chance is given once. If he be wise, he seizes it. Then his future is assured. He becomes great. If he be a fool, he lets it slip. Then Providence passes him by, leaves him in the gutter, gives him not another. Brundrith saw that the door was open. He put in his foot; where he put in his foot, there he thrust in his knee; where the knee went, the thigh followed. Then came the shoulder. He was in, and shut the door on others. Sally has been carried in with him, and the herrings and peppermints left outside, for such as stood rubbing their hands and asking themselves whether the door was ajar or not. The red herrings by the pennyworth and the peppermints by the ounce is all they will have. Everything else that the world can give is for Brundrith, because he saw his chance and took it. The salt was the means. The salt has been turned into gold. What Brundrith has done, another can do, when the chance is given him."

"No such chance has been offered you, father."

"Chances do not come always in youth. They come, no one knows when. Now the opportunity has come."

"Whence, father?"

"From Heaven. Where else could it come from?"

"And you will lay hold?"

"I—if it rested only with *me,* there would be no doubt whatever. I am not one to fly in the face of Providence. I am not one to shut my eyes on opportunities. You are other. At one time I could count on you. But since that circus girl came into my house, you have been other than you were. I do not say that you are wholly given up to skipping-ropes, butterflies and all that, but you are no longer reliable."

"But what do you wish me to do, father?"

"It is this in a nutshell—nutshell. Don't think I forget that nutshell at the undenominational meeting. That was a token of how you were going. When I heard it crack, I felt that my confidence in you was broken. I will tell you what the chance is. You take it and we are made men—you and I. Refuse it, and we are left outside, with the red herrings for a penny and, please, sir, an ounce of peppermints."

"What is this chance, father?"

"In a word—Ada Button." Jabez Grice paused, clenched his teeth, and his dark whiskers formed a halo round his mouth, broken only by the nose. "It is this," he continued, after having eyed his son with that commanding, threatening face that made Andrew quake, as it made every workman under Grice quake. "Tom Button, Nottershaw and I have a scheme. We are going to set up a salt factory at Button's and run against Brundrith. Button furnishes the land, Nottershaw the men and the material, I the brains. If we get the thing afloat, we are made men. Brundrith must come to terms, buy us up, and take us into partnership. Then the salt will not be turned into gold in Brundrith's pocket, but in the pockets of Brundrith, Grice & Company. The public demand salt. They must have salt. They will pay for it anything in reason, from four-and-six up to twenty shillings a ton. We have a vast market—the British Isles, Canada, the States, India. Pshaw! Brundrith has nibbled. We will bite when we are Brundrith & Grice."

"Are you going to give up your situation at Brundrith's?"

"Not yet. I keep in the background. Brundrith is not to know that I am in the scheme. Button and Nottershaw show till I am ready. But Button and Nottershaw can do nothing without me."

"And what has Ada with this?"

"I am not going into it unless you marry Ada Button. Old Tom is slippery. Always has been. I must have him bound down, that his interests and mine shall be one. By some means or other I have a chance of sinking money in the concern—not my money, but other money trusted to me—and I must make sure of that. Unless I am quite satisfied that Button is safe, I'll not trust a penny on this land. The sum is three thousand pounds or thereabouts. Nottershaw will supply the remainder—all rests with you. Ada is my guarantee."

"And you are sure that this scheme will answer?"

"Absolutely certain. It cannot fail. You and I are made men. Have you been to Brundrith's place? Have you seen the house, the park? Do you know whose they were?—they belonged to the Marquess of Caistor. Where are the Caistors now? With horse-racing, cards and the divorce court, gone to pieces in every way; and in their mansion that has been theirs for ages—on their land that was theirs from the Conquest, sits Jack Brundrith, the bargeman, who, not thirty years ago, would touch his cap and say 'Thank'ee sir!' for a shilling. There is a room in that house, where once a lady of that family refused a king—so the story goes—though he knelt to her. King or pretender I cannot say which; I know and care nothing for history. But in that room sits now old Sally, smoking cigarettes against her asthma, and cackling with mirth as she tells the story how she sold pennyworths of red herrings and peppermints by the ounce. You have been about. You have seen some of the grand estates and noble houses round Delamere. Which would you like? You can have anyone. But a few years, and we can pour out gold like water, and buy land where we will."

Andrew's cheek flushed, and his eye sparkled.

"That is not all," continued Grice. "I do not care for show. Conservatories, and pineries, and preserves, and carriages, and livened servants are not what I covet. A few years and I shall be M.P. Brundrith might have been member had he chosen. He did not care for politics. He liked business. Business with me is but a passage leading to political power. Wait, Andrew, till I am in the House. Then there will be a name by which reformers will swear, and that will be Grice. When I am in Parliament, then the Lords may say good-bye to their House, and the Crown will have to do without royal grants, and the Church get on in disendowment and disestablishment, and the Colonies will have to shift for themselves, and England learn to do without a foreign policy. Look here—" A fly was on the mantelshelf. Grice leaned forward with his hand bent into a curve, whisked, and the fly was caught. He crushed it, and threw it on the table before his son. "That's your chance; catch, and you are made!"

"You spring this on me, father."

"How long do you require in which to make up your mind?"

"Give me a week or two."

"Not above a day or two. Chances must be caught like that fly—at once—or they spread their wings and are gone—gone for ever. Providence will not endure fooling. With it, it is Yes or No."

"Give me till Thursday."

"Thursday at 4 P.M., not a minute beyond. At 4 P.M. I have your answer, and I go at once to Nottershaw and the thing is done. To-morrow you go to Button's."

"On what excuse can I go?"

"None—but that you go with me."

In the perplexed situation in which Andrew was placed, or had slipped into, he was prepared to accept the proposal of his father as the best means of escape from his difficulties.

A man not strong by nature, and debilitated still further by reliance on a strong will, and who is conscious of this weakness, is ready to act with rashness in matters of importance, and by so doing to exhibit most conclusively his own feebleness.

The situation in which Andrew found himself was such that he could extricate himself from it only by doing violence to his heart or to his head.

He was sliding further and further into love with Queenie, retreat was difficult, and he shrank from going forward. The only escape from his dilemma was that offered by his father—that of throwing up an insurmountable barrier between himself and Queenie—by that means alone could he be saved from her—could he be saved from himself. His father had condemned Queenie and commended Ada. Andrew never stopped to question whether his father's judgments were well grounded. With some folk an assertion is accepted as equivalent to a demonstration, especially if the assertion be made in a loud voice and without hesitation.

The prospect of wealth opened before Andrew dazzled him, but did not influence him to anything like the degree that did his desire to put himself in a firm position, and escape from the difficulties into which he had allowed himself to be drawn. Next day, Wednesday, he accompanied his father to Button's.

On leaving, Jabez said,—

"All is in train now—everything awaits your answer."

"You can have it immediately," said Andrew in a despondent tone. "I have been talking to Ada. It shall be as you wish."

"Caught! Andrew! Caught! Well done, Andrew!"

XXIII

BUTTONS

"QUEENIE! MY DEAR LITTLE QUEENIE! I am so delighted to see you. It is an age since I saw your bonny face."

One minute later,—

"How do you do, Ada? I hope you are well, and that your father's lumbago is better."

The first at the door, the second in the parlour. Unhappily, the exclamation, the salutation at the door were perfectly audible to the person addressed in the parlour.

Ada Button, with a face of marble, received Andrew. With a slight curl of her thin lips she said,—

"You seem to be vastly pleased to see *her.*"

"Queenie! Oh yes. It is a week—no, nine whole days since we met."

"Oh, you count the days, do you?"

"I cannot help knowing how the time passes, Ada, I have so much to ask her."

"Exactly—to inquire whether she is ill-treated in this house, given enough to eat, bread and butter or bread and scrape; what she thinks of me, whether she approves of me—and so on. Thank you. I should prefer not to be discussed with a domestic."

"I did not mean that. Indeed, I did not. And your father's lumbago?"

"It is we who suffer from lumbago when he pretends to have it. We suffer—whether it be from lumbago or not, I cannot say. The house is unbearable on such occasions. Perhaps you want to discuss the manners and temper of my father with that girl?"

"You mistake me, Ada. I am sorry you are put out."

"Put out! Such matters do not put me out! But I do not like to see you demean yourself. *Dear little Queenie!*"—she imitated Andrew's salutation. "This dear little Queenie, remember, is a common circus girl."

"She is my cousin."

"She is no relation of yours."

"She calls my father uncle, and my aunt is her aunt also."

"She calls them uncle and aunt, glad enough to hang on to respectability as best she may."

"You wrong her, Ada."

"Of course. She is all that is dear and good. I am all that is objectionable and bad."

A silence ensued. Andrew was afraid to say any thing. He looked in her face. No emotion was visible in it, and he hoped that her words were sharper than her feelings.

After that the silence, had been prolonged sufficiently to become embarrassing, Ada said,—

"I suppose you know, Andrew, the new arrangement?"

"What new arrangement?"

"You have not been consulted. Nor have I. It is not the way with fathers to consult their children, but to decide for them. All has been settled, independently of our wishes, by the two who rule our destinies. My father has for some time made no secret of his impatience to leave this house. He never allows one to see exactly what he wants. If he professes something very strongly, I expect to find him manoeuvring in an opposite direction. But in the matter of wanting to get away from here I believe he spoke the truth. He intends to leave as soon as we are married. As the works are to be here, he says the place will become intolerable. But your father is the leading spirit. He is to take the complete management of the salt factory; he and father have set their heads together to start. As that factory is to be here, here Mr Grice says he must be. We are to occupy this house and be saddled with your father. There has been no question whether I should desire this or not. In his peremptory manner he has settled it all, and we must sigh and endure. Where my father is going, I do not know and do not care to ask. I should not be in the least surprised if he went to America!"

"America! But he is to be one of the firm."

"Yes. He will give the land. What does he know about salt manufacture? So long as he has his dividends, his money, and can amuse himself, he will be satisfied. I suppose he will be of no more use after he has lent his name and delivered over the land. He will draw a revenue from the factory, get his share of profits, and spend it as he pleases."

"You surprise me."

"Don't take me as your authority, and proclaim that he is going to America. I only think he has it in his mind, because he talks so much of sticking to the old country. That makes me suspect he intends to turn his back on it. What concerns me is, that, having been rid of his humours, we should be afflicted with your father's despotism. He had far better spend a hundred pounds and build a lodge at the gates, and settle in there. He will be a nuisance in the house with us."

"My father never can be that. You really will see very little of him, he is in such request. Besides, he will be so greatly occupied on the works."

"It is always said that young people when they marry should be together, and no third party be with them. I foresee unpleasantnesses."

"I assure you, you will find my father of value in the house. You can consult him in any difficulty, and when in doubt."

"I—consult! I consult no one but myself!"

Andrew had been happy about his engagement. He felt a sensible relief at having his future marked out for him. The only occasion on which he had deviated from his father's wishes he had been landed in embarrassment. Now there was nothing to vex him. He had not to rack his mind as to alternative courses which he might pursue. His line of life was mapped out for him, and he was content it should be so.

He had no great affection for Ada. He did not dislike her; he rather liked her. She was decided in her views, knew exactly what she wanted, had marked dislikes, and that was satisfactory. It would save him trouble. She was very good-looking; cold she certainly was, but as in Andrew there was no ardour, he was content that the courtship should be conducted at a temperate heat. Flames and raptures were not demanded of him by Ada, and Andrew was content not to have to furnish them. A cool, practical lovemaking was all she expected, and all that he was prepared to supply. Never before had he been witness in her of an outbreak of something like jealousy, and what was certainly a display of bad temper. He was offended at the way in which she disparaged Queenie, and at the contemptuous allusions to her own father and his.

As Andrew left, he walked slowly down the drive. The moon was near its full, and was shining out of a cloudless sky; the laurel leaves were converted into plates of silver, and the snowberries were little globes of light, stars amid the dark bushes.

At the gate into the drive, Andrew found Queenie leaning against the post, waiting for him. She had nothing on her head or shoulders, though the night air was cool.

The young man came up to her without a word, and then she said in a low tone,—"Oh, Andrew! Is this true?"

"What, Queenie?"

"You are not surely going to be married to *her*?"

"Yes, indeed I am."

"Oh, Andrew!"

Queenie turned away from him, leaned her elbows on the top rail of the gate, and folded her hands and looked over them into the road, upon the meadows and fields bathed in moonlight.

"From the tone of your voice I can find that you do not approve."

"I am sorry—sorry for you, Andrew. But I will say nothing more."

"I should have been glad had you been contented. I value your approval very greatly, little Queen of Love. But we must not speak together about her. She is already nettled, thinking we have discussed her between us, and we have done nothing of the sort, for I have not met you since we parted on this gate in the setting sun. I have not had the chance of meeting you, though I have been to the house repeatedly. Have you been hiding from me?"

"No, Andrew; she sent me into the laundry."

"And how are you?"

"I am well."

"Do you like being here better than at Alma Terrace?"

"That is not a fair question, especially as you have forbidden me to speak of her."

"Well, we must hope for the best. When I come to live here, we shall see each other every day, and see a great deal of each other, and I will do all I can to make you happy."

"You are coming here?"

"Yes; and Mr Button leaves. My father comes as well. That is the arrangement."

Queenie continued looking at the moonlit fields from over her folded hands.

"Poor Andrew!" she said, musingly, and the words escaped her involuntarily. "Poor, poor Andrew!"

The young man, still smarting under the sharp tongue of Ada, was afraid of hearing words relative to her, of doing what Ada had told him he was intending to do—of discussing her with Queenie.

"My father is so sanguine," said he. "He feels confident that we shall become very rich, he and Mr Button are going to start a pump here, for extracting brine from the run under our feet. And we are to have pans here and make salt. In a few years we shall be as rich as Brundrith; and I need not tell you, Queenie, that, if I get rich, you shall share in all."

"Thank you, Andrew; but riches will not make me happy."

"Are you unhappy, little Queen?"

She did not answer at once. Presently she said,—

"I suppose I am in a wrong place. I am a peg that does not fit in any hole to which I am applied. I was out of place at the Rainbows' cottage; I was out of place at your house in Alma Terrace; I am out of place here. I wish a circus would come by, then I would run away, join it, and, I daresay, would be happy again, for I should be *in* place in a tent."

"Oh, nonsense! It is only that the life into which you have been put by Providence is strange to you. Now, let us talk of something else. I suppose you will be bridesmaid at the wedding."

"I—I, Andrew?"

"Yes; has it not been settled?"

"No; certainly not. It cannot be."

"Why not?"

"She manages that. She will never ask me."

"Let me speak to her about it."

"On no account, Andrew. It is not possible."

"Well, all will mend when I am married. Then I shall be in the house, and I will see that nothing worries you—that you are made comfortable and happy."

"You think so?"

"I am sure of it. I love you too well, little Queen, not to do everything for you that is in my power. Give me your hand."

"My hand—why?"

"Because we must part. You must go in. The night is cold, and you have nothing over you."

"My hand as good-bye—yes."

She extended one hand to him, without removing the other from the bar of the gate, or turning her head to look at him. He pressed her hand. Then he opened the gate, and, in so doing, had to make Queenie step back. She did so, and remained with her elbow as before. When he was through, she replaced the arm that she had extended to him as it had been, and continued looking at the silvered landscape.

"Queen of Love!"

She started. A man's voice! She looked round. A man had stepped into the drive out of the bushes, between her and the house.

XXIV

ROARING MEG

Rab Rainbow had settled into his employment as under-keeper in Delamere Forest, and found, to his surprise, that honest work was more grateful to his feelings than idleness, broken only by occasional poaching excursions.

His contentment would have been unbounded had he not been consumed with the daily desire to see, or at least hear of, Queenie, and had he been able to entertain the smallest hope that his suit might in the end be successful. He surmised rather than knew that she preferred Andrew to himself. When the tidings reached him that young Grice was engaged to Ada Button, his heart leaped and his hope revived.

Then an overwhelming desire came on him to go to Saltwich and see both Andrew and Queenie. He was filled with an almost passionate gratitude to the former for having stepped out of his way. Andrew had discovered what was obvious to Rab—that he was not suited to make the little Queen happy. He had considered that the claims of Rab on the girl were so great, that he could not justly oppose them. How that Andrew, having to choose a wife, could take Ada Button, when he might have Queenie, was explicable in no other way.

Therefore Rab Rainbow longed to see his late rival, to clasp his hand, and tell him he had acted like a man; and that he, Rab, would ever be to him a faithful and devoted friend. He would say to him: "Andrew, whenever you are in necessity, call on me. Command me for what you like. You might have had the Queen of Love, and you have stood aside and left her for me. You have taken one who is not comparable to her, whom you cannot love, because you saw that Rab Rainbow, who had saved her life, had the first right to her; because you saw that she could never be happy linked to one so prim, so grave, so dull as yourself. God grant that this other one, this Ada Button, may recompense you for what you have given up." Thus would he, Rab, speak to Andrew, when they met. But he would see the Queen of Love also. Now, surely, she would acknowledge her debt to him, and recompense him with the only recompense he desired. Now he was in work, he had taken a cottage in the forest near Oak Mere, where he managed for himself. It was snug, it was spacious, it cried out for a woman to be therein and make of it a pleasant home. What objection could Queenie find against him now? He had hardly been to a tavern since he had assured her he would be sober. He had cast off his old evil life, he had entered on a new and good one, and she must crown this new life and assure him against relapse.

Hip-ho-la! Rab leaped as he went along.

When he came home from his work, from ranging the forest, and threw open his door, he would see a slim little figure seated by the fire, throwing on pine cones, bushes of heather, and making a glorious blaze in which she would shine as an angel of light.

Hip-ho-la! He would dig up the garden before the cottage, and plant it with sweet lavender, with white lilies and yellow marigolds. He would train a monthly rose about the window, which would flower till the New Year came. He would have pots of geranium in the little window, hang bunches of wild thyme from the ceiling, making the atmosphere sweet.

Hip-ho-la! as he stood in the door, with his gun slung at his back, then little Queenie would start from her seat by the fire and come towards him, with arms extended, with the sun in her golden hair, and love in her dancing eyes, with a flush purer than the pink of the monthly rose in her cheeks—all to welcome him home.

Hip-ho-la! He stumbled, and at that moment Mr Nottershaw drove by.

"Heigh!" shouted Rab, and pulled a red-spotted kerchief out of his pocket, and swung it over his head.

In his impatience to reach Saltwich he was ready to have recourse to a trick so as to get helped on his way.

The builder and surveyor drew up.

"What is the matter?"

"You have dropped your pocket-handkerchief."

Mr Nottershaw felt in his greatcoat pockets before he looked at that offered him. When he saw that in Rab's hand, he said,—

"Get along—that is not mine. I do not use such rags as that."

"Then, if you will not own it, I shall pocket it myself. Would you mind, sir, now you have stopped, giving me a lift to Saltwich?"

"I'm not going to the town, but to my place."

"That's just above Button's?"

"Yes, and I shall turn off the road and cut across by Chadwick's and the Bramble Brook."

"All the same to me. I want to go to Button's."

"Then jump in, and welcome. The Bramble Brook way ain't a very good way, but it cuts off a couple of miles, and saves going round by the town. Jump up beside me, Rainbow, and you can open the gates for me, and save my descending. The cob is not amiable over gates."

Rab mounted the trap. A vacant place was beside Mr Nottershaw.

"What are you going to Button's for?" asked the builder.

"My fortune, sir."

"What—are you going into the salt concern?"

"I do not understand."

"You haven't heard? Button and I are going to open a campaign against Brundrith, and see if we cannot make our fortunes out of the salt as well as he, and draw to us some of the custom of the world, instead of letting him monopolise it."

"No, sir, I've nothing to do with salt."

"Then what is the fortune you seek at Button's?"

"Only a girl, sir."

"A girl! Is she an heiress? Andrew Grice has been before you, Rainbow, and snapped up the lovely Ada. Will you step down and open that gate? We turn off the main road here. It ain't much of a road, but we have light, and shall get along."

Rab jumped out of the trap and threw the gate wide. Before them was a footpath and tracks of wheels; obviously not a much-frequented way, nor one maintained by the parish. There was a right across the fields and down the valley of Bramble Brook for foot-passengers; no objection was made to the path being taken by a buggy or cart, but there was no right for wheeled vehicles on it.

Rab re-ascended to his place.

"So—a girl's your fortune," said Nottershaw. "I did not know there were other gilded girls available, save Ada Button."

"She as I seek has no other gold but what grows on her head. I want no money—I want but her. If I have her my fortune is made."

"But how so?"

"I am made—she can do what she wills with me. If I do not get her, then I am utterly undone and cast away."

"That is folly, Rainbow. I know you have turned over a new leaf, and very glad have I been to hear that it was so, but good conduct should not hang on to a woman's petticoat."

"A chap must have an object; he cannot work without hope. If you have a fire in your heart—a fire of disappointment and love that is not quenched—you go mad, you do what you can to forget about it. You are reckless when the morrow will be to you as to-day—without a hope. So it is with me. If I don't get her, I shall go to pieces again—I know it."

They had crossed the field, and now were in a lane that led down hill, in the Bramble Brook Glen.

"Hold hard!" said Nottershaw. "What is that noise?"

A howling, bellowing, hissing was heard.

"It is Meg roaring," shouted Rab. "Get down, sir, it is not safe to proceed."

"We will tie up the cob, said Nottershaw. "I've heard of Roaring Meg, but never have seen her in one of her fits."

"Step warily," cautioned Rab. "When Meg roars, there is mischief somewhere."

The builder and contractor fastened his horse to a gate, and then came on down the lane.

Suddenly Rab stood still, and as Mr Nottershaw was about to pass him, he extended his arm and checked him.

"Look, sir, the roadway is gone."

It was so; a funnel-like gap had opened in the path, and went down, it was not possible to say how far. In the failing light, it seemed an entrance to the bottomless pit.

"The water has not come—it will be here soon. Look at that holly tree."

In the hedge was a bush, almost a tree, and Nottershaw, now that his attention was drawn to it, saw it sink; first the hedge in which it grew disappeared, then the trunk, then the leaves.

Rab ran back the lane to where he had seen a rick of straw. He hastily tore out a bundle, came down the lane again with it flaming. He had struck a match and kindled it. Now he held the blazing straw over the gulf, and Nottershaw could see the reflection in the glossy leaves of the holly as the tree went down. Presently they ceased to reflect the light—all was black below.

"The water won't come till Meg has done roaring," said Rab. "Come on, sir, and see Meg at it."

He climbed the hedge, and the surveyor followed him. From the top of the bank they could see some way down the valley. About four hundred yards off a geyser-like spout was visible, blowing out of the side of the hill, flinging about lumps of gypsum and stones. It was white as steam.

"Jump, sir!"

Rab leaped from the hedge into the field, and ran on, the builder after him, till they came near the orifice, whence burst the column of foam. The force and fury with which it raged were alarming. The noise of the roar was deafening. Rab and Nottershaw stood above it on the slope, out of the way of the jet; every now and then a ball of marl or crystallised mass of gypsum was shot like a rocket far beyond the body of white foam. No steam rolled away, so that it was evident that the jet was in no degree warm. It sent waves down the brook, sweeping over the fields, and washing about the trunks of trees. A mile below was a mill. In a minute or two the mill-pond would overflow.

"I've known the miller grind corn for a couple of days, the wheel turned by strong brine. That which Meg is spitting forth is all brine."

"It is very strange," said Nottershaw.

"The way I explain it is this," said Rab. "The salt rock comes near the surface somewhere, and the water gets to it, dissolves it, and then there is a reservoir underground, unsupported in any way, save by the sides, which are continuously becomin' consumed by more water eating into them. Then at last the roof falls in, and when it falls in, it drives the brine forth at the weakest place in the surface of the land, and that is here, where Roaring Meg is spouting. There must be as much brine come away as there is earth falls in. There's Chadwick's orchard, where I've stolen bushels of apples as a boy, is now all down, and a flash in its place. You see the crust of earth has given way in the lane. It's fortunate we heard Meg roaring, or we might have driven on and been swallowed up like that there holly tree."

"I'll go back, and get out of this lane as fast as I can."

"We cannot go for'ard—that is impossible. We must go back and get into the high road, and go round by Saltwich."

Both returned over the field, and across the hedge to where the cob and buggy had been left. The horse was munching grass, ripping it from the hedge in unconcern.

"I'll have another look at that hell-hole," said Nottershaw. "Hold my hand. By ginger! I don't half like going near it in the twilight."

The surveyor approached cautiously.

"A precious uncomfortable thing it would be to go down there," said he.

"I don't know that one sort of death is much worse than another, if die we must!" answered Rab.

"I ain't superstitious," said Nottershaw, "but I wouldn't be easy in my mind if I thought *that* was to be my end."

"Who goes in there never comes out again. No coffin, no Christian burial for him. The sea may give up her dead, not the breast o' mother earth. When she opens her mouth and gulps, there is no casting forth agin till the Judgment Day."

"Wrr! I don't like it. By ginger! Rainbow, I could almost fancy I saw the red eyes of the Evil One looking up at me from below! Let us get away as quick as we can. I shall dream of this. Wrr! it has made my blood run cold!"

"They say that when Meg roars she is askin' for a life."

"So long as it is not mine—I am content. Whom can she be calling for now?"

"Ay—who?

XXV

A Promise

"QUEEN OF LOVE!"

When the girl turned, she recognised Rab.

Rab had been set down by Nottershaw in Saltwich. He had gone to Alma Terrace and inquired for Andrew. Miss Grice was at home; she informed him that he had gone to the Button's.

Accordingly, the young man walked to the Button's gate. He did not feel justified in going down the drive, and knocking at the house door, and inquiring after Andrew or Queenie. He accordingly secreted himself among the evergreens, and waited. Andrew would leave shortly; then he intended to speak to him, and get him to contrive for him a meeting with Queenie.

He had not been long ensconced in the bushes before the girl herself appeared alone. She went to the gate, and leaned on it, looking at the moon.

Rab's first impulse was to issue at once from his hiding-place and speak to her. But he desisted from so doing, as almost immediately he heard the front door of the house opened and Andrew's voice bidding good-night to his intended bride.

Then a feeling of curiosity came over him to see how Queenie and Andrew met, and to hear what they would say to each other. Something relative to himself might be dropped, which would indicate to him whether he might hope or not.

"Don't cry out—it is I—Rab Rainbow," said he. "Let none know that we are together, and none hear what we have to say to each other."

"What have we to say to each other, Rab? You must not tease me—I gave you your answer."

"Queenie! I have become another man, all to please you. It is in your power to make of me a saint or a devil. And now—now—I came with my heart full of goodness. But all has turned bitter as gall. Look here, Queen of Love! Whilst I have been among the evergreens, beside me was a yew tree, and the yew tree bore, as its fruit red, fleshy cups, and in each cup a grain. The cup is meat, the grain is poison. As I waited for you, I ate the red cups that I picked. Now I could swaller the grains—it would be as well so—I should die. I would do it, but that I cannot leave you here, with none to protect you from him—from yourself."

"What do you mean? You frighten me, Rab. I do not wish to be caught here speaking with you."

"Yet you came here to speak with him. Queenie! be pitiful, be tender-hearted towards me! I am a poor chap, but honest—honest now. These hands do no wrong to nobody. I'm sober now; I have touched nothing save water since I saw you last. Do not fear for me. Do not suppose I have been sober only because I have been in the forest, away from public-houses, out of temptation. No, Queenie, not so! I have gone to a tavern. I have sat with the rest, with my own old comrades, and have drunk nothin', not a drop. I did it on purpose to show my old chums that I was changed. I did it to prove my own self—I can stand. I have a resolute will. What I mean to do, that I can do. Queenie, I cannot force you to take me, but I cannot live without you. Drive me away, and I shall do somethin' desperate. I feel it in my heart, in my brain, in my blood. I forewarn you, Queenie, that you are in danger. This cannot, must not, go on. As I came from my cabin, my bosom was full of gratitude, of love for Andrew Grice. I came to Saltwich, I went to his house to take him by both hands and tell him what was in my heart.

And here—as I stood among the evergreens—what did I overhear?"

"What did you hear?"

"I heard more than the words spoken. I never could have supposed him—the serious Andrew—so great a rascal. He marries one girl but loves another. Are you blind, Queenie, or are you bad at heart?"

He grasped her by both her wrists. He held her so tight that she cried out with pain. His face, his plain, uncouth face, was changed in the moonlight to something terrible and majestic.

"Rab—do let me go. You need not grasp me so tight. I will not run away, I will speak to you."

Then he let go his hold, and folded his arms over his bosom, sank his chin on his breast and looked at her intently from below his heavy brows.

"Rab, I have thanked you for saving my life. I have felt very grateful to you. But now I think it would have been better had you let the creamies trample on me, had you let me go down into that rent in the earth. Had I died then, when my dear father died, I would not have known the care, the misery that I now feel. Rab! I am at home nowhere. Your mother was kind, but I could not make her house my home. I was not at home at Alma Terrace. I am, least of all, at home here with the Buttons. What will happen I do not know. I look forward to the future with fear and with deadness of brain."

"Queen of Love, you must forget Andrew. Put him out of your head and heart."

She was silent—she bowed her beautiful head. Rab knew that she was crying. He did not speak. He was sure that, as soon as she had acquired sufficient strength, she would speak.

Bats whirled about their heads in the night air.

After a full five minutes, Queenie looked up and looked into Rab's eyes.

"I cannot forget Andrew. I cannot put him out of my mind."

"Do you know what you are saying?"

"Rab, forget me—put me out of your heart."

"I cannot do it."

"Nor can I forget Andrew and put him away. I cannot help myself. I love Andrew. I know that he is going to be married to another. I shall have to see it all. I shall be in the house. I know more than do you. I know that he cannot love Ada. When she is his wife, then he will learn what she is, and that it is not in his power to love her. Then I know his heart will speak out and it will return to me. And I shall see his misery. I shall see how he is tortured by that woman, how he will writhe and suffer. And I shall pity him as I love him. What will come of it all, God only knows. What is in store for him—for me—what untold wretchedness—I seem to see and shrink back; and oh, Rab, I wish you had let me die!"

Rab stood as one turned to stone. His head sank lower on his breast.

"Queen! Was it to hear this from you that I came from the forest?— this—this!"

She burst into tears.

"Do not cry. I cannot bear to hear you," said he. "When you were at your father's funeral, every time you wept I sobbed in my heart." He put forth his finger and touched—stroked—her hair that was silvered in the moonlight. "Queenie, I cannot bear it!"

She controlled her emotion, looked up at him through her tears, and said, in a choking voice,—

"You are good indeed, Rab. You have been so kind, so very kind to me. I would not pain you if I could help it. I would love you if I could. Indeed, Rab, I would. If things had been different—if I had never been taken to Alma Terrace—I might have learned to love you as I came to respect you. I see that there is far more in you than I thought at first. But you see how it is with me. I cannot help myself. I know that I have no right to think of Andrew, but think of him I do. I know that when he is here, and I see him every day, I shall be unable to drive from me the love and sorrow, the regret I shall feel for him. I have nowhere else to go. I must stay here, and yet it will be anguish to me to stay, and—oh, Rab, I do not know what it will all end in!"

"Leave the place. Come to me."

"I cannot do that, Rab."

"Then go to my sister."

"I must be where Mr Grice places me. I am his ward. He had put me here, and here I must remain. Of one thing I am glad—he is coming to this house. He will be some check on her. He will be my refuge. If I can bear my pain no longer I will tell him all, and he will send me elsewhere."

"My sister's house is open to you. She is a good woman."

"If I must leave, I will think of this. But I will watch myself. I will fight with myself. I will be as much out of his way as I can. I will work hard so as to have no time for thought."

He was breathing heavily. He trembled as he stood before her in the moonlight.

"I know what I owe to you, Rab, and I wish with all my heart that I could love you. I will try my best. I will strive with my heart, and endeavour to turn it to you. When my thoughts go to Andrew, who has done nothing for me, I will give them a twist and make them look to you to whom I owe my life. I must not think of Andrew. And he must not think of me. I know all that. I know it too well. But I will try to care for you. I will indeed, Rab. It will be my only chance of escape from what threatens."

"Thank you, thank you, Queen of Love!" said the young man, and again he clasped her hands.

Then timidly, hesitatingly, he stooped and kissed her head, her golden hair; then let her go. He was happy. She had promised. He knew that she would strive against a passion that was sinful, and he trusted that out of this struggle would spring up a pure, deep love for himself. So he went along his way, in the sweet moonlight, looking up into the grey-blue sky; and he could ill restrain himself from shouting as he walked through Saltwich. When he found himself in the forest, he sang for joy.

XXVI

SHUT OUT

ADA BUTTON REMAINED A FEW minutes only in the house after Andrew left. She went in quest of Queenie, and could find her neither in the kitchen, nor in the laundry, nor in her own room.

Convinced that the girl had gone out so as to have some conversation with Andrew, Ada stole forth into the garden to catch her with him, or to listen to what passed between them. She was too late to find her with Andrew, but she overheard a portion of what passed between her and Rab Rainbow, whom she did not know. Unhappily, Ada had caught precisely that which it would have been well that she had missed. She had learned how Queenie regarded Andrew. The tone in which Andrew had greeted the girl had aroused jealousy in her mind, along with the suspicion that he was much more really attached to her than he was to herself, who was to become his wife. How Queenie regarded her personally was to Ada a matter of indifference; the way in which Queenie had spoken of her left little doubt in her mind that she had not gained the regard of the circus girl.

If Ada Button was not passionate in her attachments, she was strong in her resentments. She was like a flint which would flash out with sparks when struck, but which contained no fire in itself, no warmth when not smitten.

Ada was not the person to hesitate what steps to take on an occasion affecting herself. She returned to the house with her thin lips closed, her heart contracted, and with relentless resolve already formed in her brain.

After Rab had gone, the little Queen remained for a few minutes alone, musing, standing in the moonlight, in the midst of the drive, with her back turned to the gate, and the shadow that she cast lying short on the gravel before her.

A night bird cried out in the bushes. An owl snored like a sleeping man. As she gradually disentangled her senses from the thoughts that engrossed them, Queenie became conscious of this strange sound. She was no country girl, familiar with, and aware of, the meaning of the various notes and noises that break the stillness of night. The sound alarmed her. It was so thoroughly that of the long-drawn breath of a heavy sleeper. Where was the man who snored? Was he in the evergreens? Or was the man, whose breath she heard, really asleep? There are waking as well as sleeping snorers.

Queenie began to feel uneasy. A chill crept down her back. Her heart fluttered in her bosom like an imprisoned butterfly, and she hastened to the house, treading cautiously lest she should arouse the attention of the snorer. She went round to the back yard and tried the kitchen door. It was fast. She tapped lightly at it, waited, listened, and heard no step approach in response to her knock. She put her ear to the keyhole and heard the loud tick-tack of the clock. She could hear nothing else. She then went to the window and pattered at the glass with her finger-tips, and then discovered that there was no light in the kitchen; the lamp was out, the fire in the grate extinguished, or banked up for the night. Feeling alarmed, she now went round to the front entrance, and gently turned the handle of the door. That was also fast. The house was locked up for the night.

Surprised, disconcerted, Queenie returned to the back yard; although the household had retired, yet all were not asleep. There was a light in the servant's bedroom. She could see the glow of the lamp through the blind.

The girl picked up some gravel and threw it at the window-panes. Then she saw a shadow against the blind, and a hand draw the linen aside for a moment. She again cast a handful of sand.

Cautiously the blind was drawn aside, and a girl's head appeared. The casement was partly opened, and the servant put forth her head, and said in a whisper, so as to be audible in the yard,—

"It is *her* doing. She ordered me upstairs. Wait a bit. I'll throw you your shawl."

The blind fell, and the shadow disappeared. Presently the blind was again drawn, and again the girl appeared. She thrust forth an arm and dropped a woollen wrap at the feet of Queenie, then hastily closed the casement and withdrew from the window.

The night was cold. There was frost in the air. It was damp, as is usual in autumn. The chill had affected Queenie, and she was shivering. Grateful for the shawl, she threw it over her head and shoulders. What was to be done? There had been a stove alight all day in the laundry for keeping the irons hot. If the door was unfastened, Queenie might creep in there, and pass the night in tolerable comfort. She went to the laundry and tried the handle. The door was fastened. Even the coal-shed was fast with chain and padlock.

There was no help for it—she must rouse the house.

Accordingly, Queenie went round once more to the front and looked up. There was a light in Mr Button's window on the left. The window on the right was dark, but that belonged to the best bedroom. She stepped round the further corner. The second window on the east side was that of Ada's room. The curtains were drawn, so was the blind, but there was a light in the chamber. Satisfied that the master and mistress of the house were up, Queenie pulled the front door bell, and rapped with the knocker. The bell was timidly drawn, and the rap given nervously and apologetically. Then she waited, trembling with cold and apprehension.

No answer was accorded to her summons. She panted, shivered, clung to the door and listened. Then she knocked again, louder.

Cautiously the window-sash of the bedroom on the left was thrust up, and Mr Button's head appeared. He leaned forward and said,—

"It is *her* order. Very sorry. Here's half-a-crown. Get a lodging elsewhere."

And a coin chinked on the doorstep and rolled off on to the gravel.

"Mr Button! why am I shut out?"

Down went the sash; she received no reply. What course should she take? Queenie wrapped the shawl tighter about her and seated herself on the step, with her back to the jamb, leaning her shoulder and head against the door. She would remain there till, in very shame, the Buttons let her in. They could not intend to exclude her altogether. Ada may have found that she was out of the house when she gave orders that the doors should be fastened for the night, and have been annoyed, and was now giving her a lesson. But she would surely admit her presently.

Queenie must wait patiently, and endure the exposure till Ada relented. Accordingly, she remained seated, the cold entering her bones, and in the stillness heard the snoring owl again.

There certainly must be some one secreted in the shrubs. How cold he must be! Was he a tramp? Would he live through the night, lying out in the dews and frost? Perhaps the man was ill, was dying; she had heard it told that dying men breathed hard, stentoriously. If so, the snore would presently cease when the spirit fled. Then among the bushes next day a dead man would be found. She must not suffer the poor wretch to lie there exposed to die. She must entreat that he should be admitted, even if she herself were excluded.

She sprang to her feet, and loudly, almost imperiously, rapped with the knocker, and pulled the bell. Then she held her breath and hearkened.

Was that a step she heard descending the stair? A little strip of orange light was visible beneath the door. Through a knot in the wood an arrow of fire shot, struck her and disappeared. Then she heard the sound of a chain being undone, next of a bolt being withdrawn.

Queenie stood back deferentially as Ada Button opened the door and came forth, holding the carriage whip in her right hand. With the left on the handle she drew the door behind her into its place, and closed without shutting it. The moon was full on Ada, painting a black shadow behind her, turning her face to Carrara marble, and glistening in her eyes like crystals. She was tall and slender, finely proportioned; and with her dark hair about the head, and the inky shadow on the door, she looked like a Diana of half-animated marble.

For some while she gazed steadily at the shivering girl, whose eyes were ever-flowing and her bosom heaving. Then suddenly she raised her hand, and with the butt end of the whip struck her on the cheek and said,—

"I have owed you this—now I have repaid the debt!"

Queenie, staggering back under the weight and sting of the blow, uttered a cry and clasped her hands to her face.

Ada reversed the whip in her hand, and said between her teeth, that gleamed in the moonlight,—

"Come to the door again, disturb the house once more, and I will beat you, beat you, beat you as a dog!"

Then the sash of the bedroom window was raised and again Mr Button looked forth and said,—

"Never mind, my girl. It is her way. We all have our backs broken in this establishment. It is your turn now; it has been mine. Here is another half-crown."

Again down went the sash as a coin tinkled on the gravel.

Ada remained immovable in the doorway, holding the whip, and looking at the sobbing girl without a muscle in her cold face moving, without a tremor in the eyelid, any relaxation in the set lips.

Presently, with the lash, she struck at the coins that shone in the moonlight on the dark red sandstone gravel, and said,—

"Take these and begone! Send here to-morrow for your box. Send—do not come for it. Never set your foot here again! Never in future appear before my face. Go—go where you will! Go to Andrew, if you list—what care I?—or to your other lover. It is all one to me. Go—let me be rid of you; that is all I desire. Go! In the field is a pit; cast yourself in and be lost for ever! It is all one to me what becomes of the circus girl. What care I?"

She put up the whip to her lips, bit the lash, spat it out, laughed,—

"Father's cow went down there alive—into the heart of the earth. Go there too! Go—still your sobs there. Cease your weeping there. Forget your Andrew there. Forget that other lover! Go! What care I?"

She went back through the door, facing Queenie still, and the black shadow, of the lintel fell over and eclipsed first her glittering eyes, then her cold cheeks, then her frozen lips.

She slammed the door, thrust the bolt in place, put up the chain. The strip of orange light under the door disappeared; once more through the knot shot the fiery dart—as a stab into the night aimed at the outcast—and her feet slowly ascended the stairs as she sought her chamber, her warm bed and downy pillow.

XXVII

The Ranger's Lodge

I n her trouble, pain, bewilderment, Queenie no longer heard, thought of, feared the snoring in the bush. She ran down the drive and out at the gate, holding her bruised cheek. It was not till she was in the road that she found that a decision of some sort must be made as to whither she should go.

White before her, in the moonlight, lay the old Roman road—the Wattling street—stretching away to Chester on one hand, and to Manchester on the other. Of the cities that lay on the right hand and on the left, of the direction taken by that ancient way, Queenie knew nothing, or, to be more exact, her knowledge was limited to the fact that if she turned to the left she would come to Saltwich, if to the right she would enter the vast solitude of Delamere Forest.

Through that forest she had travelled, with the caravan of horses and circus vehicles, on her coming to Saltwich with her dear father. Then the long tracts of pines and oak, of heather and sand, had interested her. And she had been told by the maid, Jemima, that, outside the gate of the Buttons, lay the road that led, on the right, into that waste and solemn region.

Now, as she stood in the highway, looking up and down it—uncertain what to do, where to go—she saw the forest, like a mass of ink stain under the moon on one side, so dark that no rays of the orb of light could illuminate it, and she recoiled from the thought of losing herself in a wilderness where were no habitations, and which, for aught she knew to the contrary, might be haunted by savage beasts. Her education had been neglected in the horsemanship. She had not been taught that the last wolves were exterminated under Edgar the Saxon. There might be worse than savage beasts in the forest—wandering spectres, white, filmy, that froze the heart with the mere look of their lantern eyes; worse than spectres—wild and lawless men. Therefore Queenie turned her face in the direction of Saltwich.

To the house of the Grices she could not go. She shrank from again meeting Andrew. There was no alternative before her save a return to Mrs Rainbow, in Heathendom.

Accordingly, she took her way thither, with the shawl drawn well over her face, that she might not be recognised. The hour was not late. At the Button's, the house was not wont to be closed so early. She was confident that Mrs Rainbow would be engaged on some work or other at that time; for usually, when others became heavy with sleep, a spell of activity took hold of this woman, and engaged her in making a rummage and a noise till past midnight.

It was so on this occasion. Mrs Rainbow was going to have her chimney swept on the following morning. Therefore she was occupied turning over mats, covering tables, veiling her rack of crockery and her bottles of sweets, and putting her stores of oranges in drawers. The oranges at this time of the year were very hard, pale in colour, and sour. They would prove even less attractive if covered with a powdering of soot. As for the ginger beer bottles, Mrs Rainbow let them stand where they were. The season for ginger beer was over; a little more dirt on them would not signify. Moreover, the bottles were brown, and not calculated to show the soot, like the pale skins of the oranges.

When Queenie tapped at the door, Mrs Rainbow threw it open. She had tied up her head in a pictorial kerchief, on which were represented the uniforms of the British Army, in lively colours. It was knotted at the corners, forming horns. Her gown was tucked up under the string of her apron, and the apron tucked up with it, exhibiting a rather short petticoat, very dirty and ragged, and below that a pair of colossal legs in black stockings, with holes in them, shod in slippers burst at the sides, and down at heel.

At the fire, cowering before the operations of making ready for the sweep, was Seth White, the circus boy, who had been reared by Signor Santi.

"Thunder in my bones!" exclaimed Mrs Rainbow. "Whom have we here? Not the little Queen of Love again? Surely, never!"

"It is I," answered the girl. "I have been driven away from the Button's as I was driven out from the Grices. I do not suit in such houses. I was never brought up to their ways."

"But, curdle my wig!" said Mrs Rainbow. "Come in and let us look at you! What is the matter with your face? You have had a blow on your cheek."

"I ran against something; my eyes were full of tears, I could not see."

"I believe you've been struck—I do! Shiver my chignon! I believe you have. Who did that? If Rab knew, he'd kill the fellow."

"Never mind about that, dear Mrs Rainbow," said Queenie. "Can you shelter me for the night?"

"To be sure I can. There is the room you had before. Rab is away, trying to live respectable. Hope he likes it. But it ain't in him. I expect him every night to come tumbling in, broken out roaring drunk. But I sha'n't shelter him no more. I've took in Seth here as a lodger, and let him have Rab's room; so if Rab does turn up, I'll put him in the fowl-house where he'll get bitten with fleas, and serve him right for getting fresh."

"Queenie," said Seth, coming forward, his face shining with pleasure, "it is a joy to see you. Here have I been a-tryin' to get work and can't find none—and in a day or two I was goin' off to seek some show in which I could earn my bread."

"Seth," said the girl, "I am sure you will do something for me!"

"Anything," he answered readily.

"Then you will go to-morrow to Button's for my box. And if you hear of a show, where they want a little girl who can ride, and who is getting on to dance on the tight-rope, write and tell me, and I will come at once. I am fit for nothing else, suited to be among no other people but show folk and vagabonds."

On the morrow Queenie left Mrs Rainbow, much to the disappointment of that good woman. But Queenie had made up her mind to try whether she could live in peace with the Gerards, as Rab had proposed. What Rab had said of his sister pleased the girl. She would not allow her box to be taken to their house, till she had herself seen Mrs Gerard, and obtained leave from her to shelter in her house.

From Mrs Rainbow she received instructions as to her way, and she set out alone to find the cottage of the ranger.

The instructions had been somewhat diffuse, nevertheless Queenie started, animated by hope and rendered confident by the assurance, often repeated, that it was not possible for her to lose her way. Queenie did not, however, find it as easy to discover the cottage of the Gerards as she had been led to anticipate. In fact, it lay off the high road, down one of the lanes cut through the forest. It was an old house of the Cheshire type, built when oak was abundant, and the oaks were of centuries of growth. It was large, rambling, of many gables, a structure of black oak and plaster between the beams. The porch protruded, and had seats in it; and there were projecting windows of many sides. The whole was roofed over with russet tiles the colour of beech leaves when turned by frost. Before the house—it could not be designated a cottage—was a garden, with tall hollyhocks of many colours—spires of rich colour against the broken walls. The frost had nipped the leaves, but the flowers were as yet uncut.

As Queenie approached the house, much of the doubt as to the welcome that would be extended to her faded away. There are houses that repel, others that invite, some that throw out their arms and smile on the visitor, that seem to say "Come and nestle into my lap and lay your head on my breast and be cosy." It was so with this ancient timber and plaster building. The soft tones of the roof, splashed with yellow lichen, the pale blue smoke wreathing from the brick chimney, against a background of Scotch pines, the laughing garden, the wide porch, the twinkling windows, like eyes full of happiness and goodwill, spoke of hospitality and love to the fluttering heart of the lonely child, and drew her on, as had not the cottage in Heathendom, nor No. 4 Alma Terrace, least of all the box-like mansion of the Buttons.

Queenie passed through the porch and the open oak house-door, and tapped at that leading into the hall or kitchen.

Almost before she had lowered her hand, the door was flung open, and in it stood a bright, pretty, smiling woman, in a lavender cotton dress, with white apron, her sleeves rolled back, and her fresh, rounded bare arms extended.

"I knew you would come! I was sure it would be so!" she said. "Rab told me to expect you, *some* day; and when I heard you were at the Buttons', then I knew the some day must be soon. I knew you at once when I saw you coming through the garden. I was at the circus that night when it came down like a house of cards. Richard never let go my arm—Richard is my husband—and he dragged me out. *He* never lost presence of mind. Never saw such a man for coolness. It is always so with him. He knows at once what is to be done, and where to go. I said, as soon as I saw the sun shining on your pretty hair—just like stonecrop—I said—'There that little dear comes!'"

What a kitchen! How clean, how beautiful, how comfortable! A wide hearth with a fire of wood smouldering on it; above, on the mantelshelf, polished brass candlesticks and canisters scrubbed with sand—in cleaning, the hand had been twisted till the canisters were covered with a pattern as of frost-flowers. A rack of guns surmounted all. The walls were panelled with black oak, and above the panelling were stag skulls and antlers. Queenie looked round in wonder. She had never seen anything like this.

"'Tis an old-fashioned place," said Mrs Gerard. "Folks do say it was once a royal hunting lodge, but I'm no scholar, I don't know; now it's a keeper's cottage. Such is the way of things. What was good enough for kings at one time, passed on to gentle-folks in the next generation, then it wouldn't do for any but farmers. Next generation the farmers was too grand for such, and so it came to be handed on to labouring people. Well, we're comfortable enough in it. Next generation I won't say but that tramps'll turn up their noses at it, and say—'We can't stand a place, even for a night's lodging, that hasn't got hot water laid on, and not even a bagatelle board pervided.'"

Martha Gerard had inherited her mother's love of talking, and also her good looks. Poor Rab's features were the family rummage-heap of all that was plain and shapeless. He had some of the slatternliness of his mother; Martha her energy. Unlike her mother, Mrs Gerard turned her energies to good account. The house within was in perfect order; every metal article sparkled with cleanness, and the linen and drapery were without spot or tear.

"Did Rab really say I was coming?" asked Queenie, bewildered, her heart swelling, her eyes filling, her lips quivering with feeling at the kindliness of her reception.

"My dear, when he said you were at the Button's it was enough. I was there once—in service. I remained one month, and then Richard fetched me away. He saw I was getting bad. I could not have stood it longer. The old gentleman's harmless—he has his ways, but they did not concern me—but Miss Ada—she has a rare way of breaking folk's backs—as the old gentleman calls it. I doubt if there is another like her. It's a gift or a misfortune." Mrs Gerard went to a flower in the window and began to pick off the withered leaves. "There, I will say no more; I cannot tell how to stay my tongue when her name comes up. Sit down, dear, and welcome."

"How good you are to me!"

"Not at all. It is I who am in debt to you. Poor Rab! he was going to pieces altogether, and somehow, since he had known you he has been an altered man. He was the despair of his mother and a distress to his sister. He got among bad companions, got into bad ways, and he was falling into much such a wreck as did your circus. But there always were threads of good in Rab. You laid hold of them and have drawn him out of evil. He saved your life when you were enveloped in ruin, and you have saved what is better than life in poor Rab. Go on and finish what you've begun in him, and I will do anything for you—kiss your feet and be your grateful servant. There—come—this is your home now, and here—come to my arms and let me be mother and sister to you, my little wandering Queen of Love!"

XXVIII

ANATHEMA!

T HE MARRIAGE HAD TAKEN PLACE.

It had taken place in the most ordinary, undemonstrative manner possible. Even the bells of Scatterley were not pealed; but for that there was good reason, as the announcement as to when the wedding would take place had not been made to the ringers.

Jabez Grice, who ruled everybody and directed everything, ruled and directed that so it was to be. Why all the pomp and circumstance of hymen? The marriage was a matter of business, and let it be conducted in business-like fashion. He would have desired the ceremony to have taken place at Little Bethel, but to this the Buttons objected. A matter of business the wedding was, for it was a principal item in the compact between Tom Button and Jabez Grice.

Already, for three weeks, workmen had been engaged on the ground, within a bow-shot of the house. They had sunk a shaft through the usual boulder clay, red marl and gypsum. They had broken through the "flag," and at once the brine, hissing, had rushed up the shaft.

The walls of the sheds were rising—they were of boards on a basement of brick—and the roofs were being got ready. The structure was not solid—it might be said to be flimsy—but it sufficed for the end in view. A salt-boiling factory does not require very substantial buildings; and in this case, expedition in getting to work was the main consideration. The foundations of the chimney were laid. As the farm of the Button's was at a sufficient distance from Saltwich, no necessity existed for carrying the chimney to an extraordinary height. The smoke might blight the evergreens in the drive, kill some of the hedge trees, but would incommode nobody save the Buttons. As soon as the shaft had been begun, Jabez Grice had thrown up his situation at Brundrith's, and his son had necessarily seceded with him. This was a declaration of war that astonished and alarmed Brundrith.

The management of the works, the control of the men, the threads of the business, had been placed unreservedly in the hands of Grice, whom the proprietor had trusted as a faithful servant—almost as a friend. Now, suddenly, Brundrith was bereft of his services, and found this confidant, with all the intricacies of the concern at his fingers' ends, converted into a foe, or, at least, a rival.

There was, at the moment, no one capable of supplying his place; now, when too late, Brundrith regretted that he had not sufficiently considered the value of Grice's services, and had not dealt more liberally with him, given him some share, if but a small one, in the profits. Of course, it is an allowed maxim that every man must do the best he can for himself; and Brundrith felt that he was not wholly free from blame in the matter, yet he entertained considerable resentment at the suddenness and completeness with which he was menaced with a rival business, and one that robbed him of his almost indispensable man.

Jabez Grice, Tom Button and John Nottershaw had calculated on the effect of their surprise sprung on Brundrith, and for this reason had kept their counsel, not letting their intention transpire till all was ripe for execution.

When they had resolved on beginning operations, not a moment was lost in taking them in hand with energy. The energy and promptness that marked their undertaking were due to Grice. He was aware of the annoyance caused to his late employer, and though he was a man of no fine feelings and delicate scruple, he somewhat shrank from taking a lead in the concern. It sufficed him to be the main-spring behind the other two, who were put forward as the ostensible organisers of the Company, and speculators in it. Grice had not been for thirty years with Brundrith, without being well aware in what manner to undermine his prosperity, to pluck to himself some of the custom, and to entice away all the best work men.

Now it was that the influence of Grice over men became conspicuous. The hands at Brundrith's were ready to follow him to the new factory. Love of change did not explain this tendency to secession. It was due to the commanding force of Grice's character and manner. The men did not love him, but they believed in him. They trusted his judgment; they lost confidence, when Grice had withdrawn. Extravagant expectations of success were raised by his giving his adhesion to the new Company.

The confederates had everything ready for beginning and carrying out their scheme with expedition. The land was Button's. Grice sold out the securities of which he was trustee for Queenie, but took care to have a mortgage executed on the land to the full amount before he would embark any money in the concern. Nottershaw had at the time no contract in hand; he had an army of masons, brick layers, carpenters, waiting to be engaged, and in his yard was any amount of the material required.

Accordingly, the execution of the plan was carried out with celerity. The shaft was proceeded with night and day, till the brine-run was tapped, then the pump, ready at hand, was adapted to the bore. A reservoir was excavated and lined with brick to receive the brine pumped up. Pipes of communication were laid, connecting the reservoir with the wych-houses. The pans were riveted together and set on the hypocausts, and the flues were carried under the stove house.

During the day Grice never left the works, and he kept Andrew in constant employment as deputy over-looker. Other arrangements of a private nature had been made, but with these Nottershaw had nothing to do. Though they concerned the young people to a large extent, they were not taken into consultation; all was determined for them between Grice and Button. The latter was to leave the farm on the day of the wedding. He had never taken cordially to agricultural life. It would be hard to say to what he would take with sympathy if not enthusiasm. He was tired of farming, glad to remove from proximity to the stable and cow-house; and temporarily, till his future residence was determined on, till the affairs of the Company were placed on a solid foundation, he would move into No. 4 Alma Terrace, where Aunt Beulah would see to his comforts.

Miss Grice was not desirous of moving from her old quarters. Button's was too far from chapel, from her Dorcas and missionary meetings, which were the satisfaction of her soul. Moreover, she did not cordially like Ada. There was something in the girl that repelled Beulah; she herself could not say what this was, but she was conscious of entertaining a doubt whether she would be able to get on happily with Andrew's wife under one roof. Mr Button professed that nothing would suit him better than to spend the rest of his days in Alma Terrace, and lay his bones in Saltwich. When he declared this, and insisted on it, Ada curled her lip, and said in his presence,—

"Father is scheming to leave the place; you must always read him by contraries."

Grice was indifferent where Tom Button went after that his presence was no longer required, till Brundrith had been brought to terms, or the new Company had started in permanent opposition. Button was at first needed, as he was to be the ostensible head of the concern and the negotiations with Brundrith were to be carried on through him.

Button knew nothing of salt-making, nothing of the construction of a factory; he was, therefore, of no use on the spot, whereas Grice had to be there daily, hourly, and much time was consumed by his travelling to and fro between Alma Terrace and the works.

The fact that he was required on the scene of operations necessitated his taking up his abode with his son and daughter-in-law. It may be said that although these matters were arranged between the fathers, yet necessity, or circumstance, had compelled them to the arrangement.

The wedding had taken place.

There was to be no honeymoon excursion to the Isle of Man, the Lakes, or to Jericho. Of what use would such an excursion be? What pleasure could it afford in the fall of the year? It would be throwing good money away, and squandering more precious time. Andrew was

wanted at the works, and the utmost holiday that could be accorded
him was the day of his marriage. Ada raised no objections; she seemed as
indifferent to the advantages of a honeymoon as was "Hammer" Grice.
So long as she secured Andrew as a husband—young, good-looking,
amiable—that was all she desired. It was no secret to any who knew the
Buttons—except the Grices, those most interested—that Ada Button
had not been successful in love affairs, had, in fact, been fought shy of
by the marriageable young men.

There was no wedding-breakfast, no bride-cake, no health-drinking,
no speech-making. As already said, no marriage bells rang out. No
flowers were strewn, no rice cast, and it was hardly possible to throw a
shoe after a bride who did not leave her home.

Into the recondite question whether a trousseau was obtained for
Ada, the writer is unable to enter, but he can aver that no expense was
incurred by Andrew, or for Andrew, in the matter of dress.

"You have the suit ordered for Sant's funeral—that will do admirably
to be married in. You have four day shirts, six pocket-handkerchiefs,
eight socks and a box of paper collars. That will suffice.'

The dictum was that of his father, and it settled the matter of Andrew's
clothing. The same coach and the same driver that we saw conducting a
deputation to Button's, and again engaged for a funeral, now conveyed
the wedding party to the home of the young people.

No sooner was Andrew in the house, arrived from the ceremony at
Scatterley Church, than he looked eagerly about him, and asked,—

"Where is Queenie? She should be here to congratulate us. I have
not seen her for an age."

"Nor are likely to see her for another," said Ada. "She is gone."

"Gone!" repeated Andrew, starting and staring at his wife with dismay
in his open blue eyes.

"Gone these three weeks," replied Ada, indifferently.

"Gone—where to?"

"How am I to know?"

"But—good gracious! Queenie gone! and you do not know where
she is!"

"I do not know—I have made no inquiries."

"Then you should have done so."

"Of course I am in the wrong. No sooner are we married than you find fault with me."

"But this is frightful. When did she go?"

"Are you deaf or stupid? I have already said, three weeks ago."

"Queenie gone!"

"She took herself off with a play-actor or mountebank—I do not understand distinctions among that class of people."

"But—does my father—"

At that moment Jabez Grice entered the room.

"Father!" said Andrew, in great excitement and agitation, "Ada says that Queenie has gone—has run away."

"Why was I not told?" asked Mr Grice. "When did this happen? Give me all particulars and I will have her recovered."

"It is too late," said Ada. "There was some fellow loafing about the place at night, and Queenie continually out talking with him. It was a scandal to a respectable house like ours, and I really was relieved when she ran away with him."

"I don't believe it! I cannot believe it!" exclaimed Andrew, pacing the room.

"So—you give me the lie with almost the first words you use in the house after our marriage!" said Ada bitterly.

"But what grounds have you—"

"I will not answer your catechism," retorted Ada.

"But I insist on knowing; you will answer me," said Jabez. "I am her guardian, and know I must, and I will."

"I will tell you," replied the young wife, "but not Andrew, who asserts that I am a liar, and bids me prove my words." She turned her head and looked at her husband, and her thin lips were drawn. "After this sort of scandalous proceeding had been going on for some time, she eloped with the fellow one night, and sent next morning for her box by this man, who told our maid he had been one of the company in the circus."

"She cannot be far off," said Andrew, in the greatest distress. "Oh, father! what is to be done?"

"I will make inquiries at once," replied Grice. "If it be as I anticipate, and the sow that might have been, but was not, washed, has returned to her wallowing in the mire, then nothing can be done for her. Not one penny of what her father left shall she have. The man—the only man with whom she could have gone—was Seth White, for he alone of the troupe of tumblers and buffoons remained in Saltwich. If I ascertain that he disappeared at the same time that she did, then—" For a while "Hammer" clenched his teeth, and his face assumed a hard expression. "Then," he continued after a while, "then I shall withhold what is placed in my trust. Queenie must show that she deserves to have it—prove it to my satisfaction—before I give her one penny. My conscience will not suffer me to surrender what I know would be spent in debauchery, in every kind of vicious and riotous living. Andrew, I shall make inquiries at once. If what Ada says proves to be the case—and I do not doubt for one moment that it will do so—then I insist that this miserable, depraved girl's name be never mentioned again between us. Let her be to us as one that is dead, nay, as one who never has been. Let her be to the church in this serious household, Anathema Maranatha, Amen!"

XXIX

UNDER THE
GREENWOOD TREE

QUEENIE'S JOYOUS NATURE, THAT HAD been beaten down at Alma
Terrace and the Buttons, recovered its elasticity at the Ranger's
Lodge. Her happy spirit, that had drooped as a flower buffeted by
winds and battered by rain, rose buoyant in the sunny atmosphere at
the Gerards.

There are homes in which reigns perpetual spring, in which the sun
always shines, and the May breezes ever waft. Such was the house of
the Gerards.

Dick Gerard and his wife, Martha, were ever cheerful. They were
God-fearing, humble folk, making no pretence to be serious, not setting
themselves up to be models, and condemning to outer darkness all such
as did not regard them as patterns, and conform to their mould and
imitate their example. The birds of the air, the beasts of the field, the
fluttering insects in the sunbeam are happy, and follow the law of their
nature without self-consciousness and trumpeting their orderliness,
and the Gerards led an innocent, joyous life in their pleasant cottage,
and were unaware that there was anything extraordinary and imitable
in their mode of life, in their manner of enduring the sorrows, and
gathering in the gladness, that fell to their share.

A ranger's life is certainly not one of great hardship, but it has its dangers, and a keeper's wife may enjoy the happiness of having a healthy-minded and hale-bodied husband, but she has also her cares when the poachers are about, and at intervals they travel in gangs and give notice beforehand that, if the keepers attempt to obstruct them, they will do it at their peril. But, whatever the difficulties and dangers that were before them, the Gerards looked forward with quiet trust, and with light hearts bred of trust. If a dyke ran across their course, they leaped it, hand in hand, with a laugh.

It was wonderful how much they had to talk about when together. There was always something to tell, some question to be asked, some proceeding to be discussed, often some little joke to be bandied about from one to the other. And how they laughed over trifles—like children. There was, of course, some domestic strife, caused by one endeavouring to overreach the other—she by smuggling into his plate some choice piece of food that had been put on hers, he by surreptitiously doing some of her more arduous bits of work when she was otherwise engaged.

The ranger and his wife had a child, a daughter of twelve, who was paralysed in her lower limbs. She had met with an accident—a chill—and had never recovered the use of her feet. She sat all day in a little rush arm-chair, sometimes by the fire, sometimes in the sun. Her mother talked to her whilst engaged on her work, and it was possible that the habit of incessantly talking which Martha Gerard possessed, if inherited as a faculty from her mother, had been largely developed by the necessity she felt of amusing the child—of preventing her from feeling her infirmity.

The little girl, Jessie, required a good deal of attention; she had to be ministered to as a babe in arms, though she was handy with her fingers and could knit stockings and darn rents, plait straw and weave osiers. At times she suffered much rheumatic pain in her joints, but, nevertheless, the drawn, white face was ever cheerful, and the child looked forward into a future that could never be one of soundness, into life that could be nothing but a painful existence, without a murmur, even with a smile.

What a contrast this house presented to those in which Queenie had been sheltered hitherto! There was none of the grumbling, fault-finding fussiness of Mrs Rainbow, none of the disorder of tidying that was perpetual in her habitation. There was none of the repression of animal spirits and cultivation of an artificial conscience, that damned what was natural, and blessed what was unreal, such as had been the moral atmosphere of No. 4 Alma Terrace; there was none of the harshness, heartlessness, snapping, rending that she had encountered from Ada at the farm, hidden under a smooth and cold exterior, like a volcano buried in snow.

Here were cheerful innocence, frank cordiality. The Gerards made a pleasure of work, and a holiday of every day of drudgery; for, somehow, they had the wit, whatever they undertook, to discover in it something conducive to happiness, and to find a pleasant, easy way of executing every duty.

It was a wonder to Queenie to hear the sick and suffering child sing to herself at night when she was in pain that precluded sleep. It touched her to the quick to see how her mother fondled the girl, and laughed, and told funny stories to her, whilst her eyes were full of moisture; and to see how the child, in response, though biting her lips to prevent herself from crying out in her spasms, smiled and caressed her mother's cheeks. The father was, moreover, as devoted to his crippled girl as was the mother, and it was a pretty and pathetic sight on Sundays to watch him as he carried the child lightly in his arms, as though she were no heavier than a dove, to the foresters' parish church in the merry greenwood.

One evening, when the patient was in bed, Queenie ventured on the remark,—

"What a sad thing that Jessie is so infirm."

The ranger looked surprised, thought for a moment, and then said,—

"I don't know! I shouldn't have loved her half so much, nor would her mother have cared for her as she does now. And I doubt if Jessie herself would ha' been so happy."

In such a house, where all seemed so complete in itself, an intruder ran the risk of disturbing its equanimity; but Queenie found that she

fitted into her surroundings without an effort, and filled a place as
though forming an integral, part of the whole. Her own bright nature
was in accordance with that of the Gerards, and she felt none of that
restlessness, that craving after amusement, which had forced her to
commit extravagances under the repression to which she had been
subjected at the Grices. Yet as Queenie looked back to the time she
had been in Alma Terrace, she could not refuse to acknowledge that,
notwithstanding the exaggeration and restraint there, she had learned
something, and that a something of immense importance to her—the
lesson that she should be ruled by principle, and not be swayed by
caprice, should live to fulfil duties—not be the creature of impulse. She
had acquired the conviction, mainly through Andrew, that life was not
a soap-bubble, to be blown about in irridescent emptiness till it bursts,
but a something with definite purpose to guide it, with an object to
which to attain, and a course marked out which it must pursue. What
she had learned at the Grices as a theory, that she saw put in practice
at the Gerards. But she would never, perhaps, have understood what
governed the Gerards, had she not been shown the motive-principle
at the Grices.

How was it that her mind reverted to Andrew so frequently?
Andrew—what was he now to her? What could he be to her for the
future? She persuaded herself that the reason why she thought of him
so much was because she pitied him greatly for the prospect that lay
before him—the prospect of a life of contention—when married to
Ada Button, and she pitied him for the estrangement that must ensue
when he came to really know her.

Andrew was rushing into this union, without a suspicion as to the real
character of the woman to whom he was about to link his life. What
there was in Ada that could have induced him to propose, was a puzzle
to Queenie. Ada had indeed a prepossessing exterior, but her manner
before strangers was cold and repellent. Only among her familiars and
when there was no need for disguise, or when the furious passions in
her breast broke forth, did she fling aside this frozen demeanour, and
then those who saw her longed for a return to her former frostiness—
that at least was tolerable.

Queenie had no right to think so often and so long of Andrew; she knew it, and strove to turn her thoughts to other matters.

She was helped to do this by Rab, who was not long in discovering where she was, and whose delight at finding her with his sister was boundless. He did not venture to press himself on Queenie. He did not speak to her a word about his feelings. He talked about his sister, the crippled niece, about his life as an under-ranger, about what alterations and improvements he was effecting in his cottage.

Often, in the evening, he sat over the fire and smoked with Dick Gerard, and spoke about poachers and game. Rab knew intimately the ways of both. But what a field for observation, what an eternal spring of interest were the forest and the cover! How inexhaustible is the study of animal life, and how full of mysteries it is!

Queenie listened whilst this conversation went on, and it greatly entertained her. Animals she had ever loved, but the wild animal and its ways were new to her.

When they were alone together, Rab spoke to Queenie of all kinds of matters except of his love. Of that he never spoke. To it he never alluded. Once only, humbly, shyly, he inquired if it were unpleasant to her that he came so often to the Ranger's Cottage. Let her say so and he would stay away.

She could not find it in her heart to tell him that his presence embarrassed her—yet it was so. Martha saw the good influence exerted over her brother by the girl, knew the state of his heart, and would allude to the change wrought in the lawless, headstrong youth, and express her hope that Queenie would continue to control him, and would finally reclaim him altogether.

But the girl could not entertain towards Rab any deeper feeling than regard. If he were content with that, with being treated as a brother, she would give him true fraternal affection. But she knew too surely that what brought him so frequently from his distant cottage was a hope that some day he might win something better than sisterly regard. She often formed the resolution to tell him that his hopes were in vain, but never could muster up the courage to do so; she hinted as much to Martha, but Mrs Gerard was of that sanguine disposition which disregards things contrary to what is desired, and hopes for what is wished for in spite of every discouragement.

He brought her small presents—a bunch of moss with Jew's ears of brilliant scarlet, a jay's wing, a cluster of cones growing into a ball, a late-blooming blue borrage, hazel nuts. She accepted these little presents. She could not wound him by refusing them. It would seem wanton ingratitude to bid him take them elsewhere.

But these little gifts were a vexation to her. It troubled her that she was so unwilling to receive them.

Why should she not like Rab better than she did Andrew? Andrew belonged to another, and Rab was free. Andrew, after he had known her, had cast himself at the feet of Ada, but Rab had been her faithful, devoted swain since he had rescued her from the fallen circus, and Rab had never had another love.

Why should she dream of Andrew, and not of Rab? Why should Andrew occupy so much her waking thoughts?

Alas! the heart is not under the control of reason. It is wayward and capricious.

XXX

IMPROVING THE OCCASION

"I THINK NOW THAT WE will improve the occasion," said Jabez Grice.

"What occasion?" asked Ada, sharply.

"The marriage—the solemn union of hearts and hands."

"It might be improved with advantage," said the bride. "Certainly with advantage, when Andrew begins by calling me a liar and asking after a common circus girl the moment he sets foot in the house."

"If you will ring the bell and call the servant, I will do my best—"

Ada interrupted.

"She is engaged."

"But it is my wish," said Jabez, peremptorily. "When I say a thing, I mean it to be done." He went to the bell and sounded, then to the door and called down the passage,—

"Jemima, bring the lamp."

"Oh! the lamp. I have no objection to that," said Ada with a sneer.

When, however, the servant entered and placed the lighted oil lamp on the table, shut the shutters and drew the curtains, Jabez approached his chair to the table, opened a big book and waited till the operation of excluding the last rays of departing day was over.

Grice watched the girl with a somewhat grim face. His son had dutifully drawn up his chair. Then said Grice,—

"Jemima, sit down. I am going to draw out certain serious and edifying considerations from the event that has this day taken place."

Jemima curtseyed and planted herself near the door.

Ada, who had been by the fire, started up, went to the window and withdrew the green kerchief that had been thrown over a canary cage. Then she returned to her seat by the fire.

"What is the meaning of that proceeding?" asked Jabez.

"You will learn presently," answered Ada.

Hardly had Jabez Grice begun to harangue, expound and develop his subject, before the canary, roused by the brilliant light and animated by the strong voice, struck up a tweet-tweet! and then broke into shrill, rapid song. Jabez stopped speaking and looked indignantly at the bird, thereupon the canary also ceased. No sooner, however, had he recommenced, than the bird also resumed its shrill strain.

"Silence that creature!" ordered Grice.

No one stirred.

The canary rang out its thrilling song, merrily, defiantly.

"I said, 'Silence that bird!'" repeated "Hammer."

"Shall I remove the cage?" asked Andrew. "Anything for quiet!—strangle it. I cannot hear my own voice."

"I will throw the cover over the cage," said Ada.

"Why did you remove it? asked Jabez.

"I thought to increase your congregation."

She went to the window, and, with a contemptuous jerk, threw the green kerchief over the cage, but so that it hung down more on one side than on the other. The canary at once ceased to sing. Grice resumed his discourse.

It was his wont, when addressing an audience, whether a small one in a room, or the public in a hall, to look around him and mark the effect of his words on those who listened.

After a while, and a look or two at the maid, he said severely,—

"Jemima! there is no need for you to watch the bird-cage!"

"No, sir, certainly."

"I will trouble you to keep your eyes on me."

"Yes, sir, certainly."

Nevertheless, furtively, whenever she thought she would not be observed, the girl's eyes did revert to the bird-cage.

"Tweet! tweet!" sang the canary.

Mr Grice paused, shut his mouth and frowned.

"Tweet! tweet!"

The bird was waking up again. It surely was not singing in its sleep!

Grice looked hard at it, and saw that the ill-adjusted cover was sliding off. As he watched, down it came, and fell in a heap on the carpet. At once the canary resumed its song in full flow and acute shrillness.

"This is intolerable!" said Grice. "Andrew, remove the cage."

His son stood up, got a chair, and, whilst Jemima looked on in breathless interest, unhooked the bird-cage, and then stepped down.

"Take care, sir," said the girl. "You're spilling the bird's drinking water."

When the canary had been taken into the company parlour, and the doors shut, and Andrew had resumed his seat, "Hammer" returned to his topic, and continued as though his discourse had suffered no interruption. But his own attention was speedily distracted. Ada was obviously signalling some instructions to the maid. She was at the fire, behind Grice's back, and he could not see her without turning round, but he observed that Jemima looked inquiringly towards her, then down on the carpet, then back at her mistress, then gave a nod and look of comprehension, and stooped from her chair to pick up something from off the ground.

Again the speaker halted in his discourse, and in a tone of irritation asked,—

"What is it now?"

"Please, sir, only a bit of groundsel dropped by Mr Andrew as he was carrying out the cage."

"Put it on the table and be still!"

"Yes, sir."

He resumed. But he had not proceeded far before he heard Ada at the fire-irons. She was poking the fire.

He paused and coughed.

Then she began to rake out the white ash in the corners of the grate.

Jabez looked over his shoulder.

"How long is this noise going to last?"

"Till the fire is in good condition."

He turned to the subject of discourse.

Then he heard the shovel grating against the bricks of the hearth. A red-hot cinder had been raked out, also a lump of coal blistering and spurting forth flame. Ada was picking these pieces up on the shovel to lay them on the fire again. Grice coughed again and moved impatiently in his chair. He raised his voice and spoke loudly and rapidly so as to drown the noise of the shovel. Then Ada took the hearth brush and swept together the ashes under the grate. This fidgeted "Hammer" still further. He lost the thread of his ideas; he became confused in what he said. Then he turned about in his seat and said imperiously,—

"Have done! This is insufferable."

"I'm not going to have a dirty hearth," said the bride.

"Have you finished now?"

"Yes."

No sooner, however, had he recommenced than, in putting back the brush, Ada touched the fire-irons that she had stood up at the side of the grate, and they came down with a crash.

Grice shut his book with violence.

"Never, never, have I endured such contradiction; never such interruption before!"

"Jemima," said Ada, ignoring his wrath, "bring in supper, and don't forget my stout."

"Stout!" echoed Grice. "Stout, did you say? Do you not know that I never allow alcoholic drinks on my table—in my house?"

"This is neither your house, nor your table. Bring the stout, Jemima, and a corkscrew in case it is not up."

"I will not sit at the same table with you if you touch it," said "Hammer."

"Jemima," ordered Ada, with undisturbed coolness, "put a napkin on the corner table before the shell-flowers, and lay Mr Grice's plate and knife and fork there."

The maid did as required. "Hammer" was unable to speak for astonishment and wrath at the effrontery of his daughter-in-law. He had said he would not sit with her, and he could not retract, or go from his own words that evening. He was constrained to submit to be put in the corner at a little rosewood table, the surface of which was very polished, and was, moreover, encumbered with a stand, on which stood a vase that contained artificial flowers, made of sea-shells, under a bell.

Jemima took a glass paper-weight, in which, beneath the convex surface, might be seen a view of Peel Castle, and an inscription—"A present from the Isle of Man"—and placed it on one corner of the napkin.

"I think, sir, that will hold it," said Jemima confidentially; "but you won't fidget, will you, sir? The table is awful slippery."

Sullen, silent, uneasy at the novelty of his position, hardly knowing what steps to take to establish his menaced supremacy, Grice seated himself at the corner table, with his back to the lamp and the supper table in the middle of the room, and to his son and daughter-in-law. In his vexation his hand shook, and he knocked over a spoon that fell on the floor.

"Now, then, that is of silver," said Ada. "Don't you know that every time a bit of plate goes down, a penny is struck out of it? How clumsy some people are! What will you eat?"

"Hammer" Grice, conscious that his position was undignified, even ludicrous, that Jemima was laughing at him—worse than that, pitied him—looked surlily over his left shoulder and saw that in front of Andrew was cold mutton. He turned his head, and, looking over his right shoulder, saw hot beef steak pie before Ada.

He wanted hot beefsteak pie. He disliked cold mutton, but he was too offended with Ada to ask for some of her dish, to subject himself to the annoyance of being given too little crust and too much fat and gristle. She was capable of doing this out of sheer wantonness. In a tone of irritation he said,—

"Andrew—mutton!"

Then the maid-servant came to him, stooped, and, offering a dish of boiled potatoes, said, in a tone such as she might have used to a peevish, naughty child,—

"There, sir! You'll have some potato; won't you, now?"

He resented the tone, tossed his great head, and said roughly,—

"I'll eat bread."

"You'll be careful—do now—about that napkin. The table is terrible slippery."

Grice had got his mouth full of mutton, when he heard Ada say,—

"Andrew, be so good as to cut the strings to my cork; don't be afraid, the stout isn't very much up."

"Do nothing of the kind!" ordered "Hammer," as soon as he had bolted the mutton.

He could calculate on obedience from his son; but he was too late—Andrew had done what his wife required.

"It is up, Andrew," said Ada. "Pour the stout out carefully—not like that. Who but a fool would hold the bottle in that fashion? So—sideways. Gent-ly, gent-ly; I don't like froth! Will you have some? There is plenty for both." A long breath. "It is de-licious."

"Andrew! I forbid you."

"Father, I am drinking skimmed milk."

"Hammer" continued to eat till he had cleared his plate. Then he sat scowling at the shell-flowers, with his hands on his knees under the rosewood table. Occasionally, as a spasm of anger came over him, he kicked out at the leg of the table. Then came in the sweets. He would not look round, and he accepted with a churlish growl what was placed before him. As the lamp was immediately behind him, the shadow of his broad person was cast over his plate with its contents, and he ate in obscurity and discomfort. He was too angry to pay heed to, certainly to enjoy, his food, and the shadow was too deep to allow him to observe it well. He heard his daughter-in-law, whose spirits had risen under the influence of the bottled stout, talk cheerfully, if not flippantly, to Andrew, but he gave no heed to what she said. He chafed at his humiliating position in shadow in the corner. Presently Ada interrupted what she was saying to ask,—

"Any more, Grumps?"

"No."

Then he could have bit his tongue out for having answered her when she spoke to him so insolently.

"Do you like it, Mr Grice?"

"Middling."

"I thought you would. Have another spoonful. It is TIPSY CAKE."

"What!" roared "Hammer," bounding to his feet, and, in so doing, he pulled down napkin, plate, spoon and tumbler, also the present from the Isle of Man.

"What!" thundered he. "I'll tell you what—once for all. Understand! Where I am, there one of us—you or I—goes to the wall—you or I!"

"Quite so! And I am sure that will not be *I*." Then, rising from her place with a mocking laugh, Ada asked,—"This evening, which of us has best *improved the occasion*?"

XXXI

A Basket of Blackberries

JABEZ GRICE'S MOOD DURING THE ensuing day was not cheerful. He was angry with himself for having borne the humiliation to which he had been subjected; angry with Ada for having humbled him; angry with Jemima for having assisted in his humiliation; and angry with Andrew for having witnessed his deposition from the first place of authority. He showed his ill-humour at the works; nothing pleased him. The men engaged were idle, clumsy, stupid. The bricks were bad, the wood rotten, the lime poor.

Mr Button came to the place and buttonholed him.

"Well, Grice, how do you get on with Ada?" he asked, with his cunning eyes screwed up.

"Hammer" growled an unintelligible answer.

"Oh, I see," said Button, "begun to break your back, has she? How long before it is broke, eh?" And he went away cackling with laughter.

Resentment rendered Grice's heart bitter, and he resolved to make a determined stand against Ada. He had quelled all Saltwich into deference—that is to say, that part of Saltwich which was worth consideration—and was he to be defied by one girl? He would speedily show her which was master—what he, "Hammer" Grice, was.

On the previous evening Jabez had not smoked. He was fond of his pipe; he could ill get on without it, accustomed to it every evening. For once, the night before, he had not pulled it out and puffed. Tom Button was no smoker; there was no savour of tobacco about the house. Rather than engage in a fresh contest, he had foregone his pipe. From something let drop by Ada, Grice felt sure that she would make a stand against his smoking in the sitting-room. He would draw forth his pipe that evening; it should be no calumet of peace, but a bone of contention. Over that pipe the battle should be waged, the issue of which would determine who was to be the governing power in that place. He ruminated over the future. Should he achieve one splendid victory, and then retire and go back to Alma Terrace? But that would be a confession of defeat. More than that, the house, No. 4, could not receive him. Tom Button occupied his room. When Queenie had been received, an additional bedchamber had been taken at No. 5, and into this Andrew had been removed that she might have his vacated room. Now that was given up, and the third apartment at No. 4 was occupied by a servant, engaged because Tom Button was exacting as to his comforts.

Moreover, whilst the works were in progress, it was advisable that Grice should be on the spot to superintend; when the factory began work, as the boiling was to be continued night and day, it was essential that he should be at hand throughout the twenty-four hours.

No, it was not practicable for him to retire now. All the more important that a brilliant and decisive victory should establish for ever the fact that his will must be supreme, his word the law governing the new establishment.

Having determined on the field of operations and the plan of campaign, Jabez Grice felt more easy in his mind, and his former confidence returned. He would waive the objection to sitting at table with Ada whilst she imbibed stout—at all events for that evening. He would not again insist on a domestic harangue till he had achieved his great success in the battle over the pipe.

When Grice had come to this resolve, his equanimity of temper returned. His anger entertained against Ada was not abated, but the great disturbance of mind due to a sense of reverse became allayed. He contemplated the prospect of paying Ada off with interest for her audacity in attempting to resist him, in having put on him affronts.

In his excitement and indignation, Jabez had not thought of Queenie. It was other with Andrew. Having obtained leave of absence from his father, he made his way to Saltwich and inquired into the proceedings of Seth White. He speedily learned that the fellow had lodged with Mrs Rainbow, and also that he had disappeared three weeks ago, somewhere about the time when Queenie had left the Buttons.

Then Andrew went to Heathendom to question Mrs Rainbow herself. He found that lady loquacious, but uncommunicative on the point he desired to have cleared up. It was true that Seth had been with her, and that he was gone. He had departed on the trail of a circus visiting Yorkshire, in the hopes of getting an engagement therein. When, however, Andrew mentioned Queenie, he could not gather from the woman whether she had seen her, and whether she knew what had become of her.

Hesitatingly, guarding against allowing her to suppose that he gave credence to the surmise, he mentioned what had been said in his presence—that Queenie had gone off with Seth.

Mrs Rainbow laughed.

"I'll soon set your mind at rest on that," said she. "I've a letter from Seth somewhere—I got it three days ago. Lor' bless me, wherever can it be!"

After long searching it was discovered in a cup on the mantelshelf. She handed it to Andrew.

"I can't read myself," she said, "but that will show you Queenie ain't with him. More I won't say."

The letter began with an account of how Seth had followed a circus from place to place till he had finally overtaken it at Hull, and how that he had met with disappointment there. The season was at an end. Not till next spring would companies be on the move, therefore he must make shift to keep life in him during the winter months by following some other trade. The letter concluded with, "My respects to the little Queen, and please to tell her there is nothing to be done through winter."

"Why!" exclaimed Andrew. "You know where she is."

"How do you make that out?" asked Mrs Rainbow.

"By the letter. He sends a message to her by you."

"It don't follow I knows," replied the woman. "He may think she is still at the Buttons."

"How can he? According to your own account he left Saltwich four days after the disappearance of Queenie. He must have known of that. He had been her play-fellow from childhood, Come, tell me! Where is she?"

"I know nothing. Don't ask me. Now I'm off with my wheelbarrow selling herrings, and I can't attend to you."

Seeing that the woman was resolved to say no more, yet convinced that she could communicate further information if she chose, Andrew turned disappointedly to the door, when it opened and in came Queenie with a white rush basket in her hand, looking brighter, more fresh in colour, than he had ever seen her before.

She started, and so did he; and both stood for a moment contemplating each other with some embarrassment. He recovered first, and advancing to her took her hand.

"Queenie—only yesterday did father and I learn that you were not at the Buttons; that you had run away."

"Run away, Andrew! That is an odd way of putting it. I was—but no, I will say nothing about it. I have heard the news. You are married!"

"Yes, Queenie!"—involuntarily and unconsciously he sighed. "Yesterday the knot for life was tied."

"Poor Andrew!"—involuntarily, unconsciously she said it.

Then both were silent.

Queenie looked down at the basket, and that enabled her to escape from the embarrassing situation.

"See here, Andrew, I heard of it and I thought I must give you and *her* some little present. I have no money, so I give you what I can. I have been all the morning in the forest picking blackberries—they are as big as mulberries. I have put in only the finest. Did you ever see blackberries of such a size as this, Andrew? and they are sweet as honey and melt in the mouth. And I wove the little basket myself. I have learned how to do it from that poor crippled child"—Queenie checked herself and, colouring, said,—"I do not want you to know where I am. I am very happy. I am with the kindest people. But I do not wish you to come and see me. I do not wish your father to know where I am, or he may use his authority to order me away, and place me where I could not endure the life. Put a beef steak before a horse and he will turn away his head. Give a man a handful of grass and he will toss it aside. You must give the beefsteak to the man and the grass to the horse. Your father tries to feed me on what does not suit my nature. Now I am where—being a mere animal—I can eat grass, and gather blackberries, so I can trip and sing and laugh and be happy. I brought this little basket here to-day for Mrs Rainbow to take to you as a present from a friend and to name no names; but, oh Andrew, you have caught me and now you will know whose fingers picked the fruit. Well, I fed you with nuts the first time I saw you—take these now."

The blackberries were superb; she had chosen only the largest and ripest she could find, and had arranged them tastefully along with many tinted leaves touched by the transforming wand of autumn all enclosed in the pretty white basket.

Andrew thanked her with gratitude, but yet with consciousness of some restraint. It was so strange, so unsatisfactory that this child, for whom his father had made himself responsible, should be thus adrift, lodged temporarily he knew not where, among persons he knew nothing of, possibly exposed to danger and certainly without means.

As soon as he had taken the basket, Queenie slipped away, saying,—

"Do not follow me, please Andrew; it is best for both of us that we should see as little as possible of each other."

Then she was gone.

Andrew returned thoughtfully to the Buttons, carrying the blackberries.

He found his father talking to Ada in the drive outside the house. It was necessary or advisable to include a portion of the garden in the precincts of the works. This Jabez was explaining to his daughter-in-law, who received the information with a bad grace.

"I know what the end will be," said she. "We shall be able to have neither vegetables, nor shrubs, nor flowers. Everything will be poisoned. Very well, take in a bit more of ground you are going to blight. It matters not!" Then, turning to Andrew—

"What have you got there?"

"Blackberries—a wedding present from Queenie. Father, I have seen her."

"Queenie! Queenie again!" exclaimed Ada.

"You have seen her?" asked Jabez. "Is she not gone with that circus rider?"

"No, father. Nothing of the sort."

"Where is she?"

"I do not know."

"That is false," said Ada intervening. "You gave me the lie yesterday; I return it now. Of course you have found her, for you hid her."

"Do not be unreasonable, Ada," said Andrew, in a soothing tone. "She ran away because she could not fit herself into the surroundings here any more than she could at Alma Terrace. Till yesterday, I did not know she was gone. Now I do not know where she is in hiding. She would not tell me. It is by the merest chance that I lighted on her. She had heard of our marriage, and had been in the forest collecting blackberries for us as a humble offering, and she brought them to Mrs Rainbow when I happened to be there inquiring about Seth White."

"Seth White!" sneered Ada. "What care you about Seth White! You went after that circus girl."

"I went to ask what had become of White, as I gathered from you that you supposed he had taken her away. It turns out that you were wrong. He is in Hull; she is somewhere in the neighbourhood."

"Why need you inquire after her?"

"Because my father is responsible for her. She is his ward. He has, I believe, money that he holds in trust for her. We are bound to ascertain where she is and how she fares."

"You leave all that to me," said Jabez. "I did not ask you to meddle. As to her money, she must satisfy me that she will make a good use of it before I trust her with any."

"But, father, she is without a penny. She picked these blackberries because she could buy us nothing."

"If she were leading a reputable and honest life, she would not be in hiding. That which is of the truth cometh to the light. That which is of evil flieth the light and conceals itself. Where is she? Let her come to me, tell me whom she is with, what she is doing, confess that she has been a prodigal and is a penitent, and I will let her have money—not till then!"

"I am certain you misjudge her, father!"

"I never misjudge. I take you to witness. Did not I declare destruction would come to that circus, even before it fell? When I shook out my green umbrella against it—did I not therewith shake it level with the dust? It went to destruction. Even so I know—I possess moral certainty that this unhappy girl is going fast to destruction, if she be not lost already."

"But—what grounds have you, father, for this judgment?"

"Grounds! grounds! Are you catechising me as you catechised your wife yesterday? I want no grounds. I have a moral conviction it is so, which stands above all grounds. There are certain matters one knows by an inner light. By that light I know that she is lost—a child of perdition."

"Give me that," said Ada, pointing to the basket.

Andrew handed her the pretty little vessel, with its dainty arrangement of many-coloured leaves and fruit, every one of which seemed to have been placed in order with a study of effect.

Ada no sooner had the basket in her hand than she flung the blackberries and fluttering leaves away among the bushes, over the gravel and the grass, and then, casting down the basket itself, she trod it out of shape, saying, "I would it were her head!" There were blackberries still in it, some under her foot, and the ripe juice oozed out. "I would," said Ada, "that were her blood! I hate her!"

XXXII

A BROKEN BACK

WITH A SANGUINE HEART AND sure confidence Jabez Grice looked forward to the conflict that was to take place in the evening over his pipe. If he chose to pull it out, to stuff it with tobacco, to light and puff at it, Ada might give him black looks, cast at him sharp words, but she could not prevent him from smoking, any more than he could prevent her from drinking stout. He saw his mistake on the previous evening. He had protested against that which he could not, without violence, withhold her from doing. Also, in the matter of the harangue—improving the occasion—he had laid himself open to annoyance. But it was another matter altogether with a pipe. She would be powerless to interfere effectively. He chose his own ground as did the English at Crecy and at Waterloo, and the secret of success lies very generally in that. After supper, Jabez drew out his account books, opened them on the table, and then, with his eye fixed on Ada, he extracted his pipe from its case and stuffed it with bird's-eye.

"I am not accustomed to tobacco," said she at once. "I object to your smoking in the house."

Jabez made no answer. The pipe was between his lips, he stooped to the fire, kindled a piece of paper, applied the flame to the bowl, and drew the first whiff, with his eye fastened on Ada.

For a moment she seemed disconcerted, then sat down, accepted the inevitable and said no more.

The tobacco glowed in the bowl of Grice's pipe, but hotter glowed the sense of triumph in his heart. From his nostrils he exhaled two columns of smoke, and about his brain rolled the fume of the incense of self-laudation at having thus decisively shown that he would not submit to dictation from his son's wife.

"If you dislike smoke," said Andrew in a half whisper, "why do you not go into the drawing-room?"

"In a house like this," answered Ada, "every smell, every sound is in all the rooms at once."

"I will take in a candle and accompany you," said Andrew.

"I will go there when I choose, and by myself."

Jabez Grice remained by the fireside for some minutes, doing nothing save enjoy the sense of triumph, but he was not a man to remain inert, and he presently turned his chair round, took up his pencil, and began his accounts.

At once Ada also rose and lighting a candle, left the room, and in so doing forgot to shut the door. The chamber was, perhaps, somewhat close, and Grice had no objection to the admission of fresh air.

After a while, however, he looked up, with an expression of annoyance on his face, and said,—

"Andrew—the door."

Ada had retired to the drawing-room, that formal apartment which, in middle-class houses, is never inhabited, only visited on solemn occasions of state. It contained a pianoforte, rarely used and sadly out of tune, for Ada, though at school she had been taught to play, was not musical, and rarely touched the keys.

Now, in a spirit of perversity she seated herself at the instrument, lighted the candles on it, opened her school exercises and began to strum.

Not only was the piano out of tune, but an F was mute. The wire was broken. Had she chosen a composition in which the F sharp was required and not the natural, this would have been of little moment; but as if out of wilfulness, she played all her pieces in that series of keys in which the F natural is an indispensable note, so that everything she played proclaimed the defective condition of the instrument. Moreover, Ada played badly—out of time, without feeling.

Jabez Grice had begun a calculation of the outlay in wages on the works. To calculate he required to be undisturbed. This detestable and defective strumming irritated his ear, teased his mind, distracted his attention.

"Andrew," said he, "go and shut the drawing-room door. That woman has left it open as well as this."

The young man left the room. He entered that in which was his wife, and waited at the side of the piano till she had finished one of her pieces, that he might remonstrate.

But she did not stay to finish. She interrupted her performance in the middle of a run, and asked,—

"Well?"

"Dear Ada, my father is adding up his accounts now, and this disturbs him somewhat."

"He should not smoke."

"Can you not play when he is not in the house?"

"And he—can he not smoke when he is out of it?"

"Ada, you should consider him, it is his habit, and at his age a man can ill break himself of an inveterate habit."

She struck the keys, made them jangle.

"Andrew," said she, "his back must be broken."

"Good Heavens, Ada, what do you mean?"

"If I do not break his, he will break mine. We shall see. Give me twenty-four hours more. I'll do it."

Again she struck the keys and produced a crash of discords.

Andrew, incapable of effecting anything in the way of compromise, returned to the parlour, where his father was, after carefully shutting each door behind him.

"It is this wretched house. These square houses are odious. As she said—the sound is everywhere. I am glad to think the smoke is also everywhere!" said Grice, grimly, and he shut his account books. "I will do these sums when all are in bed. Then I shall have quiet."

The battle was a drawn one. "Hammer" Grice had not achieved a decisive victory. He thought to himself—"If she tries this on again, I will cut the wires."

Next day, Jabez was much occupied on the works. The chimney was rapidly progressing, and the first pan was being set up in the wych-house. In a fortnight, he calculated that the factory might start work—sufficiently to show Brundrith that they were in earnest.

Mr Nottershaw went over everything and expressed his satisfaction.

"We shall do a stroke of work here," said he, and rubbed his hands together.

Mr Button arrived.

"Well, Jabez," he asked with twinkling eyes, "how is your poor back?"

"I don't understand you."

"Ada."

"Oh! Humph! to be frank with you, she is not the daughter-in-law I had expected; far too self-willed, and lacks respect for her elders and betters. In a little time I'll bring her to know her place."

"You think so?"

"Sure of it."

That evening, at supper, Ada was unusually cheerful—she was even amiable—and Andrew's heart, which had felt an oppression since he made her his own, was momentarily relieved.

Ada could be vastly agreeable when she pleased. She was clever, and had some humour, though the latter was of a caustic nature. On this occasion she was apparently endeavouring to make amends for the unpleasantnesses of the past evenings. Grice looked at her with watchful and studious eyes. He was puzzled. Did she suppose by this means to gain her point and win of his good-nature that he should abandon his pipe? He would know only when the table was cleared and he pulled forth his tobacco pouch.

Accordingly, he waited with some impatience till the supper was removed, and the window had been thrown open for a moment to ventilate the room. Then, watching Ada, he drew out his meerschaum, and felt for the tobacco. She uttered no protest, did not even raise her eyes from the fire, to which she had turned. The pouch was empty.

"There's some baccy upstairs," said Grice, and left the apartment.

He went leisurely up the stairs to his room, which was immediately over that in which meals were taken, and the little family party sat.

In another moment Andrew heard his father descend the stairs more rapidly than he went up; the door was thrown open, and in it stood "Hammer" Grice, looking angry and saying,—

"Ada, the maid has not made my bed. The room has not been touched since I left it this morning."

"Well; make your own bed."

"I am not accustomed to do these things. Send Jemima."

"I have told Jemima to go to bed."

"There is my ewer with no water in it."

"Fill it yourself."

"I tell you, I am not accustomed to do these things."

"Nor am I accustomed to tobacco."

Grice stood in the doorway, silent, glowering at Ada. She looked him straight in the eyes, without rising from her chair, without wincing.

"I cannot sleep in a bed that has not been made."

"Then make it yourself."

"I cannot wash unless my ewer be filled."

"Then fill it yourself."

Grice remained uncertain, livid with anger, ashamed to confess his mortification. Presently he slammed the door behind him and went upstairs.

Andrew was too astonished to speak, too dismayed to protest. Ada put one knee up, and rocked it, singing or humming an air from "Traviata." A stumping and banging about of furniture overhead, was audible. Then Ada laughed, and dropping her knee said,—

"Old Grumps is making his bed!"

"Oh, Ada, how can you serve my father so!"

"If he will not consult my comfort, I will not consult his. If he makes himself disagreeable to me, I can and will make myself disagreeable in return. Andrew, let this be a lesson to you; it is best that the controversy should be between your father and me, and not between you and me. If, in spite of warning, you oppose me in the way he has done—in any way, in anything—then consider how intolerable I can make life to you. Hearken! there is your father lumbering downstairs with his jug to get water."

It was as Ada said. No sooner had Jabez Grice made his bed to the best of his ability and knowledge, than he took his ewer and descended. He liked to have plenty of fresh water in his room. He loved to souse his head every morning.

When he entered the kitchen carrying his jug, he was surprised to find Jemima there, eating her supper.

From what Ada had said, he had not expected this, and he had thrown off his coat and waistcoat whilst making his bed.

"How is this?" asked Grice. "I have been given no water in my room, and my bed has been neglected."

"Please, sir," said Jemima, rising, "missus said I was to leave it all in a muddle."

"Never mind what she says; I will have my necessities attended to. Where is the pump?"

"In the back-kitchen, sir. If you will hold the jug, sir, I will work the handle. I am very sorry, sir, very sorry, but missus gave me such particular orders—"

"Never mind the orders. Pump!"

"Shall I bring the lamp, sir?"

"No need—I suppose one can get water in the dark."

A few strokes and the ewer overflowed.

"Now, then," said Grice, "I insist on your taking the jug upstairs. If I had not myself made the bed, I would drive you to do it. But I will not do everything. I will not be turned into a maid-of-all-work by my daughter-in-law. I will not be beaten at every point in my contest with her. Take the ewer immediately."

"Please, sir, I daren't!"

"I say you shall. Carry it to my room."

He pressed the jug on her.

"Oh! what will missus do?"

Then they heard a sharp rap on the kitchen table. Ada was there with the carriage-whip in her hand, and she had struck the board with the plated handle.

"Come out from that dark hole, you two," she said. "Grumps, what frolics are you about with my maid?"

Grice and Jemima emerged from the back kitchen. The girl frightened, "Hammer" confused and angry.

"What are you doing there? In the scullery, in the dark?" asked Ada, and she rapped the table again,

"I came after water," explained Grice.

"In this indecent condition, showing your braces! You came on the excuse of water! You came in reality after the girl. Because Jemima has been taken from the workhouse and has no parents, no friends, you think her fair game. Come, carry your water, and be off—sharp, I say; be off, you scandalous old Turk!"

Grice looked at this insulting, outrageous woman with his jaw quivering, his face bloodless, his eyes glaring with hate.

Ada had reversed the whip in her hand, and she now switched the lash about between him and herself. Then she laughed.

He remained immovable, clutching the water jug, but now he had set his teeth, and his huge jaw was fixed. His eyes glowed like steel at white heat.

"I know the very thoughts of your heart," said Ada, looking dauntlessly into his eyes. "You are meditating to knock me down on the kitchen floor. Do so. Nothing would please me more. Then you will have done for yourself utterly, irretrievably, not in this house only, but in Saltwich, in the whole Serious World."

She cracked the whip.

"Go along with your water jug."

And he went without a word.

Next day Button was at the works.

"Well, Grice—how is your back—broken, man?" Jabez scowled, but made no answer.

"Ha! I thought so. Broken—broken. I knew Ada could do it—ay— and would do it!"

XXXIII

DOMESTIC THORNS

IT DID NOT TAKE A fortnight for Andrew to discover that, as far as his happiness was concerned, he had made a mistake in following his head instead of his heart. In that fortnight a root of bitterness had thrown its fibres through his soul—bitterness against his father, who had urged him to a union which would blight his life.

In all matters external, the match had promised well, and was likely to keep its promise. Ada Button was the daughter of a yeoman of reputed means, whereas Andrew was a mere workman in a factory; the son, indeed, of an overlooker, but not of a partner in the business. He had done well for himself, therefore, in the opinion of most people in Saltwich.

Others, however, had shaken their heads. The bride might be his superior in position and in fortune, she might be handsome, and with good manners, but—it was remembered that others had fought shy of this cold beauty, who, in spite of her icy exterior and haughty demeanour, was reported to have the temper of a dragon.

When the pair had stood before the altar at Scatterley, in the parish church, and Andrew had taken the thin white hand in his, and the Reverend Edward Meek had demanded of him his solemn oath to love, honour and cherish the woman at his side, then Andrew had responded not with his lips only, but with the fervour of his heart, and had sworn to hold to her and to her only as long as life lasted; to her only till death parted them. He had said to himself,—"Now I have my wife. She may be frosty as a March day, but I will be the sun to shine on her cold boughs and make them bloom with the May flowers of love. Hard she is not really, only reserved. It is better for a man to have a woman as his wife who treasures up her feelings and pours them forth into her husband's bosom, than one who is gushing to all alike. The sourest apples give the sweetest cider. She is mine, for better, for worse—I will be true to her in thought, as well as word and deed."

As he thus mused, he pressed her hand. She did not divine what passed in his mind.

Thus it had been at the wedding. That same evening a cloud had troubled the sky. She had insulted his father. On the morrow, matters had not much mended. On the third day the breach with the old man was complete. Andrew loved his father and respected him. The indignities offered to the elder offended the young man. His remonstrances with his wife were unheeded. He had himself come in for some sharp words, and for galling disregard of his prejudices.

It seemed to Andrew as though his wife cast aside all semblance of amiability when the necessity for disguise was over, as if she thought that having obtained a husband, she might treat him and his father with disrespect, lack of consideration, even with open outrage. It was as though hitherto she had worn her cold exterior, and assumed a placid, even engaging manner as a mask, and that she now regarded the time for masquerading as over, or, at all events, that the mask was out of place in her own household, before her own family.

What Andrew began to fear in the first few days of marriage, within the fortnight became with him a certainty. He would not find love—though he might find jealousy—at home, and the domestic hearth was to be a scene of perpetual strife, or of submission to his wife's caprice, resignation to the outpour of her bitter temper.

But this disappointment was not the only fly in Andrew's cup. His confidence in the judgment of his father had received a rude shock. He had married Ada in compliance with the wishes, if not at the command, of Jabez. His father had represented Ada as precisely the daughter-in-law that would suit him—punctilious in the performance of her duties, and austere in her demeanour. Not even Queenie could have proved so disturbing to the happiness of the elder man, so wounding to his self-respect, as had this elect woman. Queenie might have irritated Grice by her thoughtlessness, but would never have deliberately jeered in his face. Queenie, if by chance she had offended, would have pleaded in the prettiest, meekest way for forgiveness; Ada exulted in having beaten down and trampled on the wishes, and in having humbled the dignity of her father-in-law. Jabez Grice claimed to judge men and women by intuition, an illumination of the mind which dispensed with evidence. By this inner light he had approved of Ada; and, as the event showed, had erred. Was there any reason for holding that his judgment in condemning Queenie was sounder? But there was worse behind. Andrew had begun to doubt his father's rectitude.

Jabez Grice was trustee for poor little Queenie. He had received her money—some three thousand pounds—that had been invested by her father. This money Jabez had realised, and was now sinking it in the new speculation he favoured. As far as Andrew could see, there was no prospect of any loss falling on Queenie, ultimately. The money was secured by mortgage on the land and on the buildings it served to erect. So far, Jabez Grice was not acting against her interests and differently from the wishes of her father, even though out of this capital he schemed to make a great fortune for himself. But why did not his father concern himself about the child? Why did he allow her to run about the country, and take no trouble to discover where she was, what sort of people she was with, and whether she were in comfort. How much of the interest of the money Santi had left was given to his child? Not a penny. As far as Andrew knew, two shillings was every bit of coin that Grice had allowed her. He had, indeed, furnished her wardrobe, had housed and fed her for a brief space of time. But three thousand pounds at four per cent meant a hundred and twenty pounds per annum. It seemed to Andrew hardly just to the orphan to be employing her capital to the advantage of the trustee, and giving her no interest; making absolutely no provision for her.

This thought had so lodged in his mind and worked there that it became dominant; it preyed upon him and drew off his thoughts from his own unhappiness. In one unfortunate effort to be frank with Ada, and gain her confidence, he spoke about this in private. She flared up at once.

"Queenie again! Yes; I know very well to what this introduction leads. You want her to be brought back into this house. Never! Do you hear this, Andrew—never!"

"My dear wife, do be reasonable."

"Reasonable! You charge me with lack of sense now! I was a liar, and now am an idiot. Thank you! I have my reason. I know what marriage vows mean. I am not going to open my doors to all the rag-tag and bob-tail, to women of doubtful character and no reputation, so as to gratify you. In that one particular your father has shown discretion. He has not asked me to take her under my roof again."

"I have proposed nothing of the sort."

"No—not proposed it. You were sounding before you did so. It is in your mind. It was in your purpose."

After this brief and painful scene, Andrew went forth into the night. The air in the house stifled him, the walls of the square rooms closed in on him. He must breathe fresh air and feel that he was in open space.

The heavenly vault was besprent with stars. Andrew walked with lowered head along the drive. Something light was under the bushes—was it a cat? He stood still and looked. It did not move. He stooped and picked it up. The starlight had brought into prominence the crushed, little white basket made by Queenie's fingers, in which she had sent her modest wedding present.

It was trodden out of shape; it was wet with dew, no doubt soiled with clay. Andrew took it in his hand, went to the gate, leaned his elbows on the rail upon which he and Queenie had sat. He swung the battered basket with his fingers against the rail, drew a long breath, and sighed—"So—so—married!"

He remembered that kiss given to Queenie as he held her sitting on the rail; a kiss that had assured her that he loved her, and which had convinced him, by the answering pressure, that his love was returned.

What had he done after that mutual confession? Rushed into an engagement with another. He thought of his parting with Queenie that moonlit night after Ada had just shown him a glimpse of her real nature. He knew that he had then, by his manner, in spite of his efforts to conceal it, shown Queenie that she still had possession of his heart.

Then a new train of thoughts arose. That same was the night on which the orphan girl had left Button's—had gone away of her own accord, so Ada had represented it.

Ada said that Queenie had been meeting and talking with a man outside the house, and concluded that it was with this man that she had probably eloped.

"Why!" exclaimed Andrew, "it was with me she was speaking that night. She had come out here to have a word with me."

He was now aware of the jealousy with which Ada regarded the girl, the hatred she bore her, and which was manifested when she trod under foot the harmless little basket with its well-meant present. Was it not possible, was it not probable that Ada had followed him when he left the house that night, and had overheard his conversation with the girl, and then, moved by jealousy, had driven her away?

Driven her away—at night. Driven out the orphan child who had neither home nor friends. There boiled up in his heart a flood of rage and indignation. The thought that Ada, out of jealousy, had exposed that innocent, helpless child to the worst peril, was like the borer driven through the crust that overlies the reservoir of brine; there was an uprush in the heart of Andrew; it seethed in his veins, it hissed and foamed in his brain. Regardless of everything, he walked back to the house, went upstairs, and shutting the bedroom door behind him, said, in a tone such as he had never used to any human being before,—

"Ada!"

"Well! what now?"

She looked at him sneeringly, but was momentarily quelled by the fire in his eye, the drawn lines in his face, the resolution set on his brow.

"What now?—this. I will learn the truth about Queenie, how it was she left this house."

"I have told you, she met a man among the bushes."

"She spoke with me. She had something to say to me."

"Oh! you—was it?"

Ada laughed.

"I insist on the truth. My belief is that you turned her out of the house."

His young wife was silent.

"I am resolved to know the truth. If you will not speak, I shall summon the maid. She will be communicative. She must know some of the particulars."

Ada hesitated. She looked again at her husband—he was transformed. This was no longer the timid, yielding Andrew—the Andrew on whom she could put her foot, and he writhed like a worm. He was strong, ruthless in his wrath.

"As you will—I turned her out," said Ada, sullenly.

"And it was I who spoke with her. We were as cousins—had been companions. She naturally desired a word with me. If you wish to know about what—it was to ascertain from my lips whether it was true that you and I—you and I"—there was bitterness as of death in those words—"you and I were to be married."

Now it was Ada's turn. With an air of triumph she said, and her voice shook with rage as she spoke,—

"After her parting with you, there was the other lover hiding in the bushes."

"What other lover?"

"The fellow with whom she went away when I shut the door against her, and refused to have such a jade pollute the threshold with her foot."

"I tell you that fellow, Seth White, did not go away with her. He is in Hull; she is somewhere not very many miles distant."

"I care not—it was a man. Any man would suit her, doubtless."

"What sort of man was he?"

"I don't know; he wore gaiters and a baggy shooting-coat."

"Why! it was Rab."

"Rab or Seth—it is all one to me. You are not the only person that the jade has had dancing about her. Know that, and may you relish the knowledge."

XXXIV

WILKES

JABEZ GRICE HAD A BROTHER-IN-LAW of the name of Wilkes—a life-long friend, who shared his views on most subjects, though a very different man in manner and habits. It was, in fact, their early friendship that had led Grice to marry the sister of Ezekiel Wilkes.

Wilkes had never married. He was a lively, pleasant man, and was employed as a salaried agent to the political party to which he belonged, to look up the lists of voters, whip in such as had not registered and were sure to vote true, and to object to the claims of such as could not be calculated on, or who were known to be adverse in opinion. His function, moreover, was to go round and stir up enthusiasm wherever it flagged; and, when an election was in prospect, to spread abroad such damaging reports relative to the honesty, the morality of the candidate for the opposed party, and to make such extravagant promises on behalf of the candidate of his party as would materially affect votes, but which could be disclaimed by the candidate if brought to book for false allegations or impossible promises. In all political canvassing Ezekiel Wilkes was absolutely unscrupulous, but he was, in every other relation, an honest, admirable and kind-hearted man.

As the member was in bad health and it was rumoured that he would shortly resign, both political parties started into activity, and their agents were sent to prepare the ground for the candidature of the representatives of the orange-and-blue interest on one side, and the red interest on the other.

Hitherto, whenever he had come to Saltwich—an important political centre—Wilkes had been the guest of his brother-in-law. Directly Jabez heard that Ezekiel was coming to the place to spend there a few days looking up voters, seeing to the registration lists and spreading reports, he wrote to insist on his accepting, as usual, this hospitality. This, he assured him, he would be able to offer with a freer hand, as he was moving, in consequence of his son's marriage, into a larger house, in which he would live on a better footing.

Wilkes had accepted the invitation before Grice had transferred his quarters from Alma Terrace to Button's, and now a note from him reached Jabez, naming the day on which he would arrive. Perhaps some hesitation arose in Grice's mind as to how Ada would receive the announcement. With unwonted lack of courage, he remitted to his son the duty of preparing her for the visit of Wilkes.

Accordingly, Andrew took his uncle's letter to Ada, who was in her room, and said,—

"He is coming. We have expected him for some time; and now he says he is longing to make your acquaintance, Ada."

"Who is it?" asked his wife, with indifference.

"My uncle—my mother's brother—Mr Wilkes. I am sure you will like him. He is a very agreeable person."

"I dare say. He is coming to Saltwich, is he?"

"Yes; and we must receive him here. He may be with us for a week. He has business connected with the coming election which will engage him."

"If he will be busy in Saltwich, why does he not put up at the 'Salters' Arms?'"

"Because he is my uncle. He was my father's dear friend before my father married."

"I don't see that we can take all your relations into this house."

"It is not all—one alone, and that for a few days; a week at the outside."

"It can't be done. Your father has the bedroom that my father was wont to occupy, and we are in what was formerly the spare room. As you see, it is engaged. I am not going to turn out for any Wilkes under the sun."

"My dear Ada," said Andrew reproachfully, "why are you always so full of objections and ungraciousness? I do not wish to turn you out of your room. Such an idea never crossed my mind. There is your old chamber, to the sunrise, that is unoccupied, and there is a bed in it."

"He cannot have that room—I keep my clothes there."

"Only in the wardrobe; we can have that moved in here."

"I have the drawers full of things also."

"We can have them cleared."

"I will not consent to have everything upset for the sake of someone I know nothing about, and do not wish to see, who comes here not to please me, but about his own business. The house is not an inn. This is the thin end of the wedge. You begin with this Wilkes, next will come Beulah, and then, as the climax, the mountebank girl. I will not suffer it."

"There is the other room—that looking west— it is unoccupied."

"It has no furniture in it to speak of."

"I will have your old bed moved, and other articles."

"My old bed and tables and drawers—thank you!"

"You cannot use every article, Ada! My uncle is coming and, as he comes, he must be put somewhere. He shall be accommodated."

"As you like," answered Ada, and shrugged her shoulders. "I don't want to make the acquaintance of and to be pestered with all your kith and kin. Heaven knows what they are! Some, I am aware, were circus folk. Does this man stand on his head? I presume he will not take his meals with us in his shirt sleeves."

"I leave you to arrange about the room. But, mind me, Ada, he is to be accommodated here. If you choose to make a display of bad temper before him, then he will think ill of you, for which I shall be very sorry. I would wish him to say,— 'Andrew, you are a lucky dog! you have got a lovely and an amiable wife. I wish you joy.'"

A few days after this conversation had taken place, Wilkes arrived—a little, round man, with a quick eye, grey, bushy hair and whiskers, and an abrupt manner. He was welcomed by Andrew and his father. They shook hands warmly. The old fellow continued to hold and shake the hands of his nephew.

"Well done, my pippin! You have feathered your nest well. This is a change from Alma Terrace. Ah! you young rogue, with your blue eyes and fresh health, you conquer girls' hearts and they throw themselves into your arms with all their fortunes, and think you cheap at the price. Where is she? I must see her. I suppose I may snatch a kiss! It is the privilege of an uncle and of an old man."

"Come to your room," said Grice.

"Which way?"

The lively old fellow went out at the door, and trotted up the stairs. On the landing, Ada passed him, cold, haughty, and without looking in his direction.

"Stay, uncle!" shouted Andrew from the hall floor. "There is my wife."

"What!" exclaimed the stout, little man, turning round and catching her by the shoulder. "What! passing me like a stranger! without a word, without touching hands! Come, come! I knew your Andrew when he was a child; I knew him as a boy—I have never known him anything but the best of good fellows—a Nathaniel, in whom is no guile. You are happy in your choice."

Ada removed her shoulder from his grasp, gave a slight inclination of her head, and accepting his hand with manifest reluctance, said coldly,—

"I am glad to hear this."

Wilkes said some words of courtesy—but his intent to offer a kiss was damped in the bud. He felt restraint, and—wonderful for him—shyness, before the icy, repellant young woman.

Grice conducted him to his apartment; when the door was shut,—

"Jabez, old bird, is she always like that? Say it is a stiff neck!"

Then Grice's face darkened.

"Ezekiel," said he, "I suppose every man makes a mistake some time or other in his life. I have made one in getting Andrew to take her. For him it matters little—he is young and yielding. So long as she has

good looks and money, he doesn't care; but for me it is different. She
is intolerable. You shall judge for yourself. I couldn't help it. We must
have had Button's ground, and there was no other way of securing it.
Tom is a slippery party."

At meal time the presence of Ada made a sensible change in the
condition of affairs to what they had been in Alma Terrace, when
Wilkes was guest to his brother-in-law. It was like the presence of
an iceberg. It chilled cordiality, it checked conversation, it impeded
confidence; it even deprived the food of relish and took the aroma
off the tea. The rooms were larger and better furnished than at
Alma Terrace, the victuals were better, and better cooked; there was
apparently more of comfort in every form, and yet, in actuality, there
was less. The moment Ada left the room every heart expanded to
its old geniality; when she returned all were equally oppressed and
contracted.

After supper, Andrew said to Mr Wilkes,—

"Uncle, do you mind a stroll along the road with me, I have
something to say to you?"

"Your servant at any time," said Wilkes jumping up. "Glad to get out
of the room for a little, and warm my blood with a walk."

When they were beyond the gate, Wilkes put his arm within that of
his nephew and said,—

"Come, boy, I desire to say a word of congratulation. You have a wife
who, I must admit, is one in a thousand. Never saw her like—never.
You need not fear for her fidelity—she'll keep every one at arm's
length. I'd have kissed the red-hot poker before I ventured on her lips.
She's calculated to be a marchioness—by the piper!—a duchess. She
has aristocratic pride in every fibre of her body—if it's not aristocratic
pride, then it's pride that comes from something else. Nothing plebeian
about her, my boy; none of your vulgar *bonhommie*; she is none of your
Bouncing Sallies or Jumping Joans. Every man has his own ideal of
what woman should be. I didn't think you looked so high, Andrew."

The young man hardly knew how to take his uncle's words, whether
spoken in commendation or the reverse. He accepted the dubious
praise in silence.

"I'll light a pipe," said Wilkes. "Your father gave me a hint she didn't like tobacco fumes. Well—never offend the ladies. Now, what is it, boy? Nothing about domestic broil, I hope—for you know the song:—

> When man and wife are flouting,
> If a stranger pop his snout in,
> He is sure to get it tweaked for his pains!"

"The matter I desire to consult you about, Uncle Ezekiel, is that of Queenie. You have heard about her?"

"Yes. Grice wrote to me, told me that poor Sant was dead and that he had left the child in his charge. Where is she? I want to see the little dear, see if she has inherited any of poor Joe Sant's good looks."

"I do not know where she is. She left this place rather hurriedly, and is hiding somewhere. You see, she and father did not get on happily together. She is frisky, like a little grasshopper, and my father does not understand that sort of thing."

"But he knows whereabouts she is?"

"No; he does not."

"He must ascertain. If he does not, I will. She is no relation of mine, but I knew something of her father in old times when he was a boy. It was bad enough to have her running from one end of the island to another with dancing bears, tumblers and horse jockeys—but her father was with her. Now she has no one to guard her. Your father must pursue and recover her."

"You see, uncle, he is very busy just now."

"Busy or not—it is a duty. Bless my soul—what matter a pump and a brine-pan when an innocent child is in jeopardy."

"He does not see it in this light. I wish he did."

"There is no other light in which it can be seen," said Ezekiel Wilkes vehemently. "What is she doing? Is she starving? Begging her bread—bless me! among thieves and pick-pockets. She must be found."

"She may be found; but then—when found—where is she to go?"

"Take her with you."

Andrew shook his head.

"That cannot be. She would not stay in our house. From it she ran away. She is as incompatible as a companion to Ada as she is to my father."

"I can believe it. I would take her myself, but I am a bachelor and a rolling stone. She must be found, that is the first thing. Next, as to her money—where is that?"

"Sunk in these works."

"But the interest of it?"

"Till her place of concealment is known, my father, even if he wills it, cannot help her. And he has peculiar notions on this head."

"Look here, Andrew, you go and find her. When she is found, then we will consult what is to be done for her. Leave your father to me. I will speak to him."

"But when am I to go?"

"To-morrow, Andrew; not a day is to be lost."

XXXV

A Visit to Rab

ON THE MORROW ANDREW HAD disappeared. He had said nothing to his wife, nothing to his father. There were obvious reasons why he should not tell Ada that he was in quest of the orphan girl she had driven from the house. He left his father to learn what had taken him away from Mr Wilkes, who had undertaken the communication. He was not home at supper. He did not return all night.

With some malice, Mr Wilkes asked Ada if she knew where he was. She replied curtly in the negative.

"Something may have happened to him," said Wilkes, curious to see whether alarm for her husband would cause Ada to throw aside her frozen demeanour.

"Something—he has lost his head," said she. "I am not going to concern mine about him."

Andrew had gone first of all to Mrs Rainbow, and had in vain endeavoured to extract information from her. He knew nothing about her having a married daughter. Had he been aware of that, he would have gone to find the daughter. Mrs Rainbow declared that she had seen and heard nothing of Queenie since she came unexpectedly into the house with the basket of blackberries. When

Andrew pressed her to be more communicative, she became stubborn and sulky.

The reason of her reticence was that she knew of Rab's attachment, she saw the transformation it had wrought in him, and she surmised that, unless he met with success, he would fall back into disorderly ways. Queenie was with the Gerards in the place where Rab's suit could best prosper, for it would be warmly seconded by Martha. Were the place of Queenie's retreat to become known, then Grice, her guardian, would certainly remove her, and she would be placed among surroundings and under influences adverse to Rab.

Loving her son, jealous for his happiness, the mother obstinately refused that information which, if given, might jeopardise his happiness.

Andrew told the woman that his father had money in trust for the girl, and ventured further to assert that some money was due to her.

"Very well," said Mrs Rainbow, "let that be left with me—if Queenie is anywhere near, and comes to Saltwich, she will assuredly come to see me, and then I'll give it her. Here's an old sardine tin, there's a mouldy fish in it and some oil—I'll pour out the oil and eat the fish, then you can put the money in and I'll hide it in my mattress till Queenie turns up."

This Andrew naturally declined to do. In the first place, as he informed Mrs Rainbow, because he had not received the sum due to her; in the second, because that sum must be paid into the ward's own hand. His third reason—that he had no confidence in Mrs Rainbow— he did not state.

Disappointed in this quarter, he resolved to visit Rab. He asked the old woman how he was to find him, and she gave him but vague directions. It took up a good deal of Andrew's time to ascertain where Rab was, and what was his employment. It was queer to him that the thief had been set to watch thieves, the poacher turned into a gamekeeper.

When he had learned this, and also where Rab Rainbow's cottage was in Delamere, he departed for it, and on reaching it found the house locked up. Rab was away on his duties. Andrew was pleased to see how tidily he kept his little habitation, with a garden before the door. Nothing was now flowering in the latter, as the season was so far advanced; winter was stealing over the country and blasting the vegetation.

The days were short and the light began to fail whilst Andrew hung around the cottage.

One thing was certain—Queenie was not there. He looked in through the window. There was no fire on the hearth; the whole aspect of the cottage was that of a bachelor's habitation.

Whilst waiting, Rab came up with his gun over his shoulder.

The two men looked at each other in silence, each hesitating what address to make to the other.

Presently Rab, unslinging his gun, rested his crossed hands on the barrel, and said,—

"Late to be here, Andrew Grice."

"I came to find you. I have been waiting for you several hours. You do not suppose that I would have left my business and wasted a day without good reason. I have matter of importance I wish to speak of with you."

"Well! come in," said the keeper.

He unlocked his door, threw it open and entered the cottage. Andrew followed him. Rab put his gun in a corner—he would clean it presently, it was foul—and seated himself on a bench. He pointed to a chair, the only one in the room.

"I have not much furniture; a lone man does not require much, and I rarely have visitors."

"I am rejoiced to see you in a house of your own, and engaged in honest work," said Andrew.

"You did not leave your business and come this distance, nor wait for me some hours, to tell me this. To your point, Andrew."

"It is this, Rab; I am here concerning the Queen of Love—do you know where she is?"

The ex-poacher looked hard at his questioner, and answered,—

"That is no concern of yours."

"You are mistaken. It is; that is to say, it is a concern of my father, who is her guardian."

"Why is not he come in search of her, instead of you?"

"For an excellent reason—that he is engrossed in this new concern Button and Nottershaw are starting."

"If he cared for the Queen, and knew his duties, he would have come.

"Surely, Rab, a father can trust his son!"

"He has left his duty for a long time unattended to."

"We knew nothing about the disappearance of Queenie at first. I will not say that we were purposely kept in the dark, but it so happened that we knew nothing at all about her not being at Button's till full three weeks after she had left the place."

"Left!" laughed Rab bitterly. "That is a strange way of putting it. Left! Do you, call that leaving when you are thrust out, the door locked on you, and you are denied admittance?"

"Never mind about the circumstances of her departure. Neither you nor I can help them. They are of the past. What concerns me is the present. Come, Rab, tell me where she is."

"How should I know? Why do you ask me?"

"I will be open with you. Your mother certainly is aware where Queenie is, or, at least, has had some knowledge. I have ascertained that Queenie was speaking with you on that night when she was turned—I mean when she left."

"That night!" exclaimed Rab. "Yes, and she was speaking with you as well. I saw you with her. I overheard what was said."

"There was nothing said which you might not hear. Come, Rab, be frank. I know very well that you have had little Queenie in your heart. Is it so still?"

"That, I say again, is no concern of yours. You have your wife."

"I have, and for that reason I can speak openly to you. Queenie is to me a sort of cousin. She is a responsibility. My father has charge of her money. He undertook to care that she should come by no harm. Let us know where she is, that we may find her some home or place of shelter."

"Has she got none? No shelter for her little golden head in this winter storm? No home—no prospect of any?"

He looked about his own modest cottage.

"What do we know? Nothing. These winter storms. Exactly! We are troubled at the thought that she may be out without cover in them, and exposed to worse than winter storms, with no one to look after her, no one to be solicitous for her."

"Andrew," said the ex-poacher in a low tone, but full of feeling, "do not fear that. She has one who will never, never suffer harm to come to her."

"Rab! Are you going to marry her?"

The young keeper looked at Andrew steadily, with an earnest, sad light in his eyes.

"I don't know."

"Rab, I must come to the bottom of this matter. Where is the Queen of Love? Where are you concealing her? You do know where she is, or you would not talk of watching over her."

He spoke with vehemence—a storm was working in his breast; his heart beat so that its throbbing was echoed in his temples. Was he jealous of Rab? Was this hidden commotion in him due merely to solicitude for a strayed cousin? This impatience to find her, occasioned by concern that his father should fulfil the duties of his trust?

The searching eye of Rab was on him.

"Andrew," said the young ranger, "don't be a scoundrel. Don't get into the way of some of your set and begin by deceivin' your own self before you come for'ard to impose on others. You had the choice before you. There were the two girls—Ada Button and Queen of Love. It was not a choice between one rich and one a beggar, for if Miss Button had land, if what I hear be true, Queenie had money. You had your choice. The field was open; I did not stand in your way. You chose Ada Button and turned away from Queenie. By your choice you must abide. What you chose you cannot get away from, without bein' a rascal, in your own eyes, and in those of all the serious—all of your profession in Saltwich."

Andrew listened, and lowered his eyes involuntarily.

"It is all very fine your pretending that you come here in fulfilment of a dooty. The dooty is the mask, Andrew, you put on to hide from yourself your real motives. You came here because you want to see little

Queen of Love once more; because your heart aches, and you already repent the choice you made, because you say to yourself:—What a mistake I fell into—nay, what a mistake I went into with my eyes open! Lovin' one woman, I married another whom I did not love, to please my father, with the prospect of becoming rich."

"No, Rab, not that."

"Well, let be. It was not that. Then it was because you did not value the little Queen. You saw that she did not belong to your set. She did not think quite as you thought. She did not grow prim, stiff, and dingy like an Irish yew, but bore light and widespread branches, like a silver forest birch. She did not care to peck and cluck on a dung-heap like a barn-door fowl, but darted and twittered as a swallow. Therefore you said she will not do for you. You had eyes and saw not—log of wood that you were—you saw not that hers was a braver, purer, more generous nature than your own. That was why you did not take her. She was beyond your narrow range. You saw not that she cared for you, and that she would ha' given to you happiness such as you will never get with that other. No—you saw not that. You were blind as an owl in daylight. Now it's too late. You must keep away from her, and she must be kept away from you. If your father desires assurance that she is in safe hands, I can give it him; if he purposes sending her money, I bid you inform him that she needs none; she has friends as will provide for her all that she requires. Now, no more. Are you goin' back to Saltwich? If so, keep to the road. Beware of the way down Bramble Brook. Roaring Meg spouted there some while agone, and the earth fell in right across the road. If you were to follow that way, it would take you to your long home. You would see neither your wife, nor Queenie again for ever."

Then Andrew rose and left. But he did not return to Buttons. He was not in the mood to do so. He took a bed at the "Forest Inn," on the outskirts of Delamere. He desired not to see his wife, his father, his uncle, till the morrow, when his mind would have recovered its composure.

XXXVI

A TRIAL

ANDREW SLEPT BUT LITTLE THAT night. He had much to think about. As he had sat in the tavern eating his supper at a table in the corner, there had been men drinking nearer the fire, nearer the light than himself. He had declined to have a lamp on his table. He preferred not to be observed. The men were joking and speaking about their wives.

Said one,—"When my good woman begins to rattle her tongue, then I take up my hat and come here. I know that at this moment she is abusing the walls, the floor, the ceiling. All that abuse would have fallen on my head and shoulders had I not made off."

"Yes," said the other; "but when you go home, Jack, how then? Don't you get a double amount? Mine bottles her wrath up till I come home—and then—there's fine games!"

"If she begins at me—I shall return here. Drink's the only cure to the poison of a woman's tongue."

Andrew had listened to this conversation with a sad heart, and he wondered that the fellows could laugh, and have the stomach to drink, when their homes were so wretched. Could they quench their heartburn thus? Could they drown remembrance of their troubles thus?

Would the same medicine heal him? No—he must bear his burden without help from such means as sufficed these fellows.

Did ever any man have a wife so hard of heart as his own? And yet Ada was not harsh and repellant to everyone. She was not unkind to Jemima. She was amiable to Beulah. She was charitable to the poor. When some persons in need were sick, she sent them puddings, wine; she inquired repeatedly after them. She was even thoughtful of the comforts of people whom she was not bound to consider. But the fact that she owed care and graciousness of manner to her husband, to her father-in-law and to their friends, was apparently resented, and discharged her from making the effort to fulfil this duty. Kindness, graciousness she could show—but only as works of supererogation—she would not exercise them where they were obligatory. It had been so in her conduct towards her own father. Andrew was able to judge, by the manner in which Tom Button spoke of his daughter, that she had taken no pains to please him, and now that this feature in her character was known to him, it explained the eagerness shown by Button to leave his house—an eagerness that had been previously enigmatical to Andrew.

To animals, Ada could be kind—she had her pet cat, her tame canary, her fan-tail pigeons. The cat loved to lie in her lap, and to be talked to and caressed. The canary would fly to her when the cage was opened, hop on her finger, and peck food from her lips; the pigeons responded to her call. Why was it that so much affection could be shown to dumb creatures, and that to her husband should be reserved stubborn defiance and acrimoniousness? Why was it that she drew and loved to draw animals to her, yet took a moody pleasure in repelling those of her own household and family.

Andrew retired early to bed. His room was above that in which the men drank, smoked and talked. He did not mind the smell of tobacco. He was accustomed to it. That of spirits disgusted him, and his bedroom reeked with the fumes. The men below became uproarious; they shouted, sang coarse songs, quarrelled, made friends, and then swore at each other. It was long after the hour when the taverner was bound to shut his ale-house that these half-tipsy men reeled away or were dismissed.

But even after they were gone, and Andrew had heard the steps of his host and hostess retiring for the night, he could not sleep. His eyes were burning, his head aching, all his nerves were on the quiver.

There were thousands in the world who had been bankrupt in their domestic happiness, and they accepted their condition and made the best of it they could. Why should not he? He had sworn to take Ada for better, for worse, little dreaming then what the "worse" was. But he had received with her a good house, well furnished, an estate of many acres, and the prospect of a great fortune. There is something to counterbalance every advantage given by Providence. If perfect happiness were accorded in this world, men would fall in love with their existence in it, and be loath to leave it, unwilling to believe in and hope for a better life beyond. Every good thing has to be bought at the price of tears. If Providence passes over the counter so much wealth, so much land, such and such a habitation, it demands in payment so much heart's blood, so many anguish drops, so many sighs. Well!—he was now paying for what he had received. Tears in his burning eyes for the turnip field—ten acres; heartache for the shrubbery, gnashing of teeth for the house, humiliation for the vegetable garden, an aching heart for the garden gates—and so on. He was discharging his bill to Heaven for all the material goods he had received. That man downstairs, who had drunk and laughed over his wrangling wife, had not he compensation for this? He enjoyed his coarse pleasures, was able to smack his lips over the landlord's villainous ale, puff with satisfaction his cheap tobacco, relish a brawl, and laugh over insipid jokes. He had been granted by Providence the faculty to reap pleasure out of what bred disgust in the finer mind of Andrew. How would it have been with him, questioned Andrew, turning from left to right in his bed, had he followed his heart and taken Queenie? Was it—as Rab had said—that the little girl had been willing to be his? He knew that it was so. She had given him her young heart, and he had refused the gift. He had been shown one who would have suited him, perhaps not in every particular, but in a thousand more particulars than the woman he had chosen. Queenie might have been moulded, but there was no possibility of making any change in the icy woman he had taken to his side. He might throw some of the blame on his father, who had proposed and urged on the match, but not the whole of it. No man can be driven into union with a woman against his own consent. His father had left him free to decide, and had done no more than fix the date at which the decision was to be made. He had made his election a day before the date appointed.

Again, solemnly in his heart, Andrew vowed that he would be true to his marriage oath, in thought as well as in deed; that he would not relax his efforts to win his wife by love and forbearance. He had done wrong in taking her when he did not really care for her. It was probable that she had discovered his lack of love and resented it. He would strive to make what amends he might to her, if she would suffer him—if—

Next morning, Andrew started for home. As he was walking towards Button's from Saltwich, he encountered his uncle.

"Well, old boy! Found her?"

"No; I am no further than I was."

"Let us sit down. Come inside this field gate; there is a roller and the hedge will keep off the wind. It is pleasant, in the last smiles of summer, to receive the benediction of the dying sun. It is that of Isaac:—My son, I give thee the fatness of this earth and the dew of heaven from above."

They went in at the gate. The ploughed earth was steaming in the hot sun. The hedge was hung with dew that gleamed as diamonds.

"Well, boy! I have spoken with your father. For the first time in our life, in my experience, we have disagreed, and almost quarrelled. Unhappily, he does not see it. He maintains his position. The girl has left the house where he put her; she has fallen into bad ways; and, till he can be satisfied that she will spend the money properly, he will do nothing for her. It is monstrous—it is immoral, but your father is incapable, I believe, really incapable of seeing the matter in any other light. Then out came a reason—the worst of all. He has spent all her money. He has turned it to the last penny into bricks and mortar, into railway trucks for the salt, into boiling pans and slack to burn under them, into pumps and pipes, into chimney and stove house. He has spent all—every farthing, he avers—and therefore could do nothing, even if he willed. The capital is safe, he protests, and so I believe it is, but in the meantime where is the interest? What is the child doing? Who is looking after her? What profit is she getting from the sum her father bequeathed? I am angry and uneasy."

"I am sure that Queenie is not far distant; in a little while she must be found; but, so far, I am not certain where she is. Only in this am I confident, that she is in good hands, and we need not be anxious on that score."

"If you are satisfied, it is well. You are a judge. But do not intermit your efforts to find her. It is a duty owed her. If your father will not see after her unless she be a girl precisely to his mind, then you and I must do so for him. Now about yourself. Andrew, I am sorry to say it, but I must. Old boy, you may as well open your heart to me. I have known you since you were a child, and I am your nearest kinsman, next your father. What I say, he feels, but he is ashamed to admit it. I have some scruple in speaking out, but it is better to speak plain than hide in the heart what works therein. Andrew, my pippin, that wife of yours don't please me. I'm sorry to say it, but she is heartless—hard and white as a bit of scale from your pans."

Andrew dropped his head and covered his face.

"I did not think matters were as bad as they are," continued Wilkes. "When I arrived, she chilled me by her reception. I have since observed you and your father. He is one man outside the house—the old man with his old weaknesses—no, with strength accentuated—more dictatorial, more impatient of opposition, more ready to browbeat, than he was of old; but within doors, he is limp and weak, he hardly speaks, hardly raises his eyes from the ground. And you, boy—I had hopes of you. A little infirm of purpose, a little overawed by your great and noble father—great and noble he is—a little too much given to trust him to judge for you, and to take all your opinions second-hand from him; nevertheless there was, I saw, sterling stuff in you, the promise of an upright and useful man. Now, I fear all the good will deteriorate, all the promise come to none effect, through that woman. If she has quelled your father, she will quell you, and there is nothing in you to paralyse but what is good and vigorous. Therefore I say—she will be your moral desolator."

Wilkes paused and looked at Andrew, who remained with his eyes covered, speechless.

"At first," continued the old man, "I thought that there was hope. Hers was a self-enclosed nature, but if I could discover the key to her heart, I believed that I would discover that it contained much wealth. I know there are such natures, and happy are the husbands who have wives of this description. It is better that they should not wear their hearts on their sleeves for every daw to peck at. But the conviction has been forced on me that she is not such as I had hoped. Don't be angry with me when I tell you she is not the woman for you."

Andrew looked up, and tried to speak, but could not.

"There is no hope for you, boy, but in a separation."

"A separation?" gasped Andrew.

"Yes, you and she do not fit each other. She will be the death of all good in you, and you can do her no good. She is like a cold, damp mattress that will suck the vital heat out of you—and leave you a rheumatic wreck. Come to some arrangement between you, and part."

"It is impossible. I have made my bed, and so must I lie! Oh, uncle, uncle! I might have had another."

"Another!" exclaimed Wilkes. "Leave that thought out of the question altogether. Is it, think you, the knowledge of this that embitters her? If so, the blame adheres to you in a measure."

"Uncle, it is impossible for us to separate. The house, the land are hers—that is, her father's. Queenie's money is sunk in it. All our prospects depend on it. Father has thrown up his place at Brundrith's, calculating on this new business. Everything that concerns our future is in her hands. What would become of us if I were to say, I will not endure this life—I will go back to Alma Terrace; you shall bear my name and have no further part in me?"

"So, for the sake of a beggarly sum of money, for the sake of your prospect of becoming a rich man, you will continue to hug this lump of ice, to sip this cup of gall. I am angry with you. Don't talk to me of Queenie's money—that is secured by mortgage. No; if you remain at Button's it is because your eyes are dazzled with the prospect of becoming a millionaire like Brundrith. You have a pair of strong arms, fresh healthy blood; cast such a thought from you and go back to Brundrith's, or go elsewhere and earn your seventeen shillings a week in peace and comfort, without this devil of a woman to madden you!"

Then Andrew stood up, his weakness was past. He spoke firmly as he answered Wilkes.

"No, uncle, it is not that. I have no doubt I could earn my bread anywhere. I have no doubt that I should have tranquillity round about me. But I would carry away with me an undying torture within, disturbing my inner peace."

"How so, boy? I don't see it."

"Uncle—I swore before God to take her for better and for worse, and to hold to her till death. I swore that in the church when I held her hand. I swore it again last night on my bed. I cannot, I will not, seek a separation—but not because of money prospects."

"On my word! boy"—the old fellow also sprang up—"you are right. I was wrong. So far from killing out all that is good in you, this woman is bringing it to light. Here's my hand. God be with you. You have a future. God help you!"

He turned away, walked hastily through the gate, and took the road to Saltwich, whilst Andrew turned—home!

XXXVII

In Death we are in Life

T HE WEAVING TOGETHER OF OSIERS into game-baskets, as well as into such as were ornamental, was an employment that brought in money; and Queenie was happy to have acquired the art from the crippled Jessie. In the season of the year, when the leaves are falling, and when Christmas is looked forward to, there is a demand for small hampers.

Saltwich, lying near the royal forest of Delamere, as well as numerous preserves of noblemen, was well supplied with game. The poulterers' shops were furnished by the poachers and by the gamekeepers, perhaps almost as much by the latter as by the former. Some of the landowners disposed of such game as they were unable themselves to consume, so that there existed the excuse for the serious wherewith to salve their consciences in buying at the poulterers, that it was possible, just possible, that the hares, pheasants, partridges there exposed may not have been come by dishonestly.

At Christmas there would be a great sale for geese and turkeys, and in the game season, and the Christmas season, the good folk of Saltwich were wont to send hampers to their friends. Moreover, the owners of preserves asked for hampers by the hundred in which to disperse their game over the county among their friends.

To meet this demand the crippled child and Queenie were busy with their fingers. It proved that they had hardly osiers enough in the neighbourhood to keep them supplied. Accordingly, Gerard talked of making an osier bed, and asked his brother-in-law if he would cut a dyke to bring water into the pan where he would stick willow slips, because he himself, as ranger, was too much engaged with his duties. Rab's time was of less value.

Rab took for the occasion a day after a frost, one of those wondrous November days that intervene between storm and gloom, when the year enters on a second childhood, recalling early spring, with its crisp air, bright sun and its twitter of birds. And yet it is not spring. Nothing is budding, the leaves touched by frost are falling, the broad chestnut hands are all down, the male ash is bare as a skeleton; only the female still holds her fingers over the bundles of keys that contain her seed, and which she screens from frost as long as possible. In the hedges stand up the scarlet heads of the wild arum, the hollies are red already; the improvident birds are desolating the mountain-ash in wanton thriftlessness, strewing the ground under the trees with the sweet berry. About a stone on the ground are strewn broken snail shells that a blackbird has been shattering, that he may take a surfeit of the glutinous morsels before they retire underground for the winter.

The sun is sufficiently hot to bring out faintly the aromatic breath of the pines, that was so strong in summer. Owing to the stillness of the air, the patter of falling acorns can be heard, also the tap-tap of a green woodpecker running up the trees and testing the bark for insects.

Lovely though the day may be, the loveliness is that of a dying year. The air is charged with the scent of death, of the fallen leaf, of the decay of vegetation. The frost has smitten the flowers, their late-formed seed-pods are rotting, not ripening. Green though some elm leaves may appear, the sap is out of their joints, and with the first gale they will be torn from the boughs.

And yet, in the midst of death we are in life. As the leaves sail down, they reveal the already formed bud, in which is the promise of leafage and flower for the ensuing year. Already, out of the ground are shooting some precocious seedlings, themselves doomed to death, but harbingers of others following at a safer time.

Cheshire is a land of meres, the blue eyes of the county rivalling, not excelling, in blueness the tint of those of its girls, as limpid and bright, as inviting—and sometimes as treacherous.

The forest of Delamere occupies a tract of land not very fertile. The soil is of a hard, argilaceous-crust, locally termed "fox-bench," lying in beds of from six inches to three or four feet, strewn over with a light, poor soil. In its eagerness to procure money, the Crown in former days has disforested portions of what was once a vast wilderness, and has given up tracts to cultivation, with but mediocre success. The forest-land is useful as forest, profitless under the plough. For the same reason, with the improvidence of a wastrel, in the days of George IV, it hewed down its magnificent oaks, the wood of which is hard as iron, and now Delamere Forest consists mainly of plantations of firs and pines of no age nor dignity of size.

Yet wild nature is never without charm; and if the upper growth be of no great grandeur, the undergrowth is full of riotous unrestraint, variety and caprice. The bramble flings its streamers at large, the heather mantles every open patch, the ivy runs up the trunks like a squirrel, and, like the squirrel, strives to reach and destroy the leading shoot of the tree. Moreover, there is wild life in the forest. Not so much as there was when Delamere was a wood of oaks, for the bird little loves the pine; nevertheless, there can be no tract of country, in which man has his habitations thinly sprinkled, to which the wild creatures will not fly, just as the Pixies and Brownies, driven from the lowlands by the plough, have made the unenclosed and silent moor their last refuge.

Rab Rainbow was engaged on the trench he had been sent to cut. A piece of low, bad ground was separated from the mere by an undulation of the surface. It needed but a channel driven through this ridge to let the water run into the "pan" and make it sufficiently soppy to favour the growth of osiers. The fold was apparently of "rammel," first cousin to "fox-bench," and grew nothing but a little stunted broom. But the low-level soil, to which the water was to be introduced, consisted of clay. This was baked hard, and cracked in the summer under the hot sun, as also in early spring, under the March wind, precisely at those periods of the year when the willow ought to be making growth. Should this pan be flooded the osiers would thrive where now nothing grew but coarse grass and moss.

"Confound this darned rammel," said Rab. "It's enough to turn the point of one's pick. What was it ever put here for—I suspect to prevent the farmer coming this way with his plough, that there might be in the world some free land not hedged about. What is that? A quartz stone. How came that here? Such stones don't grow nowhere in Cheshire, no nearer than Wales, and it has been rolled over and over in water till the edges are worn off. I guess now this was all sea at one time; and, sure enough, it must ha' been, for the salt is below."

"You have a tough job there, Rab?"

The young man stood up. Queenie was on the bank watching him.

"It is slow work, is it not, Rab?"

"Rayther; this rammel or fox-bench is so hard! But I'll break through."

"Shall I help you, Rab? I have nothing to do."

"You—Queen of Love! You are not strong enough!"

"I can use the shovel"

"Pshaw!" he continued, working with his pick.

Queenie turned up her sleeves, exposing delicately moulded arms, and each elbow was like a rose.

"You will see," she said, "I can work. Set me where to begin."

"If you will—shovel out the soil behind me."

He had marked the line that was to be followed, with pieces of bough stuck into the ground, pieces on which still hung green leaves. The trench was three feet wide—Rab had cut to the depth of his knee; before him rose a hillock. There the trench would be six feet deep from his own cut level, and before the water could be introduced he must go a spade-graft deeper still.

"Hulloo!" said the young man. "This is spade ground. We are at the end of the rammel. What is the meaning of this? Here is another white spar standing in the side. It seems as though they had been set on end."

"And this?" asked Queenie, as she stooped and picked up a small, reddish-brown stick with a knot at both ends. Then she dropped it. "It is a bone."

Rab continued to dig—the earth was now black, no longer red, and, as he struck, he disturbed pieces of pottery, very friable.

"I said it had been meddled with," said he. "Someone has been chucking old crocks here. The weather is warm."

He paused and looked behind him.

The pretty golden hair was glinting in the sun. Queenie had thrown back her straw hat and freed her head. The hat hung by the ribbons that had been fastened under her chin.

As she worked, thoughts chased each other and turned in her brain; when Rab ceased driving his pick, she ceased shovelling.

"I have had a letter," she said. "It was left at your mother's. It is from that good Seth. He is in Hull now, but has got no work that will keep him through the winter. He has seen Genaud, the great circus owner, and he will take me on with the new season, so I need no longer be a burden to your sister."

"Queen of Love!" exclaimed Rab, and dropped his pick. "You are not going to leave us in spring!"

His face expressed his concern.

"Indeed—I am only of use in a circus. I have not been brought up to anything else."

"It ain't so. Martha cannot praise you too highly. You earn money with your hamper and basket weaving. You are of use to her in looking after Jessie, and—she will cry her eyes out if you go. As for me—for me—"

He took up the pick and recommenced work. He remained silent, with his back turned to her, and dug vehemently into the black earth.

Queenie watched him for a while, then resumed her shovelling, but did not throw out much earth.

She expected Rab to speak, but he would not. Presently she said,—

"You are not angry with me?"

"You know I'm never that."

"Then why do you not speak?"

"I'm thinking."

Again he dug on and said no more. She waited, then threw out a little earth, and waited again. He paid no further attention to her. She touched and plucked at his sleeve.

"Rab! You are angry with me!"

"I am not; if you will go—go, and there's an end o' my hopes!"

"What do you mean?"

"I shall have nothing to live for when you are away. I do not know how it will all end—I had light before my eyes—now all is dark."

"Oh, Rab, it is my profession!"

"May be—"

He dug his pick into the earth and out rolled from under his feet, along with the black soil, something globular. Queenie put her hands to it to throw it from the trench. It was too round, too big a lump for her shovel. Then she dropped it and uttered a cry of horror. It was a human skull. It lay in the black trench before her, staring up at her out of its hollow eyes, grinning with its white teeth.

Rab turned at her cry and saw the girl shrinking from the ghastly object.

"What the parson says is true," he remarked. "'In the midst of life we are in death.' I believe surely we have dug into a grave!"

"Oh, Rab, desist! Dig some other way."

"I cannot. We will put this into the earth again. But I must go on. We have disturbed the dead, but these can be no Christian bones—there is no church yard here. Look—what have I here?" He stooped and picked up a flint polished axe-head. "It's a thunderbolt," said he. "I've heard tell of them. This old, ancient fellow was killed with it whilst sitting under a tree, and they heaped the earth over him where he was struck."

Queenie was by no means eager for a return to circus life. She had tasted the peace, she had seen the beauty, enjoyed the comfort of a quiet cottage home. She delighted in the freedom of the forest and the beauty of nature. She loved Martha Gerard as she had loved no other woman. She was warmly attached to the crippled Jessie. Beside this sweet, pure life, so tranquil, so blessed, that of a caravan, with its restlessness, its noise, its unreality, had ceased to attract. If she must go back to the old life, it would be because she had failed to take root in the new existence. She had no claim on Mrs Gerard. The ranger's wife had not kept a servant, and could hardly be expected to entertain a lodger who paid nothing. Queenie had her clothes, but these would wear out; the soles of her boots already required mending. She needed sundry trifles, and every trifle cost money. She could not be a burden to her kind hostess, and the produce of her weaving would do little more than pay for her food and shelter. Probably the girl was in no way irksome to Martha, but Queenie was sensitive—had been rendered so by the manner in which she had been treated at Mrs Rainbow's, at Alma Terrace, and the Buttons.

The sun was warm, the air still. From the sides of the trench a fresh scent of mould entered the nostrils. If this were a grave they were cutting through, it was one that had lost the savour and horror of death.

Rab turned round. The skull lay between him and Queenie. He had cut so far into the hillock that he was down in the trench to his shoulders. He put his foot to the skull.

"I wonder who he was," said Rab. "If he'd been a good man and respectable, he wouldn't ha' been buried here. He'd have been took to the church. Here he lies all alone, none near him. I shouldn't be surprised as he was such an one as me—a chap as had a lot o' bad in him, but one day he came to know a girl, with golden hair and dark eyes, and she laid hold of him and drew his heart after her, and he came to leave his bad companions and give up his wild and godless way of life, to see a bright, beautiful world of happiness open before him. But she didn't care for him; she didn't think he was good enough for her—which was true. And so she went off and left him in Delamere Forest under a tree, and he sat there, and God O'mighty in His mercy struck him dead wi' a thunderbolt, to save him from doing something desperate."

He turned over the skull again with his foot.

"Rab," said Queenie, "how can you speak like this to me?"

"Because, little Queen of Love, your presence or absence is life or death to me. If you go"—he leaned on his pickaxe—"if you go, then I pray the Lord to strike me down with a thunderbolt."

"Rab," said the girl, "I will not go. I will remain here in dear Delamere. I love the forest. I love the life. I love you all."

"What—and me?"

She hesitated.

"I like—I respect you, Rab."

"Will you come to be mine? Then Delamere is the Garden of Eden again."

She put out her hand—over the skull.

Rab seized it.

"Queenie, in the midst of death we are in life. I thought it was all up wi' me when you said, 'I will go.' Now you will stay. Now you have put your hand in mine, it is all hope and joy and new life—sprung out of death.'

XXXVIII

REBELLION

WHEN ANDREW REACHED HOME, HE went at once in quest of his wife, and found her in the little parlour engaged with her canary, to which she was supplying fresh water. He put his hand on her shoulder with a word of welcome, but she did not look in his direction, and answered his salutation with,—

"Take your hand away. I don't want to be touched by *you*."

"I am sorry I could not return last night, Ada. One or two matters stood in the way."

"It is of no concern to me. You were welcome to remain away altogether. I would not have run after you—you may be sure of that; nor would I have cried my eyes out had you never returned."

"Ada—how cruel you are!"

"Of course, I am in fault. Never was a wife treated as I am—neglected by her husband, browbeaten by his father, and insulted by every Jack and Tom they choose to invite into the house."

"We have invited none save my uncle, and he would never insult you."

"He gives me black looks—in themselves as great an insult as a word or a blow."

"Ada, he came here prepared to be friends and to love you as a dear niece. It is yourself who has chilled and alienated him."

"Again, of course, I am in the wrong."

"Never mind about these little frets and sores, Ada. Be loving and bright. I am so glad to see you again."

"There you have the advantage of me. As I said, it would have been a matter of indifference to me if you had never returned."

"Ada, for shame!"

"What am I in this place but a means to an end? You wanted my land for a factory, you wanted my home as a count-house, you want my garden for a reservoir, and to cut down my trees and stub up my shrubs to light your fires with, and, finally, you want my spare room for your vulgar uncles. I hate this sort of thing. I won't have it. I am made worse than a servant. A servant can give notice and leave. I am fast here, to see all my plants poisoned, my birds made sickly; my canary is unwell to-day."

"She is moulting. We are not responsible for that."

"And then you go off without a word, without a good-bye, and do not say whither you are going, whom to see—though I know well enough—and you return just when suits you, not to me, but to your brine-pans. I don't flatter myself I am the attraction. I know better than that. The attraction that draws you back from Delamere Forest, or wherever you have been, is the new salt factory. That interests you, that engages your thought. You have some feeling for bricks and pumps, but none for your wife whom you swore to cherish."

"Ada! you know this is untrue."

"No sooner are we married than you tell me I am a liar; my wishes you take a pleasure in disregarding, and now you desert me to run after yellow-haired circus girls."

"Ada!"

Then in came Mr Grice.

"Father," said Andrew, "I am glad you are come in at this moment, for there is a matter that must be settled between you and me and Ada once for all. It concerns little Queenie. My uncle and I have had a talk about her, and he and I are of one mind. By his advice I went yesterday in search of her, but unsuccessfully. She is somewhere within reach, but where, exactly, I do not know. I saw Rab Rainbow, but no one else. He is acquainted with her place of concealment."

"Why does she remain concealed?" asked Jabez.

"She does not desire to return to this house."

"I would not let her come inside the doors," said Ada.

"Very possibly she knows that," pursued Andrew; "and she has no wish to go to Alma Terrace."

"There is no room for her there," said Jabez.

"That also, perhaps, she may know. I believe she prefers to find quarters for herself than take those provided for her by you, father. By some fatality, she has been placed in positions of constraint and contrariety unsuited to her light and elastic nature; she was unhappy at Alma Terrace, unhappy here. I do not suppose she found much comfort with Mrs Rainbow in Heathendom. What sort of a house she is in now, I do not know. Among what sort of people she is, I do not know."

"She is in a public-house. She is gone as bar maid," said Jabez. "That is the sort of situation into which the natural Eve in her will have thrust her."

"I do not believe she is in such a place," said Andrew. "Rab is reticent, but he assures me solemnly that she is in the best hands, and in a place where she is well protected from harm."

"Rab!" said "Hammer" Grice, roughly. "What is his word worth? What does a poacher, a drunkard, a debauched scoundrel like that know about respectability? If he is the guarantee, you will find Queenie in the worst quarters."

"You mistake Rab."

"I—I mistake! I know what he is; not only by the inner light that illumines me, but also by public testimony. What is Rab but a drunken blackguard?"

"He was such. He is reformed."

"An Ethiopian does not lose his colour if he scrubs himself. His wickedness is in the grain. He is a 'backslider.' He knew better at one time; and now there is no place left for him, though he may seek it. Don't talk to me of Rab. He is a worthless vessel, pre-ordained to destruction."

"I differ from you," said Andrew, with decision.

His father stared. What spirit had come over this young man that he should dare, not merely to differ in opinion from "Hammer," but to proclaim it to his face! Had his marriage done this? Grice thought so. He turned pasty in colour with anger, and said,—

"Because your wife flouts me, you hide behind her petticoats, and make a feeble stroke at your father as well."

Andrew coloured.

"You are mistaken," he said, with an effort to maintain his composure. "I have to judge by what I see. I have had more opportunity of observing Rab than you have had. I trust his judgment."

"His—not mine!" bellowed "Hammer." "Trust that tavern sot, that pothouse brawler, that poaching thief, rather than your own father, the most respected man in Saltwich!"

"I trust my own judgment, formed on observation, rather than your prejudice, father. But enough of that. It is not concerning Rab that I am seeking an interview. It is concerning Queenie. You are trustee of her property and her guardian."

"And you are neither, and therefore not called on to interfere."

"I must interfere. I conceive that a great wrong is being done her. In the first place—as her guardian, you are not taking any steps to obtain for her a place of security and comfort. I believe she has found both for herself. I believe it on the testimony of Rab Rainbow. If you disbelieve his word, and think him incapable of judging, then the more the obligation lies on you to see after her, take her from where she is if the place prove unsuitable, and put her where she may be better looked after."

"Andrew—the father in the parable did not run after his prodigal son into his riot and beggary, and pluck him away. He waited till he returned a penitent."

"The cases are not parallel. This is not a son but a little girl, and you have voluntarily taken on you the responsibility for her well-being. But next, and this is now the serious question—What about her money? You have made use of her capital. You have taken it out of the bonds and other securities where her father had placed it, and where it brought in, say three and a-half or four per cent, and have expended it in bricks and mortar and machinery. Where is the interest? What do you show for this capital of hers? Let her have three and a-half if you cannot just now pay four per cent, but, for Heaven's sake! do not defraud her of everything."

"Defraud!" said "Hammer"; "you dare say that to me?"

"I am sorry to offend you, father, but I know no other word to express what is being done, when a child is left, possibly to starve, without one penny, when she should be in receipt of just over a hundred a year—enough to keep her in comfort—whilst you are making use of her capital to build up a fortune for yourself. You must remember what you said to me, father—that you looked to our being rich as Brundrith, to buying a park and mansion, to your entering Parliament. This is all to be gained through poor little Queenie's capital, whilst she is ignored, cast out, and nothing is done either to see that she is among respectable people, or that she is not suffering from want."

"When the prodigal returned, then the father slew the fatted calf and brought forth the gold ring and raiment for his son. He did not send him the joints of veal to consume with harlots; he did not forward to him ring and raiment wherewith to make a display at his riotous feasts. I shall not defraud the child of one farthing, but I will pay over to her the money I have in trust, as well as arrears of interest at five per cent, not three and a-half, when she is brought to her senses, acknowledges her sins, and comes to me in repentance. I hope she is starving and in rags, eating the husks that the swine are given. So only can she be humbled in mind, and so alone come to realise her present lost condition."

"I have spoken my mind before Ada," said Andrew, "because she is annoyed at my going in search of the poor child, and puts a wrong interpretation on my acts. I wish her to understand how matters stand relative to her and you, father, and how I am concerned in the matter. I do not think your actions right; and if you will not see to Queenie, I must, or get Uncle Wilkes to do so. His time will be so taken up with electioneering matters, that he can ill afford space in which to search for Queenie, but he and I will provide for her, if you refuse, father, to do what he and I regard as your duty to her."

"I am to be taught my duty by a boy!" shouted Grice, and flung out of the room.

"And, let me tell you, none of my money is to be spent on her! Where will you get money? Are you receiving wages from your father now? I laugh at your undertaking."

Then Ada, carrying the bird-cage, left the room as well.

Andrew walked to Saltwich. He desired to see his aunt and to have a word with Mr Button.

As he passed the shop of Mr Poles, his eye was arrested by a collection of pretty little rush baskets in the window, among his collection of paper. The pattern was identical with that of the basket of blackberries Queenie had given him.

He instantly entered the shop.

"Mr Poles," said he, "whence did you get this supply?"

"You may well ask why they are in my window," answered the paperhanger. "But there is a reason. I wish to oblige a very worthy woman—Mrs Gerard, the head ranger's wife in Delamere; she is sister to that queer chap, Rab Rainbow. You'd hardly think it—she is a good creature, and has a crippled daughter. The child makes these, and I don't see but what there's as good a chance of their selling in my window as in that of a fancy shop. So I'm taking charge of them and making no profit by them. Some folks rather fancy this sort of thing. Will you be pleased to buy for Mrs Andrew Grice?"

Andrew had discovered what he was desiring to find. He remembered that Queenie had said she had learned plaiting of a crippled child. Undoubtedly, she was with the Gerards. He did not know the family, but Mr Poles's word of commendation was a guarantee for their respectability. With a lighter heart he took his way to Alma Terrace.

XXXIX

WALK!

THE SALT FACTORY WAS IN working order—nay, it was even in work. Much money had been spent thereon—all Queenie's little capital and some of Nottershaw's savings; not altogether in the form of gold, but in that of material, bricks, lime, iron, wood, slate. The firm had supplied itself with covered trucks on the line, built at Chorley, and each truck cost £102. 10s. and held from six to seven tons of salt. Grice had introduced into the works an improvement of his own—a rotator—a species of flexible belt that travelled on a level, and carried along with it baskets in which the moulded salt from the tubs was tossed. These blocks were then dropped, or tilted over, as the belt turned, into the receiver of a mill of revolving steel rollers that ground the salt to dust. The idea had long worked in Jabez's mind, but he had not been able to carry it out at Brundrith's. Now, to his delight, it was in working order, and he looked with pride at the white blocks travelling along, and then dropping into the hopper which discharged them under the roller. It was an invention destined, as he said, to revolutionise the trade. Those who bought and employed the flour of salt for the table, would never afterward return to the coarser crystals.

Already the chimney was pouring forth its volumes of smoke. Already the pans were in ebullition. Already the trucks were being laden with "butter salt" for the East Indies, and women were employed packing table salt for the home market in water-tight bags and jars. Already barges were drawn up at the wharf, and salt was being tipped into them.

Brundrith began to fidget. Brundrith became sensible that his interests, his all-but monopoly, was menaced. Brundrith began to move in the direction of Button. Brundrith began *pourparlers*, and *pourparlers* introduced negotiation.

Nottershaw was in high glee. He came to the works and button-holed Grice.

"I say"—he removed his finger from the button-hole to rub his hands, then hooked his finger in again—"I say, all is going splendidly. Brundrith is holding back only because he and Tom Button can't come to precise terms. It is a matter of a few hundreds only that divides them. Jabez, that invention of yours is famous. It tells. It has troubled Brundrith's dreams. That means some hundreds more than the mere plant and ground. By ginger!—"

"Hush! don't swear."

"I'm not swearing. Ginger comes from Jamaica. It is imported in pots, which my daughter paints for bazaars when they have been cleaned out. Old fellow! never you take ginger with port wine—it is fatal. It spoils the palate."

"I never touch alcohol in any form."

"To be sure, I forgot. But bother the ginger. Let us back to our muttons. Grice, I wonder, what the figure is at which old Tom is sticking?"

"Don't you know?"

"How should I. Tom Button has not told me."

"Nor me. It is odd. He has not consulted me as he should have done."

"Tom is a sly dog. I wish we had not made him our plenipotentiary. It all comes of your wanting to hold back and not be brought to close quarters with Brundrith. And I—you are to blame, Jabez. You thought

I was an orange to be sucked and cast aside. I know what your scheme was, to use me and then pay me off, and exclude me from the ulterior benefits—not take me into partnership. By George!—"

"Hush! I cannot allow of oaths."

"I am using none; my great-uncle was George Hamlet. He was an admirable man; whenever I am serious and think good thoughts, I recall George Hamlet. He had lumbago very bad, and was accustomed to sit with his back against a roaring fire, exposed to its full heat; it drew out the rheumatism, he said. He lived till he was seventy-four and five months. He was a very worthy man, was George. Two drops of turpentine on a lump of sugar—that was what he took internally, and exposure of his loins to a roaring coal-fire—externally."

"Never mind George Hamlet."

"But I do mind George Hamlet. I owe a great deal to him. He gave me a complete collection of Simeon's skeletons—I mean skeleton sermons— to do me good internally, and left me seven thousand pounds for my external advantage. But, as you say, to our muttons. I tell you, Grice, we have put too much power into Button's hands. You have sunk money on his land, and I have done the same. What hold have we on Button?"

"His daughter is married to my son."

"Yes; but I have no hold on him," said Nottershaw.

"For all I have advanced, I have the security of a mortgage on the estate."

"Yes; but I have not. Of course, there is the fabric, there are my books to show the expense to which I have been. But I am not altogether easy. Button is sly as a badger. You are a serious man, and I rely on your character. It isn't worth your while to fiddle me; so I build on you. But Button—" He shook his head. "He ought not to have been invested with such powers. There has been the mistake."

"You should have looked after him. I am engaged on the works."

"That is all very well, Jabez," said Nottershaw, "but I have not a defined position in the concern. You two fellows have desired to keep all in your own hands, so that, when a partnership is declared, it may be Brundrith, Grice & Button—and Nottershaw not even as a Co. I was to be paid for the bricks and slates and so on. A little profit—not much—and the grand harvest was to be yours and Button's. Well, I put in my claims. But I'll tell you what troubles me. Here, have we been, all three, combined to overreach Brundrith, and, as far as might be, to overreach each other. That is to say, you and Button wanted to get the better of me. I hope Button won't be fishing for his own basket, and forget Jabez & Co."

"He cannot do that. My son has married his daughter."

"Much he cares for Ada," laughed Nottershaw. "You would toil, and lay by, and sacrifice yourself for sweet Ada, I have no doubt. By ginger!—I mean preserved ginger—there is the man himself."

"What! Button?"

"No—look! Brundrith in our works. That is what I call impudence. He will not pass over your rotator and crusher without realising its importance and taking note of the construction. Will you go and meet him?"

"I had rather not. We are not on the best of terms."

"Let us go behind this wall of salt blocks and observe him. It will be larks, by Jove!"

"No oaths, please!"

"Jove was a personage in the heathen Pantheon. Very consoling to a Christian to consider, the victory of his religion over Jove's and all that sort of thing, so I mention him occasionally to stir up a thankful spirit in me. Come along, Grice. I'm going to watch him from behind this mountain of salt loaves."

"If you think that I am going to hide from Brundrith you are vastly mistaken. I wouldn't get off the pavement for the Queen, and I'm not going to stir from the floor for Brundrith. If he chooses to come my way he can do so. But it is impudence on his part, and I have half a mind to order him off the premises. He's walking about as if the place belonged to him."

"He is indeed, by jiggers!"

"Jiggers! I really wish, Nottershaw, in the interests of our serious profession, you would be more choice in your speech."

"Jiggers! There's no harm in jiggers. It is wrong not to enlarge the mind. You keep yours on brine, and never look beyond your pans. I do;

my intellect sweeps the horizon, and I consider the gold fields where jiggers are used for the sifting and washing of the ore. Brundrith is coming towards us."

Peter Brundrith, the great salt man, was, in fact, in the new works, looking round them with critical eye. He was a broadly-built man, with a clumsy walk, white whiskers, a somewhat flat face, and dark, beady eyes. He went about with his hands in his pockets, and occasionally removed his right fist from where it lurked, and rubbed his lips and nose with it, clenched into a ball. It was a trick he had brought along with him from the lighter to the mansion, from the times of his early life when he used no pocket-handkerchief. It was now merely a trick.

Brundrith looked hard at the rotator and the mill, and nodded with a grunt. He turned his head to Grice who was near, and said,—

"So, you have carried it out. It's not bad. I shall make some out of it."

Jabez opened his eyes.

"You've not patented it, I suppose?"

"No."

"I shall. I have taken the lot."

"I don't understand you," said Grice.

"Hope you made good terms. You'll get nothing more from me. I paid damned dear."

"Look hear, sir!" said Grice. "As long as you were master and I man, I couldn't rebuke you for your profane speech. Now we stand on one level—I and you—and I can speak. If you had been godly in your conversation and had refrained from oaths, I would not have left your service as I did. But when a man gives loose rein to his tongue, then one who is serious in his profession deals without scruple with him. I left you in the lurch. I know you missed me. I have drawn away your best work men. I have attracted to me some of your best clients. If you had been godly in speech and had attended chapel, and sent things to bazaars, that would not have happened. Now you and I are on one footing as masters, and I can tell you my mind plain."

"Now, I don't understand you, Jabez," said Brundrith. "And don't care to do so. You behaved scurvily with me; so I shall make no bones with you. Walk!"

Grice stared at his old employer.

Brundrith turned to Nottershaw.

"Mind this—no bills. I have accepted all as paid for. I take over the whole concern."

"What concern?" asked the contractor.

"This."

Brundrith turned his sharp eyes on Grice, and said,—

"As there's a woman in the concern, I won't be too harsh. But I expect you to clear out at your earliest convenience."

"Clear out—of what?"

"Of Button's, to be sure. I've taken over the whole, concern. As for you—walk out!"

"Walk out of what?"

"Out of this shop. It's mine. Bought everything—land, house, factory, stock, stables, your invention—everything! Going to run Button's along with my old affair."

Grice and Nottershaw were speechless.

Brundrith trotted into the stove-house.

Grice and Nottershaw looked at each other. The former recovered himself, and went after Brundrith, touched his arm and said,—

"All very fine this, but we are partners."

"We—who?"

"I and Nottershaw."

"Partners out in the cold! Walk!" Then in came Andrew, looking hot, and caught his father by the sleeve and drew him into the walling shed.

"Father, have you heard the rumour?"

"I've heard something that has set my head spinning."

"Button—father."

"What of him?"

"Bolted, and taken everything with him."

"Then we are done for," gasped Grice, and sank on a salt tub.

"Everything gone but the mortgage."

An imperious call from Brundrith,—

"Now, then, Grice—walk!"

XL

RUIN

JABEZ GRICE COULD HARDLY HAVE been more dismayed had his
favourite preacher danced a hornpipe in the pulpit of Little Bethel,
or his pet Missionary Society had organised itself into a Co-operative
Slave-hunting Company.

The news, borne in on him at both ears—from Brundrith on one side,
from Andrew on the other—was but too true. Tom Button had outwitted
all with whom he had been in conjunction. He had sold his land, his
house, and the factory for a lump sum to Brundrith, and had departed
with the money in his pocket, no one knew whither. Brundrith had
therefore acquired everything—not only the factory—but also Grice's
invention for grinding salt into gold, also the house in which Jabez and
Andrew with Ada were living. Whether Nottershaw would be able to
recover for material employed in the fabric was open to question.

Button had assured Brundrith that every account was settled. Thus
both Grice and Nottershaw had been overreached; but Brundrith did
not escape scot free, for no intimation had been given him that there
was a mortgage on the property.

It had been understood between Jabez Grice and Tom Button that
one of the stipulations of the sale was to be that both of them were to

be constituted partners in the newly-organised Company. Button had not concerned himself about this; he had sold everything for a lump sum, and, with that lump sum in his pocket, had gone chuckling into space, taking with him the satisfaction of having "done" his fellow conspirators against Brundrith's monopoly, of having done Brundrith in a matter of three thousand pounds, by concealing the fact of the mortgage, and of having paid off Ada, his daughter, for many a slight. The sinking and completion of the brine shaft had cost about £800; each salt-pan had come to nearly £600. The grinding mill had cost £300. Over the "common" salt there had been no permanent covering set up, but the "butter" salt had exacted roofed sheds, so also the stove for "handed squares," and the stove room with a loft over it. The reservoir had cost much money. Not only was every penny of Queenie's capital disposed of, but also several thousands of pounds that Nottershaw had advanced either in material or in wage to workmen.

Now Grice was left out in the cold. He had lost his employment at Brundrith's, and would find none in the new factory under the man whom he had attempted to injure. He could not call the house he inhabited his own; even Ada must turn out of it. That thought was the only one that gave him a gleam of satisfaction. But the gleam was a mere flash as from a spark of magnesium—instantaneous, and leaving behind a sense of more profound gloom.

In came Mr Poles. He was in excitement. He had been in Liverpool and had seen Tom Button by accident, and was confident that he had started for New York. He was sure it was Button, though the man was disguised in an outrageously fast costume, and with jewelry on his fingers, and in his scarf. He had a somewhat bold-looking, dressy lady on his arm. They were leaving an hotel and starting for the wharf —much luggage in very new portmanteaus and boxes on the roof. On one of the latter the initials U. C.

"Uriah Something-or-other," suggested Poles. "It is remarkable," said he, "that U and C are the letters that follow on T and B, the proper initials of Tom Button. I am not sure, but I fancy he saw me, for, directly I recognised him, he jumped into the cab and pulled up his greatcoat collar to hide his face. I was so taken aback that I did not at the moment know what to do. I asked the waiter at the hotel door whither the gentleman had gone, and he said that the gentleman had informed him he was off with his missus to New York by the Caledonia—I think that was the name of the ship. That puzzled me. Tom Button lost his missus twelve years ago."

"I'll go at once to Liverpool," said Andrew. "We must make sure of this without delay."

Jabez Grice was as one stunned, unable to advise a course, unable to see any way out of the cloud. But his eyes kindled and he set his teeth.

"This comes of Ada," he murmured; "she turned away from her the heart of her own father."

Andrew was about to leave, when he heard these murmurings. He said in a low tone,—

"Father, I will go. But remember one thing. If you speak to my wife about this matter—not a word of offence, understand! I will have her respected. She is not to blame. The blow will fall heaviest on her."

"Respect such a woman as that!" scoffed the old man, losing all command of himself. "Such a woman, who has driven her father from her! Such a woman, who has insulted, outraged me!"

"I will not leave the place," said Andrew, "unless you pass to me your word, as a serious Christian, to address her with decorum."

"I won't speak to her at all. I shall go to Alma Terrace, to Beulah. Now that scoundrel is away, I can have his room."

"No, father. There must, under the circumstances, be some one in the place. Do you go to Liverpool; I will remain here."

"You go," said Jabez, sullenly; "I will not look at, I will not speak to Ada. I will persistently turn my back on her."

Andrew went to Liverpool, and the result of his inquiries was that no doubt was left in his mind that Mr Button had departed for the United States under an assumed name. Mr Nottershaw accompanied Andrew. He was in a fume, afraid that he had lost his money, uncertain whether he could come down on Brundrith. He ran from one solicitor to another to obtain opinions, which were conflicting, partly because he was unable, in his then condition of excitement, to state his case clearly

Andrew learned more concerning his father-in-law than he expected. Button had been wont for some years to visit Liverpool, and had fallen into extravagant ways, had borrowed money, and must have been in embarrassed circumstances when Jabez Grice proposed to him the project of the salt factory.

When Andrew returned to Saltwich, he found that the news of the disappearance of Button was known to every one, and on reaching the house, further discovered that the bailiffs were in possession, with a bill for £37 10s. 4d. They had been put in by a spirit merchant.

Jabez Grice was hardly able to command himself. The destruction of his hopes was more than he could endure with equanimity. He wandered about the house, the grounds, the factory, without a purpose. He paid no attention to his son's report. He had already convinced himself that he must accept the worst. He had no money of his own. Ada had none in the house. Even if he had been rolling in gold, he would have refused to satisfy the claim of the spirit merchant as immoral. His brother-in-law, the only man who could have soothed his mind, was away, and would not be back till night!

The old man sat and listened to his son, gazing into the fire, and as Andrew spoke, the canary sang in shrill and ever shriller tones, as though laughing and mocking at their misery.

Then Andrew ascended the stairs to his wife's room. He had been told that she was above; she had not shown herself since the appearance of the bailiffs in the house.

Before her door Andrew turned for a moment and drew breath. His heart ached for Ada. The blow to her must be crushing—to lose her father with such ignomy, to have to endure the disgrace of the odious men below, and to see the prospect before her of being constrained to leave the home in which she had been born. Worse still, she, who had been reared in comfort, in self-indulgence, must be prepared to settle down to the level of a labouring man's wife, in a cottage, without a servant, would have to scrub the floor, do the washing, light the fires herself. She had not behaved kindly to him. Who could tell! might not this humiliation be the rude shock which would result in a softening of her heart, lead to an improvement in her manner, and thus that great good might come out of present evil?

He had not liked Tom Button; had not felt the least love spring up in his heart towards his father-in-law, but his daughter must surely have felt attachment towards the author of her being, though with her lips she had spoken irreverently of him.

Now, almost for the first time since their marriage, was Andrew conscious of entertaining love for his wife. Out of the pang of his great pity for her, love took birth. He resolved to exercise the utmost forbearance towards her; to veil, as far as possible, the greatness of her loss, and the scandal of her father's conduct.

Then he softly turned the handle of the door, and entered her room.

Ada sat by the window knitting, and, as he came in, was counting the stitches.

He took a chair, drew it opposite her, and waited till she had done counting. Then he laid his hand on hers and said,—

"Dear Ada, a word with you."

"Well!" she looked at him with a cold glitter in her eye; yet he could see, from the redness of the lids, that she had been crying. "I have come upstairs to be away from those fellows—I suppose I am not to be allowed the satisfaction of being left alone, even in my own room, but am to be pursued thither by you. I am sorry there are no attics to this house, or I would have fled to them."

"I hardly know, Ada, how much has been told you. I do not wish to distress you more than need be—"

"Then leave me to myself."

"Ada, I have seen Brundrith. He has no wish to behave ungenerously; on the contrary, we are welcome to remain here till Lady Day. Your father has sailed for New York, but I can hardly believe he intends to leave us completely at the mercy of the creditors."

"Then you know very little of my father. He cares for no one but himself. Did not I warn you that he was making for America? I saw, from his manner, that he had some such scheme brewing. As I said it, of course you paid no attention. I am a liar and a fool in your eyes."

"You are neither—but an unfortunate, unhappy young wife."

"Thank you! I want none of your pity."

"You have it, all the same. And in a pitiful condition you are."

"How do you know my father is gone to America?"

"He left his hotel at Liverpool for the boat—he said he was off to New York."

"He said that?"

"Yes, Ada—at the hotel."

"Then—he is not started for New York yet."

"Ada, prepare your mind—your heart I would rather say—for what is before you. Our prospects of making a large fortune are at an end. But God has given me wits, strong arms and hearty resolve. I have made up my mind as to my course. As I tell you, I saw Brundrith. I went direct to him when I returned from Liverpool. I told him frankly how matters stood. I could see by his manner that, though angry with my father, he is placable. I will again go to him and ask him to overlook the past, and take my father on as foreman and me as waller in this new factory. I believe he will readily agree. We have perhaps behaved badly to him, but he is a worthy man and does not harbour resentment."

Ada laughed bitterly.

"This is what it has come to! That I—I am to be degraded into a common, vulgar workman's wife. This comes of marrying into a family of beggars."

"Ada!"

The blood mounted to Andrew's brow.

She started from her seat, and flung her head on the pillow of her bed and burst into tears.

Andrew went to her. He could not bear to hear her sob and weep. He laid his hand on her head. She passionately withdrew from the pressure, raised her head and said,—

"If I am unfortunate—unhappy—it is because I have you as my husband and cannot rid myself of you. I do not care if I never see you again. You married me for the sake of this house and ground, and the brine-run under it—not for my sake. For me you never cared. Now that what you wanted goes from you, you hate me."

"Ada!"

"Leave me in peace. The sight of you makes me mad."

"And the sight of you makes me despair."

He could have bit his tongue off that he had allowed this cruel word to escape him. But so it was with Andrew; the softer his heart had become, and the warmer his feeling, the greater the revulsion when wounded, and when his kindly feeling was repulsed. Whenever he was indifferent to his wife, or felt an inarticulate aversion, he remained calm, spoke with gentleness, could not be goaded to a harsh speech; but whenever a warm and powerful gush flowed through his arteries, and a mild and sympathetic light kindled in his eyes, then disappointment made him lose command over his words.

He left the room, shut the door behind him, and said to himself,—

"My father was right. Once in man's life does Providence offer him a great blessing—if he puts that from him, then he is shut out for ever."

XLI

By the Mere

·

QUEENIE WAS NOT HAPPY. SHE had as much as engaged herself to
Rab. When she put her hand into his, with a sudden impulse, he
had accepted it as her concession to his wishes, and she had herself, at
the moment, so intended it to be taken.

The desire to return to the stir and change of the circus had passed
away from Queenie in the fragrant and peaceful forest. It had not been
a deep-rooted desire in her. It had appeared to her as the only means
possible of earning her living, as a condition of life more pleasant than
the perpetual fidget at Mrs Rainbow's, than the dull oppression of the
mode of existence in Alma Terrace, than the hard despotism of Button's.
Now she had found a sphere that suited her exactly. It was full of
beauty and calm, and so commended itself to her innate artistic sense;
it was a home of love and true piety, and so was a sweet resting-place
suited to her moral sense. She could stretch her limbs and swell her
lungs on the heath among the forest tracts, and enjoy physical life. Wild
nature proved an inexhaustible store house of interest, ever feeding her
intellectual life.

But when Queenie came to ask herself whether Rab was as
congenial to her as was the life in Delamere Forest, then she faltered in

her answer. Rab was a better man than he had been represented. He had been bad. Usage goes a long way towards effacing dislike to what is ugly. She had thought him at one time very ugly, then had come to consider him plain. Now she did not consider about his features; she regarded them as passable. He certainly had good eyes, full of intelligence and a kindly light. He who had been a loafer was now an energetic keeper. His conversation conveyed information; he earned a wage, had a nice cottage pleasantly situated, and could maintain a wife.

One who could love so faithfully without encouragement, and out of love break with bad habits and reform himself radically, was surely the man on whom she could rely to be true and devoted through life. Were she to break off her engagement to Rab it would drive him desperate.

Queenie said to herself,—"I am not too good for him. I am not good enough. Why, then, do I hesitate? Why am I so uneasy?"

And the answer came—"I do not love him."

That was at the bottom of it all. She could not get further than liking Rab. Would she be able to love him when she became his wife? Was it right for her to become his wife when no love for him woke in her heart? when she saw no prospect of love coming? How would he endure that—to have a wife and to discover that she respected him, but did not, could not, love him? When she questioned herself further, and asked why she did not, could not love him, her pulses beat faster, her cheek mantled; she started from her place and walked fast over the sandy soil, and strove to stifle the answer that rose up in her soul, for it frightened her. She went to the edge of the mere, to the point where the little dyke had been cut by Rab to let the water flow to the low plot that was to become a willow bed. A soft haze like steam hung over the water and tops of the trees, playing among the heads of the pines, and trailing over the silver surface of the mere. The sun shone, but was shorn of all its gold—it was as a burnished silver salver set in the sky, and the blue of the heavens was suspected rather than seen, athwart the gauzy veil. The air was warm, very little wind was stirring, and that only at long intervals. Nature was dozing, in the doze that precedes death, beautiful in her last sleep, and still, so that but for the occasional sigh that stirred the leaves and brought them down in a golden shower, and clouded momentarily the polished face of the lake, it might have been thought that all life, all motion, was extinct.

Water was flowing through the cutting formed by Rab, and a flotilla of fallen leaves had gathered about the mouth through which the current ran. The leaves were of all sorts—maple, beech, birch, plane, oak, bramble; of all colours—yellow, crimson, brown and green.

As Queenie stood watching the clear stream flowing through the cutting, she observed the leaves detach themselves from their fellows, enter the current and sweep along with it, sometimes singly, sometimes in combinations of two or more together. Their fates were different. Some shipped their way along without ill hap, and dived into the deep cleft cut through the prehistoric burial mound. Some caught against a fibre of heath-root, and remained at anchor. Some couples parted; one lagged behind, then the foremost caught against the bank; that which had been first arrested disengaged itself, swam onwards, caught up its partner, and carried it forward with it, or else remained along side, or even, occasionally, sailed by with callous disregard.

It amused Queenie to watch the leaves—to see which associated together, and how they got along together. Then she saw a little primrose-tinted birch leaf, light as a feather, shoot from the flotilla, pursued by a dull, brown, oak leaf.

"There am I—there is Rab!" said Queenie. "And see! ahead is poor Andrew struggling along with that wicked Ada."

"Andrew is not ahead; he is at your side."

Queenie started, as though shot through the heart, and turned white. Had he heard what she had said? Had he divined her thoughts? She hardly ventured a glance at his face. That glimpse sufficed to show him to be sad and careworn.

"What are you doing here, little cousin?"

"Andrew—amusing myself!"

"What at?"

"Only watching the autumn leaves."

She pointed to the two pairs sailing along the stream.

"Ada and I—you and Rab; is it so?" he spoke and sighed.

"Yes, Andrew," she sighed in echo.

Neither spoke. They were watching the leaves. The first pair consisted of a beech leaf and a dark green, prickly holly leaf. They made their way slowly—the beech leaf held by the needles of the holly. Then suddenly, whether caught by a puff of air, or by a ripple of the water, the beech leaf detached itself; and at that moment, moved by the same force, the birch foil escaped from its companion, shot along the stream, caught up the leaf of beech, and the two slid along together, leaving their companions grounded.

Queenie started and withdrew from the streamlet, her brow flaming. Andrew followed her. He did not altogether understand the mystery of the leaves; did not know which represented himself and which the others named, consequently he was unable to see what had produced such agitation in the girl at his side. Queenie seated herself on a bank of dry heather. She endeavoured to conceal her confusion under an appearance of ill-humour.

"What have you come here for, Andrew? I wished to be left to myself."

"I came to see you."

"And I did not want you to come."

"Queenie! matters have reached a crisis. I have been forced to pay you a visit. I inquired after you from Rainbow. He would give me no information. Then, by a lucky chance, I discovered your hiding place."

"Lucky! I think it the reverse."

"I daresay. It is no lucky matter that brings me here. So, Queenie, is it to be as you said—Rab and you?"

"Yes, Andrew."

"I suppose I must wish you joy."

He spoke with an effort.

Then she hid her face in her hands and burst into tears. He did not speak, but quietly took a place by her side.

"Well, Queenie, we all have our troubles, our sorrows, our disappointments. We must bear them. It is God's will, and by them He fashions us to the shape he chooses."

She raised her head and looked in his eyes.

"Andrew, I do not love him, and yet I have promised to marry him. I do not think that it will ever be possible for me to love him with the love that is due from a wife. Tell me, ought I to take Rab? Ought I to marry one who has not, and never can, have my heart?"

He shrank from a reply. What could he answer? Had he not done that very thing which she meditated? He left her question unresponded to.

"Let us leave that matter to be considered at another time," said he. "I have come to tell you how matters stand with us at Button's."

"How? Matters between you and Ada?"

He shook his head.

"What, then?"

"All is ruined. Mr Button took advantage of the trust reposed in him by my father, and sold the land and factory—everything—to Brundrith, and ran off to America with the money. We are left in a desperate position—father and I thrown out of work, bailiffs in the house on account of Button's debts; the only thing saved is your little fortune. That my father had secured. He holds a mortgage on the estate for three thousand pounds, or thereabouts, which is the amount bequeathed by your father. I am so thankful that has been preserved, but my father is an upright man. He thought to make much more for you out of the factory than could have been made out of the South American bonds. You are in no worse position than you were. It is we who are in a bad way, but I do not feel discouraged; I have in me the will and the power to work."

"And Ada! how does she bear it?"

"I have not been able to see much of her. I do not know that she realises the terrible downfall. She will have to leave Button's."

"Andrew," said Queenie, "as to my money, I am glad it is safe, not on my own account but on yours—that is to say on your account, your wife's and uncle's. I do not want it. It can do me no good. It may serve you in this difficulty, and help you to get out of your present distress. I do not understand about mortgages, and bonds, and investments. You can, I suppose, get my money out from that into which it has been put. Well, take it; do with it what you will. I am content; I shall be very happy to think it has been a means of relief to you. I ask but one thing in return. Tell me what I am to do about Rab. I cannot love him—I cannot love him, for—"

He put out his hand to ward off more words.

"Queenie," said he firmly, "let me say it—not you. It is perhaps better spoken than allowed to remain burning under cover. You and I have loved each other ever since we knew each other. What you saw in me I cannot think, but it was so—somehow we came to care for each other very, very much. You, in your fresh, innocent, child-like frankness, told me as much! I said nothing, or very little, yet you knew you were dear to me. Then came my father's influence, and my doubts about you on account of your education, and I flung myself from you at the feet of another, whom"—he lowered his voice—"I did not love, and who I now know, from her own lips, has never loved me. Such is the condition of affairs. We parted on the rail at Button's, and then—if there had been any secret between us before, all was revealed at that time to each other. We knew each other's hearts then. But I was mad; I dashed head long into an union that promised fair, though it was one against which my heart protested. Now it is done, it cannot be undone. I know, Queenie, that we must not meet. I know that we must fight against that which is in our hearts. I do not blame anyone but myself, least of all my wife; for I was wrong in offering her my heart when it was given to another—to you. You and I have bravely struggled against ourselves, and, Queenie, we will struggle on. I am bound to Ada, and I will never be false to her in any way, as far as lies in my power. Now, Queenie, you ask me if I counsel your doing that which I did. No! a thousand times no! Unless you love, do not marry. You prepare for yourself unspeakable anguish, and—"

Suddenly, overcome by her impulses, Queenie threw herself in his arms.

"My poor Andrew! My dear Andrew—I can never love any but you."

He quietly, gently unlaced her arms that clasped him, raised her weeping face from his breast, and thrust her from him.

"Queenie," he said, "you must be a brave little girl and do what is right. I would not have spoken, but that there was no advantage in concealment, and it empowered me to say plainly what my advice was. Hear me out. There is no hurry. You are young. Ask Rab to give you time. You may not be able to love him now. In a year or two it may be different. Then—then take him, but not till you are sure you can give him what you vow shall be his. Now, as to your money. Dear child, we cannot owe that to you. I came here to assure you of its safety, to assure you that I would see that you lose nothing. I feared you might hear the news of our disaster, and be in alarm for your own inheritance. It shall suffer no further risk. Now, good-bye once again. Now all is spoken out, and I go to my work and to my trouble; you to yours. Take Rab when you can love him. Do not take him unless you can, or not till love comes. Goodbye!"

XLII

A BROKEN LIFE

MRS GERARD WAS CLEANING A copper pan after having made apple jam in it. That was a task she imposed on no one, for she thought that she could trust no one save herself to do it thoroughly and so obviate all risk of poisoning the family with verdigris.

Whilst thus engaged Rab burst into the house. When Martha looked up she saw that his face was red as blood, his eyes were wild, and his hair in disorder. He cast himself on the bench in the window and drove his fingers through his shaggy hair.

"It is my fate. All is against me. I have struggled, and now it is over."

"What is gone wrong, Rab?"

"Everything. Thrice have I been present when Andrew and Queenie have met. First when they began their acquaintance, then when he got engaged to Ada Button—and now that he is married. It is all up with me!"

"What is it, Rab?"

"It is too hard," said he, and his whole body shook.

"What, Rab? I thought all was going on well now."

"Yes, so it ever is with me. The clouds lift, and then down they come again darker than before. It is night now—black night upon me."

"I do not understand you, Rab," said Martha, abandoning her copper pan, and coming to him in the window. "Brother, you were very happy a little while ago."

"That is true which they said once in chapel—that Providence orders all things, determines who are to be saved and who lost. And them as is to be lost, they may fight against their destiny, they may strive to be good—and it's no use. They must go down and be lost eternally. It is true. I thought it queer teaching when I heard it, and I didn't believe it. I do now. I've proved it in myself."

"Rab! what has come over you?"

His sister strove to take his hand, but he with drew it.

"I will tell you all. It may do me good. I don't know that anything can; but you are a kind lass, and I'll tell you everything. The first time I saw her—"

"Whom?"

"Queen o' Love, to be sure. There is no other. The first time I saw her was talking with Andrew Grice, and I thought then I'd never seen a girl as was her equal. She sort of threw a charm over me then, and I could think of nothing but her. Yet even then it was Andrew she talked to, laughed with, to him she gave nuts. And he—he was frightened to be found with a circus girl, as if it were something wicked. I felt a hate for him then, because she chose him out to chat with, and had no eyes, no words for me. That was the first time. Yes—" He paused, put his hand into his breast pocket, drew out a note book, opened it and unfurled a leaf. Within lay a withered rose. "There, Martha—she did give me this. I don't know whether to mock me, or because she pitied me. I don't know," he added bitterly, "whether it weren't the doin' o' Providence as had ordained my destruction, drawin' me to damnation, as you draw on a rat to the trap, wi' a trail of anise seed."

"Rab! Rab!" His sister shrank from him. "How can you say these terrible words? You know that she has been a good angel to you."

"Yes—she has been a good angel so far; but now, after she has drawn me up out of shipwreck, she is ready to cast me down the cliffs again. Listen to me, Martha. You know how I saved her life when there came that sinking of the ground by Saltwich Flash, right under the circus.

Well, that finished what she had begun with the yaller rose. After I had held her in my arms, then it was over with me. I could think of nothing but her. She was my sun; I could have light only from her. She was my goal; I could run only to reach her. She was the one pearl for whom I would fish all my life on the chance of bringing her up in my hand."

He beat his brow, then laid his open hand on the table, and proceeded:—

"It is folly that a man should take such a matter to heart. Folks say there are more fishes in the sea than those taken out of it; that there are as many flowers in the field as there were after it has been picked over, as many stars in heaven after it has rained sparks. To me there is only one prize, one flower, one star. I want no others. I can see no others. She did not encourage me. She told me she liked me, but did not love me. She was grateful for the life I had given her, but she would not yield up that life into my keepin'. I was a fool, I suppose, to go on hoping. I saw that she loved Andrew, not me—no, not me. God help me!"

He bowed his head; he could not proceed. Martha remained silent as well.

"Then came Andrew's engagement to Ada Button. It was for money. He did not love her, but she was rich, and his father persuaded him to it, and, perhaps, he was right. The Queen would not suit that serious family. She and Jabez, who ruled everythin', could not agree, and he would have driven her desperate. Then came the second time that I caught Andrew with Queen o' Love. It was when he was partin' with her, after he had bound himself to Ada Button. Then I learned that she loved him, and that, although he was to marry Ada, he still loved Queenie. He could not help it—I mean, he could not help lovin' Queenie, none could; but he should not, loving her, have taken that other woman. Well, Martha, then, when he was married, I thought all was clear before me; that she would get over her fancy for Andrew— and he is a good chap, that I do not deny, and I well knew he would fight agin his love for Queenie, as a sinful thing to harbour. She gave me some encouragement then. She did not say she did love me, but would try her best to do so. Then I was a happy man. Then I sang at my work; I was like a bird in spring. At the time when I was discouraged I did not drink. No ale, no spirits could give me pleasure, could quench the fire that burned in me. I did not try to look at, think of, other girls. He who has seen and been kindled by Queenie can look at, think of no one else. So, when she promised to try to care for me, I rose up and felt strong. All my bad ways fell from me like the cords that went to pieces on the arms of bound Samson. Everythin' smiled and laughed in and about me. The sun and the moon danced in heaven. Then, presently, whilst I was cuttin' the channel to let the water on to the osier bed, we came to some sort of understandin' that she would take me as her own. Then there was in my heart as the blast of a trumpet."

He leaned his elbow on the table and laid his head on his hand. The sweat ran off his face in streams.

"To-day I was cuttin' osiers for the bed. The boy Fred Fellows was with me. I fastened the twigs together; he did not understand how to take a bind and twist it so that it held. I gave him my knife that he might cut the twigs; and, when I had enough, I hoisted the bundle on my shoulders and went towards the new bed to which the water is let in. I forgot to ask him for the knife again. I came to the place for the willows, and what did I see by the edge of the mere but Queenie and Andrew. If they had not been so full o' each other, they must ha' seen me. This is now the third time I've come upon them when together—and the third time is fatal one way or other. I could not quite hear what they said. I stood at a distance and looked on. They was seated and speakin' to each other, and their eyes were fastened on each other. Then there sprang up in my heart a Roaring Meg of bitterness and foaming hate. What did the man mean—this Andrew, bound to another by his own act—comin' between me and the girl who had promised to be mine? In my fury I felt for my knife; I could not find it. I could not tell what I had done with it. A guardian angel watched over them. If I had found my knife, Andrew would have been a dead man."

"A guardian angel watched over you, Rab," said Martha—"and saved you from a dreadful crime."

"May be." He put up his other elbow, and threw his head into the hollow of his other hand. "May be. I care not. Then I cast down my osier bundle and clenched my teeth and my fists, and I went round till

I could see her face in full, and then I shifted about till I could see his in full. Neither had eyes for me. Neither could see anything save each other. I do not know what they said. I did not go nigh enough to hear. I could not have heard. Roaring Meg—the bitter jet in my veins—was boilin', hissin', spittin' in my ears. I could hear nothin'. Then he stood up—so did she. They were very earnest—he speakin'—and all at once she threw herself into his arms. I cried out. They heard me not. A flame of fire passed before my eyes. When I saw clear again, he was biddin' her leave—wavin' her from him, and himself drawin' back. I was in the wrong; Andrew is not a bad man. Can he help it that he loves her? It is his misfortun', it is his misery; as it is my misfortun' and my misery. He will do her no wrong. He knows what is right and he will do it. No—I am glad I did not kill him. I pity him as I pity myself. He and I love the same Queen of Love, and she can never be his—and now I know that she can never be mine."

"Not yours!—"

"No. Andrew stands between us. She loves him. He cannot help it—it is so ordained. It is inscribed on the black heaven that scowls down on us, that he should love her, and she him, who are and must now be separated. It is woe to him. It is woe to her. It is woe to me. We three must bear this consumin' fire eatin' into our hearts, a fire ever burnin', a worm ever bitin', a fire never quenched, a worm never glutted."

He clasped his head in both hands, and a gulp like a sob burst from his throat. Martha trembled. She saw how deep was the agony through which Rab was passing, and she could do nothing to help him. A man sobs but twice in life—once when his heart is broken by the woman he has loved; once when he stands self-convicted and penitent under the eye of God.

"She cannot be mine," he said slowly. "I could not take her, knowin' that her heart was elsewhere. It would be too cruel to her to constrain her to fight the battle between dooty and her own heart. He has to do that. It would be a twofold pain to me to hold her in my arms and know that the shell was mine, the spirit was elsewhere; to see her every day strivin' desperate like to force a love that would not come. I must consider her. She knows that Andrew is not for her; and with time she may come to think of him with more calmness. But it would make the struggle much more cruel if she had at the same time to pretend to care for me, and to know that I saw through it all and was suffering."

"Then what will you do, Rab?"

"I do not know. I cannot stay here and see her. It would be a daily trial to her; it would be bad for myself. Gerard, I dare be bound, can get me shifted to some other station. I must go. But keep little Queen of Love here. There is no one else but me to protect her, and she needs protection from herself. I cannot tell—man is weak, and principles give way. She must be protected also from Andrew."

Rab stood up. The strong man looked as if he had passed through a long sickness; he shook, he seemed haggard. He picked up the withered rose, and folded it again in his pocket-book, and replaced it near his heart. Then he held out his hand.

"Good-bye, Martha."

"Are you going?"

He nodded.

"Whither?"

"I cannot tell. My head swims."

XLIII

FRESH TIDINGS

Andrew walked on to Saltwich, his mind occupied by many cares that not only possessed his mind but oppressed his heart. The future before him was dark. Personally he concerned himself very little about the defeat of the scheme which was to have landed him in opulence. He was not ambitious to be rich. His tastes were simple, and he was humble minded. That which touched him to the quick was the ruin in his domestic happiness. There was no prospect of any improvement in his relations to Ada. If she had not been softened by what had happened, bowed to shame by her father's conduct, nothing would avail. Hard and malicious she would remain to the end of the sad chapter of their married life.

Andrew had been accustomed to work as a waller for his living, and to walling he would return. He could earn from fifteen to eighteen shillings per week, and there was the hope before him of rising, like his father, to be an overlooker at forty shillings.

But he was not alone. Alone he would have faced the prospect cheerfully; but, linked to Ada, he saw in it a vista of contrarieties, recrimination, heartburning. He was united to a woman he could never love, and was separated from her to whom still his heart clung.

He dared not allow his mind to rest on Queenie. He dared not make further inquiries about her lest he should excite the jealousy of his wife; if he did seek her and concern himself for her, it must be in secret, with all precaution, as though he were committing a crime. How would his father bear his disappointment? What would he do? Jabez had offended Brundrith too seriously to be taken back into his service, even if Jabez desired it; and that was not probable. In all likelihood "Hammer" Grice would seek a situation in a Northwich or Winsford salt factory; his ability was known, he had a large body of adherents at his back who would urge his claims, and an employer would gratify this party by engaging him; but it would be a severe blow to "Hammer" to have to leave a town where he had been a figure of so much consequence and to have to beat out for himself a career elsewhere. Elsewhere there were to be found other men, positive, self-assertive, who would not step aside to make way for the newcomer.

The young heart is rarely hopeless. Its sky, however dark, is not without a glimpse of the blue. But to Andrew there was no lightening of the shadows, no gleam to lure him on.

As Andrew walked through the forest, he had no eyes for the wild nature that surrounded him—contrary to his wont, which was to rejoice in all that was fresh and beautiful. A squirrel watched him with bright eyes, and gathered from his manner that it need apprehend no danger from him; it therefore disdained to abandon the cone it was shredding for the seeds. Crows croaked; he had no ear for their harsh notes. Yellow leaves strewed the road, as though it had been strewn with gold. In the Norse legend, the flying hero, escaping the treachery of the Swedish king, scattered bezants in his way as he rode from Upsala, and his pursuers halted to collect them. So was the flying sun scattering autumn gold over every path by which he withdrew.

On reaching the little inn where he had slept on a previous visit to Delamere, Andrew entered and asked for bread and cheese, and found the same two men seated there as he had seen and listened to on the former occasion. And, precisely as before, so now did the ill-humour of their wives, and their own indifference to it, form the seasoning of their conversation.

Again Andrew listened and wondered, as he had wondered before, at the bluntness of the feelings of these fellows, who could go on, year by year, enduring their domestic miseries, perhaps wantonly provoking them, and always bearing them with light heart. Was drink the panacea for such evils? Did it deaden the nerve that it no longer felt acute pain? Andrew mused, sighed, paid for his simple meal and left.

On reaching Saltwich, Andrew's way led past the paperhanger's shop. He found Mr Poles at his door, in conversation with Mr Nottershaw and Mrs Rainbow, and, the moment they caught sight of him, they signed to him to join them.

Mrs Rainbow had received a letter from Seth White, who was back in Scarborough. Mrs Rainbow, being unable herself to read, and not being confident of the ability or reticence of her neighbours, was wont, on the receipt of a letter, to apply to Mr Poles to decipher it for her and write the reply. She supplied the paperhanger with eggs and fruit, and she accorded him her custom, when she repapered a bedroom, which was once in fifteen years; and then she purchased of him four pieces at four pence per piece. As she gave him her custom, she considered that she had a right to his services *gratis* in such a matter as the conduct of her correspondence. Mr Poles did not mix freely in the same society as that in which Mrs Rainbow moved, consequently he was not likely to divulge those matters contained in her letters which were not for the public ear.

On receiving a letter, which the postman assured her was for herself, Mrs Rainbow had gone with it to the paperhanger's. John Nottershaw came into the shop just after Poles had read the letter aloud to the lady, and, as it contained matter of importance that concerned Nottershaw, he obtained permission from Rab's mother to give him a sight of it.

Seth White began by informing Mrs Rainbow that, on mature consideration, thinking that the circus was overstocked with male riders and tumblers, he had come to the opinion that it would be advisable for him to strike out a new line for himself. Having made the acquaintance of an optician at Scarborough, he had arranged with this man for the loan and ultimate purchase of a telescope. With this glass Seth stationed himself on the Parade. During the day he invited the loungers to look through it at some steamer or coal-barge that was passing, at a penny a peep; at night he was ready to exhibit the crater on the lunar disc, the rings of Saturn, the red spots on Mars, the satellites of Jupiter.

Seth enlarged on his prospects. If the sky remained tolerably clear, he was able to reap a harvest of pence in an evening. He sent his respects to Queenie, and his assurance that it was "Hup with circus riding, at all events for men. But 'an'some gals could do middlin'!" He added that there were more competitors for a vacant place than ever, and "accidenks," which provided vacancies, were fewer than in the good old days. He sent his regards to Rab, and hoped he was doing well. Then this marvellous effusion proceeded—we copy it with all its grammatical errors:—

By the waye, if you seez Misteer Andru Grise, you give, him my complermints. I seed 'is wenerable farther-in-lore pass to-day with a dashing feemal on his harm, and 'ee all bedeked with jowls. I persuaded 'im to 'ave a spy throw my glass, and 'ee guv me saxpince. I knowed the hole chap at oncit. I s'pose he's hout on 'is 'unneymoon. 'Ee didn't know me, in corse, and I didn't make that baold to interdooce myself. I knoze my persition.

Mr Button at Scarborough! Mr Button not gone to America! Why— he had announced at his hotel that he was off to New York, and had engaged his berth in the *Caledonia* under a feigned name.

Had he taken the alarm when he saw Poles? or was it all a blind against being followed that he had conceived from the first?

What was to be done?

Nottershaw had not hesitated for a moment after having read the letter. He wired to Seth White:—

Keep eye on Button, and mum's the word. Five pounds reward.

Then he hastened back to Poles, and then it was that he met Andrew Grice returning from the forest.

"Now, then," said the builder, "Andrew, I ain't going to stand no nonsense. I'm off and then I'll have him arrested. It's fraudulent conspiracy. Sorry you've got such father-in-law, Grice, but can't help it—I must get my monies."

"I will go with you," said Andrew. "If we can induce him to refund—and he is sure to have the money with him—you will not take extreme proceedings?"

"I don't care a hang for the man. I want my monies."

"I care for my wife. I must do what I can to save her feelings."

"You'll not give him the hint to slip off?"

"You may trust me, I think, Mr Nottershaw. Besides, it is not to my advantage."

"Excuse me. One is surrounded by rascals. You are right; I know you too well to doubt you."

"I must consider my wife. If you can get him to surrender a fair sum, you will not take further action—we must avoid a scandal."

"I want my monies, not his blood. Let him go with his 'jowls' and his 'dashing feemal' where he likes—through the telescope into Venus, I care naught, and you will be well rid of him."

"Mr Poles," said Andrew, "will you be so good as to run to Button's and tell my father and my wife about my departure. Say I'm off to Scarborough, and add what particulars you like to Ada—except about the dashing female—nothing of that, mind. Spare her all you can."

"We'll tackle the party!" said Nottershaw, rubbing his hands. "Ginger! It will be fun to see him when we come on him and clap him on the back!"

Poles accepted the commission. He was a weak man—too weak to refuse it, and too weak to execute it. He did not tell Andrew to his face that he was indisposed to go to Button's, because he did not like to admit the reasons why he was indisposed. He accepted the commission without serious intention of personally executing it.

Had he been open and declined it, then a whole series of events that will have to be recorded would never have occurred, and the conclusion of this story would not have been what it must be.

Mr Poles did not deliberately undertake to acquaint Grice and Ada with the fact that Andrew had started for Scarborough, with the formed purpose in his mind not to discharge the office that had been pressed on him. Being an eminently weak man, as said, he received the commission with inward repugnance, and a resolve to delegate it to someone else, as opportunity came, or to postpone the communication till it suited his own convenience.

There is more mischief done in the world by weak people than by wicked people. We guard ourselves against the wicked, we are off our guard with the weak.

The reason why Poles was reluctant to take the message to Grice, and why he actually neglected to do so, must be explained in the next chapter.

XLIV

THE BRINE-PAN

JABEZ GRICE WAS UNABLE TO rest after he had heard of the disappearance of Button with the money paid him by Brundrith.

Throughout the day he wandered about the house or grounds. Now and then he entered the factory, examined the works, looked at the wallers, inspected the mill, then came home and pulled out his books, but found himself incapable of fixing his attention on his accounts.

He was beset with difficulties. In the house were the bailiffs. He could not get rid of them if he would. He had not the sum required. He was not bound to pay the drink bill of Tom Button. He could ask no one to relieve him of the annoyance of their presence by advancing the money they demanded. In the interests of morality he sincerely hoped the spirit merchants might not be able to recover the sum owed them.

If the vexation of the presence of these two men had fallen heavily on Ada, Jabez might have reconciled himself to it; but she had retired to her room, and left it for her meals only. She would not enter the kitchen where they sat; she refused to hold communication with them, even to see them. She maintained before her father-in-law a cold indifference of manner that irritated him, because he was himself in agitation of mind and soul.

Grice needed money for current expenses. He knew very well that he would have to leave Button's. A couple of months ago he had possessed savings in the bank; but he had withdrawn every penny, and now had nothing to fall back on, nothing to maintain him till he found work elsewhere.

Jabez had jumped at one resolution, and to that he held fast. He would separate from Andrew. His son was cumbered with that woman Ada, and "Hammer's" eyes flared whenever he thought of her. The single alleviation to his distress lay in the consideration that now he would be able to shake himself free from association with Ada. Andrew was married and bound to her—not he. Andrew was a fellow with some good in him, but as he was fettered to that woman, "Hammer" must free himself from one as well as the other.

If Andrew chose to make his peace with Brundrith, let him do so; but he, "Hammer," would never stoop to express regret for the past and to ask a favour for the future.

He shrank from leaving Saltwich, where he was esteemed and followed. But what was he to do? To return to the drudgery of work under an employer was repugnant to his pride. He had lifted himself out of the artisan class; if he could help it, he would not drop back into it again. Was a fortune to be found only at the bottom of a shaft? Was Button's the only sphere in which his abilities might win him riches and renown? Jabez had a long and shrewd head, and he had looked about him whilst employed on Brundrith's works. He had had other schemes floating before his eyes, and the only difficulty which had occurred as a stumbling-block in the way of starting these schemes had been lack of capital. One of his schemes was connected with the water-carriage on the Weaver Canal. At the time it was conducted by isolated individuals, men who owned each his "flat" or barge, and who acted independently. He was satisfied that an organised service of barges to carry the salt down to the mouth of the Mersey would be of immense advantage to the manufacturers, and would absorb or displace individual venture. Whoever succeeded in this scheme would make his fortune.

All that was required, as a start, was capital for the purchase of several "flats," and the engagement of men to work them, that would form a nucleus certain to expand. Happily, through his own foresight, everything had not been lost. Queenie's little capital was safe. Why should he not remove it from its present investment, and employ it for his new venture? That would not be cheating his ward. Brundrith would almost certainly desire immediately to free the estate from its charge. He, Grice, would pay her four and a-half per cent interest out of the profits. He would begin in a small way, gradually crush out all the little men, establish a monopoly, and become as wealthy by this means as he might have become on the salt venture. He resolved on no account to take Andrew into partnership, not that he bore him a grudge, but lest Ada should reap some advantage by it, be made well-to-do, comfortable, happy. She deserved to suffer mortification and poverty on account of the dishonesty of her father.

Some fine day in the future he would drive by the red brick cottage in which she and Andrew "pigged it," as Grice said to himself, and he would laugh to observe her haggling with Mrs Rainbow over the price of a peck of potatoes, or shaking the mats on the doorstep.

Suppose he made a fortune! He would leave it all to the missionaries, or to found a chapel—not to Andrew, lest Ada should enjoy it. Hatred of his daughter-in-law, the outcome of wounded pride, was now the strongest passion animating "Hammer"; it oozed up between the joints of all his thoughts; it entered into and poisoned all his expectations. Then his mind turned to Phineas Poles, the sheep-faced—an intimate friend, as far as intimacy can exist between one who commands and another who is commanded.

Poles was credited with being well off. He had no family, lived in a modest way, subscribed liberally to charities, did much business in various ways, in and around Saltwich, and must, accordingly, have made money. If he had made it, he must have laid it by. It was owing to this, as much as to his perfect respectability, that Mr Poles was put forward as a man of prominence in the serious world. His sheepish face proclaimed his guilelessness; his comfortable little property assured him regard; his contracted intellect qualified him to follow a leader with docility.

If Grice had controlled the opinions of Poles in matters religious, political, philanthropic, educational and sanitary, it was probable that he would have little difficulty with him in negotiating a loan on so sound a security as the mortgage.

Accordingly, Jabez resolved on applying to Phineas, not in an obsequious, apologetic manner, as soliciting a favour, but haughtily, as conferring a favour.

Poles, undoubtedly, had made money. It must have come in through several channels; and though only as a dribble through some of them, yet a combination of dribbles makes an abundant stream. All mighty rivers are, in fact, but the combination of confluent dribbles.

Poles hung paper, and supplied the papers; he painted, he plumbed, he framed pictures and sold them; he illuminated addresses in the Old English characters; he even heraldically decorated carriage panels. He sold valentines and funeral mementos. Recently he had added to his business the disposal of wickerwork baskets.

The public reckoned that Mr Poles made money by all these means. It was known that at his breakfast he never went beyond a rasher, and at his dinner a chop or steak—that he was very economical about his clothes—never eating anything fatty without pinning himself about with napkins. He spent very little money, therefore he saved a great deal. Rumour set him down as a capitalist.

Jabez sought him in his shop.

"How do you do, Phineas?"

"Middlin', thanky, Jabez. Got an elongation of the uvula and a hirritation of the glottis; I've gargled alum and cayenne but have not been relieved. Would you condescend to look down my throat and pass an opinion? Dr Birch recommends that the uvula should be snipped, and a slice taken from the tonsils; they are enlarged and ulcerated. Do, please, look. Sorry about this affair of Button."

"It is touching that I have come."

"My dear life, you don't say so!"

"That scoundrel, Tom Button, has sold house, land, factory, everything to Brundrith, and has bolted with the proceeds; that you know—but what you do not know is that I have three thousand pounds secured on it by mortgage."

"I'm glad to hear it. I feared all was gone."

"It is safe as the Bank of England, and I want you, Poles, to take over the mortgage and find me upon it the money I want."

"You are sure it is safe? After Button's bolt—nothing seems safe."

"There is the land. Brundrith has it. Brundrith has taken it burdened with the mortgage. You can't lose a penny. I won't deal with Brundrith; we are not on good terms."

"Have you the mortgage with you?"

"Here it is. Look it over."

Poles perused the deed with attention.

"Three thousand pounds," said he. "But would you first look down my throat; the uvula is like a bell-rope, it tickles me, and I can't think of any thing through the irritation."

"Presently. But you will take the mortgage?"

"And the glottis—Dr Birch says it is pink as a cherry."

"You will furnish me with the money?"

"My dear Jabez! All my money is locked up in house property. I couldn't do what you propose, not till my throat was better; and I couldn't sell house property right off on end. Do you pass your opinion on my tonsils."

This conversation took place some hours before Poles read the letter of Seth White to Mrs Rainbow. Now it may be guessed why Mr Poles shrank from going to Button's. He knew that he was irresolute and weak. He knew how resolved and strong Grice was. He feared lest, in another interview, Grice should over-persuade him, and force him to find the money with which he was reluctant to part. When he had received the commission,—

"Dear, dear!" said Phineas, "the evening chills are bad for sore throats. I'll see; if anyone comes this way, I'll send him; but it might prove fatal for me with my elongated uvula to breathe the night air, impregnated with the savour of the fall of the leaf. I'll not be going to Button's till tomorrow, but I'll send if I have the opportunity. Grice is an overpowering man, and after this affair of Tom Button, one can't be too cautious."

When "Hammer" Grice returned to Button's, Ada met him at the door with the question,—

"Where is Andrew?"

"How can I say," answered Jabez; "you must ask someone else."

"Someone else!" exclaimed Ada; "you insult me!"

"I don't understand you."

"I know very well whom you mean by Someone else. It is that Someone else who takes him away from me when I am in trouble, when the house is in an upset, when I have lost my father, when ruin stares me in the face—and you connive at his desertion."

"I do not pretend to fathom your hints and sneers."

"A fine scandal this will cause in your solemn and canting world," said Ada with bitterness and heat. "A pretty scandal when it gets abroad that pious Grice's pious son is dancing round a circus girl, to the neglect of his newly-married wife."

Jabez stared at his daughter-in-law, and his jaw fell. Was this true? That it was possible, he saw at a glance. It was no secret to him that Andrew was deeply attached to Queenie. Andrew had shown, by the persistence with which he had urged her rights, that he still cared for her. Now that Ada—the hated Ada—was no more desirable as weighted with lands, and plated with gold—was it possible that Andrew meditated breaking the bonds laid on him, and escaping to her whom he really loved?

The thought filled Jabez with dismay. It numbed his brain, it sickened his heart. If this were to happen, then it would prove an almost fatal blow to his moral supremacy in Saltwich. But further—it would mean more than that—that Andrew would block his way in the realisation of his new scheme, would insist that the capital of Queenie was not employed in lighters, invested to Grice's advantage in a manner justifiable, but not perhaps legitimate.

With this new trouble haunting the chambers of his soul, Grice went into the factory.

The day-gang was leaving. The short winter period of light was at an end, darkness was settling down over the land and filling every shed with night, casting shadows over everything that was bright, veiling all forms with a drapery of crape. Jabez Grice went into the store. He lighted a lantern and looked about him. The only men now engaged in the factory were a couple of wallers and a stoker. The shed he was in was empty of hands. He looked at his rotator and mill—the invention that was to have brought him so much money, but which now would grind wealth for Brundrith. His heart glowed within him, glowed with resentment against every one and everything—against Andrew for this new scandal, against Poles for not coming to his aid, against Ada for the many humiliations to which she had subjected him, against the spirit merchant for putting the bailiffs into the house, against Tom Button for his rascality, against Brundrith for having reaped where he had sown. Looking at his machine, this last consideration for a moment prevailed over his other resentments. He snatched at a long handled hammer, set down the lantern, and with mighty blows beat to pieces every part of the mechanism that he could reach, and which he was capable of destroying. The sweat ran off his brow. His teeth were clenched, his breath came in snorts through his distended nostrils. In a quarter of an hour he had shattered or disabled machinery that had cost hundreds of pounds to construct. If it had been possible he would have effaced every indication of the method whereby the object aimed at was attained. Then, panting with exertion, his head reeling with excitement, he cast the hammer on one side, snatched up the lantern, strode through the stove-room, where the intense heat struck him in the face like a fire-blast, dried up the moisture streaming from his pores, and shrivelled his hair, and next moment he threw open the door into the wych-house and entered. The steam rolled in his face and blinded him. In his intoxication of resentment, without considering why he was there, without forethought, without purpose, he strode forwards, tripped on the rib that edged the hurdles, and in a moment went over, with the lantern in his hand, into the pan of boiling brine.

XLV

A MAN OF SALT

No cry for help broke from the man in falling. No shriek of agony was heard when he went into the scalding fluid.

The brine-pans were attended by two wallers, one on each side, holding wooden rakes. One of these saw Grice stumble and pitch into the vessel, and he screamed to his fellow for aid.

Jabez had fallen his length in the shallow pan—no pan exceeds eighteen inches in depth. He at once staggered to his feet. The hand that held the lantern had not been submerged. Instead of relaxing his hold of it, the spasm of pain had made him grip the metal ring more firmly. Bewildered, enveloped in steam, Grice was battling with the boiling waves, plunging forward into the middle of the pan, wading further up it, towards the furnace.

The wallers called to him, but he did not hear; signed to him, but he did not see. He reeled in his agony, went down on his knees, was up again, and then, caught by the men's rakes was dragged to the edge, along with a salt scum that formed a foam about him, and was drawn out into the "stand-inside," then further upon the "hurdles." The hot brine that ran off his sodden clothes—the hot cloth itself—scalded the arms and hands of the men as they heaved him out of the pan.[1] Then

the wallers shouted for the stoker, Robert Gelley, who was below, at
the fire under the pan. He came up at a run. The three together lifted
Grice in their arms, carried him into the store, and leaned him against
some loaves of salt.

"Cut along, Jim! run for a doctor," said one of the wallers to his
mate.

"It is useless," said Grice. "I've seen a score go in, and none recover.
I want no doctor."

He paused and raised an arm. Already the salt was crystallising on the
sodden sleeve, and as he lifted his arm the cloth cracked.

"Go to the house," he ordered; "bid them come—whoever are
there—Andrew, if back, and Wilkes."

Jim departed.

Gas had not been introduced into the factory. The distance from
Saltwich, and the precipitation with which the works had been started,
had prevented this being done. Consequently, the factory was lighted
with lamps. There was no lamp in the storehouse, as this was not
occupied by workmen during the night. The stoker unhitched a lamp
from the wall of the wych-house, and brought it where Grice lay, for
the lantern emitted but a feeble glimmer through its smoked sides, over
which, moreover, salt was forming like frost leaves on a window pane.

Sam Verdin, the waller, and Robert Gelley, the stoker, were alone
with the parboiled man. Jim had gone to summon his relations. They
fetched bags of table salt that had been ground in the mill of Grice's
invention, and arranged them under his shoulders and head. He would
not allow himself to be laid prostrate. He insisted on being given a
sitting posture, but with an incline backwards. When he was made as
easy as was possible,—

"Verdin!" said Grice, "you know me; you have been with me these
fourteen years. Now, it's a dying man speaks to you; it's no use holding
out hopes; I know there are none. There can be none to him as has
gone into a pan. I've seen many cases. I have an hour, perhaps I have
two—not more—nor shall I be conscious all of that time. So I must
make haste—haste with what I have to say. No doctor on earth can help,
can prolong life, can lessen my pain. It's up with me. There's one or two

things I care for before I go. My call has come, and I'm not afraid. I'm ready. I have been ready for my call forty years. I've been a leader and a light to them as sat in darkness. I've been a standard-bearer in Israel. I've been a prophet in Jewry. Now I want you to do one thing for me."

"I'll do it, Grice."

"I'd have you, when scaling your pan, drive the chisel through the bottom in three or four places and damage it all you can. I don't want Brundrith to have all profits out of his bargain. He spoiled my game and I'll spoil his as much as I can. You understand?"

"Yes, 'Hammer.'"

"Stay," said Jabez, "when I think on it, I know of a better way. When the brine is all evaporated, let Robert keep his fires up furious, mass on the burgey, make the draught strong that the bottom of the pan may become red hot; then, Verdin, you can drive holes through with ease and riddle it well with a crowbar."

The two workmen looked in each other's faces and signed to each other. What they said without words was, "Humour him, consent, but darn us if we do it."

Jabez remained silent for a few minutes, contending with his anguish. Then he continued:—

"There's something better than this that I lay on you as a dying man's injunction. You two fellows cut or unfasten the nuts and clamps that hold up the pump on the beams; let it fall down the shaft, and it will sink into the brine-run. That will spoil the shaft for ever. Brundrith will never be able to get it up; I doubt if he can put another down in the same place. It will be a damage to him of a thousand pounds. You'll do that for me?"

"Yes, Grice."

At this moment Wilkes entered. He was greatly agitated and alarmed.

"Jabez! Good gracious! This is too horrible! I hope—I hope and pray you have not been gravely scalded."

"Gravely!—about as gravely as may be. Thanks be—my head did not go under water."

"Jabez!—you suffer."

"Of course I suffer. A chap don't get into boiling brine and come out without pain."

"I've sent for the doctor on Ada's horse."

"It's a waste of money. I have not an hour's life left in me."

Wilkes signed to the two workmen to withdraw. The men obeyed, retreating to the door of the stove-house, where they remained within call, but out of earshot, talking in whispers.

"Jabez, old fellow," said Wilkes, "this is a terrible affair; if it be as you say, and as I fear, no time is to be lost. You must prepare for the great change."

"I've been prepared these forty years."

"Yes, old fellow, in a general way; but have you nothing of which to repent?"

"Repent! What do you mean? Repentance is not for such as me I had done with that forty years ago."

"I mean—have you committed no wrong to anyone, acted in any way wrong, anything for which to be sorry?

"Sorry! I!—committed wrong? I! I am one of the Elect. I can do no wrong. I have done only what is right and good these forty years. I am sealed." Then, with a gesture of impatience, "This ain't the sort of comfort you should give. You've been going back to the weak and beggarly elements for some time, Ezekiel."

"But, surely, Jabez—how about Queenie Sant—and her money?"

"Her money!" repeated "Hammer," slightly raising himself and staring round.

He saw Ada enter. She stood startled, awed and cold, looking at her father-in-law with stony eyes, and without uttering a word.

"Her money!" "Hammer" turned his head from Ada to Wilkes. "Yes; I am glad you spoke of that. It might have escaped me. Queenie's money. When I am gone, Andrew will step into my place as trustee. He will be responsible for her money. Wilkes, keep your eye on him. Though she is not akin to you, you take an interest in her. Look after her concerns."

"You may be sure I will do that."

"Yes, do so, lest Ada get any advantage out of Queenie's money. Do not let Andrew make use of the money so as to advance himself and make *her* position"—he looked round at Ada—"make her position more tolerable. Take care that he invests the money so as not to be of any use to himself, lest *she*"—he again looked at Ada—"lest she get more comforts than she deserves. Do not let him borrow it so as to extricate himself out of temporary difficulties he may be in. Do not allow him to speculate with it"—again he glanced at Ada—"lest the speculation should succeed, and *she* be lifted out of beggary. Mind that!"

He drew a heavy breath that rattled in his chest, and he righted his head on the bags. He could not raise it; his hair was stuck to the canvas by salt. Although his head had not gone under water, yet the brine, spirting about as he fell and as he floundered, had dropped on his hair and wetted it. The moisture now evaporated and the brine crystallised, and in crystallising had sealed his dark hair to the bags on which his head reposed.

A strange and ghastly transformation had come over the man as the brine dried on his clothes. First there ran over him a pallid tinge as though he were being covered by a growth of mildew. Then the whiteness intensified, and every particle of his clothing which had been immersed or was splashed was covered with a film of salt like the formation of rime, then became more dense, so as to resemble a powdering of snow.

The dark fringe of hair that encircled his face, running from his cheekbones under his chin, was frosted; it changed from black to white, as though, with the deadly pangs he endured, his hair was bleaching.

"Ezekiel Wilkes, Sam Verdin, Robert Gelley, Jim—all!" said Jabez, "I'm going fast out o' this vale of misery and rascality into the blessed land of Total Abstinence from everything as I don't approve of, where there are no public-houses, no skipping-ropes, no butterflies nor vanities, no spangles, no tight-rope dancing and no circuses, where" —he tore his hair from the bags, as he forcibly raised his head and glared at his daughter-in-law,—"and where there are no Ada Buttons." He let his head fall again. "I'm going to that blessed land from out of which I shall look as from a window and see my enemies burning, burning—for ever and ever, Amen! I have done."

He clenched his teeth. His solid jaw set like a steel rat-trap. His heavy brows contracted to a frown, and his face became scarlet. His eyes

looked straight before him, and a glaze came into the irises, as though
the salt had entered them also, and was frosting and obscuring them.

His bosom laboured, he breathed heavily, nosily. Wilkes spoke to
him, but received no answer. Not a cry, not a moan escaped his set lips.
How great was the anguish he endured might be conjectured, but could
not be gathered from any token he gave. Strong, resolute, dauntless the
man had been through life, he was strong, resolute, dauntless in death.
Gradually his breathing became more difficult. So little token of life did
he give, that Sam whispered to Jim,—

"He's asleep."

Then Ada, looking deadly white, withdrew silently, and as she opened
the door to escape witnessing the last scene, the surgeon entered.

As the waft of cold air swept through the shed and blew over the
face of the sufferer, he snorted—defiantly it seemed, as though about
to encounter a political or religious antagonist, and then the whiteness
that was spread over his clothing extended also to his features, the
rigidity of his garments communicated itself to his muscles. The heavy
jaw fell, as though he were opening his mouth to command attention,
and then stiffened. The contracted brows set hard in their contraction.
Wilkes, who had passed his arm under the back of his brother-in-law,
withdrew it with a sigh.

Jabez Grice had passed into the World of Great Surprises, where the
first and greatest surprise that awaits man is the vision of himself, not as
he supposed believed himself to be, but as he REALLY IS.

1. The reader will hardly credit the particulars of this struggle in the
    boiling brine, and what ensues. The writer gathered them on the spot
    from an eye-witness of similar accidents.

XLVI

A TERRIER

ADA HAD WITHDRAWN FROM THE salt store to avoid the last scene, and had returned to the house. She did not enter it immediately; she halted moodily on the doorstep.

Ada had entertained no affection for her father-in-law. She was shocked at the accident—in her cold fashion she pitied the man for his sufferings—but she said to herself she could render no assistance; the sight of her incensed the dying man, and, therefore, she were better away. With his last words, he had shown that resentment against her rankled in his heart, unsubdued by the pangs his body endured. She was no hypocrite to feign love and regret for a man who had disliked her, and who had been repugnant to herself. But now came the consideration. What was she to do? Where was Andrew? She was exposed to every sort of annoyance, and her husband, her proper protector, had chosen to absent himself.

Again she asked, what was she to do?

She was no longer mistress in her own house, which was in the charge of the bailiffs. Jemina was in a condition verging on insubordination; would ask for her wages and depart unless these men were withdrawn. Then, what was she to do? She would not demean herself to cook and bake for these bailiffs; and further, when the dead man was brought into the house, she was wholly unprepared for the novel and unpleasant obligations that might be imposed upon her.

Ada entertained an unreasoning dread of death. She could not endure the thought of remaining in the house, with the corpse, till the funeral. Grice's room was immediately over that in which the meals were served; it adjoined her own, separated from it by a thin plaster partition.

Grice alive had been objectionable, dead he would be intolerable.

Ada had made no friends in Saltwich. There was no one in the neighbourhood whom she could ask to receive her.

By the death of Jabez Grice, and the departure of Andrew, she was left in the society of Wilkes, whom she had offended.

The desertion by Andrew had put her in one of the most desperate predicaments in which she could have conceived herself placed. Her sour heart became more acrid with resentment towards her husband.

Where was he? He had parted in dudgeon, taking offence at some words she had said. No doubt he had gone to Queenie. He concerned himself about Queenie more than about herself. He had taken up Queenie's cause against his father; he had never interfered on his wife's behalf with "Hammer." If he had not gone to her, why was he away so long? Andrew knew that she was in difficulties, and yet he deliberately absented himself.

Not a touch of self-reproach mingled with her meditation. It never occurred to her that she might have so embittered the life of her husband as to have driven him to desperation.

"There they come!" exclaimed Ada as she saw the four men—Wilkes, Sam, Jim and Robert Gelley—issue from the factory and approach the house, bearing the dead Jabez Grice between them. As he was brought nearer he seemed to be a snow man whom they had picked up, and who, on being taken into the house, would dissolve. "I will not remain! I cannot endure this!"

She darted within to be out of the way, and retreated to her own room. In such a house, square as a die, again the fact became obvious that every sound was audible. She heard each step as the bearers carried the corpse up the steep stair; she heard the whispers of the bailiffs and of Jemima, who had issued from the kitchen, and stood watching the scramble of the bearers with their white load up the steep stairs. She heard the bang and creak of the banister as, on the narrow stair, one of the bearers swung himself against it, or leaned heavily upon it in the labour of ascent. She heard each low-breathed word of advice and encouragement spoken by one to the other.

Then ensued the trampling in the adjoining room. She trusted she would not be asked to go in, asked for anything that might be required. Go in she would not. Help she could not directly. She would commit her keys to Jemima, and let her attend to the requirements of Wilkes and the other three.

Then she locked her door.

Presently the men descended.

Remain in that house, divided by a thin partition from the corpse, she would not.

Ada was not superstitious, but she was unacquainted with death. She had never looked in the face of the dead. She was not unaware that she had incurred the animosity of the man between whom and her intervened six inches of lath and plaster. What if he were not dead—if he were in a swoon only? What if, in the stillness of the night, he were to wake up and wander about the house? What if, waking up, he were mad with pain, and in his madness broke into her room to vent on her his resentment? She had locked her door. Ay! but he might break through the plaster. She had heard of such cases as men supposed to be dead coming to life again. What more likely than that, under his suffering, "Hammer" had fainted? He had but to drive his foot against the wall, and laths would fly and plaster fall down. Then he would thrust his hands in and rip and break till he could get his scarlet face through, with the frosty, crystallised hair bristling round it, and then work in shoulders and body, and so reach her, and in his rage and agony rip her as he had ripped the wall.

"I will not stand this! I will not stay here! I will find Andrew!"

In nervous terror, but without her face being more blanched than usual, or any quiver in the muscles of her limbs, Ada put together a few articles in a bag and descended the stair, went into the yard and ordered the boy to harness the cob into the carriage.

Then a bailiff emerged from the kitchen.

"It ain't allowed, ma'am. Nothing may be took away!" He protested with a clumsy apology,—"it ain't me, ma'am; it's my dooty. It's the sperit merchants has had me and t'other chap put in."

Ada was constrained to start on foot for Saltwich. She had formed her resolution what to do. Beulah was the proper person to attend to her dead brother. Beulah was old—had experience. Beulah was the only woman to whom she could turn. She would despatch Miss Grice to Button's, and remain herself over the night at Alma Terrace, and next day go in quest of Andrew. It was all Andrew's fault. He should not have allowed his father to take up his quarters along with him. If Jabez had remained in Saltwich, this would not have happened.

The night was dark, but on nearing Saltwich she came within the circuit illumined by gas lamps. First she reached some hideous cottages, built of burnt slack—hard, black cinders—with red brick facings. Then came the town itself, of smoked and soiled red brick.

Ada stood at a fork, where one street, that to the right, led to the lower town, and passed the shop of Mr Poles, whereas that to the left led to the upper town, where stood Alma Terrace. At this fork of the ways Ada halted for consideration. She doubted whether to go to Mr Poles or to Miss Grice. She shrank from breaking the news to Beulah. Ada's nerves were in an irritable condition. She was indisposed to witness a scene, and a scene of cries and lamentation, of tears and perhaps hysteria, such as might be expected would occur when Beulah learned that her brother had been scalded to death.

Was it possible for her to escape this? Certainly, she might go to Mr Poles and commission him to inform Miss Grice of her loss. But there was a consideration that militated against this. Poles was a chatterbox; he was sentimental, sympathetic. There would be a mingling of tears, attempts at consolation, and much time wasted, whilst Ada remained at the shop and wearied herself with looking at the patterns of wall-papers there. Also, Mr Poles might forget to inform Beulah that she—Ada—intended to remain the night at Alma Terrace.

As Ada stood irresolute, she observed a little terrier, that had lost its master, also standing at the fork, and as irresolute as herself. A gaslight was burning there, and she could see the animal distinctly. It was whining. It ran a little way down the right-hand street, then retraced its steps with a piteous note, and snuffed the air, then the ground on the left-hand turning.

Ada stepped forward. The dog saw her, looked back and snarled. She had not touched it or attempted to touch it. It barked at her, showed its teeth, then revolved and again questioned in which direction it should seek its master.

The comical little dog cocked up his ears, his tail wagged, not with pleasure, but with nervous query, and with sharp jerks he turned his head from one direction to the other, then started, shook himself, whimpered, dropped his little black nose, set it up again and danced on his small paws.

All at once Ada heard a whistle. The terrier also heard it, and with a short, joyous bark scampered down the right-hand street. He had heard, seen, his master issue from Mr Poles' shop. The master waited for the dog, and then went into the paperhanger's shop again, taking the terrier with him.

"Very well," said Ada. "That settles matters. If there's a man with Poles, I'll go the other way. After all, it does not matter much."

How often in life's journey do we come to points where ways diverge, and we stand in indecision as to which course to pursue. There is nothing to determine our election. One road presents as much or as little attraction as the other. Yet an election must be made, and eventually we discover that the whole tenor of our after life depended on the selection—a selection made with eyes blinded to the consequences.

There was, however, a reason why Ada should have chosen the left-hand course which led to Alma Terrace, for, had she possessed good feeling, she would have known that it was her place to gently break the shock to Beulah. Had she turned to the left, inspired by this feeling, it would not have altered the course of events, but it would have modified our view of her character, and have awoken some pity for her.

Had she not gone to the left, but followed the right-hand road, she would have entered the paperhanger's shop and have learned from him that Andrew had gone to Scarborough, and that it would, therefore, have been in vain for her to seek him in Delamere Forest.

The terrier, having lost his master, was the occasion of her selecting the left-hand road. Had he not stood whining and snapping there, she would not have known that Poles was engaged with a stranger, and would have sought his intervention.

Poles had not taken the message, for the reasons already given, but he had told Mrs Nottershaw, who passed, and he trusted that, in a roundabout way, the tidings would reach Jabez and Mrs Andrew Grice. Having done this, he felt himself absolved from further obligation.

Ada was thus left in complete ignorance as to the reasons which had determined Andrew's absence, and was ignorant as well whither he had gone.

Before entering No. 4 Alma Terrace, she had resolved not to tell Beulah the worst, but to say that Jabez had been badly scalded, and that the presence of his sister was urgently needed. This would precipitate Beulah's departure.

She, accordingly, adopted this line with Miss Grice, professed that she knew no particulars, and had come off at once to urge her to proceed to her brother without a moment's delay.

"I will remain here," said Ada. "You will have to spend the night at Button's, and I will occupy your room until your return."

Then Miss Grice departed.

Ada made herself comfortable, and slept soundly.

Next morning she locked the house, put the key in her pocket and started for Delamere Forest. The Watling Street that passed the entrance to Button's led into the forest, but Delamere extended in another direction as well—it enfolded Saltwich on the north and west, and she knew that Rab's dwelling lay in the direction at right angles to the Watling Street, and was to be reached by quite a different way.

She supposed that Queenie was either with Rab, or with his sister. She recalled the invitation he had given to the girl on the night on which she, Ada, had locked the girl out.

"Where Queenie is," said Ada, "there Andrew will be."

What she would say to her husband did not trouble Ada; she would find suitable words when they met. She had cowed and crushed her father and her father-in-law, and would find no difficulty in quelling

Andrew. Jabez Grice was a man of iron, yet he had been subdued by her. Andrew was malleable and pliable; she would do with him what she chose. He had not power to resist her.

She did not know where Rab's cottage was, and she went towards Mrs Rainbow's house to inquire, but found the same terrier at the door, and the little dog barked and snarled at her again.

"No!" said Ada, "I will not inquire of his mother. Anyone else will be able to tell me where he is."

Again her ill fate pursued her. Dick Gerard had come in to see his mother-in-law and bring her a message from Martha. It was he who had been in the shop of Mr Poles the previous evening.

Had Ada gone into Mrs Rainbow's, she would have heard what she wanted to know concerning Andrew.

For the second time the little dog served to alter her determination. The master of the dog was in Mrs Rainbow's shop. She considered that, when alone with Mrs Rainbow, it would have been difficult to ask for the habitation of the ex-poacher without giving a reason for wanting to know where it was; it would be impossible for her to do so before a stranger.

Thus, a second time, Fate, with a drawn sword, stood in her way and kept her from taking that course in which lay her sole chance of safety. By her own determination, formed on the slenderest reason, and without in the least perceiving the importance of her decision, Ada elected to do that which led to—But we must not anticipate.

XLVII

ONE MAGPIE

EVERY PERSON, IN HEATHENDOM, KNEW Rab Rainbow. Ada found no difficulty in obtaining the direction she required. It was one thing to ask in a casual manner where was his cottage, and to make that inquiry in the street; another to enter his mother's house and formally inquire there.

The inmates of Heathendom were a frank, garrulous people, fond of airing their opinions; the mention of Rab's name set tongues wagging.

Some good women rejoiced that Rab was a converted character, and that without the intervention of preachers and amid the excitement of a revival. A man said that he was gone stupid. A poacher could always make on an average his seven shillings and sixpence a day, whereas an under-keeper got but half a-crown, which proved that Rab was stupid to the tune of five shillings *per diem*.

Ada took the road that had been indicated to her.

The way led between fields on the outskirts of the forest. Before her lay the gold-green sea of Delamere, the deciduous foliage yellowed by frost. She had no eye for Nature, no feeling for the beautiful, and she regarded nothing that lay before or around her, till a magpie rose, flew a little way ahead, and lighted.

"One for sorrow! Jabez Grice is dead. Bad for Beulah!"

Then she returned in thought to the misdeeds of Andrew.

Imagination plays tricks with men; it runs riot in the brains of women. She saw Andrew with Queenie, looking at her with enamoured eyes, telling her how unhappy his wife made him; how she affronted his father, engaging Queenie's sympathy for himself, intensifying her dislike for Ada, speaking of his wife with sneer and ridicule, finally declaring his purpose to leave her; he had married her for land and money; now that land and money were no longer hers, he would sever the connection.

"There is that magpie still!"

Ada walked fast. When the mind is in combustion the limbs move swiftly. At last she reached Rab's cottage. The walk had occupied a long time, but it had been one to brace the nerves and exhilarate the spirits, had not her brain been in a ferment and her heart overcharged with ill humours.

After a careless knock delivered at the door, without waiting for a summons to enter, Ada stepped inside. Rab was within, at his fire, cooking a rasher of bacon. He looked up in surprise, but did not desist from his occupation.

"This is Rab Rainbow's cottage?" asked Ada.

He nodded.

"And you are Rab Rainbow?"

"This is my house, and I am he. What do you want?"

"I am Mrs Andrew Grice of Button's. You have doubtless heard of me?"

He nodded, and continued to fry his rasher, looking into the fire.

Ada waited for a word. He gave her none. Then she raised her tone to one of sharpness.

"This is not Cheshire courtesy nor Cheshire hospitality. I have walked all the way from Saltwich to see you."

"No—not me."

"I have come to ask you a question—to obtain information which you can give me." She seated herself. "You have not offered me a chair. I will take one. I am very tired. Moreover, I am hungry with my walk.

Give me some food, and I will pay you. It may be some time before I get back to Saltwich."

Rab rose somewhat surlily and put the rasher on a plate. Bread, steel fork and knife were already on the table. So were a glass and a jug of water.

"There!" said he, "eat."

Then he returned to his place by the hearth, took his knee in his hands and looked broodingly into the red embers.

"Will not you eat also?" asked Ada.

"Not with you."

He remained in the same position, without speaking. He paid no attention to the guest who had forced herself on him, till he heard her rap the pitcher with a coin to attract his notice.

"I have eaten. Here is a shilling," she said; "now, perhaps you will be more gracious and speak with me."

He looked at her with a lowering brow, and when he rose, roughly thrust back her hand, then changed his mind and said,—

"Yes; I will give you nothing; let me have the shilling. There is no hospitality where coin passes from hand to hand."

"Do you object to offer me hospitality?"

"Yes!" Then—"What do you want? You did not come here for me."

"I have come to know where Queen Sant, the circus girl, is. I believe you can tell me."

"She is with the Gerards."

"Who are they?"

"Martha Gerard is my sister. Dick Gerard is a head ranger. She is well where she is."

"Do you often see her?"

"Yes."

"And others—has she other visitors?"

"She has not many friends, but some enemies."

"Enemies! A person must have some significance to have enemies. I would not have supposed a poor tight-rope and horseback jumper could have been of sufficient importance for anyone to think of her with love or with hate."

"You are wrong. She has those who love her—"

"*Those!*" repeated Ada with emphasis. "Oh yes! she has plenty of lovers. An easy, loose minx!"

"Take care what you say!" shouted Rab; he snatched up his stool. "I swear I'll kill you if you say a word against her."

"So—you are one of her lovers!"

Rab, looking from under his bushy brows, answered,—

"And you—one of her haters."

Ada tossed her head contemptuously.

"I'm sorry," he said, "you are the one an' only person in this world as does, as can hate her—and you because you have a deadly, evil heart."

Ada was incensed, darkness formed in her cheeks—no red came there, shadows only. She said with a sneer,—

"You do not care that she has many lovers."

"I do not deny it," he answered—"that she may have many; she is welcome to have many to love and admire her. The sun has every flower, every bird, every insect to look up to it and love it. But she—the Queen of Love—has no thought of any save one."

"Of you?"

He drew his stool to the fire, poked the embers about with his foot and did not answer.

"Of you?" repeated Ada eagerly.

"No!" he answered; "no, not of me."

"And you endure this!" exclaimed Ada, folding her arms and standing before him, every muscle in her frozen face set hard as steel. "You—with your gun—you allow this! You men, you are weaker than we women are; you—a ranger—you, a fellow that was a poacher—you admit a rival! You suffer him to step between you and your game! I snap my fingers at you—milk-sop!"

"What! would you have me shoot him? Do you know *whom* she hangs to with heart and soul?"

He looked her steadily in the eyes, and she met his gaze firmly at first, then a quiver came in her lids, and she lowered her eyes.

"No!" said Ada in a low tone. "No, I do not say kill him; but why do you suffer another to stand in your way? Why do you not go in and capture the object of your affection? When she is yours, then that other one you speak of will not dare to come near your house; if he should venture to prowl around, then I give you leave to shoot him, as you would a fox that sought to rob your fowl-house. Make her your own. She is worth it. She has money."

"I care not for her money."

"You care for herself—for her doll's face and wig of yellow hair?"

"You are right there. I love her for herself."

"She is not insensible to you. I know it."

"How can you know that?"

"She was in my house. She told me as much."

"That is a lie; she never said it, least of all to you."

"You are very insolent."

"I owe you no civility; you drove her out of your house."

"She left—she had too many lovers."

"Take care! You lie!" Rab clenched his hands and approached her threateningly. "You slanderous, cruel devil!"

Then the rage, the hate in Ada's heart flared up in one blinding flash before her eyes; it dissolved all her coldness, it overcame all the caution, and it revealed the full malignity of her heart.

"You—you are a man. Ruin her, cast her off—rid me of her as you see fit—only keep her out of the way of my husband, Andrew."

Rab drew a long breath that hissed between his clenched teeth.

"So! that is what you desire! You have come here to say that to me—to me. You, who hate the Queen of Love, you say that to me who reverence, who love her above the light o' day. You shall come with me and see her again—once again—her whom you bid me—"

He seized her wrist and drew her from his door.

"You need not drag me along as a prisoner. I go voluntarily. I desire to see her."

"She is at my sister's house."

"And is Andrew there also?"

"Come and see."

As they issued from the house, a magpie—perhaps the same Ada had seen before, probably another—rose and flew before them.

"Again—one magpie!" she said.

XLVIII

ROARING MEG AGAIN

Dick Gerard sat in the window bay of his house with his crippled darling on his lap. Before her was a table on which she had arranged acorn cups, and an acorn converted into a miniature teapot by the insertion of a tiny bit of stalk as spout, and another bent in a bow to serve as handle. On a dry oak leaf were some grains of sugar, on another crumbs of bread. Opposite the infirm child crouched Queenie on her knees; she was invited to tea with Jessie, to eat some cake and sip tea out of the acorn cups. Queenie was a child as truly as Jessie. The latter was the youngest by some years, but she had been aged by pain. Queenie had but just begun to enter into the school of privation and responsibility. She was young for her years. She laughed and enjoyed trifling with these woodland toys as much as did Jessie.

"Do you like your tea sweet?" asked the crippled girl.

"Thank you—sugar, please."

"I like sugar too," said Jessie, "but must not take it because of my rheumatism."

Then both girls looked up. Rab had entered along with Ada Grice.

"Oh! my husband is not here!"

Ada looked about her. Her eyes penetrated to every corner of the room, as though expecting to find Andrew secreted somewhere.

The ranger Gerard stood up from the stool on which he had been seated, and gently placed the child in her chair.

"Are you Mrs Grice?" he asked.

Ada nodded.

"My husband, Mr Andrew Grice, has not returned to his home since yesterday morning; in fact, he has disappeared, and we are becoming alarmed. There are matters of extreme urgency demanding his presence. Whilst others are inquiring elsewhere, I came to seek him in this quarter. I thought it possible, just possible, he might—"

"Excuse me, have you not heard?"

"Heard what?"

"That he is at Scarborough."

"My husband at Scarborough!"

"Before leaving Saltwich he asked Mr Poles to let you know that he was called precipitately away."

"But what in the world has taken him to Scarborough?"

Richard Gerard looked a little confused.

"Well, miss—I beg your pardon, ma'am, I mean—he heard that your father was there—Mr Button."

"My father not in America!"

Ada laughed. There was no merriment in the laugh; in its intonation it resembled a sneer.

"He is at Scarborough. Mr Nottershaw resolved on going there after him, and your husband at once determined on accompanying him. He laid it on Mr Poles to see you and explain the cause of his hasty departure."

"Poles has said nothing—I had no idea. But for how long will he be away?"

"That is more than he could tell. My mother-in-law got a letter from an old lodger, now at Scarborough, and in it he said he had seen Mr Button. Thereupon Mr Nottershaw started, and Mr Andrew Grice, for some reason or other, did not like not to be with him; he thought perhaps that Mr Nottershaw would be too sharp with the old gentleman, and seeing Mr Button was your father—"

"I am much obliged to you," interrupted Ada. "This is very astonishing to me; I had no conception of it. Mr Poles has been remiss in his duty. He has occasioned me the greatest possible annoyance and alarm. I thank you. I will intrude no longer. I must hasten home to Button's immediately."

Without a word to Queenie, Ada was leaving the room, but the girl sprang from her seat, ran after her, caught her hand in the porch and detained her.

"May I say a word?"

Ada hesitated, then, with an attempt to disengage her hand, said coldly,—

"I do not think we have anything pleasant to say to each other. I am in haste. I want to get home."

"I will not keep you above a minute," said Queenie. "It is but this. I know that you have been, and that you are, in trouble. I have been told that there has been great loss of money. I am unhappy concerning it. There is my three thousand pounds—you are welcome to a part—if need be, to all of it. I place it at your service. I really do not need it."

Ada looked coldly at her.

"You are under a mistake, or else—you desire to make a cheap show of having a good heart. We are not in trouble. We have had no loss. We may for a moment have supposed that we had, but it is over. My father has plenty of money; he has gone for a change of air for a few days to the seaside. That is all. We cannot think of standing indebted to—to—you. Certainly not to you."

Releasing her hand, Ada signed to Rab Rainbow, and said,—

"Be pleased to show me the shortest way back to Button's, and you shall have a shilling. Hah! there is that magpie again."

As she waited in the porch, Rab stepped before her and said,—

"Have you nothing to ask of the Queen of Love?"

"I?—most assuredly not."

"Not—forgiveness?"

"Forgiveness!"

"Forgiveness for a deadly insult offered her when she was in tears at her father's funeral. Forgiveness for turning her out, friendless and homeless, at night into the world. Forgiveness for a cowardly and cruel blow."

"Oh! she has been whining and telling tales!"

"She has not been whining or telling tales. What I know has been wrung from her 'gainst her will."

"I am in haste, let me pass," said Ada coldly.

"Oh, Rab!" exclaimed Queenie, "do not go back to all that. It is every bit forgiven and forgotten."

"Forgiven by you; not forgotten or forgiven by me," said Rainbow. "Once again, and for the last time, Mrs Grice, will you ask forgiveness for these wrongs done to a helpless orphan? I give you a last chance. Go down on your knees to her."

Instead of answering, Ada thrust past, stepped into the garden and walked through it.

Rab went after her. He said no more, and paced silently on the other side of the road, a step or two ahead of her.

After they had gone some way, this silence became irksome to Ada, and she said haughtily,—

"Why do you not go home? I don't want you."

"I am about to show you the short cut. I expect the promised shilling."

"I forgot. True. I am tired. The distance round by Saltwich is much longer. Go on. You shall earn the shilling."

Ada Grice had not the least suspicion that she was the primary cause of the devastation that had been wrought in the prospects and present happiness of the family at Button's. Yet it was her own indifference to the feelings of her father which had led him to seek comfort elsewhere, and had made him careless for her welfare. She, and she alone, was the cause of the unhappiness of Andrew, and of her own troubled heart. It was true enough that he had not loved her, and that he had loved another when he married her, but he had manfully striven to overcome the passion it was no longer lawful for him to harbour, and he had done all in his power to win his wife's affection and to become himself attached to her. So far from reproaching herself for misconduct, she threw all blame on her father, on Andrew, on Jabez Grice, on Queenie, and now on Rab for not having freed her from annoyance through Queenie. The more bitter her heart was, the wider sweep did that bitterness take in its overflow.

She, walking on one side of the road, silent, and Rab on the other, also silent, had reached a gate. Here the young man halted.

"This is the turning," he said; "here leads the way down Bramble Brook."

At that moment a boy ran up.

"Mr Rainbow," said he, "here is your knife—the knife you gave me for cutting the willow slips. You went away without my seeing you to return it."

Rab took the knife, opened it, closed it again, and returned it to the lad.

"You may take it," he said; "I give it—I shall not want it again."

The boy overwhelmed him with thanks; Rab waved them away.

"Here," he said, "you may do one thing for me in return."

He took his pocket-book from his breast, opened it and drew forth the white sheet of paper that enclosed the withered rose-leaves. With a pencil he wrote something on the paper, then thrust it back into the pocket of the book and handed it to the lad.

"Take that, Fred," said he; "take it at once to the Queen of Love at Gerard's house. Give it to her—give it into her hands and hers alone."

Then he threw open the gate, and, looking gloomily at Ada, said,—

"This is your way."

"Please, Mr Rainbow, Meg is roaring," said the boy.

"Right! I hear her voice. I know what she says. Take the pocket-book and be off."

The lad, skipping with delight at having acquired a strong and serviceable knife, bounded away along the road recently traversed by Rab and Ada.

"This path leads through the fields," said the latter.

"There is right of way," answered he.

"I must rest here a moment," said Ada; "I am dead beat. I have been on my feet all day."

"You will have rest enough soon."

"Yes; if this track cuts off two miles, I shall be home shortly.'

Already the dusk was closing in. The days were very short now. Moreover, a dense mass of cloud, the concentration of the haze that had hung over the land for a couple of days, lay half way up the sky, dark as night, a frown on the face of heaven, a menace of destiny.

"So you write letters to Queenie Sant!" said Ada after a while, with mockery in her tone. "How often do you correspond?"

"I wrote but one word."

"And that?—"

"Farewell."

"Farewell!" exclaimed Ada, and started from the heap on which she had seated herself. "You are surely not going to leave her?"

"I shall see her no more."

"Coward! Fool!" she cried. "You leave the field—you are beaten out of it—and retreat without a blow before—Andrew!"

He did not answer, but strode along through the field.

"Have you not another knife—a knife you can give me; that I may go back and run it into her heart? Tired as I am, I would do that rather than leave her to Andrew, and if you go away she is so left."

Her breath came quick. Rab was walking fast; she kept up with him, running at his side. They had entered the lane. There were high bushes of holly and hazel on each side. In the track between them the soil was wet, the feet plashed in water or sank in mud.

"Do you remember?" said Rab in a low tone, "the day when the Queen of Love's father was buried? Do you recall how you struck the coffin wi' your whip—and what she said?"

"It was an accident," replied Ada.

"But—her words—have they lodged in your recollection?"

Ada shrugged her shoulders.

"It is dirty underfoot, and dark between the hedges here. No; I give no heed to such things."

"I do. She said to you,—'May you never have a coffin, never enjoy Christian burial.'"

"I had forgotten such silly words."

"I have not."

They walked on. The lane descended.

"This is very lonely," said Ada. "What is that noise? Are we near the railway?"

"That noise? Old Meg is roaring."

"Meg? What Meg?"

"Listen!"

Rab halted; so did his companion. They could hear the hissing, spluttering, bellowing of the brine-jet, which had again broken forth, after quiescence, on the hillside down the glen.

"I heard Mr Nottershaw say he had seen it, and also a subsidence somewhere in this part."

"Yes; Meg was not fed then. She is hungry again."

"Fed—with what?"

"A human life. She is clamourin' again. Water don't slake her thirst. Earth and stones don't satisfy her hunger."

"You are leading me the right way?"

Ada was becoming alarmed. The manner of her companion was strange. His words were not reassuring.

"Yes; I'm conducting you the only way that lies open for you and me."

Then she uttered an exclamation. She had lost her shoe in the clay. In the darkness she could not see it.

"That matters not," said Rab. "Here goes my hat—they will tell that we came this way."

"What do you mean?"

"The boy saw us turn down the track."

"What of that?"

"We shall never leave it."

Ada was becoming momentarily more uneasy; would have been exceedingly so had not her attention been distracted from Rab and engrossed in the search for her shoe.

"Rab!" she said, "I cannot walk home barefooted."

"I will carry you," he answered, and, stooping, snatched her up in his arms.

"Let me go—help me to find my shoe."

"Your shoe will tell the way by which we came."

He strode forward a couple of steps, carrying her, then he said,—
"Ada Grice, do you think that we two are two too many?"

"What do you mean? Let me go!"

"I will not let you go. Listen to me as I carry you for'ard."

"I will not be carried further."

"Hearken to what I say, Ada Grice. There are those two, Andrew and
Queenie. They loved each other—they are fitted for each other—they
will never, never be happy apart. But you and I stand in the way. There
is no peace, no joy for them whilst you are the obstacle—and to me no
peace, no joy anyhow. She don't love me; she never will do so. And I—I
could not live to see her happy wi' another."

Again he strode forwards, bearing Ada in his strong arms. She had
been paralysed at first by fear; her alarm augmented with his words.

"You are mad, Rainbow. Let me down on my feet!" she screamed.

"Yes; I am mad—mad with love, mad with despair."

She struggled in his grasp, battling with hands and feet. She
shrieked—in hopes that she might call someone to her assistance.

"Silence!" cried Rab. "Or—if you cry—cry to God and not to
man."

Before them, in the way, lay a black blot, beyond it the hedge was
in motion. The pit that had sunk when Rab had been that way with
Nottershaw was enlarging its dimensions, and, as it did so, the brine
roared forth at the vent lower down the valley.

Now, and now only, did Ada see whither she was being borne; now,
and now only, did a notion of her danger flash through her mind. She
was in the arms of a madman, resolved on self-destruction, resolved on
carrying her to death along with himself. Now, and now only, did she
see the nature of the death that lay before her. In a paroxysm of terror
she thrust her left hand into the hair of Rab; with her right she gripped
his throat. She tossed herself from side to side, she writhed as a serpent
under the foot, she shrieked in ever-sharpening shrillness, and her cries
mingled with the snorting of the brine geyser. In one of her desperate
struggles she almost threw Rab down; he reeled from side to side, lost
his balance, slipped to his knee. She planted her foot on the ground; she

drove his neck back, she tore out his hair, she bit at his hand, and for a moment disengaged herself by her frantic efforts, her terror lending strength, and she ripped herself from his arms.

Then he threw himself forward, caught her by the skirt, gathered her garments in his arms, clutched her with the grip of a vice below her knees and rolled over.

They were at the edge of the abyss—the earth crumbled—it sank under them.

Meg ceased to roar. Meg was satisfied.

XLIX

BONAVENTURA

"DEAR ME! THE *BONAVENTURA*! A screw. Can you see her, my love?"

A gentleman with a pasty face and a stoop in his shoulders was peering through a telescope at a distant vessel passing in the offing. The telescope was on a stand and belonged to a professional show man—in fact, to Seth White.

The gentleman was in a stooping posture. He had both knees bent, and had clapped his open hands on his legs above the knees as he peered through the glass. The attitude was inelegant; but it is open to question whether one that is graceful could have been assumed by a person somewhat stiff in his joints and wearing stays, when engaged on studying a distant object through a telescope.

"*Bona-ventura*," continued the gentleman. As he bowed, his heavy gold watch-chain hung pendulous below his breast and tinkled against his eyeglass. "*Bona* means good—I know so much Latin; and *ventura,* I think, means about-to-come; that is to say, good luck. Let us take it as a good omen that I see the *Bonaventura,* and can read the name through the glass. Do you see her, love? Next week, with good luck, we shall sail to New York."

He addressed a smart woman who stood near the showman.

"*Bona-ventura*—well met! Good luck! we have caught you, Tom!"

A hand was clapped on one shoulder.

"Mr Button, well found!"

A hand was clapped on the other.

The gentleman rose upright as quickly as the stiffness of age and the constraint of a tightly-laced pair of stays would allow him, and looked blankly to one side—and encountered Mr Nottershaw, then to the other and saw his son-in-law, Andrew.

"Now, look here, Tom!" said the contractor, "I ain't going to stand no humbug. You shell out without obliging me to have recourse to the law. I have a warrant in my pocket. There are others beside myself on the alert for you. I don't care a snap for your feelin's, but Andrew is more humane. He comes to induce you to disgorge without making the scandal public."

"Ah, ha, ha!" exclaimed Mr Tom Button, in the tones of a peacock, and extended both his hands. "Glad to see you both! Glad to see you, Nottershaw! 'Pon my soul! And you, Andrew! I was feeling out of sorts. Beulah Grice is a charming woman, but cooks abominably—converts meat to india-rubber—and she upset my digestion. So I run off to Scarborough for a change of air, before winter is quite upon us, and Christmas with its bills and boxes. Glad to see you. Always a pleasure to meet friends, specially when it is unexpected. What brings you to Scarborough?"

"What brings us? You, to be sure!"

"Bless my soul! You don't say so. I didn't know I was a man of so much importance. What is it? Ah! there is to be a testimonial and a dinner to me at Saltwich? or do you want a subscription for a new chapel? But stay—I haven't introduced you to Mrs Button number two."

Button's eyes looked shiftily from side to side. He was searching for a means of escape. There was none. Andrew held him on one side, Nottershaw on the other.

Some time elapsed before Button could be induced to accept seriously the fact that he was caught, and that he would have to make terms with Nottershaw to escape being committed to the custody of the law. He attempted all kinds of evasion of the subject, and would have given his captors the slip had they not kept strict guard on him. In fact, there was clearly no security with Button till Nottershaw had got hold of a certain small portmanteau in the hotel, about which Button seemed to be least solicitous, and on which alone his eyes did not rest with an expression of anxiety. Nottershaw was frank to brutality with the man; he insisted on having his keys, and he examined that particular portmanteau first of all. He had learned, by experience, what was well known to Ada—that Button's words and acts were to be read by contraries.

When nearly the whole of the spoils were in Nottershaw's hands, then, and then only, was old Button amenable to arrangement. With the lightest spirit he bade his fair companion remain at Scarborough till his return, and he put into her hands a little money for present necessities.

"Business—business," said he. "I can't give you more. You see, my dear, I can't; 'pon my word, I can't. I've fallen among thieves, who have stripped me and left me half dead."

Nottershaw was a man of decision.

When Button saw that there was no door open by which he could escape, he resigned himself cheerfully to his situation.

"I'd got tired of honeymooning," said he. "I'm most thankful to you; I shall be eternally thankful to you, John, for delivering me. That woman—she has her fascinations—she held me as a cat holds a mouse. She grows desperate tedious. A man can't dance attendance all day, even on a new wife. I am most obliged to you for coming when you did, and freeing me. 'Pon my word—*bona-ventura*—it was good luck to me. I can't help laughing. It is killing! It is positively killing! Whilst I was looking through the glass at that steamer!"

Nottershaw, having taken possession of Button's money, paid his bill at the hotel, took tickets at the station, and he and Andrew escorted the old fellow back to Saltwich.

"Upon my life!" exclaimed Button, as Saltwich was neared, "I smell the burgey. Never was a bean-field sweeter; the scent is like that of the Garden of Eden to me. How certain smells bring back old times. After all, there is no place like home. Come, sing the chorus to 'Home, Sweet Home' with me; I'll troll out the song:—

'Mid pleasures and palaces tho' we may roam,
Be it ever so humble, there's no place like home.
A charm from the skies seems to hallow us there,
Which, seek through the world, is not met with elsewhere.

Andrew! Nottershaw! roar it out!

Home, home—sweet, sweet home!
There's no place like home!"

Turning to Andrew,—
"How did you leave the lovely Ada? You must be pining, son-in-law,
for the smiles and kisses of your amiable wife."

There was malice in this speech; there was mockery in his song of
"Home, Sweet Home." Andrew's sensitive spirit winced, and the crafty
eyes of old Button observed the pain he had caused.

Surprises of the most thrilling nature came upon Andrew on his
arrival at Saltwich—surprises not only to thrill but to stun. He arrived
at Button's to find his father dead—awaiting burial, and to learn that his
wife was also dead and was buried, having disappeared down the abyss
opened in Bramble Brook Valley. That she and Rab Rainbow had been
lost there admitted of no doubt. He had left the Gerards along with
her to guide her homewards by the short cut which led down Bramble
Brook Glen; they had been seen turning into the field by the gate from
the high road by the boy to whom Rab had given his knife, and her
shoe and Rab's hat had been found near the edge of the hole.

That Rab was aware of the chasm which had opened there and
engulfed the path a few months previously was well known. But on
that same evening on which he took this path, Meg had again spouted,
and the spouting of Meg was a sure token of another subsidence;
indeed, the blowing off of this blast was an effect caused by the falling
in of the crust of the earth over a subterraneous cavern half filled with
brine. On examination of the locality, it was discovered that a second
conical depression had been formed, a second crater had opened,
connected with the first, so that the two together took the shape of

the figure 8, and that simultaneously the upper abyss had enlarged its circumference.

The marks of feet in the marl showed that Rab and Ada had come down this lane together to the point where the land began to crack. Then ensued a confusion of footprints. Ada's shoe was embedded in the red clay. Here and there was the print of one shod foot and the track of one unshod; Rab's bootprints were seen to be depressed. It appeared as though a struggle had taken place, and yet even this was doubtful, as the impressions may have signified no more than the going over the same ground in the dark several times in search of the lost shoe. Beyond the chasm were no traces. In the hedge was no token of a scramble over it; in the meadow grass no dints of feet having sought to circumvent the pits. That Rab and Ada had both been lost in the abyss could not be doubted. That their bodies would never be recovered was equally certain. There was no reason to suppose that the fatality was due to anything but accident. Rab was, indeed, a strange fellow, but of late he had put off his old violence, abandoned the public-house, had not been seen in liquor for months, and had conducted himself rationally and honestly. No motive for a crime could be suggested, and, when the disappearance of Rainbow and Ada Grice was inquired into, the judgment given on it was accidental death—a verdict with which public opinion was in accord.

One person alone suspected that there was more behind than appeared on the surface, and that person was Queenie. At the inquest, the boy, Fred Fellows, had not mentioned the fact of the pocket-book having been given him by Rab for the girl. He mentioned the present of the knife. But what was there in that? Most boys receive such presents. Every man who wishes to afford a boy pleasure thinks of giving him a knife. Had the question been asked of the lad, did Rab Rainbow deliver you a commission? then the fact of the pocket-book having been sent by him would have come out. Had that fact transpired, Queenie would have been questioned, and she would have been compelled to produce the paper containing the rose-leaves, on which was scribbled in pencil,—

Farewell.

From RAB.

Queenie did not consider herself morally obliged to produce this evidence when she was not called upon for it. Its significance she herself did not understand. It was capable of the most varied interpretation. Rab might have resolved not to visit her again. He might have meant abandonment of his claim on her hand. He might have determined on leaving that part of the country. He might have scribbled those words out of presentiment of coming evil. He might—Queenie's heart stood still with a sickening horror—have deliberately destroyed himself and Ada so as to clear the field for herself and Andrew.

She put from her resolutely this latter solution of the mystery, and snatched eagerly at one after another of the others. Gentle herself, incapable herself of strong passion for more than one moment, ever ready to forgive, always eager to spare others pain, generous in her judgments, she could not bring herself to believe in such a solution; nay, even in such a self-devotion as that implied by the last explanation. Thus the deaths of Rab and Ada remained to her a mystery into which she feared to look.

The condition of affairs at Button's was materially altered. By the urgency of Andrew, Nottershaw was persuaded to conceal the fact that Mr Tom Button had been captured and compulsorily brought back to Saltwich. Mr Button himself, with cheery effrontery, went about calling on his friends, informing them how much better he felt in health for the sea-breezes of Scarborough, expatiating on the superior advantages of the east to the west coast, as though his departure from Saltwich had been openly planned and talked about beforehand, and as though such persons as supposed him to have bolted with money were to blame for their lack of charity in thinking evil of him. He was more sedulous in his attendance in the morning at Scatterley Church. He volunteered to take a class in a Sunday school. His constitution and spirits, he averred, had been greatly benefited by his excursion to the seaside. And a few days later arrived the person whom he proclaimed to be his new wife, with whom he trotted about in cheery mood, and to whom he insisted on introducing his friends, or rather acquaintances, for of friends he had actually none.

Nottershaw and Andrew Grice between them managed the many concerns of Mr Tom Button. They paid off his debts. They returned to Brundrith the three thousand pounds of which he had been defrauded by concealment of the fact of the mortgage. Nottershaw had had enough of the salt speculation, and he contented himself with being repaid his outlay with a handsome margin of profits. Brundrith showed himself a straightforward, kind-hearted and forgiving man. He had made no pretensions to seriousness, was not able to pose as a converted character, had never gushed with unctuous spiritual maunderings, and had enjoyed his glass of sherry—nevertheless, he was straight, as a rule, in all his business transactions, tender in his judgments, and ready to forgive every wrong done him. He was forward to make such arrangements with Andrew as were to the advantage of the latter. He took him into partnership, and constituted him manager of the factory at Button's, partly in consideration of the value of his father's invention; partly, also, because Button's was likely to be an important addition to his business and could not be trusted to an underling; partly, also, because Brundrith estimated highly the integrity and intelligence of Andrew.

When Tom Button's debts had been paid, there still remained a sum which was fairly his own, and this was handed over to him. Button at once disappeared with his wife, and it was believed he had gone to America, mainly because he had talked much of starting a great mission for the conversion of souls at Homburg—that seat of gambling and dissipation. Therefore it was concluded, by such as knew him, that he had started in a direction exactly opposite to Homburg, and that the conversion of souls was about the last thing to which he purposed applying himself. Before leaving Saltwich he had put down his name as a liberal subscriber to every description of charity, and when he departed it was discovered that not one of these subscriptions had been paid.

L

THE YELLOW ROSE-LEAVES

FIVE YEARS HAVE PASSED, AND they have seen many changes. For five years Queenie remained in the house of the Gerards, as simple, happy and useful as she had been when first taken in. She received her allowance quarterly, and esteemed herself rich. She spent it wisely, in part in taking lessons in music, in English literature, and in the French language. She had a pony and drove him into Saltwich almost daily—to her teachers.

In the house she was like a bird, bright, cheery and full of merry music. Jessie loved her devotedly—so did the Gerards—husband and wife.

Only occasionally did a shadow steal over her bright face, and the sparkle fade from her sunny eyes. That was when she thought of poor Rab, and puzzled her head over the mystery of his death and that of Ada.

During the autumn of the fifth year, the feeble life of Jessie became more feeble, her pains increased, the stiffness that had held her lower limbs invaded her back. The face became whiter, the eyes more lustrous, the voice weaker. But cheerful, trustful, loving she remained, and to the last a little hypocrite, concealing her sufferings from the eyes of those who loved her, simulating an ease she did not really enjoy.

Finally, as the birds began to sing in spring, the flickering life went out, as her mother was kissing her, Dick was kneeling sobbing by her bedside, and her wasted hand clasped Queenie's fingers.

Meanwhile, Andrew had been working hard at the new salt factory. This had been greatly extended; what had been run up temporarily had been replaced by permanent erections. Both the old works and the new were in full swing.

Brundrith found no reason for regretting that he had taken the young fellow into partnership. Andrew, freed from the numbing influence of his father, expanded in every direction—in his opinions, in intelligence, spiritually as well as mentally. He took pains to acquire cultivation, for he saw that the partnership would be the means of his becoming eventually a rich man, and he had sufficient self-respect and ambition to resolve not to be a rich boor.

The house at Button's was pulled down when it began to lurch, through the sinking of the foundations; then Andrew built himself one in better taste on a tongue of red sandstone that did not overlie salt rock, and was yet near the works and to the west of it, away from the drift of the smoke, and close to Delamere Forest. When the house was finished, then he invited Queenie to it, to reign there as sovereign in his household, as she had long reigned over his heart. After a brief honeymoon they returned to Saltwich, and their first expedition was to the Gerards.

"We will walk home," said Queenie. "Please Andrew, send the carriage round by the road. We will take the short cut by the Bramble Brook."

The time was summer.

The evening sky was full of light, the birds sang, the hedgerows were ablaze with flowers, the air was balmy with the scent of white clover.

As they walked along, Queenie, whose heart was full, said,—

"Andrew, dare I say to you a word about your father?"

"I had rather you did not," he answered; "you never understood him, as did I, who saw him always, and who alone have a right to judge his character. I know, from many little indications, that you misconceive him. It is I, therefore, who am glad of this occasion of speaking to you about him. My father was a strong man, and among so many who are weak, that is something. But he was something more than strong, he was a conscientious man, and he was sincere, down to the ground. What he believed to be right and true, from that not the whole world—no power in heaven or in hell—could turn him. What he hated, that he hated simply because he believed with his entire heart that it was false and wrong. What he did for me, that, please Heaven, I shall never forget. He formed in me the sense of duty; he gave to me the mainspring of principle to direct my life. Whatever is good in me, that I owe to him; whatever is weak and bad is due to myself. But he erred, as all men are liable to err, whatever be their creed, religious or political, to whatever church they may belong, to whatever party they may be attached. His error lay in rearing all his superstructure on a false basis, and that false basis was self-confidence. On the absolute conviction of his own infallibility—on that rock he built his church; and, believe me, Queenie, it is on lowliness of mind that we must lay our foundations."

They walked on. For many minutes neither spoke. Presently Andrew and Queenie reached a spot where the lane ceased at the edge of a broad "flash" or lake covering three acres. This was the spot where the subsidence on the Bramble Brook had occurred. The aspect of the spot was completely changed. There was now no longer visible a funnel-shaped crater, but a broad, placid mere, in which wild duck swam and sported. Around it the fields were wrinkled like the face of an old man, for the surface of the land was gradually but surely sliding down into the depths of the mere, and the sheet of water was annually extending itself.

Those passengers, who had been wont to use the old lane, had broken down the hedge on one side, and had formed a path in the field circumventing Bramble Mere.

Andrew and Queenie stood silently looking at the sheet of water that shone like burnished gold, reflecting the sunset evening sky. Presently Queenie said,—

"Andrew, I must tell you something. Here lie Rab and—Ada. Do you know that, before Rab turned out of the road to come here, he wrote on a slip of paper the word 'Farewell,' and sent it to me? The paper contained faded rose-leaves—the faded leaves of the yellow rose I pinned in his cap the first time that we met. Andrew, when I think how he valued those leaves, and how, when he first had them, he vowed he would never part with them so long as he lived—then I think—I think—oh, Andrew! something so dreadful. Martha Gerard has told me that he, poor fellow, saw us meet by the mere when he had cut the trench, and that he then knew, from my foolish way—when, do you remember? I sprang into your arms, and you very rightly repulsed me—then he realised that he could not be happy with me, for he saw that I loved you and you only. He was just. He admitted that you were not to blame. He thought that you could not help yourself; that I could not help myself—and then he had no hope any longer for himself. Oh, Andrew! what do you think? It troubles my mind—can Rab have—have—done such a wicked thing as—as to kill himself and Ada?"

Andrew did not reply at once. He looked intently at the golden, shining water. Presently he drew a long breath, and said,—

"The death of those two is as great a mystery to me as it is to you, Queenie. There is one truth I have learned from experience, burnt into my heart and mind, and that truth is, to be very slow in forming a judgment, even of acts which men condemn as crimes. It is likely enough that they may be mercifully judged elsewhere, where motives are read in clear light. I have learnt, also, that the best Christians are not those who blow a trumpet before them and occupy the chief seats in the synagogues—but that they may be found, if sought, perhaps in a wandering circus, perhaps in squalid Heathendom, perhaps in the depths of the leafy forest. What are you doing, Queenie?"

She was scattering the withered rose-leaves over the shining pool.

"I was doing something he bid me long—long ago," she said.

"And," answered Andrew, as he took her arm in his, "and we will take to heart a certain saying on which the preacher spoke in chapel last Sunday, but which, somehow, he did not make clear, because I think he did not understand it himself as I think I do—Judge nothing—no, nothing—whatever complexion it may wear, before the time, until the Lord come, who both will bring to light the hidden things of darkness, and will make manifest the counsels of the heart; and then—how strangely the sentence ends, Queenie; how unlike what we should have supposed. It goes on to say—then shall every man have, not blame, but *praise* of God."

THE END

ALSO AVAILABLE IN THE NONSUCH CLASSICS SERIES

For forthcoming titles and sales information see
www.nonsuch-publishing.com